Time's Bloodied Gold

L. J. Hutton

ISBN: 13: 9781791925215

Published by Wylfheort Books 2017

Copyright

The moral right of L. J. Hutton to be identified as the author of this work has been asserted by her in accordance with the Copyright, Designs and Patents Act 1988.

All characters in this book are fictitious, and any resemblance to actual persons living or dead is purely coincidental.

All rights reserved. No part of this publication may be reproduced, stored in a retrieval system or transmitted in any form, or by any means, without the prior permission in writing of the author, nor to be otherwise circulated in any form or binding or cover other than in which it is published without a similar condition, including this condition, being imposed upon the subsequent purchaser.

Acknowledgments

I would like to thank Teresa Fairhurst for her continued support and discussions on mythology, and for also being the one who demanded to read more of Bill Scathlock after his appearance in a short story, and then again as a 'walk on' part in *The Room Within the Wall*. Since then Bill has continued to mentally 'poke' me to keep writing about him, and he appears again in *Green Lord's Guardian* and there are other plots lurking as work-in-progress at the time of writing.

Mary Ward has continued to provide food for thought with discussions on Old English poetry, which led to some moment of inspiration for this book, and which have provided some much needed intellectual stimulation. It's harder than you might think coming up with convincing dialogue in an archaic language that nobody speaks any more, and Mary has (through her PhD dissertation discussions) kept me alert to the pitfalls of translation.

Thanks also to Ann Farr, who made a few but very pertinent suggestions along the way, which helped no end in creating the final package.

And of course to my husband for putting up with me being in a different world for large chunks of a day. He's also the arch-pedant who double-checks my work for those 'dyslexic finger' moments that spell-checkers just don't get, and walks our lovely lurchers when I just need to get 'one more paragraph' down. Our three lurchers are my sanity, and one or more of them is inevitably on the chair beside my desk as I write, making sure that I don't miss important things like dinner times!

Thank you, every one of you!

Danny – February

Danny was running as hard as he could, and it wasn't enough. He knew with horrible certainty that it wasn't, and that nothing short of a miracle would save him now. He could hear an engine coming downhill towards him, but was that his friends escaping or his pursuers catching up with him from behind? And if it was his hunters, would they get out and search on foot, or stay in the Land Rover? They had no need to be quiet about it. Not rowdy, of course, they had to be quieter than that. Not whilst in a built up area like this and in the depths of night. However, Tenbury Wells wasn't such a smart little town that sounds which could be attributed to a bunch of men merely coming home very late after a night out would cause comment. He, on the other hand, was desperately trying not to signal where he was to them, and although he was still a very long way from being in their sight, noise carried uncannily clearly through the empty night. It didn't help that he was hampered by the two little girls he was carrying, one on each hip and clasped to him as tightly as he could without hurting them.

He looked up and swore, glad that neither child understood English enough to know what he'd just said. Tonight February was slipping into March, but the still long nights wouldn't help him, there was too much moon tonight. Not that Danny was kidding himself that hiding in the dark would ever be an option – there weren't enough places, and any he'd passed were so obvious that he knew them to be utterly useless. He was also desperate to shake his hunters off his trail before the town woke up and people began to go about their daily business, for he was only too aware of how suspicious his actions would look to those who didn't know.

A man running through the streets with two little girls and pursued by two or three others – it was a thing the red-top papers thrived upon! And he knew that if someone caught hold of him, and detained him in a fit of good citizenship, that his hunters would be quick to feed into that kind of misinterpretation. They would feed into those fears of child abduction, he knew, painting themselves as the children's saviours, not what they were – their greatest danger. Or if such good Samaritans believed him and argued back, they would be in as much danger as he was, because who could defy Mikhail when he was in this mood and in danger of gunning down anyone in his path?

Anyway, he wouldn't dream of endangering an ordinary member of the public by actively seeking their help in this, and was praying he didn't come upon them by accident. For a start off he was pretty sure that Ulryk would be armed with the remaining semiautomatic from the farm, and God alone knew what nasty weapons Mikhail had in the pockets of that bloody great jacket he insisted on wearing whatever the temperature. Even a couple of unsuspecting coppers in a patrol car would be easy prey for those two! Worse, any situation where his true profession was exposed to his hunters would ensure beyond doubt that the next thing anyone saw of DS Danny Sawaski was his body floating down the River Teme.

Luckily he paused before emerging out onto an open area again. The night breeze suddenly brought him a whiff of Russian tobacco, and when he strained his eyes in that direction he was quick enough to catch sight of the momentary flaring of a lighted end as someone drew hard on the cigarette. Crouching down with a hand gently over each of the girl's mouths, Danny was rewarded with the sight of Dymek and Piotr stepping out of the shadows. Neither was searching very hard, and Danny offered up a prayer of thanks that it was those two who had crossed his path. Maybe, just maybe, Dymek had told Piotr all of the plan, and he, too, was as disgusted as Danny with Mikhail, and as a result he might risk being less than conscientious with the search the gang leader had triggered. Please God that was so. Danny urgently needed that kind of break.

As they turned away he made for the town proper in the vain hope that he might spot a taxi, or even a late night bus – anything would be good! Anything which got him in amongst people and moving fast towards Worcester would be a surfeit of riches, but instead there was a big, empty nothing. Given the lack of such an escape route, though, he'd not done badly to get this far, Danny thought wryly. But now that he could breathe again he could think straight enough to know that carrying on running wasn't going to be the way to escape. Holding the two girls' hands firmly, he led them carefully deeper into the undergrowth.

He saw open countryside coming up ahead of him again as a mass of different shadows to the sharp outlines of houses as he got closer to the river. Here at least he might stand a chance. Was there anywhere he might safely leave the girls? A playground, maybe? Somewhere where mothers and kids would come in the morning and where they'd be found? That way, he could move faster and decoy the men away from them, and be running faster himself. A large clump of bushes came up ahead and he slowed and slipped into the undergrowth, desperately trying to pull some much needed breath into his wheezing lungs for a moment while he rested the two girls on the ground, although still holding onto them tightly. So far they hadn't cried out, and he could only hope that the women had explained things as best you ever could to a five and three year-old who'd been yanked from their home into a foreign land. They weren't even crying, and that said a lot about the violence they had witnessed of late. He had to get them to safety, he had to.

As he sucked air in and tried to ignore the pain of the stitch which was twinging under his left ribs, Danny tried to think. Tonight he thought he'd never felt less as though he was living up to his anglicized version of his name – Danny Savage. Far from feeling savage he was scared to death. He hadn't really thought this through, but then there hadn't been time to do any kind of planning. What plans he'd had in mind for getting away from the people traffickers had only ever involved himself; always having the codicil of him coming back with a very large number of heavily armed colleagues afterwards to rescue the people being held. In truth, though, he'd long had his doubts about the last bit, but until these last few days he'd never quite allowed himself to believe that he'd been totally abandoned. Yet now he could hear his old boss, Bill Scathlock's, scathing words in his head.

"That's the trouble with you, Danny! You don't bloody think, do you? Not really think. You go steaming ahead with your grand plans, your head filled with some bloody daft idea of how you'll come out of it smelling of roses. But you don't think about the fallout hitting the poor sods around you, do you? That if you win someone else has got to lose! Or at least come out of the situation less well-off than they might have done. Oh you're always sorry afterwards, after the damage has been done. But it's not enough! ...I've had enough! You can't get away with just being sorry for ever, one day you too will feel the pain! And I won't be there to haul you out of the fire, either."

Time's Bloodied Gold

At the time Danny had made some equally scathing remark about not needing Bill to pick him up because he wasn't going to live the rest of his career in Bill's shadow. Now, though, he'd have given just about anything to be able to make a call to Bill and see the big man coming over the horizon.

"But what choice did I have this time, Bill?" Danny whispered to the darkness with the faintest of breaths. It had been mere chance that he'd heard Mikhail telling the gang to get rid of the two girls. To drown them like unwanted kittens! That was when Danny had felt the dread certainty of knowing that the day had finally come when all of his options had run out. That he couldn't go on one day more, couldn't get up and face himself in the mirror if he didn't do something this time. Yet therein also lay Danny's biggest problem, because never in his craziest dreams had he imagined going on the run with two children. But if he was going to even have the wildest chance of success then it had had to be done right there and then, there couldn't even be a minute's delay once he knew what was planned.

It had been easy enough to get the girls out once he'd mimed what was going to happen to them to the prisoners. Their parents grasped that, and that their children's only hope lay with this stranger who was opening the door of their caged area while looking so scared himself. With the door unbolted and left that way he'd been out of the farmyard in seconds, but getting far enough away was another nightmare altogether. He hadn't dared try to take one of the cars. The noise of starting the engine alone would have brought trouble down on him in seconds. As it was he reckoned he'd had about five minutes' start on them – and of course they didn't know which way he would run, which might give him a few minutes longer – but that would count for nothing soon. Again, if he'd had time to properly plan this, he could have found an inconspicuous spot and created a hideaway, but these last couple of days had taken all of his energy in concentrating on maintaining his undercover façade and surviving, rather than allowing his mind to drift off to plan for something that might never happen.

Plunging on through the darkness, he was glad to reach the backs of some buildings around the riverside part of the small town which might be occupied, glad to be amongst signs of humanity even if they were of little help. But as he strained his hearing to make sure that the worst two of the gang, Mikhail and Ulryk, weren't right on his heels with those bloody guns of theirs, he caught something else. A car coming and pulling up not far away beside the bridge, and then the door open and the car springs give a small creak as somebody heavy got out. Oh God, was that Mikhail in his car? Had he grabbed Danny's VW instead of one of the gang's Land Rovers? In his panic Danny couldn't remember whether he'd left his keys behind at the farm. Was this where it all ended? A bullet in the head for him, and a drowning for the children?

Nine months earlier

Half of Hindlip Grange, the headquarters of West Mercia Police on the outskirts of Worcester, must have heard the argument. Danny Savage was venting again, and those in the know wondered how long this could possibly go on for. Some thought acting-DCI Bill Scathlock had been far too patient already. Being open to the ideas and opinions of those working for you was one thing, but Danny Savage was taking the piss these days.

"This is going to come to a head soon," a passing sergeant said to his friend as they walked past the gents where the almighty row was going on. "Someone senior is going to do it for Bill if he doesn't act soon."

"You deliberately sabotaged my promotion!" Danny yelled, Bill's voice calmly responding,

"How many times more do I have to tell you this? I'm only an acting DCI, and because of that you're only an acting DI. I can't make your post permanent, Danny, you know I can't. It's not in my power to do it."

"But you could recommend it! You could make them see that I'm ready to be promoted!"

"Make who see? The Super'? The Chief Super'? Who, Danny? Who the hell do you think is going to listen to the likes of me when everyone can hear you gobbing off like a spoilt teenager? How many people have passed the door here already? And this isn't the first time, is it? For fuck's sake, wake up! It's on the cards that they're getting rid of the DCI posts anyway. That's not me talking. The union reps have been warning us about that for ages. The future is all specialized departments. Serious Crime Squads and the like, each one run by a Super' with DIs and sergeants running their arses off under him or her. You need to start getting on with people, mate, 'cause at the moment you're seen as a major pain in the neck, and that will get you stuck on the sidelines faster than anything I do or don't say."

"Oh yeah, right! Like the word of Bill Scathlock doesn't get taken seriously around here!"

"You daft pillock! There's a world of difference between the blokes we work with getting on with me and maybe respecting my opinions, and my word being taken as gospel by those above me. Jeez, Danny! What's the matter with you these days?"

"What's the matter? I'll tell you what the matter is: if I don't move on pretty soon I'm going to end my career no further than I am now, as your bloody bag carrier! Well I'm better than that, you arrogant bastard, and if you didn't stop running me down behind my back I might be able to prove that."

There was the sound of a door being punched with those last words, and then Bill emerged from the toilets saying over his shoulder,

"I'm not staying here to have you throw accusations like that at me. I've never done that, and if you stopped for one minute to think, you'd know I haven't."

The burly acting-DCI pounded off down the corridor giving a good imitation of a very angry bear, and causing people to scatter out of his way as he approached them.

Pounding outside to the car park, Bill finally stopped and drew breath. What the hell was eating Danny these days? Ever since they'd had that odd case with the Roman shrine a few months back, Danny had been getting more and more irascible. Was it that he had trouble dealing with anything a bit off the grid, a bit unusual? If so, then that more than anything would hold him back from promotion,

Time's Bloodied Gold

because these days what people would do to one another seemed to be getting stranger and sicker by the year, and with ever more bizarre motivation. If Danny couldn't get his head around that, then he was destined to stay as one of the team rather than the one heading any investigation, quite regardless of anything Bill said to anyone.

"You look like you've been chewing wasps," a friendly voice said from behind him, and he spun around to see Joe Connolly walking towards him.

"Bloody hell, you're a welcome sight," Bill said with relief. "I tell you, if I smoked I'd be doing a passable imitation of a dragon right now. ...What are you doing here? We're a bit off your turf aren't we?"

Joe worked out of the West Midlands Police Force's CID centre up in Harborne, some thirty-five miles away, which made his appearance at West Mercia's HQ a little out of the ordinary. The fact that Joe then said,

"I came to see you, as it happens," baffled Bill even more.

"Not a social call, then?"

Joe shook his head. "No ...actually I have a proposition for you. We've got a long-term operation going on, but we need someone who's not a familiar face, and I immediately thought of you. I've got an appointment with your boss later this afternoon, but I was hoping I'd get chance to talk to you first, which is why I've come early."

"I'm intrigued! Come on, I'll buy you coffee and you can tell me more."

"Well by the look of your face just now I think you might welcome a change."

Once they were both nursing a coffee and sat as far out of the way as was possible in the canteen, Joe began.

"You know human trafficking is a big thing these days, don't you? Well most folk immediately think of Nigerian or

Lithuanian prostitutes, and in fairness, that's where our investigation started and where a major strand of it is still focused. But we more or less fell over another face of trafficking in the process. One of the nasty little shits we've been targeting kept meeting with another bloke – Polish we suspect – who repeatedly offered him cheap workers."

"Can't imagine there'd be much call for that in the heart of Birmingham."

"Not the kind of workers he was offering. There's certainly a problem with Asian workers being brought in to work in family sweatshops, but they're a different kind of slave labour to the ones we're looking at. Our focus is the gangs who use the open borders of the EU to bring people in against their will – or at least under the pretence that they're coming to a better life that doesn't actually exist. Now what we're trying to figure out, Bill, is whether this is a wholly new gang who are trying to muscle in on the lucrative city trade, albeit rather ineptly, or part of an existing gang from another part of the UK. The latter is what we're more worried about, to be frank. A gang war with the potential for the bodies of innocent victims turning up in the canals of Birmingham is something everyone wants to avoid."

"And with Birmingham having more miles of canals than Venice that's a lot of water to dump corpses in," Bill sympathized, having visions of some of the muckier stretches of old industrial canals at the back of old factories, where bodies might lie for days or even weeks without getting noticed.

"Exactly! But what we also need is someone a bit more clued up on rural crime as well, because whoever this is, it turns out that they're coming into the city from well outside of it."

"Where do you think they're coming from?"

Time's Bloodied Gold

"Somewhere down here. Somewhere here in C Division's patch. Couldn't be more specific than that, but that's why I'm here for some help. How do you fancy doing a spot of undercover, Bill? We need a bloke who can handle himself, someone who isn't easily intimidated and who can't be pushed around, but bright enough to keep his ear to the ground."

Bill immediately laughed. "Get outta here! ...Aww come on, Joe, half the bad lads in Worcestershire know my ugly mug! The chances of me not getting made in the first day are remote to nonexistent."

Joe was determined not to give in that easily, though. "It would be limited danger, Bill. I know the Eastern bloc big gangs have a vicious reputation, but these are definitely small fry. The danger would be minimal."

"It's not the danger, you daft bugger. I know I'm not in the first flush of youth, but I haven't got that delicate yet. No, I meant exactly what I said. I'd be utterly useless for what you want. Besides which, I'm crap at dissembling. What I'm thinking is written across my face no matter what words are coming out of my mouth." Then a moment of inspiration came to him. "But I think I know just the lad you might want."

"Really? Who is he?"

Bill sighed. "Well at the moment he's the acting DI to my acting DCI, but that's coming to a close at the end of the month. I won't lie to you, Joe, we've not been on the best of terms of late, but I'll tell you why I think he's the right lad for you. He's hungry for promotion for a start off, and a spell on a team like yours might be just what he needs to get him seen in the right light and by the right people. But there's more to it than that. His name is Danny Savage, but he only changed it to that just before he came into the force. His real name is Danny Sawaski, and he's fluent in

Polish because his dad and grandparents always spoke it at home."

Joe's eyes lit up. "Blimey, that would be a bonus! If he can follow what they're saying in their own language that would be great!"

"Now he can be a bit abrasive, but he's the kind of lad who does well given a bit of a long leash. Not so good on the 'yes sir, no sir, three bags full sir,' stuff, but very good when you want someone who can think a bit independently. And I think it would do him no end of good to work with someone other than me for a bit."

"He's feeling a tad overshadowed?" Joe guessed and got a rueful smile from Bill in return. "Ah! ...Not much room to shine. I get it. Okay, then with your blessing I'll pass all this on to your brass and see what comes out of it."

They shook hands and Joe disappeared off to his meeting, leaving Bill sitting and thinking that this was going to turn out only one of two ways. Either Danny was going to excel and get the promotion he craved so badly, or it was going to prove that he was temperamental unsuited to the job. Bill hoped it was going to be the better of the two, but for now he was just feeling relief that he might have several months free of Danny's gripes, because he had the feeling that their senior officers might also see this as a chance to be shot of Danny on a long secondment and send him off with their blessings.

Chapter 1

February

Bill stood at the bottom of the unused underpass and watched the SOCOs doing their thing with the three dead derelicts. It had been a freezing cold night, and had come after several cold and soaking wet days, so the chances of someone freezing to death when sleeping rough were pretty high. However, that hadn't been what had done for these three, or at least not last night it hadn't. Nobody used the underpass these days ever since the council had decided that it was too much of a temptation for potential muggers, and had chained off the ramps on either side. The trouble was that a chain easily stepped over was no deterrent at all to someone going down there. It simply stopped the unsuspecting law-abiding folk of the west side of Worcester from going down there, not the rogues or rough sleepers. What it did mean, though, was that no-one had been down there in weeks until the council had sent someone to hose it down, when the residents of the nearby tower blocks had begun to complain of the stench rising from it. And that stench had come from the decomposing corpses of three men.

"Does it look like they really were sleeping rough?" Bill cautiously asked the leading pathologist, anonymous in his all-covering disposable whites. "I'm not asking for miracles, such as anything like cause of death yet, just a rough idea of whether we're looking at probable natural causes when you factor in lousy diet and freezing temperatures."

He was covertly crossing his fingers that the swathed pathologist would be saying 'yes' to that. Churlish though it might sound to an outsider, Bill had his hands full as it was, and three suspicious deaths was the last thing he wanted to land on his desk. They wouldn't be sent any higher than him, of that he was pretty sure, or at least not unless it looked like some serial killer was on the rampage, but somebody doing in tramps was still something which would need investigation.

"Look at this," one of the SOCOs said, holding out an unfamiliar medallion dangling from a chain. "You wouldn't expect a tramp to have one of these, would you?"

Bill took it from him in a gloved hand and moved into the light to see it better. It seemed to show someone who looked like a king or maybe a bishop with a sword in his hand, and Bill thought his bet would be on something religious. It had that look about it, as though someone had handled it often, not like a piece of jewellery which had just been worn. And the SOCO was right, you wouldn't expect a tramp to have something like this, because unless Bill was very mistaken this was gold-plated at the very least, and possibly good quality plate at that. Bollocks, this was sounding suspicious already, and looking like he'd be doing a juggling act an octopus would be proud of. Just what he wanted.

With nothing more to be done at the scene Bill returned to his office, but got another surprise when information on the medallion came back.

"It turns out it's of St Stanisław of ...of this place," the civilian researcher said and showed him a piece of paper with the word 'Szczepanów' written on it; "...however you say that! Apparently he's one of the patron saints of Poland. A medieval bishop whose relics are in Wawel Cathedral."

Time's Bloodied Gold

"Really? Well that's a turn up for the books. Looks like our tramps might not have been English then. Well done, Jan."

Jan left the information on Bill's desk where it was soon joined by the autopsies which, to his surprise, had been unable to confirm that the men were likely to be Polish going on their dental work and other indicators. In fact the pathologist thought he could say that they most definitely *weren't* Polish, but struggled to say where they actually were from. All that could be said was that they seemed to have had very little contact with modern life at all. In fact, cause of death seemed to be wholly natural if you took into account that there was no obvious sign of a brutal end, but that was suspicious, in the pathologist's eyes, because he could find no good reason why they had died. Moreover, one man lying down and giving up the ghost was one thing, but three together was definitely odd, especially when every drug test which had been performed on them showed no signs of them having taken anything in a suicide pact. This wasn't going to be the quickly closed case Bill had hoped for.

"Now what were you doing dossing down in a Worcester subway?" he mused aloud as he read through the details again.

Whoever they were, they'd been living in poor conditions for some time and were malnourished although not to the point of starvation. What also caught Bill's eye was a note that the men looked as though they'd been doing quite heavy manual labour for some time. Not the musculature he would expect to find on a tramp, certainly.

Then another surprise came to the surface: these men had not died in the subway, they had been dumped there and probably quite some time after the actual time of death, and that alone made the deaths suspicious. What was going to take longer, however, was determining cause of death. There were still no obvious signs of a violent death, nothing like crushed bones or any signs of knife wounds, but that didn't rule out something like suffocation when the bodies were in such a decomposed state and had been gnawed at by rats. Reporting the findings to his superintendent, Bill concluded,

"It seems likely that they died and their bodies hidden away somewhere else, and were only moved to the subway when there was a danger of them being discovered in situ. My inclination is to say that whoever did for these poor sods thought that it would throw us off the scent if they were found a long way from the scene of the crime. This is going to be a long case, boss. Trying to find someone who remembers migrant workers isn't going to happen overnight. We've already eliminated the obvious ones who came here to work and then never went back. None of the records match. These three were from much further down the food chain, unskilled, probably spoke no English, and here illegally. No farmer employing them as pickers for a season is going to admit to having had them, and they probably slept in a barn somewhere and had food brought in to them. They were effectively invisible. God help the poor bastards, but they could have died as long ago as the late autumn when the last of the pickers left ...or so the pathologists are telling me. It's not good."

The superintendent looked miserable, knowing full well that Bill was right, but also that this might well add to the permanently unsolved case list which was never a good thing.

However, a couple of weeks down the line and with little progress having been made, Bill had other things on his mind. He was in hospital having his knee replaced after what should have been a simple incident of stopping some shop-lifters had turned bad. So his cases got handed on to other officers and sidelined, and he resigned himself to several weeks of boredom.

Three weeks later ~ Thursday

Bill sat at the small table in the corner of the pub and swirled his orange juice and lemonade moodily. This meeting wasn't his idea, but then he'd never been able to refuse one of Charlie's requests. The universally acknowledged king of the police archives and cold cases – even if someone else was officially in charge – was nothing if not persuasive, and in this instance had damned near begged him to come. And Charlie had been very tactful. In choosing *The Plough* to meet in he'd placed them well away from the main police station, not that anywhere was that far away in a town the size of Worcester. But it did mean that Bill could reasonably expect not to walk into any former colleagues. Yes, he was off on sick leave, but it always felt a bit like skiving off coming out to a pub in the day, even if his hospital issue crutch was propped up beside him. It didn't help that Charlie also knew his real ale, and Bill was forced to sit here smelling the beer which his antibiotics stopped him from drinking, and that wasn't doing much for his temper either.

He was saved a return trip to the bar by the appearance of Charlie, who spotted the empty glass and gestured in query as he headed to get himself a pint. Moments later the small detective appeared clutching a brimming pint for himself and a pint of coke for Bill and smiling.

"Thanks for coming, Bill! I know you're officially off work for the next few weeks while the knee replacement takes, but I wouldn't have asked if it wasn't serious."

"I know, that's why I'm here," Bill responded. "I'd have told most of the others to piss off before they got to asking."

Charlie gave a small smile in acknowledgment, knowing that such comments were the nearest thing to flattery anyone ever got from Bill Scathlock. He reciprocated with an open question Bill could choose to ignore if he wanted.

"How's life?"

Coming from Charlie, though, it didn't feel like a meaningless question put in to fill an uncomfortable gap. And that meant that for once Bill didn't feel awkward about answering and being honest about it too.

"Pretty crap, really. The knee's still giving grief as yet, although it is improving, but it's the boredom that's driving me nuts. I guess it's the price for playing rugby all those years, sooner or later the wear and tear was going to catch up with me. I'm just praying that I'll be able to go back to active duty, because I'm not sure I'm cut out for a desk job."

"Life can be bloody cruel sometimes," Charlie sympathized, thinking back to his predecessor who had disappeared into early retirement, but whom many years previously had suffered a terrible loss of family in an accident.

"I've just found it so hard to go in one fell swoop from working all hours to absolutely nothing," Bill confessed frankly, trying to put some perspective on his complaint for Charlie, and to demonstrate that he wasn't just moaning for no reason. But Charlie was already nodding understandingly before Bill had finished the sentence, not least because he couldn't imagine how he'd have coped with such a sudden wrench. "I mean, even going for anything like what I'd call

Time's Bloodied Gold

a proper walk is out of the question for a while. I've got to do regular exercises, but the surgeon said it was a right old mess and not to expect miracles."

Charlie could understand that frustration, being a keen cyclist when he got the chance.

"So come on, then, what's got you trekking across town to meet me on the sly?" Bill asked, breaking Charlie's reverie.

Charlie took a deep breath. This was when it all became a bit chancy. How would Bill react? Only one way to find out. "It's Danny Savage," he said, coming straight out with the main stumbling block. "Have you seen him at all of late?"

Bill glowered. "Seen him? You must be bloody joking! The last time was well over six months ago and I kind of hoped it would be the last for a long time!"

Charlie nodded, staying calm. "I'd sort of guessed that's how things might be. The trouble is, Bill, he's in trouble – or at least I think he is. I can't get anyone else to take my fears seriously though."

That got Bill's attention. "How do you mean?"

"Well you know that he got seconded to a West Midlands team investigating human trafficking – former Eastern bloc prostitutes being brought over here, to put it very simplistically for now."

"Yes, I know, I was the one who put him forward for it."

"Were you, by God?"

"Yes. Seemed straight forward enough when Joe Connolly told me about it."

"Well it got un-straightforward pretty damned quickly. Our much unloved boss decided that that operation might also be linked to a series of warehouse and farm building fires on our books which were obviously arson attacks."

"I didn't think there was any evidence for that?"

Charlie shrugged. "Maybe not, but you know what Williams is like, if he could wring two investigations out of the price of one, especially with West Midlands mainly footing the bill, he wasn't going to waste that opportunity."

Bill sniffed in disgust. "Now *that* I believe."

"Hmmm ... well they've been a small but persistent and growing threat which he wants off the books anyway, because they're pushing the unsolved figures up. Fires which apparently have been burning incredibly hot for what was stored in the units, and one of the bright sparks in the pathologists' department happened to say that you could have had a body in there and they'd be having a hard time telling it from the bits left over. It seems there are fine ashes by the cart load from these scenes, but only a tiny fraction would be likely to have identifiably human elements. Short of sifting the whole lot – which they haven't got the time, facilities or budget to do – they can only do random samples and hope for the best unless we give them good reason to do otherwise."

"Okay, I can begin to see why Williams might think that there might be a link to the trafficking, even if it's stretching a point, because what else would be the motive?"

Charlie waggled a finger at Bill. "Hence the thinking that the best way of finding out would be to infiltrate someone into the gang if possible and see if there is a link. Someone who could actually find out for certain whether this is just a case of malicious damage, or whether there's something more sinister and gang related attached. Something which we could claim some credit for. The major case budget is still paying for the undercover officer, and so the local seniors were happy because they're likely to get a series of minor cases written off without spending a penny on them.

Time's Bloodied Gold

"As for Danny, well he can be a prickly sod as you know only too well! And a bit late in the day one or two people are now saying that you were the one to get the best out of him. He's gone from being seen as the bright lad with a big future, to being a bloke with an over-inflated idea of his own capabilities, and too fond of telling those above him where he thinks they've gone wrong and how he could do it better. Someone we'd be better off without."

Charlie took in Bill's little nods of agreement at these last statements. This was the placatory offering – letting Bill know that at last his assessment of Danny's behaviour had been confirmed, albeit too late – although talking to Bill himself it seemed like there was less deep-seated animosity between the two of them than office gossip had implied. If so, then that was all to the good, because now that Charlie had Bill onside he had to drop the bombshell.

"But the thing is, Bill, Danny's been gone too long. I know he can't be in regular contact on an operation like that, but Jane's been in touch – and officially too – spitting blood about how he missed sending Zoe's Christmas present and several visits."

"Missed Zoe's present?" Now Bill was sitting up and taking notice.

"I know! I mean, you and I both know how Danny and Jane had got to hating the sight of one another, but their daughter was the one thing even they could agree on. If Danny was alright he would have posted a card and a present, even if he'd had to drive for miles and post it in a motorway service station or something. It might have been some toy bought in a hurry and not wrapped properly, but he'd have sent *something*. The job was never so important that he would've let Zoe down, even if he couldn't be there in person."

"How long?" Bill was frowning and staring off into the distance, and Charlie knew that Bill's razor-sharp brain had clicked back into gear, knee operation and sick leave all on the back burner when there was something to get his teeth into.

"The last guaranteed personal contact anyone had from him was back in late November," Charlie supplied and Bill blinked and then fixed him with a horrified stare. "Since then only random emails and texts, and now they've stopped too!"

"He's undercover and no-one's *seen* him since *November*? Fucking hell, what are they playing at?"

"Well he's possibly been seen – although by someone who doesn't know him well – but no-one's actually spoken to him properly since. Now you can see why I'm worried. Three and heading for four long months, Bill! And with Zoe's birthday coming up I don't want to be taking another phone call from Jane that Zoe hasn't heard from her dad again."

"Why are *you* taking her phone calls?" Bill demanded. "Bloody hell, Charlie, someone senior to you should be fielding those!"

"They do ...in a way. But Jane remembered me and rang back to talk to me. If you'd been a bit more accessible, not out working cases, you'd have been the obvious port of call, but failing that then at least I was a remembered friendly face from back in the days when we all worked together, who wouldn't dismiss her as a hysterical bimbo. Pretty understandably, she wasn't happy about being given the brush off with lots of platitudes from the official contacts. She might loathe the sight of Danny but she's not stupid, and I think she intuitively knows something's really gone wrong.

Time's Bloodied Gold

"She asked me to dig around and see if I could find something – anything – that I could tell her which would put her mind at rest. I think she also wanted reassurance that if he hadn't been in contact then it was because he *couldn't* rather than wouldn't, if you get my drift. In her heart of hearts she wants to believe that despite everything which has gone on – Danny throwing their marriage away and going a fair way to doing the same to his career – that there were some depths even he wouldn't sink to. That there was still a vital spark of the old Danny she'd once loved which was alive deep inside him, and that in that case, maybe for once he really needs help and isn't able to ask for it."

Charlie exhaled heavily and shook his head. "Well you know me and the computers. It didn't take long to worm my way into where I probably didn't have a right to be. If people were a bit more imaginative with their passwords it would have taken me longer, but as it was I was in before you could say 'knife'. Robbie," referring to his predecessor, "always said it was dangerously easy once you knew how, and once I took over I could see what he meant. I always accessed files on the days when the men in question had been in, so there shouldn't be anything to trigger a query – like a file being opened on a day when the bloke in question was away for a week. But what I found worries the living daylights out of me!"

He handed a stuffed Tesco's bag-for-life which was obviously very heavy over to Bill, and which was clearly double wrapped to stop it bursting at the seams.

"Don't shout at me for doing this. I know the consequences …but it's the only way I could get these for you. These are printouts of all the files I could get my hands on. You'll have to bear with me on that because I used both sides of the paper and shrunk the fonts to get as much out as possible without bringing a shopping trolley! So some of the files start on the same page as the previous one, or on the backs of others, but they're all clearly marked as to which is which."

"And you want me to dig around." It wasn't a question.

Charlie nodded. "I'm afraid I've got something else plaguing me at the moment, so yes please. Or at least I want to you to go through that nasty tangled mess and tell me that Danny is likely to at least be alive somewhere. I'd do more myself, but it'll require you going out of town for several trips and I can't get out of the office at all at the moment. I've tried to do stuff myself at weekends for the couple of weeks as my suspicions have grown, but so many places where I wanted to talk to people were closed then – even here in the Midlands – it was just hopeless. Which was when I first thought of asking you, although at the time you were just as busy. And now on top of that I'm being saddled with some bloke from the Warwickshire force coming over to observe and learn how I get stuff done, heaven help me! If I've got someone looking over my shoulder all the time I shall have to watch my step for a bit. It's a pain in the neck, because normally he could stare all he liked. But the one time I want to do something a bit dodgy turns out to be the one time I can't!"

"How bloody inconsiderate of Superintendent Williams!" Bill said with mischievous sarcasm and a wry smile. He patted the bulging carrier. "Leave it with me, Charlie."

"You'll investigate?"

"I'll do my best."

"Good, then if you want to see some of the other evidence, next Tuesday would be a good day to stop by up at Himley."

Time's Bloodied Gold

Bill winced. Trapped by his own promise, the one thing he hadn't wanted to do was go back to the building while officially off.

"It okay," Charlie was saying hurriedly. "It's Terry Gething's retirement 'do' that day. You knew him well enough that no-one will think it too odd if you just swing by to say cheerio and wish him the all the best." Terry had been a desk sergeant for most of his career and was the kind of old-school policeman Bill liked and had got on with. The sort of man who'd had no aspirations to get any higher up the ranks, and who was always a safe pair of hands to put new recruits with.

"So Tel's found the escape route, has he?"

"Yes. And so I thought that, if I could get you to have a look through the files beforehand, then it would give you an excuse to come into the building. You could show your face briefly at the 'do' and then come and find me. It'll be a good day to go rummaging, because Terry's so popular everyone will be busy wishing him well. We should be able to sneak you in to see the evidence without any trouble. You see, I want you to listen to some taped conversations. I'm not telling you what just now because I don't want to prejudice your opinion before you've had chance to read all the rest for yourself. I've put my home phone number on the front page in there, so give me a ring. The golden handshake takes place about one o'clock, by the way."

"Charlie, you're a sneaky and conniving old bugger!" Bill said but without rancor. It had to be damned serious for Charlie to take risks like this. "All right, I'll have a read and ring you back."

"Great! Now I must get back and try and get some work done before my guest arrives in ten days' time." Charlie pulled a face, and this time it was Bill's turn to feel sympathy. They both had their own way of doing things which was most effective for them, and neither was happy about having to pander to others' whims and change their ways.

"Best of luck with the training!" Bill wished him with a wry grin.

"Thanks! I suspect I'll need it!" And with that Charlie took his empty glass back up to the bar and left with a cheery wave of the hand from by the door.

Typical of Charlie to take the glass back, Bill thought as he drained the dregs from his own glass and pulled on his own coat. He half thought about taking his own back, shamed into the courtesy by Charlie's actions, then thought better of it. Better if no-one remembered him leaving with the bulging carrier bag when he hadn't come in with one, quite aside from the logistics of managing the glass with his crutch and the bag. While the barman was distracted trying to find crisps for another customer, Bill slipped out unnoticed.

Outside he hobbled at half his normal speed back to his basement flat in an old Victorian house on the west side of the city, wincing from time to time. He'd had the stitches out only this week and sometimes things till tugged a bit. Inside he turned the gas fire on and pulled his chair up to the low antique chest he used as the coffee table, which was big enough to read larger documents laid out on it if he wanted. An angle-poise lamp completed the set-up, and once he'd brewed a large mug of tea, Bill sat down to read.

In truth he had to admit to himself that he was just a little grateful to Charlie for this opportunity. Not to renew acquaintance with Danny. He still wasn't sure how he felt about that and he regarded the pile of papers warily, wondering what he was going to find. On the other hand he was already bored stiff and had all too often in these last few days had found himself harking back to the incident which had been the final straw for his already dodgy knee, and had resulted in him being like this now.

It had been a dank, drizzly day. Police were surrounding a gang of hoodied thugs in the scruffy back end of a council estate, following a chase from an out of town retail park where they been halted in an attempted robbery of Halford's. Then a little girl, now clutched in the ringleader's arms, had been snatched from her mother as the gang tried to complete their escape through a parking area behind the houses, only to realize their escape route was cut off by a patrol car. Several of the other gang members still clutched in-car stereos and the like from their haul, but the leader was brandishing a very illegal large knife in his free hand and challenging the police.

"Yo' 'in' gonna shoot me, man!" he'd crowed, then sniffed hard through his drug-ruined nose. "No' wiv' der lil' bitch here!" and he'd waved the knife closer to the wailing child. "Yo' back off! ...Yo' fuckin' back off, or she gets it!" He was high as a kite, or in the advanced stages of withdrawal more like, and Bill had recognized in an instant that he was utterly unstable and unpredictable. The pathetic attempt at American urban 'speak' from someone who was resolutely white and rural might have been laughable under other circumstances, but there was nothing funny in the way that the youth's eyes were skittering all over the place, or his jittery knife hand. The scrawny lad was every bit as dangerous as some big city gang member in his current state, and Bill could still remember the prickles of fear which had run down his spine as he'd watched that knife like a hawk. This idiot could still kill the child regardless of his 'gangsta' pedigree, or lack of one, and she'd be no less dead even if the junkie would have hardly any memory of it afterwards.

When some of the uniformed officers had tentatively taken a step back at a gesture from another senior officer, others of the gang had begun whooping and hollering, winding the leader up more with his own sense of power.

"Yo! Yo' go, pigs! ...I'm der man now!" he hooted triumphantly as the little girl howled, "Daddy!" as she was swung about like a rag doll.

At that something had snapped inside of Bill. He'd been over the police car's bonnet before he'd even thought about it, and was pounding down on the teenage thug. It was a moment when Bill's colleagues belatedly remembered that he'd been a more than useful rugby player for years, as well as having been on the police boxing team when such a sport had been an acceptable thing to do. Like a raging bull, Bill pounded across the open space at a speed no-one expected. As two of the gang came forward he shouldered each of them as he would have done going for a try and sent them flying, and hard too!

Coming up on the gang leader, Bill had punched the thug to his right hard enough to put the lad out cold for two days, then swept the little girl into his arms as he head-butted the leader. The drug-skinny youth wilted with rolled up eyes, but that was when it had all gone dreadfully wrong. For as Bill had turned to lift the little girl away from the falling body, another youth had tried to grab him from behind. And although Bill had elbowed him hard in the gut and winded him, as this youth also fell, his legs along with those of the falling leader twisted around Bill's, and he too went down as his feet lost their grip on the wet ground. Even in falling Bill's reactions had been sharp, for he'd twisted so that the tiny girl came down on top of him and not beneath his considerable weight. Yet his old rugby injury had taken too much strain, and Bill's left knee had

Time's Bloodied Gold

come apart in an explosion of pain which had put him out for the count too.

When he'd woken in hospital, the consultant had told him that while they normally didn't do knee replacements on someone as young as him, in this case they had no choice. The knee joint was wrecked beyond reconstruction. "You could be on crutches for life," he'd been warned.

It was a bitter blow for a man as active as Bill, and made worse by the potential loss of a job he truly loved. No-one was going to keep an active job open for a man whom most people thought might be in a wheelchair from then on, and it was the fear of that which was also dragging him down in spirit at the moment. Come hell or high water he was determined to get back to his old level of mobility again, and if he could demonstrate that he could be useful even in this state, it might sway decisions about his future.

"Forget it's about Danny making a prick of himself again," he told himself sternly and refocusing on the document in front of him. "If you can haul his chestnuts out of the fire and without a scandal it'll look good for you. Come on, Scathlock, you can do this sort of stuff practically in your sleep, get a grip!"

He continued to grumble softly to himself as he settled down to the files, but in truth just doing this was making him feel better. It was going to be important to go through the files methodically, reading each one carefully and not skipping anything. He knew that Charlie wouldn't have bothered risking bringing anything out which wasn't really relevant in some way, and so he gave it his full attention.

As he worked he found himself swept back to old cases of his own, for names and places were sometimes all too familiar to him.

"So Morris Watson reoffended did he?" he murmured softly to himself, reading one report which placed much of the blame on Morris for two of the factory unit fires, but where they couldn't make a conviction against him personally on account of him being already inside for the fourth time. Bill could understand his former colleagues' conviction that Watson was the brains behind some of the arson linked robberies, though. They had Morris' signature all over them – small enough to be a low priority, but good enough targets to reap the fire-setter a good reward from the electrical goods taken before the fire masked their disappearance. But these weren't the ones Danny was investigating, and the first thing he'd done was go through all the files he could find and compile what he saw as anything which might be relevant.

Indeed, most of the mass of early cases Danny had brought into his review, and which Bill now ploughed through, were minor break-ins and occasionally arson events – annoying and costly to the poor souls whose property was destroyed, but nothing more than that. All were classified as rural crimes, since they took place in small factory or warehouse units made out of old farm buildings, and because of that at first several had been a low priority since they could almost have been accidental. Apart from the regularity of their occurrences they hardly posed much of a threat, for out where these places were there weren't even any animals in danger, much less humans. Only when seen en-mass were some of them potentially connected, and Bill mentally applauded Danny's thoroughness in going through the records and making his review more comprehensive than when all this had been handed over to him. He might not like what Danny had become, but he couldn't deny his former partner's capabilities – or at least when Danny chose to step up, Bill mentally added the qualifier.

Time's Bloodied Gold

Danny had come to the conclusion that of the thirty-two cases he'd reviewed, most of the arson attacks were unconnected, being either genuinely unfortunate accidents, sheer stupidity by drunken kids, or, in one case, a farmer wanting to get rid of a troublesome tenant and taking advantage of reports of arson attacks in the local papers in an attempt to cover up his own involvement. Two more of the break-in cases he'd quickly laid at the door of a known offender in the neighbourhood, and had brought about a successful prosecution on top of those laid at Watson's door.

But that still left seven incidents which looked worryingly like they were related, once Danny had sifted through the evidence and pulled out the key factors. Those all pointed to an organized and clever gang who had positively counted on their early crime spree slipping under the police radar as connected events. Danny had begun to dig deeper with a care and caution Bill was forced to admire. Disturbingly these reports reminded him all too sharply of why they had been friends rather than of why they had fallen out.

"Damn it, Danny," he muttered in frustration at the memory as he eased himself up onto his feet and went to refill the tea mug, "why did you have to start trying to eclipse me at every turn and spoil it all? I'd have given you every chance to shine, you should have known I would."

Chapter 2

Thursday

When he settled himself back down to work, the next page revealed the heart of Charlie's worries. Danny had become convinced that the gang were at least partially operating out of the Leominster area, for once properly mapped, the relevant crimes radiated around the small town without ever coming too close to it. The nearest they'd got to Leominster was the most minor of the fires close to the village of Ivington, yet revealingly, that had been just a deliberately set fire but with nothing taken and nothing untoward that anyone could pinpoint. Except for the fact that the fire investigators linked the accelerant to the other fires it would have been thought nothing more than the mindless vandalism of an empty barn. It had been enough of a blind to distract the early investigators from spotting the geographical pattern, but Danny had been the one to see the significance of it as, quite literally, a smoke screen. Forensically it was identical: a very hot fire at its centre, but one which this time had never had anything to conceal. One quite deliberately intended to throw an investigation off the scent, and it had, but Danny had also picked up on it being the earliest chronologically and wondered if the gang had been testing the chemicals to see if they would really work before they began in earnest.

He'd also been convinced that the gang probably met somewhere in plain view. Far from sneaking around, which would have drawn the attention of someone sooner or later, Danny thought that they were assembling at

Time's Bloodied Gold

somewhere like a local pub, and then going out and doing a job after closing time, making their exit seem like nothing more than lads who had joined up for a drink, and then leaving normally like all the other customers.

"But why were you focusing on the fires?" Bill asked aloud in his confusion. "I thought Joe said this was all about human traffickers?" He read another couple of pages, went back to look at the dates, and then sat back with a worried frown. "You were doing all this at Hindlip before you even got in the field, weren't you? So has the problem been that you've been trying to answer to two masters?"

He really hoped not, because if so then that could explain why Danny was in trouble if neither side of the investigation had thought he was pulling his weight. Feeling increasingly dismayed, Bill read on.

Danny had begun to visit pubs in the area, to see which he thought were the best candidates for meeting places, well before the time he was due to go undercover. Bill knew how some of the senior men would've reacted to an officer going it alone like that when they found out. It couldn't have endeared Danny to his old colleagues, and was it another reason why their boss had so happily pushed him into the undercover operation, hoping that a dose of reality might bring Danny up short quicker than all the admonishments from the likes of Bill had succeeded in doing? No, Danny hadn't been doing himself any favours despite his astute conclusions.

However, by the time he'd had the go ahead he already had the advantage of being established as a semi-regular at *The Eagle Hotel*, which was the one pub which could be guaranteed to be sufficiently busy on any night to mask a gathering because of having overnight visitors, as well as passing trade. It also conveniently had a bit of a beer garden used by smokers with its own way out, and which was regularly frequented by huddled groups of people in the dark, even in the depths of winter. Multiple ways in and out, and its location on both South Street and with a way through to Corn Street through the car park and an alleyway, made the *Eagle* the prime candidate.

At first Danny had made substantial progress. He was a slim-built man of medium height and with mid brown hair, who could make himself look smart or scruffy with equal ease, unremarkable in most respects, so that he could find himself easily overlooked. Once he'd established his targets he had adopted the guise of a travelling sales rep', disenchanted with the endless struggle to earn a decent wage when most of his remuneration was commission base. He'd propped the bar up on his visits, which he kept suitably random, and moaned about how he wished he could earn more. He didn't have to work that hard on the tale of an ex-wife who had no intention of letting him off the hook financially any time soon, so that he was lucky to be left with enough to live on. Even without having ever drunk in the *Eagle*, Bill needed to use little imagination to visualise Danny stood at the bar, at the slouch in his classic stance, fuming at the latest bill he'd been presented with by Jane.

Then he came to a report in which Danny said that he'd actually made contact with the gang and was being initiated into their membership. Seemingly his preparation work had paid off, because that came remarkably swiftly, but Bill had a sinking feeling that some might see it as happening a bit too fast, especially those whom Danny had managed to rub up the wrong way. He gave names and descriptions of those men he'd met, set up ways in which he could report back to the rest of his team at the taskforce and also to his own headquarters, and had then disappeared properly undercover in September.

Time's Bloodied Gold

At first his written reports had come in by email – always from places with free internet connections and never the same one twice in a row. There was nothing odd in the fact that they were inevitably terse and containing little besides some names or a potential target, because Charlie had included the reports from the officers who had been making personal contact with Danny, and who were getting verbal reports of a much more comprehensive nature. The cover of a sales rep had been a good choice in that it allowed Danny to seem to know people in all sorts of places. Several 'meets' had been done by the contacting officers – including regular ones by his welfare officer, who seemed to be a man called John Taylor – all playing the parts of former purchasers of Danny's wares, discussing the pros and cons of obscure computer parts until those accompanying Danny had gone off to stare in other shop windows, or play a games machine in the pub.

This had gone on nicely for the first month with someone meeting Danny more or less twice weekly, and with phone contact on days in between, but unfortunately there were no clear results coming out of the operation. Bill read the taskforce leader's comments inserted into the reports, and could see only too clearly that the only reason Danny hadn't been pulled out was because he was reporting that many of the gang were Polish, and were possibly part of the same crew the West Mid's lads were looking for. Home grown thugs were bad enough, but ones who needed deporting were definitely to be got off their patch as fast as possible.

Danny was also hinting that there was far more to this than anyone had first spotted. At first Bill thought that he was implying that this gang were attached to another one, but much bigger and nastier. Those hints made him begin to fear that Danny had got embroiled with an outlying faction of some serious organised crime, or, horror of horrors, maybe even the Russian mafia. The reports brought in from the meetings gave names which looked Eastern Bloc, and Danny himself was of the opinion that they had welcomed him because he spoke their language, but he had been able to confirm that other connections these men were speaking to were also Polish. Given the supposed connection to the ring bringing in eastern European prostitutes, it only seemed to confirm the taskforce's belief that events in the western counties were all part and parcel of their investigation, even if Danny had produced nothing more concrete as yet.

Bill had enough sense to know that massive crime networks were totally out of his experience and league. He felt a dreadful frison of fear at this stage of his reading, because if Danny had got himself mixed up with people like that then he was likely already dead, and nothing Bill did would be able to help him. It didn't affect his own willingness to carry on digging, but it was a stark reality he had to face up to – although he had a nasty feeling that Danny might have had delusions of the kind which had him cracking a major eastern crime network, and getting promoted to somewhere substantially more exciting than the rural Midlands.

He felt almost weak with relief when he read further, and realised that at least it wasn't trouble of that sort. There was no doubt that Danny had successfully made an unexpected connection between his raiders and part-time arsonists, and other crimes, but it wasn't on a mafia scale, thank God. This was maybe because the immediate financial returns weren't large enough for the really big boys to get involved. To add to their miseries those being trafficked seemed to be being used as mules, but not for drugs as might have been expected when linked with prostitution.

"Linked to *what*? Antiques?" Bill gasped out loud when he read the word. "Eh?" He scanned another couple of pages and then came back to where he was, deeply puzzled. "Ancient artefacts? Really?"

He went and opened his laptop and did a quick search on the only such thing he knew of, the Staffordshire Hoard, which had been found back in 2009. As images of beautiful small gold items came up on the screen, Bill began to get an idea of what Danny was talking about. This wasn't the stuff to put in some chic shop somewhere and flog for a few hundred. Potentially these were small portable pieces a serious collector would pay large sums of money for. Even before it had been conserved and its potential true value had been established, the Hoard had cost Birmingham Museum and Art Gallery with the Potteries Museum and Art Gallery over three million pounds to save it for the nation, so Bill could well believe that pieces which didn't need major work on them would command a very high price on the black market.

However, what Danny couldn't seem to do was find any tangible proof. Everything was based on his word alone as to what he'd heard or seen, and that wouldn't be enough to bring a conviction without something much more solid to back it up. As early as August and before he was fully undercover, he had reported that he'd witnessed shabby men, and sometimes women, being brought in to the gang's base – which he'd discovered but not been to officially yet – and then being relieved of small items which were quickly whisked away by the boss of the gang. But then Danny's trails of investigation got complicated because the artefacts went one way and the humans seemed to go another.

> Sawaski reports that he is very concerned about the mental health of the trafficked people.

Bill read in a new report.

> They seem to be deeply disorientated and do not appear to understand what is being said to them. Sawaski says that this is not simply when spoken to in English. Polish seems equally incomprehensible to them. Could they be Lithuanians and Sawaski mistaken? Taskforce evidence does not indicate potential links in any region apart from the Baltic states. Insufficient manpower to run a second investigation regarding a whole new region of exploitation in tandem with current one, Sawaski needs to be clear on the targets.

That gave Bill a shiver. What the hell was going on here? It sounded as though whatever it was that Danny had got himself into, it had turned out to be something quite separate to the main investigation, and that didn't bode well. But if the powers that be didn't want to pursue that line of enquiry at the moment, why hadn't they pulled Danny out? Then the nasty thought came to Bill that if those Danny had witnessed were people who could be classed as vulnerable, then visibly closing an investigation into them would have very negative implications if it ever came to light. However, not pouring manpower into it if it was something of nothing protected the budget too!

Time's Bloodied Gold

"Oh bollocks, Danny, what did you get into?" Bill sighed, then felt a sudden tug of guilt, because if not for a twist of fate it would have been him stuck, not Danny. He'd been the one they'd approached first of all. He was the one Joe had wanted.

And why was that? Joe had said they wanted someone who could take care of themselves, so had there always been the chance that whoever took the job would be out on their own? He only knew Joe as an acquaintance, not a close friend, but he had taken his word on this, and now it was starting to look as though he shouldn't have. This strange isolation was bad news, and while Bill knew that all undercover officers should ideally have daily contact with a welfare office, he also knew that in reality things rarely went to plan. Only recently there had been the very public scandal of a police officer sent undercover for years without proper procedures. Someone who had been – in Bill's opinion – shockingly treated by the job. Especially as that officer had consequently come into contact with other officers who'd had no idea that he was an undercover colleague; who had treated him appallingly; and who had thereby shown him a very negative side to his job just when he had been most vulnerable and unsupported.

"Christ, Danny, I hope you aren't heading down that road," Bill found himself praying. "Dear God, if I got you into something that awful, I'll never forgive myself."

By the time the next month had rolled to an end, Danny's personal contacts had been pulled back to once a week. That all by itself was a worrying shift in procedure. And what worried Bill more than the crimes was that there seemed to be a real problem with communication from this stage onwards.

Danny missed five meets in October, and then sent irate e-mails or texts within days of each one, asking where the hell everyone was. Instead of questioning what was going on, however, the leading DCI had inserted a terse note into the file that in his opinion Danny was showing signs of stress and should never have been given so much leeway when he was in that condition. Bill knew this particular West Mid's DCI by reputation, and how much he loathed their Superintendent Williams, so that note looked very much like back-covering and also a possibility of shifting blame away from the taskforce if things went wrong, since it had been Williams personally who had agreed to Danny's secondment. It also read very much as though those senior staff involved were starting to think that Danny had been sent into a situation beyond his ability to deal with.

Yet only a day later there was a transcript of an email message to a hidden account from his own division to Danny telling him to keep working on the arson cases. It was as though the left hand didn't know what the right was doing, with Danny being caught in the middle.

"Where's your bloody welfare officer?" Bill fumed, turning the latest pages back and forth, hoping he'd missed something, or the pages had got out of order. But try as he might he could find next to nothing in weeks from this John Taylor who should have been with Danny all the way. Nor could he find Joe.

Going to the pile of stuff he hadn't read already, Bill rummaged through and finally came up with what little Charlie had found for him on the taskforce. With growing horror he read of Joe being moved on to another case entirely even before Danny had gone undercover, and there was just a snippet of a memo which implied that someone very senior had decided that Taylor's experience was needed to handle a man going inside one of the more dangerous urban gangs closer to the taskforce's existing target.

"But who took over Danny?" Bill gasped.

By now he was scattering clumps of papers all over his living room floor, frantically trying to find a clue as to what had happened. Yet as far as he could see, nobody had been reassigned to Danny, and then he came across another snippet.

```
...no need for Sawaski to
have a handler from us as he
should be returning to his home
nightly and can call in.
```

"Home? What bloody home? He surely wasn't operating out of his own flat in Worcester, was he? Please tell me you didn't compromise him that much?"

Again he ripped through page after page in different piles of papers until he came to a clue – Danny had taken a tiny flat in Leominster right at the start of the operation.

"You fuckwits! Returning to a cover address isn't the same as going home! How did you think you were going to find him, eh?"

Grabbing his notepad, Bill made an immediate note of the address, mentally adding that he was going to have to mothball his beloved classic Mini Cooper for a while, and hire an automatic so that he could drive out to see this place. Thank God it was his left knee that had gone. Without the need to use a clutch he'd be fine driving with just one functioning leg.

Feeling positively shaky, Bill went and got another hot drink and stuck a curry in the microwave out of his well-stocked freezer. He would dearly have loved a stiff scotch at the moment, but the antibiotics he was on post-op wouldn't mix well with one, so he had to make do with tea strong enough to strip wallpaper off with. Fortified by the food, he braced himself to return to the papers, expecting worse to come.

Now the tone of the messages changed again, and Bill found himself reading transcripts of text messages sent from pay-as-you-go mobile phones interspersing the e-mails.

> <u>November 6th: e-mail</u>:
> Need to meet soonest. Have new information on 'Boris'. Also have evidence to hand on to you. Please meet me at the bridge in Tenbury in four days. Can't come sooner. Make it 1.00 - my minders will be in the pub and I can slip away for a few minutes!
> DS
> <u>Note from taskforce</u>: DCI to arrange for someone to meet DS Sawaski.

Bill raised an eyebrow at this. The attitude now seemed extraordinarily relaxed about it all given where Danny was. Had something gone on which was unrecorded here, or at least which Charlie hadn't been able to find? Maybe a quiet meeting between the Danny's new DCI on the West Mid's force and Williams in the latter's office, in which they had begun to doubt all of Danny's actions and motives? If they had come to the conclusion that he'd become compromised and was trying to feather his own nest as well, then it might account for the sudden coolness towards an officer who ought to have had more support under normal circumstances. There was certainly something happening in the background, off-record, and it wasn't good. Bill had once thought he would feel more satisfaction

Time's Bloodied Gold

at Danny's office-politics games coming back to bite him at last, yet now the moment had come he wasn't in the slightest bit smug, just worried sick.

He read on,

> November 9th: e-mail:
> Where the hell were you today? I waited by the bridge in Tenbury and no-one came! Suspect somewhere in Shobden a new target. Fear they have new 'goods' arriving and new targets! Contact me soonest! DS
>
> Note from taskforce: no meeting set up for 9th, no idea why he should be expecting it earlier. Officers went today, 10th, as prearranged by phone message left at station on a direct line's voicemail during the night of 8th and saw no signs of Sawaski. Left message at agreed spot - Sawaski to come in to any station and terminate the operation.
>
> November 13th: text message to direct line within the station:
> Definite new acquisitions linked to main inquiry! Arson used to dispose of faulty 'good's. Supposed links correct! Cannot ring in or come in! Am being watched closely! Next target seems very important to them! Will inform you as soon as I know. Wait for me!

> Note from taskforce: mobile number registered to pay-as-you-go phone which must have been disposed of after use. When rang was picked up by passer-by who kindly took the phone into nearby Leominster station. What is he doing in Leominster? No indication of cases needing investigation there. Officer sent with repeat of previous message to meeting point in Bromyard to await Sawaski.

Bill looked at the transcript in open dismay. What? How could they not know he'd be in Leominster when he'd been set up there? Then a horrible thought came to him. Had someone implied to Danny that he ought to do such a thing, but had it been Danny himself who had found and rented the flat? Because if it had gone through official channels then what he'd just read made no sense. And which side of the investigation had suggested it? Presumably not the ones taking the messages? And worse, it was looking increasingly like they were running out of patience with Danny, Bill thought.

Moreover, if he had been in Leominster, or any other larger town for that matter, then there were plenty of chances to go into a station and get away from this gang once and for all. So why wasn't he taking it if he was so worried? Surely he had enough on them now to be able to direct a proper raid on their hiding place? Or was he getting the sense that he wasn't being believed? And what of this fire he'd reported? Bill dived on the fire reports again and confirmed that this fire was not amongst them going by the dates. Or was that because it hadn't actually happened? Dear God, had the gang deliberately given Danny wrong information about Shobden to see if anyone turned up at the location? If they had, then the taskforce's indifference might just have saved Danny's life.

He scratched the five o'clock shadow on his chin, rasping the hint of stubble as he thought. Danny was clearly moving about a lot more than anyone had expected, but in his eyes that should have been cause for more concern, not less. Was Danny with the gang all the time, or at least a very large part of it? It sounded horribly like it, otherwise he would have been meeting officers as he had been at the start, although Bill did have his doubts regarding that by this point. So it must mean that these men, whoever they were, were also highly mobile. That might make it harder for Danny to trace a base of any kind, and it might also account for why Danny was still reluctant to come in. If he was thinking that these men were even more dangerous than anyone had anticipated, and the victims more vulnerable, it would be wholly in character for Danny to become equally more committed to bringing them in.

The tone of the messages was also get more tense and irate, Bill realised.

<u>November 15th: text message to same direct line, again one-use phone</u>:
Meet me at Leominster station at 4.00pm on 17th - last day for poss cover by crowds of school children! ½ term next week. Will bring proof of our original targets! Get to forensics soonest for all our sakes!

<u>Note from taskforce</u>: message sent to his home division for a

```
patrol car to be sent at time as
requested for presumed
extraction. No sign of DS
Sawaski.
```

Ouch! Bill thought. A patrol car! That really meant that someone was intent on getting Danny back in the fold one way or another. On the other hand, if Danny had truly stumbled on something nasty then it was a clumsy and heavy-handed thing to do, and one which might backfire on them all badly. Clearly Danny had thought so too from his next contact,

```
November 17th: text message
from public phone, Bromyard:
   WHAT ARE YOU DOING!? TRYING
TO GET ME KILLED! I SAID CONTACT
NOT A BLOODY ARREST! All you've
done is spook them badly!
```

The fact that the handling officers hadn't even bothered to deign this with a comment told Bill that they had evidently dismissed this as sheer histrionics. And why had no-one picked up and responded to the intent to bring them evidence? Presumably it would have DNA on it, and if it was something like a piece of bloody clothing then Danny had been taking a big risk holding on to it. What had they been thinking to disregard him like that?

Danny was many things, but he'd never been a man to make mountains out of molehills. Indeed, in their long working relationship together Bill couldn't think of another time when Danny had sounded so genuinely scared. He'd seen him aggravated by stupid or ill thought out actions by other officers. He'd seen him downright angry at times. And he'd seen Danny react to danger often enough to know how Danny normally covered his fear with light-

Time's Bloodied Gold

hearted banter and silly jokes, or biting sarcasm. None of which sounded anything like the tone of these messages here, and although they were written, Bill knew Danny well enough to be able to hear Danny's voice as clearly as if he were standing shouting in his ear. Danny was shit scared!

> November 20th: text message from public phone, Hereford:
> Have been taken to Kyrewood Graves. This is at the heart of things, not just a cache spot but the base I have been searching for. Have information on those targeted for next incident on next full moon! Meet me Bromyard, by sports centre, tomorrow 6ish!
>
> Note from taskforce:
> contacted home division, PC Ellis volunteered to walk by on his way home. Reports that he loitered for a while but saw no sign of Sawaski.

And there it was, the heart of the problem! Something which had been niggling at Bill ever since he'd started reading this stuff. PC Ellis was new to the force, if Bill was recalling the right fresh-faced lad whose details had been circulated as one of the new starters, and he hadn't even seen Danny before, much less worked with him, as far as Bill knew. All these people could only have had the most superficial of working relationships with Danny, especially as he'd been moved well away from his and Bill's old team.

In fact Bill was shocked, now he'd spotted it, that absolutely no-one from their old unit had been used in any way, shape or form on this operation. Forget that they might be working on other cases, it would have been the simplest thing for one of them to make a brief contact. Instead, Danny had been teamed with men who, to all intents and purposes, were virtual strangers to him. No wonder, then, that Danny's pleas were going unnoticed. They must have been judging him purely by what they'd been told by a hostile Williams and other senior officers. Men whom Danny had succeeded in alienating badly. Had these newer officers looked at Danny and thought they were seeing one of their own turning bad? Someone making exaggerated claims to cover up the fact that he was, in reality, happier on the other side of the fence, and away from the restraints of his superiors? God, Bill wanted to punch Williams out! No officer should be left like this!

Bill almost dreaded reading the final entries,

```
November 30th: e-mail:
Finally managed to get away.
Something happening here in
Bristol too. Is anyone backing
me up on this? I can only carry
evidence with me if I know
you're going to take it off me
and definitely turn up! If
they'd searched me last week and
found what I was carrying you'd
have got me killed! These people
mean business! We were right -
workers come here! Please note
AGAIN: the fires are a blind,
they cover other evidence. Look
at neighbo

Note from taskforce: e-mail
not completed, presume
interrupted. Once cafe traced,
reported no signs of a scuffle
```

Time's Bloodied Gold

```
or anyone departing under force
from others.
```

Clearly Danny hadn't wanted to just walk away from the whole thing. Bill suspected he'd feared that if he did so, the gang would tumble to the fact that they'd been infiltrated, and might step up the level of violence to those trafficked in response. Danny himself certainly seemed to have no doubts that they were capable of extreme behaviour. But the way he'd presumably envisaged things resolving themselves was for his information to lead to his superiors sanctioning others to come in mob-handed, and to clean up the whole miserable pack of miscreants he was entangled with, not leave him hanging in the wind!

```
    December 6th: text message
from one-use phone:
 You failed to turn up again!
Why are you doing this to me?
YOU requested the meet, not me!
Had to ditch evidence in the
Teme. STOP PLAYING GAMES! THESE
MEN WILL KILL MORE THAN ME!
    Note from taskforce: again no
meeting set up for 6th. Meeting
prearranged for 3rd - same
method as before, Sawaski
leaving voice message on direct
line in early hours. DS Sawaski
failed to make contact, so can
only assume situation not as
urgent as he's making out.
```

Bloody hell, Bill mentally fumed, *what in God's name were you lot playing at? Who exactly decided that it was Danny who rang you? Was it just because they gave his name?* Or did they give a name at all? Was it just implied that he was an undercover cop as bait? Bill hope fervently that Charlie would have an answer to that one, and that some of the evidence he was going into the station for would be a tape of one of those messages. *I bet you never even played it to one of our old team to see if it was actually Danny's voice*, Bill thought bitterly. *Because it's blindingly obvious now that your messages to him were being intercepted, and they've been playing Danny to see if he goes to these meetings. Are you all blind to what's going on?*

He got his answer at the end of the next e-mail.

> December 11th: e-mail:
> Meeting desperately needed! If you don't come and help get me out soon it will be too late. The heart of the operation is out beyond Tenbury! Haven't got full details but they moved some goods to somewhere else. Scared off, I think! I'm being watched almost all of the time! They think I'm checking sales reports at the moment and getting a warning from my boss, but I can't string this out much longer. Strensham services best place! Tomorrow! Wait for me!
>
> Note from taskforce: DS Sawaski showing signs of paranoia, unable to comply with request since we don't know which side of the M5 he's coming to - budget doesn't run to men on both sides all day. Unmarked patrol vehicles checked both in passing at noon without sign of Sawaski. Last reported sighting

Time's Bloodied Gold

    of him was in Bromyard on 9th by
uniformed officer. Appeared to
be alone and unsupervised but
turned and walked away when
officer made eye contact.

Dear God, they thought Danny was inventing it all! Shocking though it was to Bill, he could see all too clearly what Charlie had meant, and how horribly the wires had become crossed in this dire, tangled mess.

    December 14th: text message
from private mobile:
    House in Clifton, Bristol,
integral to op! Will be in Ross
again on 17th. Extraction needed
but NOT by uniformed officers!
Meet at roadside cafe past M50
on A40, if not there WAIT.

    Note from taskforce:
apparently stopped a member of
the public and asked if he could
send a quick text. He deleted it
from her phone so she had no
idea what it said. Supt.
Williams informed, disciplinary
note made against DS Sawaski for
potentially endangering a member
of the public. Bailey and
Shepherd went to Ross under
strict instructions to bring
Sawaski back no matter what, but
saw no sign of him.

Bill mentally gulped. Bailey and Shepherd? Who the bloody hell were they? West Mid's men? Danny must have been looking for a familiar face and they'd sent him two strangers! He could have walked by under their noses and they wouldn't have spotted him if Danny was incognito. He was hardly a remarkable looking bloke at the best of times. Fucking hell, what a cock-up! And he didn't like the sound of that last sentence at all. Bringing Danny back like that sounded like they were all set to discipline him and shove him out of the force before he could embarrass them, or worse. Bill knew that sounded ridiculous, but that poor bloke who'd spent seven years undercover had been told by his old force he had no skills they needed when he came back. He'd been shot out of the force faster than a cat skin from the back of a dodgy takeaway, and the shivers running up and down Bill's spine were telling him that Danny was heading for the same treatment.

```
December 17th: text message
from private mobile:
  Last chance! Frankley
service, M5, 8.00am on 21st.
Tell Bill S to come. I trust
him! Extract me now!

  Note from taskforce: DI
Scathlock not on this taskforce,
also known to be at loggerheads
with DS Sawaski - further
indication of increasing mental
instability? Supt. Williams
questions whether Sawaski is
really undercover or simply
delusional. Also appalled by
second use of a civilian's phone
under false pretexts. Order
issued to detain on sight.
```

"You stupid bastards!" Bill raged out loud now in his exasperation, "of course, we were at loggerheads, but that's the point! He's trying to tell you something is very wrong!

Time's Bloodied Gold

And for a start off it's that he needs to see someone he can recognise, not a total bloody stranger! Why in God's name didn't someone at least pick up the phone to me? Christ, it's not as though I'm bed-bound even now! I could've gone without any of you having to get your hands dirty!" Then a nasty thought came to him. "Was this the plan all along to get rid of Danny? Give him enough rope to hang himself and then wash your hands of him? If he came up trumps then there's nothing lost, but you expected him to get into trouble, didn't you, Williams! You fully expected him to come to grief so that you could get shot of him one way or another! You bastard!"

> December 21st: email from internet cafe in Birmingham:
> No more time left, evidence goes in 4 days. The house in Clifton has history! Why won't you help me? No chance of turning self in. THE BLOOD IS ON YOUR HANDS IF YOU DON'T!
>
> Note from taskforce: Passer-by reports seeing three men manhandling another out of the Bull Ring and reported it to police. Partial finger prints found on a post reported as Sawaski's, but second witness says he was drunk. Reported getting into a car which turns out to be hired by a Mr Savage. Supt. Williams believes Sawaski/Savage has gone across to the arsonists' side and is to be considered suspect from now on.

"Oh you are joking!" Bill gulped, feeling his stomach churn sickeningly. "No, no, no! Danny's many things, but he'd never be bent! Oh God! You let him go, didn't you! You've left him to it! And if they're caught and Danny's with them, you'll have him arrested and put in the dock as a bent copper. Jesus, Williams, if you were within reach I'd bloody kill you for this!"

```
December 28th: text message
from public phone in Leominster
by B&B housing benefit
claimants:
    Tell Bill S I forgive him!
Tell Zoe I love her.
    Note from taskforce:
virtually impossible to trace
the comings and goings at the
boarding house. No chance of
prints. No reason to issue a
warrant to search the place
either. Most residents have form
but not suspect for
current/specific misdemeanours.
No sign of Sawaski or sightings.
```

This was the last message from Danny, and Bill found himself torn between wanting to punch someone very hard (preferably Williams), and weeping at the sheer incompetence of it all. It certainly explained why Zoe hadn't had her Christmas present! Danny must have been struggling for his very life in those last few days.

Read as one body of writing he found his responses echoing Charlie's, with the sense of worry which had grown with each contact report. Maybe the men in the station just hadn't seen the urgency when they were picking these messages up days apart and while doing other jobs. Forcing himself to be realistic, Bill could see that it was unlikely that

Time's Bloodied Gold

the same person would be taking the messages over and over. With their own workloads to worry about, the weekly contacts must have read as formalities. Especially if there had been some misconception at the Birmingham end that Danny was merely pursuing enquiries on their behalf, rather than being actively undercover. His messages seen in that light would sound bizarre.

And they didn't know Danny like he did, or even as well as Charlie did. Coming from a colleague they'd hardly got chance to know before he was off into the wilds (and on what might well have been interpreted as some kind of ego trip), Bill couldn't in all honesty blame them for not raising the alarm earlier. The ones he reserved his venom for were Williams, the DCI, and whoever ought to have been Danny's welfare officer, all of whom *ought* to have known better. Thank God for Charlie's curiosity and sixth sense for things going wrong!

What worried Bill far more was that there were blatant pleas for help which had gone unnoticed. Pleas which any senior officer worth his rank should have picked up on if the whole operation had been properly supervised. Words like 'extraction' cropping up with increasing urgency. That made him angry. Really angry! Angry enough to forget all differences of the last two years. Charlie was right, something had to be done – from outside of the police force if no-one would do it from within. And Charlie had read him right too. Whatever had passed between himself and Danny, this put it all into the pale. He was going to get to the bottom of this and find his old friend come hell or high water! Bill hadn't ever lost a man on his shift and he wasn't going to start now.

Chapter 3

February ~ Friday

By the time he'd finished reading the reports Bill was shattered and too wound up to do any more that night. A good night's sleep would put another perspective on things, he knew. However, in the morning, armed with a large mug of industrial strength coffee, he sat down to read through the reports again, far more motivated than he'd been when he began yesterday. If he was to help Danny at all he needed to get his head around the crimes which had triggered this whole sorry mess. So spreading them out on his big coffee table he began to go through them again.

With Danny's comment in mind that the electrical goods had not been the primary motive, he found himself looking harder at the minor details than at the main texts. Why the super hot fires, and what had they been concealing? Then he spotted it. A common link, and it went back to what Danny had been trying to say in that email that had been cut short. In every case units close to the supposed targets had also suffered fire damage. Not as bad to be sure, and therein lay the clue – these owners were claiming for things like smoke damage to furnishings, or heat damage to delicate equipment, not wholesale destruction, so they were never seen as the targets. But many neighbouring units had been entered by the fire brigade checking for secondary fires, and so it was harder to tell whether they had been entered before that. There was the possibility that when owners had turned up, that they had no idea whether a door was not as securely locked as when they had last been in. Was that why the fires had been set to burn so hot, to be sure they affected the neighbouring units who were the real targets?

And then Bill saw something else. Something which was possibly what had tipped Danny off. The electrical workshops or suppliers were all ridiculously diverse. One unit specialized in reconditioning washing machines to be resold to raise money for charity. Another made small components for the car industry. Yet another was making incredibly tiny electrical control panels mainly to go into things used by the military but for other specialized industries too, although hardly James Bond, secret squirrel stuff. There was no rhyme or reason why anyone would want bits from all these diverse fields. As a body there was no coherence. And the disunity went on throughout the whole series of attacks. All the 'targets' had in common was that in some way, shape or form, they could be classified as 'electrical'.

Bill stared at the reports, willing them to show him what Danny had unearthed. When his stomach started growling he realized that he'd worked straight through until midday without a break. Padding through to his kitchen he made himself a doorstep sandwich of ham and cheese, and refilled his coffee mug. Then he took both to the sofa facing the big bay window, sitting at the other end of it to his chair and the oak chest smothered in papers. Bill's flat only had one of everything – living room, bedroom, kitchen and bathroom – but it was a lower ground floor flat in a large old Victorian building facing the river in Worcester. This meant that all the rooms were of a good size, for once upon a time they had been some of the public rooms of a substantial and grand home, and Bill's living room had a huge ceiling-to-floor bay window, which had glorious views over the river. Whenever anything was bothering him, Bill found himself inevitably drawn to the peaceful scene, for apart from calming him, it also helped him focus on the heart of the matter and away from any distractions. As he watched a lone seagull swooping low over the water in the pale February sun it suddenly came to him, and he hurried back to the chest.

There it was! In each case there had been someone either selling, storing or restoring antique objects in the same complex or farmyard to the electrical units. They hadn't seemed so obvious because they weren't such fashionable targets for thieves as electronics, but also because to a cursory inspection they had seemed even more disparate than the electrical goods. But now that Bill came to look at them closely he realized that they might have more in common than he'd first thought. What they definitely weren't dealing with was large quantities of furniture of the kind which eager members of the general public would buy to 'authentically' furnish their period houses with. People who owned places like Bill's flat where a large bureau or wardrobe would look very much in keeping. No, these were quite different. Quite often they were the smallest units of the ones surrounding them, the four largest being used by individual antique dealers who worked collectors' fairs and didn't have shops to store their wares at. And this was the link to Danny's reference to antiquities, because he spotted almost instantly on this repeat read through that one of them sold items such as Roman coins via an internet site.

"Sharp-eyed of you, Danny," Bill murmured in approval, sitting back to think.

Yes, that started to make more sense. If these poor unfortunates were bringing stuff in that would be classed as portable antiquities, then they could easily be stuffed into pockets or stitched into clothing, and would be small

Time's Bloodied Gold

enough to pass unnoticed. As for where they were coming from, it hardly took a long internet search to find reports of ancient places being ransacked in the current chaos in the Middle East. That could be one source, but equally there were digs in almost every western European country, and it could as easily be that stuff was being filched off an important site much closer to home and being brought here to trade onwards.

He looked at each of the seven antique dealers closer now, and found that they all had similar stock. There were certainly differences, but all stocked a plethora of random small items where it might be hard to see just what was missing. For instance, ten battered Roman coins out of close to a hundred kept in a drawer would be initially overlooked, and Bill wondered how many owners would be back in touch when they came to do a stock-take. Of course, by then whatever they had lost would be long gone. Might some of them even resign themselves to the loss and not report it for fear of insurance premiums going through the roof? That would make the targeting of small firms all the more cunning. They would undoubtedly claim for a major piece going missing, but the avarice of modern insurers sometimes made them seem worse than the crooks – they, at least, wouldn't be taking a hefty chunk out of a one-man company's earnings every single month like the insurance companies would – and some owners might therefore work on the hope of lightning not striking twice.

"But why the fires?" Bill mused, wandering over to the window again and staring at the river. "Are they just to try and disguise the fact that these places have been broken into? ...In fact, why did you need to break into them at all? ...Hmm, do you need other bits and pieces to bulk up your load? Or do you approach your customers with several items, knowing that they'll pounce on one, but working on the presumption that if you just offered them that one piece alone that they'd be more suspicious of where it came from?"

That sounded plausible. The buyers of these items weren't going to be that scrupulous, Bill knew, but presumably they saw a big difference between buying something by a devious route and something which was downright 'hot'. Some big collectors would be solitary in habits, having stuff simply to gloat over it alone, but others would want to show their acquisitions off, and it was these people whom Bill foresaw as wanting to avoid having someone say, "hey, isn't that from such-and-such a site?" This gang had been very clever in all that they had done, to Bill's mind. Clever enough to offer a bulk of modest stuff (acquired from the break-ins to match what came into them) salted with a few tasty items, but which would look normal enough to the kind of buyers who wouldn't ask too many questions.

He knew that while the Portable Antiquities Scheme was supposed to protect valuable heritage sites from being plundered by idiots who did damage to ancient monuments, and who hoped to get rich quick off finds, the reality was that very few prosecutions had been brought. Nor were the sentences that much of a deterrent to hardened criminals – a few hundred hours of community service was hardly going to have their sort quaking in their boots.

And how did things stand with stuff brought in from abroad? In theory they were protected by the Hague Convention and by UNESCO, he knew, but how effectively could they hope to be policed? He found an online reference to men who had been imprisoned for trying to sell over three thousand Ancient Greek coins looted from an important heritage site in Romania with a value of more than three million euros, but that hadn't ended well. The coins had been sold in an American auction and only a handful of them had ever been recovered. What was more, a single coin – if it was the right sort, as they had been in this case – could easily net those selling it as much as eight hundred euros each, making Bill blink at the potential rewards from such a trade. Three thousand coins at even five hundred euros each was still quite a haul for a bit of illegal archaeology.

However, Bill could also see that where the Romanian criminals had gone wrong was in stealing from an important site in the first place, and then selling their loot through a major auction, leaving a substantial trail to follow. He had a strong sense that the men Danny was tracking were being a lot craftier. Wherever they were getting this stuff from, they were disposing of it in tiny amounts, and it looked suspiciously as if they already had private buyers lined up without the need to go anywhere near an auction house. His bet would be on whoever was the brains behind this having sat in the background at many an auction before they'd ever started this, making notes of who might be approachable on the sly, and who to avoid. They would have looked for the collectors who were clued up enough to know what they were looking at without an auctioneer providing provenance for a piece. Indeed it looked very much as though they might be selling abroad. Danny had seemingly found no hint of strange sales in the UK since there was nothing in these reports to that effect.

What Bill would really have liked was a hint from Danny as to what exactly this gang was selling. Was it coins, artifacts like brooches, or even manuscripts? The latter seemed unlikely if they were being brought in by illegal immigrants, because there was far too great a chance of them getting damaged. No, it would be something a little more robust, or at the very least something which could withstand getting wet, because the odds were that at some point these poor lost souls had got into a boat of some sort.

Sighing at the realization that the solution would not be as simple as enquiring with local dealers as to whether there had been a sudden glut of Romano-British coins on the market, Bill decided that nonetheless he needed to get out and do something. He had dragged what he could out of the files for now, and sitting staring at them was only going to give him a headache. Time to get on to the local car hire firm and get mobile.

Within the hour he had an automatic Citroen sitting outside his building, helpfully brought to him by an obliging young man once he had been told of Bill's knee problem. It was ideal for Bill at the moment, having plenty of leg room and being substantially taller than his Mini, which made it far easier to get in and out of. Easing himself behind the wheel, he propped his crutch up in the passenger foot-well and set off for Leominster.

It was only twenty-five miles along the A44 to Leominster from Worcester, a short enough drive and one which passed through the outskirts of Bromyard, but Bill refrained from stopping there today, wanting to have a better idea of how Danny connected to the place – especially with regards to that oblique taskforce reference to a meeting place. Best not to do anything until he was sure he wasn't about to trigger any unwanted reactions. He knew he was also going to have to call in at the *Eagle* in Leominster, and fairly soon, but he wanted to have a better idea of who he was dealing with when he did that. Just at the moment he was in no position to be able to make a fast exit from the place if things started looking tricky. But

Time's Bloodied Gold

Danny's flat was something else, and Bill felt happier about tackling that first.

He got into the town and parked easily enough, blessing the fact that there was pay-and-display parking just off West Street where Danny's flat was. West Street was a restricted traffic section of town, and as Bill limped out of the car park opposite the *Black Swan*, he thought that Danny had made a good choice. Nobody was going to be able to drive up behind him at speed here and grab him, or at least not without attracting an awful lot of adverse attention. And the *Black Swan* was more of a hotel than the kind of pub with big screen TVs showing sport all day and every day, pool tables, and rows of over-chilled lager pulls and chemically created shots, all of which meant few rowdy late night drinkers and fights that might disguise Danny taking a beating.

Then when Bill realized that Danny's flat was in the elegant old building between the *Black Swan* and a takeaway, he had to smile. Danny had always been one for his Chinese meals, and it seemed as though he would have been well catered for here. It saddened him, though, because he could see that under other circumstances, Danny might have been a lot happier here than in his over-priced, ultra modern chicken-coop of a flat in the centre of Worcester. This was far more to Danny's taste, remembering the arguments with Jane when Danny had wanted to buy a Georgian cottage for them, even though it had been far outside of their budget.

The outer door to the flats at the side of the building succumbed to Bill's talents with a pick far too easily – the Friday afternoon shoppers all too intent on getting done, and going home, to watch a man seemingly fumbling with his keys – and soon he was walking up to the third floor where Danny's flat was. That was good attribute, Bill thought, because the only people coming up the stairs this far had to be going to Danny's attic flat or the one across the corridor. You wouldn't confuse someone coming to break the door down with people going on up to other flats. It was also good as far as Bill was concerned, because it meant that he was undisturbed as he picked this lock too.

Inside he was amazed at how like his own place this was. Was there some subconscious choice going on here with Danny? It was smaller, and the layout was different, of course, with the entrance coming in from the middle of the building and with the bathroom immediately in front of it, but the feel of it was the same. Turning right into the living room, he found it was similarly high-ceilinged to his own, although with some sloping of the ceiling from the eaves, with an attractive large window looking out onto the roofs of the building opposite even if it lacked Bill's wonderful view. However, whereas Bill had a proper kitchen, this place just had a row of kitchen units along the wall backing onto the bathroom.

"Danny, my old son, what was going on in your brain when you picked this place?" Bill murmured softly, as he began a methodical search of the place, careful to use gloves to leave no trace of being there. The place had obviously been let fully furnished, because Bill knew Danny's taste and this wasn't it. A squashy three-seater sofa under the window had probably seen a lot of action with previous tenants even if not with Danny, and Bill guessed that if anyone ever did a forensic sweep of the place all sorts of DNA would come off that. This was the kind of place that would attract young, single men looking for a first place away from home, or divorcees like Danny needing a cheap pad. A rickety bookcase, on the other hand, showed a few books, all of which Bill knew were Danny's. They were the old favourites he returned to over

Time's Bloodied Gold

and over again, and Bill suddenly had the compulsion to take them with him, fishing a carrier bag out of his pocket and piling them into it. If Danny never came back here, he didn't want the landlord just chucking them into a skip. He would take them back with him and keep them safe for Danny. The taking of the books might also signal to Danny that someone who knew him had been here if he came back in a panic, and that that person had been Bill.

However, the living room revealed nothing else of interest, and Bill walked back to the door and tried the bedroom across the tiny hall next. A double bed was neatly made and looked undisturbed, while the wardrobe built into the recess of the chimney breast contained the well-worn suits Danny wore to work, and which would have served him just as well as a rep struggling to make a living. The chest of drawers revealed only day to day clothing too, but something caught Bill's eye. The drawers were beside the sealed off chimney, whose hearth had been covered over with a sheet of hardboard and painted to match the rest of the room. However, the screw at the bottom beside the chest had lost its paint. It could have been just that it was the one most likely to get kicked and scuffed, but Bill thought it worth inspecting.

Getting down so that he could sit on the floor with his bad leg stretched out, Bill pulled his multi-purpose knife out of his pocket and opened up the screwdriver blade. As he'd thought, the screw undid far too easily for it just to have had the paint scuffed. This had been opened and closed more than once, and regularly at that. Looking at the hardboard, though, only this screw had been worked on, so nothing large could have been hidden without bending the board to near snapping point.

Very cautiously, Bill began to probe inside with his finger tips. Something moved under them and with great care he pulled it back to the opening. What came out was a memory card of the kind used in cameras, in a firm, clear plastic case.

"Oh you beauty," Bill whispered in delight, wriggling so that he could lie fully flat and shine a small torch into the space. There were two more SD cards in there, each in a tiny individual case, and Bill retrieved them both, screwing the board firmly back into place.

Getting back up onto his feet was rather more of a challenge, but he managed it by virtue of heaving himself up on the bed. Smoothing the covers straight again, he decided he would check the bathroom, just in case. He wasn't expecting to find anything much there. Danny hadn't been here long enough to find much worth hiding, and anything with the gang's DNA on it was hardly going to be here. Danny wouldn't have taken that kind of risk. It could backfire on him in all sorts of ways.

So it was more force of habit than anything else that made Bill lift the lid of the low-level toilet cistern, but then almost drop it in shock. There was a packet of white powder wrapped in several layers of clingfilm and then in a sealable plastic bag in there, and Bill knew straight away that it was cocaine. Not for one moment did he think it was Danny's, but it confirmed to him all over again that Danny was in mortal danger. Someone – and it was most likely to be the gang – had left something which would seriously incriminate him if it came to light. But why? Was it an active scheme to get rid of Danny? If so, that was an awful lot of money to throw away, which made this gang a lot better funded than anything in the reports had implied. Bill didn't think they would be shy of getting physical with Danny if they knew he was a cop, so why bother blackening his name? And there had been no mention of drugs at all, which was also worrying because it either meant that the gang had branched out, or that the background information from before Danny had gone in had been horribly wrong.

Bill stood and looked at the cocaine long and hard before coming to a conclusion. If Danny had had so much as a whiff of drug dealing he would have found some way to get it into one of those reports, even if it was just one word like 'cocaine', Bill thought. So maybe one of the gang had come up here? Somebody Danny had felt he had to invite up to keep the pretence going? Going back into the kitchen, Bill looked at the bottles in the cupboard – Polish vodka, not a drink Danny ever had from choice. So that confirmed that he'd got it in in anticipation, and going by the way half of it was gone, somebody had got stuck into it. Then he looked at the almost empty gin bottle beside it and had a suspicion. Unscrewing the lid he sniffed at it. Not a hint of gin! So Danny had been filling that with water and drinking it with the tonic water which was also there to keep up appearances, while staying stone cold sober.

But what to do about the cocaine? If he left it and the next people who came calling were men from the taskforce looking for evidence against Danny, then that could be disastrous. On the other hand, if he just took it, and the mystery man had been in here since Danny had vanished then that might endanger him just as much by suggesting Danny had backup that wasn't actually there. Yet leaving it here wasn't an option for many reasons, not least the dangers of it getting onto the streets.

"A break in," Bill sighed. "I'm going to have to fake a break in."

If it looked like random, opportunist thieves, then they could well have made off with the drugs and Danny would be in the clear. So Bill went through the flat, silently creating the kind of mayhem he knew all too well got left behind after a regular break in, including leaving the cistern lid askew to drop a hint if the gang returned. When he was satisfied that he had done a good job, he slit the cocaine packet open and deposited it in the toilet bowl. Before he flushed, though, he went out onto the stairs and stood and listened carefully. Hopefully everyone in these cramped flats was out at work, because they weren't big enough to house mums who might be at home with a small child. Certainly he couldn't hear anyone moving about, or the sounds of daytime TV or a radio on, and so he went back into the flat and flushed the toilet. Nobody came out to see who was in the empty flat upstairs, and so he risked a second flush to get rid of all trace of the drugs. Then pulling the flat door just shut, he carefully hobbled down the stairs with the bag of books and let himself out into the street.

Taking his time now, he walked the loop along West Street, onto High Street and onto Burgess Street to then come back up onto West Street via narrow back ways, in the process ramming the plastic bag from the cocaine deep into a public waste bin. It wasn't that he expected to find anything of consequence doing this circuit, but rather he wanted to get a feel of whether there was a back way to approach the flat, somewhere where Danny might lurk to see if someone was following him. However by the time he had got back to his hire car, Bill was of the opinion that there was no sneaky back approach, and that Danny's security had been safety in numbers by being so visible on West Street.

Grateful to sit down, Bill took the car on a tour of the town, cruising around it and taking much more notice of it than on previous times when he had been here. High Street was a one way, with a right turn into West Street, but a straight-on to South Street where Bill saw *The Eagle Hotel* on the left. So it was that close to where Danny was staying, was it? He didn't like that one bit. On an impulse he turned left onto Etnam Street and left again to School Lane to come around behind the hotel. However he had to make another left with the one way system before he came to the back access to the hotel. The traffic allowed him to pause and look hard at it and he didn't like what he saw. This was busy enough in the day with the shops around it, but what about at night? Danny could have been hauled out to a waiting car here with little trouble, and who would have said a thing?

Dare he go into the local station and make enquiries about any scuffles? Maybe not today. If the chaos at Danny's flat quickly came to light, it would be better that he wasn't associated with being in the area right now. But what did reassure him was that there was nothing here that screamed any warnings to him on a subconscious level. Bill had got used to listening to those internal fidgets that told him something was amiss even if his conscious brain couldn't pinpoint just what it was as fast.

So swinging the car back onto the A44 he headed back for Worcester, resisting the temptation to turn in at the *Talbot* for one of their great meals as he passed it. It would have been too much of a temptation to sit there looking at the hand-pumps of their own beers given the way he was feeling at the moment. Anyway, he had the memory cards metaphorically burning holes in his trouser pocket, and he wanted to get home and download them onto a backup. What he chose to then was still very much up in the air. He knew he should take them straight into work, but he wanted to see what was on them first. If there was something which would stand up as evidence in court then he wouldn't hesitate to hand them over. However, he had a sinking feeling that they wouldn't, because if they were that incriminating Danny would have surely used them already.

That set off another set of worries. If he did find good solid evidence on them, then that would mean that he had been wrong about Danny. He didn't think he was – would go as far as to say he was *sure* he wasn't – but bitter experience was also whispering in his ear that sometimes it was the ones you least expected who turned out to have some nasty little secret. He was just praying that Danny's didn't turn out to be a perverse enjoyment of being the 'big man' in a small and very murky pond, and with a callous disregard for the lives of those sufficiently unlike him to be able to be dismissed as if they were aliens or animals.

"Oh come on, Scathlock," he admonished himself, "stop it! After all this time you know the real Danny, you *know* you do." On the other hand, some of the senior people who had made assumptions about Danny were men he didn't know half as well. Was he going to let such men cloud his judgment? No he wasn't! "Time to get home and see what's on these bloody cards," he growled, and eased the car right up to the speed limit as it sped along the twilit country road.

Chapter 4

Friday evening – Saturday morning

Back at his flat Bill went and dug out a couple of the spare memory sticks he always had available, and then booted up his laptop again. To start with he simply copied the information straight across onto the spare drives, anxious not to even try opening them until he had backups. He also made sure he handled the originals with care and with gloves on, and then straight away put them back into the evidence bags he'd brought them home in. No way did he want to contaminate evidence, and had he not been convinced by now that Danny's life might hang on what he dug up, he wouldn't have done this but left it to the police technical experts. However, sadly he knew it was all too likely that this would go to the back of the official queue for forensic attention unless he could give someone senior very good reason to prioritise it, and that meant looking at it first.

Carefully opening the first file, Bill realised that these were all photographs. By the look of them they had been taken on Danny's phone and very much on the sly, because some of the angles were very odd, as if he'd had the phone held down by his side and had just had to hope for the best that they caught what he wanted. Often there were three of four very similar images, and Bill could believe that Danny had tried to bracket his shots, and had hung onto them all in the vain hope that if someone who knew more about photo resolution than him got at them, then they would be able to pull more out of one or other of the shots. Many of them were very dark, making Bill think that they had been taken indoors somewhere and in very gloomy light. Nonetheless, he could make out figures.

Sitting back with a sigh, Bill decided he would have to have a play around with these copies himself. He would never have considered himself much of a photographer, but last year his colleagues had clubbed together and got him a voucher for computer stuff for his fortieth birthday, and he had bought himself a copy of Photoshop. Since then he'd not done a vast amount with it, but he knew enough to know that he would be able to adjust the exposure of these shots with it. So making sure he'd got the 'how to' book he'd also bought close to hand, he began experimenting.

Luckily the first few he tried his hand at responded well, and with a little lightening of exposures soon revealed themselves to be photographs of people. Most of them were men, with only one or two women in the shots. However, what struck Bill was their expressions. These people looked absolutely terrified out of their wits, to the point of appearing almost catatonic. That puzzled Bill. He fully expected people to be scared – who wouldn't be after some time in the hands of traffickers – but there seemed to be more than that in these cases. If they had been abducted by aliens they couldn't have looked more lost and befuddled.

"Where the hell have this lot come from?" Bill asked rhetorically. It surely wasn't Poland, because even in the rural parts he was sure that they wouldn't have looked as askance at a mobile phone as two of these were doing. And then he recalled what Danny had said about being worried about the mental health of these victims. "Blimey, mate, you weren't wrong on that one. They all look like they need the services of a damned good psychiatrist."

Time's Bloodied Gold

Their clothes were odd too, once Bill started to zoom in and look at them harder. The more photos he opened and processed, the stranger things became. For a while he couldn't put his finger on what it was, even though his cat's whisker instincts were twitching like crazy. Then he got a couple of longer shots clearer, and what leapt out at him then was their footwear. Where in God's name had they come from? Because the last time he'd seen shoes like that had been on the feet of the re-enactors at the Battle of Tewkesbury Fair back a couple of summers ago. He sat back and blinked hard a few times to refresh his eyes and then peered hard again. Yes, that was what they looked like. They had the same bindings on the bottoms of their trousers, and the shoes looked handmade and more like moccasins than modern shoes.

Put into that light, it made him realise that it was also what had been so odd about their clothing. Not a damned thing looked modern. Bill was no fashion guru, and refugees hardly abounded in this area, but he'd seen enough news reports from places like Sicily, where refugees were coming ashore from war-torn African and Middle Eastern countries, to know that even they had more trappings of the twenty-first century than the people he was looking at here. No hoodies, nothing that looked as though it had a zipper, nothing that looked as though it was made from a synthetic fabric, not a trainer in sight. Every last garment looked handmade down to the cloth they were made of. Indeed, Bill was starting to see the depths of Danny's dilemma. If you didn't know Danny and were already starting to think him a liar, shown these you would think he was indulging in some massive piss-take with the aid of some re-enactor mates. Except that Bill was drawn back to the faces of the people and knew that *that* amount of blind panic was almost impossible to fake. But would that be sufficient to convince a sceptic?

Hell's teeth, how on earth was he going to convince someone as cynical as Williams that Danny was in trouble with these? He wasn't, was he? He was going to have to get a whole lot more than a few strange photographs if he was going to get a manhunt going for his missing friend.

And what was he going to do over the weekend? He could carry on reading the remaining files, but something gnawing at his gut told him that he wasn't going to find anything more solid in there. Moreover, if Charlie had already tried asking around at weekends then he wasn't going to do much better, although he wanted to hear from Charlie himself what steps he'd taken now. That would be a job for tomorrow morning, for certain.

Tuesday couldn't come fast enough now, because the thing Bill really wanted to do was to listen to those phone calls which had supposedly come from Danny asking for meetings. He must ask Charlie if he had those, because if he could listen to them and could immediately spot that they weren't Danny's voice, then that would be a great help in clearing his friend of being a time-waster. The other thing he now questioned was why nobody had wondered why Danny could seemingly make a phone call to arrange a meeting, but then send such distressed texts and emails when the meetings failed to take place. Surely that ought to have rung alarm bells with someone? Why would you dismiss such contradictions?

Unfortunately Bill could only think that it had to be further evidence of how low Danny had fallen in everyone's estimation.

"Christ mate, why didn't you pick up the phone to me? It's not like you don't know the number here or my mobile."

Time's Bloodied Gold

Having a sudden attack of guilt, Bill hurried to his main phone and checked the answer service. There was nothing there, and he had so few calls normally he would have noticed, although that didn't preclude an unfamiliar phone number being lost in the tide of unwanted cold calls he, like everyone else, got. Reaching for his mobile he checked that as well. A couple of missed call numbers looked faintly familiar and he returned to the call logs to compare them.

Swearing long and hard, Bill realised that two calls had come in just before Christmas when he'd been running round like a lunatic working on a case involving a missing teenager with Down's syndrome. The teenager had been found safe and sound in the end, but it had been one of those cases where everyone piled in to help because of the vulnerability of the victim, and Bill had been one of the main coordinators, juggling evidence from incoming calls from all over the place. That was why he hadn't spotted these – his head had been swimming with phone numbers. One had been from the disposed of mobile Danny had used on the sixth of December, and another had come in on the eleventh, which was when Danny had sent a frantic email although the number wasn't identifiable as one Danny had used. Almost certainly that had been a public phone somewhere.

"Why in God's name didn't you leave me a message?" Bill fumed. "Jesus, we didn't part on *such* bad terms!"

Then felt even worse as he realised that this might have been at the fore of Danny's mind when he'd said 'tell Bill S I forgive him.' How would he live with himself if it turned out that Danny had appealed to him for help and thought Bill had ignored him out of hurt pride, vanity or worse? That almost had him heading for the malt whisky, antibiotics or not. Then a little sanity prevailed, and he knew that Danny would have had the wits, even when half scared out of them, to know that Bill might be up to his ears in a case, rather than deliberately ignoring him. That was what he probably meant – that he understood Bill had been preoccupied and elsewhere.

"I'm not leaving you hanging, though, mate," Bill promised from the heart. "One way or the other I'm getting to the bottom of this. I just hope you'll be alive when I find you." Then added grimly, "But if you're not, by God those who left you out in the cold are going to pay for this."

After a lousy night of limited sleep, and what little he did get being punctuated by nightmares, Bill got up on Saturday morning and, after brewing up a large cafetiere of coffee, rang Charlie's home phone number.

"I thought I might hear from you today," Charlie's broad Brummie voice declared.

"Damned right! This is appalling! How the hell did it get to this state of affairs?"

"That's what I kept asking myself every time a new bit of information came to light. Honestly, Bill, I've never come across such an unholy mess."

"You're not wrong about that," and Bill went on to tell Charlie of his conclusions, finally coming to, "So what I wanted to ask you first is this, can you let me hear those phone calls supposedly from Danny asking for the meetings?"

Charlie could be heard exhaling heavily on the other end of the phone. "Well now, I hadn't thought of that angle, but I think you might be onto something. I don't have all of those calls, only the ones that came into our force. You have to understand that accessing written files is a lot easier than taped conversations. Because Danny is our officer, certain people have had to be kept in the loop so there were copies of things."

Bill chuckled. "What you're tactfully saying is that Williams ought to have kept his files more secure, and you know what's going on more than he does because you've actually read the damned things."

There was another deep sigh. "Between you and me, the man's a bloody nightmare – far too much of the political appointment for my liking. I don't snoop regularly, Bill, because I realised pretty fast that Robbie," his predecessor in the archives, "was right when he said that there would soon come a time when my conscience wouldn't let me stay silent on things I felt were wrong, and at that point it would become very clear where I had got my information from."

"Aah, I always wondered how Robbie had his finger so accurately on the pulse of what was going on."

"Yes, and he showed me the value of knowing where to look and when. So when it's something like this, I feel fully vindicated in digging in the hidden dirt. And whereas Williams sees these copies of reports as mere record keeping, and files them away to focus on other things, you and I have actually read them and seen how explosive they are."

"Explosive is the right word."

"Well we should be able to get to some of those recordings on Tuesday, but what I would say is that whoever made the calls must have sounded something like Danny. I mean, it couldn't have been one of the Polish blokes, could it?"

"No," Bill sighed. "But in a way that bothers me all the more, Charlie. While I was thinking of Danny in with a bunch of Polish rogues, that was one thing, but this implies an English element too. Someone who can pass for a

Midlander, at least, if not Danny's Potteries accent. And they have to be in on this up to their eyeballs if they're playing silly bastards trying to entrap a police officer. Do you see what I mean? There's something bloody close to a blatant disregard for the law about that. Somebody thinks not only that they can find out who is in their inner circle, but on top of that there has to be some kind of assumption that they can do something about it once they've found him, don't you think?"

Charlie could be heard swallowing hard on the other end of the line. "Christ! This is why I wanted you on board – you see things in greater depth than me. Bloody hell, Bill, that's a nasty turn up for the books! Do you think they would hesitate to kill him? I mean, are they so arrogant as to think that they can hide his body where we can't find him?"

Now it was Bill's turn to sigh. "Well the forensic people did say that identifying a body after one of those fires would be tough. Shit, I don't want to attend a crime scene like that in the future and be fretting that it's Danny I'm looking at in the pile of smoking ashes! But I think we can't afford to disregard the strong possibility that these monsters are stone-cold killers." He paused and both of them took a few deep breaths at the implications.

"What I also wanted to ask you," Bill continued, "is, where's Danny's car now? I'm talking about the hire car mentioned in the reports. Has it come up again? Because I can't imagine that the number plate hasn't been flagged up with our colleagues on the Central Motorway Police Group, quite aside from our own division."

"Ah, now that's something I can tell you about," Charlie said with relief, and Bill heard the rustling of paper as a notepad was flipped through. "That came back to me yesterday, as well, and I went digging in the system. It was

Time's Bloodied Gold

caught on a speed camera on the M5 coming north from Bristol on the thirtieth of December, and again on the same day on the A49 near Hereford. It was at night, so way too dark to see much, unfortunately, but there seemed to be people in the back seats."

Bill's laugh of relief took Charlie by surprise.

"Bill?"

"Well you can't imagine that this lot – with them having been so bloody crafty so far – risking getting caught by speed cameras, do you? But if it was Danny at the wheel, and if it was at night when his passengers might be dozing, then a good way to get himself noticed would be…"

"…To get a speeding ticket! Bloody hell, that's a relief! I've been worried sick ever since I read that report in late December that said that Danny seemed drunk that maybe he'd already taken a beating and was on his last journey."

"Oh I sympathize with that! The thought had crossed my mind too. I'm sure these bastards know how to give a man a good kicking and keep his face unmarked. And it's more typical to see someone drunk in public, especially at Christmas, so how would the civilian have known the difference between a man staggering because he was barely conscious, and one who was so plastered he could hardly keep his feet? Can you check on Monday whether Danny has been picking up any more tickets?"

"Christ, yes! I didn't think to look at this year's records, but I will now. In fact I have some news for you of another member of our secret squirrel club."

"Who?" Bill's heart sunk into his boots at his news. More people getting involved in something which could get him thrown off the force if all went wrong wasn't a good thing.

"Morag."

Bill's heart resumed its normal beating and his mood

lifted. "Mogs? How the hell has she come on board?"

"She came down to my office yesterday asking if I'd heard how you were. She's not really settled into her new job you know, there's still the heart of a detective beating underneath everything."

"Don't need to tell me that, mate. I'd have her back as one of my DCs in a heartbeat."

"Well I think she wanted to have a chat with someone who'd understand. And I brought the conversation around to Danny, as much as anything because as a Statement Reader I wanted to pump her for any times she might have seen his name, or that of Danny Sawaski, crop up. I don't know whether it's good or bad that she hasn't, but I was surprised to hear her say that she was troubled by Danny's disappearance. She's come to it from a different angle to me. While you've been off Danny's position in our division has come up as a vacancy."

"Fucking hell!"

"I know. And I'm sorry that that one slipped past me, Bill. Well, as you can imagine, you could have knocked me down with a feather when she said that, and it must have shown on my face, because the next thing is she's asking me what's wrong. Knowing you always set great store by Morag's instincts I kind of came clean – well at least in as far as to say that I'd begun digging into what had happened to Danny because I, too, was worried. The next thing I know she's having a bit of a weep in relief and starts telling me that although Danny was an aggravating little shit to work for, he was one of the few who never batted an eyelid over her being gay. It turns out that however much he irritated the crap out of her, she thought it was right that he was the one who got to be your DS out of the DCs, even though she was one of them. She was cross as hell that he seemed to be pissing the opportunity away back last year, mind you; but maybe because she's been the butt of so much vicious gossip, she also said that she could equally understand him getting ratty at being on the receiving end of so many snide comments.

"You know when he had that massive rant at you in the gents? The one that half of the building must have heard? Well she took him on one side and had a bit of a heart to heart with him about that. Told him he was being a dickhead if he thought any of his troubles started with you. And when he came to her later on about this new opening, she told me that she'd told him she would bet good money on it being you who had put him forward for the undercover operation. ...And of course that's why she's now feeling lousy, because she told him to stop fannying around and take the opportunity you'd sent his way."

Bill was stunned, but also grateful for Morag's loyalty and for her knowing him as well as she did. That Danny had gone undercover with less malice towards him than he had hitherto believed was something of a relief.

"So Morag's going to come down and join us on our little mission on Tuesday. It's a good day for her to be away from her desk without having to give excuses."

"It'll be good to have her with us. I miss her a lot."

"Just a warning, though. I get the impression that the lass she married not long ago is a bit ...shall we say difficult ...about Morag having men friends. So don't be offended if she won't come round for dinner or anything."

That didn't surprise Bill. Jackie had seemed a prickly personality on the couple of occasions he'd met her, and somehow he didn't think this was a relationship destined to last, but that was Morag's affair. "I'm glad you warned me, Charlie. I'll make sure I don't press her too hard to come for a curry with me, in that case. ...Oh, by the way, has there been any hint of a laptop belonging to Danny coming to light?"

"A laptop? No, Bill, not a peep. Why?"

"Well Danny was always one for the latest technology, but more than that, I think he'd have wanted to look at what he had on those memory cards in more detail than his phone could have given him. And that's another thing. Those photos were taken on something several steps up the smart-phone ladder to the basic burn phones Danny dumped. My money would be on his beloved i-phone. And I think that's why there are three memory cards. None of them are anywhere near full, and I think that was because he changed them to make sure that he wasn't caught with incriminating evidence on his phone. Or more likely, he linked his phone to his laptop, pulled the photos off it and onto the cards, and then deleted them from his phone. But he'd need at the very least a good tablet device for that and I'm thinking more likely a laptop, which is why I asked. Oh, and that's why I think he used other phones to call in on – he didn't want to have any evidence of him betraying them on the one they always saw him using."

"That would be sensible. Do you think the photos had anything to do with timing?"

"In what sense?"

"Well those fires took place on or around the full moon of each month, that I do remember, because at one point someone wondered if it was idiots trying to do something in the way of a pagan ritual while off their faces on drugs. The theory didn't stand up to scrutiny, but I remembered it, so have you looked at the dates on the photos?"

Bill swore at himself. "Bloody hell, how did I miss that one? I was so intent on what they were of I never looked at the encoded information. Hang on a moment, Charlie, I'm going to look at a couple right now!"

He had his laptop on already, and it took no time to plug in the drive he was working with and bring up the first batch of photos.

"Okay, the date says the twenty-ninth of October on this one."

The sound of keys clicking came down the phone to Bill and then Charlie added, "And I've just looked up the dates for full moons – Monday the twenty-ninth of October was a full moon and then Wednesday the twenty-eighth of November!"

"Jeez! Really? …Christ, the later ones on this disc say the twenty-eighth of November! He must have transferred some from another card or taken a hell of a risk in keeping the earlier photos on it. What about December?"

"Erm… the twenty-eighth again."

"Shit! That's the date on the next batch of photos! No wonder he was starting to sound frantic as the end of the month came up. He must have known it was going to happen all over again – whatever 'it' is. …Hang on a tick, just looking at the next ones. …Oh my God, Charlie, they're dated January! He was alive in January, or at least he was on the twenty-seventh!"

"And the twenty-seventh was a full moon again."

"When's this month's?"

"The twenty-fifth, shit, that's Monday! Is there any way that we can get a message to him? Some way that we could let him know that *somebody* cares, even if it's not the ones who ought to?"

Bill now had no hesitation in telling Charlie about what he'd done with Danny's books, adding, "He has to know that there are only a handful of people who would know he always had his nose stuck in the *Game of Thrones* series,

Simon Scarrow's Cato and Macro books and Anthony Riches' Roman soldier series, and that the likelihood is that it was me who would know to take them. I daren't go back to the flat in case he's there with someone, but at least he's got a chance of working that one out. Hopefully if he checks his hidey-hole – which surely he would – and finds the cards gone he'll twig that I found them too."

"*Phew*, that's a good one. And making it look like there had been a break in was a good thought. If his first time back there is with someone else he'll look suitably shocked."

Bill wasn't sure Charlie would think that if he knew of the flushed away cocaine. That was the one thing Bill had kept to himself, not least because he didn't want any glimmer of doubt about Danny crossing Charlie's mind, and drugs would be the one thing which might do that. There was a lot of stress to this job, and it wouldn't be the first time an officer had succumbed under unbearable pressure. Blessedly few, it was true, but enough for it to be something Charlie might take seriously because although he'd known Danny well, it wasn't as well as Bill had.

However, he did have a final question for Charlie. "Do you know what this Kyrewood Graves is? I couldn't make that out."

"Ah, now that I can help you with! I knew the name Kyrewood rang a bell over something, so I went and dug out the Ordnance Survey map for the Tenbury area. There's a Kyrewood House, which is big enough to be named on the map, and a hamlet of Kyrewood, but a bit further south is the even bigger Kyre Park. So a chunk of that area slightly south and east of Tenbury is known as Kyre. A bit closer to Tenbury on the south side is another hamlet called Callows Grave. Kyrewood Graves, though is right on the intersection of three counties just on the west side of Tenbury."

"What, three shires meet?"

"Yep, Shropshire is just the other side of the River Teme, and Hereford and Worcester join on the south bank of the river. It's a real old no-man's-land."

"Clever bastards!"

"Eh?"

"Well it's just occurred to me that they've picked one of our most thinly stretched patches, haven't they? Tenbury & Martley is the largest patch in the Malvern Hills District. Two hundred square miles covered by one inspector, one sergeant, a constable and two CSOs – we're not exactly in the same league as the Met for being able to cope with organized crime out there, are we?"

"Oh…!"

"Precisely! So, what else can you tell me about this Kyrewood Graves?"

Charlie huffed audibly. "There's not much to tell about, to be honest, Bill. If Robbie was still here, he'd no doubt be able to give you chapter and verse about some lost medieval village, or the like. All I can tell you is that we're talking about a proper hamlet in the sense that there's not even a church there. There's something called St Michael's marked on the map a couple of miles away, but that's not a church, it's a boarding school. But given that what we're talking about is just a couple of farms and half a dozen farm workers' cottages, there'd hardly be anyone there for a vicar to minster to. Doesn't mean that there wasn't one once upon a time, though. I don't know if you've ever been out that way, but Roachford church – just a bit further away and east of Tenbury – is a lovely old Norman church with a wonderful tree of life carved above the door. There must have been enough people to make building such a place worthwhile back in the day. I bet if you had a look around you'd find some old deconsecrated church that's been converted to make a smart stone house."

"Really? Hmm, I might go for a drive out there and see what it looks like. If I dangle my camera around my neck and look suitably like some church-hunting nerd, I shouldn't spook anyone too much. Thanks for that bit about Roachford – it'll give me something to babble on inanely about if I'm questioned."

"I'd offer to come with you, but we've got the grandchildren coming over in a bit, and Mary will skin me alive if I leave her to cope with our Denise's two monsters on her own."

Bill chuckled. "God forbid I should get on Mary's bad side! Anyhow, I'm going scouting, not launching a full-scale assault – not that I won't scoop Danny up and drive like the hounds of hell are at my heels if I get the chance to get him away from there."

"Well if you find anything, give me a ring tomorrow."

"I will. I'll keep you up to speed on what I find."

Before he set out, however, Bill decided to try one other call. It might be that Jackie was there and Morag wouldn't be free, but he'd like to speak to her even if it was only briefly.

The phone rang out and then Morag's familiar Scottish voice said, "Hello?"

"Mogs? It's Bill."

"Bill!" There was no mistaking the warmth in her voice. "How are you? How's the knee doing?"

It took a few minutes to satiate Morag's appetite for details of his health, but the way she was chatting freely convinced Bill that Jackie could not be there.

"Listen, gal', I've been talking to Charlie about Danny."

Time's Bloodied Gold

"Oh God, isn't that a mess! I know Danny riled a lot of people, but he never deserved this."

"No he doesn't. Look, are you free right now? Only I'm going out to do a bit of scouting round out where we think Danny might have been, and a couple would look less suspicious than a big bloke like me cruising around the place on his own."

"I'd love to! Jackie's away on some professional development weekend, and I thought I'd enjoy having the house all to myself, but to honest I was already thinking I would have to get out for a bit. Meet me down by Sainsbury's in about half an hour, eh?"

"Done! I'm in a big gold Citroen by the way. Had to hire an auto for a bit, so don't look for the Mini, 'cause I won't be in it."

"Gold Citroen, got it, see you in thirty, then."

Chapter 5

Saturday afternoon

"You look nice," Bill complimented his old partner as she climbed into the car. The way she blinked in surprise worried him, though. Was it such a surprise to receive a compliment?

"Well I thought I'd give the new sweater an outing," Morag replied after a moment's delay and with something of her old cheeky grin.

Grinning back, Bill declared, "Right, so we're a cosy old married couple out for a Saturday afternoon drive – or at least pretending to be."

Morag snorted in amusement. "I don't think 'cosy' is ever a word that applies to you!"

"Oh come on now, get into part!" Bill teased with a wink. "Just imagine I'm wearing a skirt if it helps!"

That reduced Morag to helpless giggles instantly.

He took the twisting 'B' road out through Martley and Clifton upon Teme as the quickest way to get to Tenbury Wells, but also because it passed by Roachford.

"I want to have the quickest of looks at this church Charlie mentioned, which turns out to be at Lower Roachford," he explained to Morag, and pointing to the camera case sitting down on the shelf where the gear stick would be on the manual version of the car. "If I get a few shots of that one, I can play the enthusiast by showing anyone who questions us the photos."

"Sneaky," Morag said with admiration. "Actually I know the church. Some friends got married there a few

Time's Bloodied Gold

years ago. It's a real pretty old place, especially when it's filled with flowers."

"Great! So you can do a bit of enthusing too."

On the short drive they chatted amicably about work and mutual contacts, with Bill carefully avoiding any searching questions about Morag's marriage. He was quietly dismayed, however, that Morag never volunteered anything. There was nothing about days out or meals with friends, and he was incredibly glad that she hadn't left the force altogether now, as she'd originally intended to do. Some day she was going to need her old friends, he suspected, just as Danny needed them now.

The church was quickly photographed and then they were back in the car and heading down into Tenbury Wells.

"Where do you want to start?" Morag asked.

Bill puffed his cheeks and frowned. "Well I reckon we might go for a swift half or two in the local pubs. It's Saturday, the Six Nations rugby games are on, and that might draw these lads out. We'll stick our noses in the doors first. If they look dead quiet we won't even bother going in, and if anyone asks, we're meeting friends who forgot to tell us which pub they are in."

It was apparent straight away that *The Bridge* and *The Ship* pubs, both on the main road and close to the Bridge over the Teme, were not what they were looking for. Both were a bit too up-market in Bill's estimation, while *The Vaults* was too small and *The Crow* too much of a local.

"They'd stand out like a sore thumb in there," Bill declared as they closed the door behind them.

Catching the eye of someone who looked local, Bill asked,

"Excuse me, mate, are there any other pubs in town? We're supposed to meet someone here but they aren't in any of these."

The elderly man wrinkled his nose. "Hmm, if you turn right at the end here, you come to the *Market Tavern*, and then as you go into Cross St there's the *Pembroke House* – that's a nice place. Of course there's the *Fox & Goose* on the Berrington Road, but I wouldn't think friends of yours would be in there. It'll be right rowdy at this time on a Saturday. I'd try the *Pembroke* if I were you."

"Cheers! Really appreciate the help," Bill said genially, and with Morag's hand looped through his crutch-free arm they strolled off.

Once out of sight round the corner, however, Morag loosed Bill's arm and said with a grin, "I'm guessing we're going to try the *Fox & Goose*, then?"

"Absolutely."

When they found the place they could see that it was a far cry from the pretty, slightly 'olde worldy' pubs elsewhere in the town. This was a typical modern, big-screen, sports pub, where the only food on offer would come with chips or in a bun. Luckily it had a decent sized car park too, and Bill immediately decided that they would go and bring the car up.

"I'm in no fit state to be making a run for it," he declared, "and it's been a year or two since you were mixing it up on the streets, Mogs. Don't doubt for a second that you remember how, but your reflexes aren't exactly going to be honed like they once were."

Morag gave a wry grunt. "No, I don't think I'd be able to explain to Jackie why I'd got bruised knuckles when I'm supposed to be being the good wifey staying at home." There was no bitterness in her comment, but again Bill was dismayed at the sound of what her domestic life was like. It wasn't his place to rescue her from that, though, and just at the moment Danny was the priority.

Time's Bloodied Gold

When they walked in through the door they were assailed by the sound of chanting at the huge screen beside the bar. Italy were playing Wales, and Leigh Halfpenny was just going for a conversion to the sound of much encouragement from the locals. Mercifully the England v. Scotland game had been last week, with England winning handsomely, so Morag's Scottish accent wasn't going to cause trouble.

Managing to catch the bartender's eye, Bill got Morag a half of lager and himself a fruit juice with tonic water.

"Antibiotics," Bill sighed mournfully at the bartender's raised eyebrows when he realised the soft drink was for him, and then got a sympathetic smile. "Can't wait to get off the bloody things and have a decent pint again."

They found a seat where they could just about see the screen and made the right kind of noises to convince others that this was what they'd come to see. However, Bill was scanning the crowd avidly even so.

"Over there, by the game machine," he suddenly said to Morag. "The big bloke with his coat still on."

Morag made a play of reaching for her glass to lean a little Bill's way and spotted the man he meant.

"He's a nasty looking bastard if ever I saw one," she murmured under cover of her glass. "He's got that Slavic look about him too. Oh, hang on, is this his mate come to join him?"

A shorter man had emerged from the gents and come to stand by the other, picking up a half empty glass and draining it. Saying he was smaller was not much, though, because the first man was as big as Bill, who couldn't help but think that Danny wouldn't stand much of a chance against those two.

"Are they leaving?" Bill asked softly, not wanting to stare.

"No. Number two is going to the bar for a refill. ...Hmm a pint for him and what looks like a double vodka for his big mate Igor. Jings, he looks like he could audition for a part in a Hammer Horror film! He wouldn't look at all out of place with a bolt through his neck!"

"He does look a nasty piece of work. That's one hell of a bottle scar on his cheek, and his nose has been broken more than once, I'd say. I reckon someone bit a chunk out of his ear too – that must have been an ugly fight." The big man was the one Danny knew as Mikail, had Bill and Morag but known it, and they were only too right in their assessment of him.

As it was Bill took in the way the barman was looking faintly worried when he realised that a second double vodka he was being asked for was for the same man as the first. You could see that he was wishing he'd not started serving this man, and that he feared a fight was brewing. Bill heard him say,

"That's the last one for you and your mate, okay? He's had enough and I don't want any trouble."

The first turned away having snapped something in Polish at the barman, which you didn't need to be a linguist to guess was not complimentary. He obviously told Mikhail what had been said, because the big man threw an nasty glance the barman's way and downed the first double in one go.

"Do we give the local lads a ring?" Morag asked softly.

"We can go back to the station, it's not far," Bill informed her. "We'll nip in and just give them the heads up. It's a good excuse to find out if they've had any trouble."

They finished their drinks and slipped out as unobtrusively as possible as half time came up on the

Time's Bloodied Gold

rugby. However, when they reached the police station it was to find it was closed up.

Morag sniffed in disgust. "You can understand why rural communities feel they've been left to fend for themselves, can't you! I mean, we know it's because the man power has been cut down to the bone, but it can't be much fun living out here when something goes wrong. How far does someone have to come from to get here? From Leominster?"

Bill grimaced. "I suspect it's worse than that. The last time I checked, even Leominster station wasn't open every day."

"What do we do if all hell breaks loose at the pub, then? I mean, we're hardly in a position to wade in, are we? I'm only a civilian attached to the police now, and you could hardly break a fight up in your condition."

Bill knew exactly what she meant. It went totally against the grain to not intervene, but at the same time she was right, what could they hope to do? Even if Bill made an arrest, how long would it take before anyone could come and take them away? In fact there was a real danger that they might break away from him long before anyone got here. Turning the car again, Bill took the road back past the pub and started up the twisting road which climbed out of Tenbury. The higher they reached, the smarter the houses got, becoming larger and more detached. That worried Bill because they didn't seem like places were the gang would be tolerated hanging around.

"How far is it to Kyrewood Graves?" he asked Morag with growing dismay, and pulled in at a farm gate so that they could consult the map. If they were virtually there already then Danny may have been mistaken and this could turn out to be dead end.

Mercifully, as they were sat parked viewing the map, and realising that they still had a way to go before they got to Kyrewood Graves, a battered Land Rover went past with the two Poles in.

"Thank God that's the pub out of danger," Morag breathed, swiftly followed by, "Holy crap, he's got to be well over the limit!" as the vehicle veered towards the far side of the road and then came back again. "I'll be dropping the hint that we need the lads out with a breath test kit when I get back into work. How many round here rely on the fact that they're unlikely to ever get stopped?"

"Way too many, I suspect," Bill sighed, pulling out and focusing now on tailing the ancient Land Rover Defender, but keeping sufficiently far back as to make it seem coincidental that they were on the same country road. The Defender was a good choice of vehicle for round here. Every farm had to have one if not several once you took workers into account. Nor was it odd for the rear number plate to be so mud splattered as to unreadable, regardless of the fact that that was illegal. "Grab the OS map again, would you, Mogs? Where do we end up on this road?"

Morag retrieved the map and squinted at it in the dim light. "If we don't turn off, in about two miles we come to the tiny village of Berrington, and then beyond that it eventually connects with the main road at Little Hereford. Before that, though, there's a turn off on our right to Kyrewood Graves. It's awfully small. Are you sure it's where you want?"

"Well it's the one in Danny's message, so yes it is."

As they approached the turning, Bill could see what Charlie had meant. There was a large farm on the left by the narrowest of turnings back towards Callows Grave on a track Bill wouldn't want to take the large Citroen down, especially when it wasn't his car. The turning to the right didn't look much better, either, and Bill pulled up. Taking the map off Morag he peered intently at it, suddenly saying, "Does that look like one of the crosses they use for a church without a tower or a spire?"

Morag looked at him in bemusement. "It looks like a spider in football boots crawled over the page! It might, and it might not be."

However, Bill grinned. "Then we have a good excuse for looking lost," and he turned the big car into the narrow track.

First they passed another three-storey old Georgian farm house, but this one looked almost derelict. A couple of big steel-framed barns were filled with bundles of something which Bill guessed would be hay or straw for cattle, but there was no sign of life in the farm yard or surrounding buildings.

"Looks like they've decamped to a more modern place," Morag mused. "Can't say that I blame them. That must have been a drafty old hole at this time of year. I bet it cost a fortune to heat."

"I doubt it ever got heated throughout," was Bill's opinion. "The old farmers were a hardy breed. You probably just put another sheep dog on the bed in the worst weather."

"Thank God for central heating and insulation," Morag declared with a shiver. "I like going home and getting into my fluffy dressing gown too much to live in a place like that."

Bill was taking the lane very slowly because the potholes were closer to lunar crater sized, however they turned a kink in the lane and came to a closed gate.

"Hmm, that's not very friendly," Bill said softly. "Oh, hello! We've attracted someone's attention."

A man in a shabby donkey jacket and wellies was striding with some purpose towards them.

Painting an amicable smile on his face, Bill opened the window, having hurriedly put the radio on to a station playing inane music.

"Afternoon!" he called cheerily.

"You're on private property," the man said tersely, with a heavy Polish accent.

"Really? Oh, I'm sorry. We didn't see any signs. We're looking for the church," and he gave the scowling man his best daft smile.

"No church here."

"Really? Felicity, give me the map. See? Here? That little cross means a small church or chapel. We were hoping another one like this one," Bill burbled on, thrusting the viewing screen of the digital camera at the man with a shot of the carving at Roachford on it.

The man was totally nonplussed, and for a second his face betrayed utter confusion, then it settled back into an angry scowl.

"Told you, no church here."

"Ooooh!" squeaked Morag, playing her part. "What, not even that gorgeous bit of gable-ended wall there? Do you think that could be Norman, darling?"

"Might be!" Bill gushed.

"Listen here, Norman, or whatever your fucking name is, piss off! There's no church here and you're trespassing. So get your fancy yellow piece of crap off our land."

Morag feigned dismay with, "How rude!" while Bill managed to look completely affronted as he declared with a sniff,

"I'll have you know that this colour is *gold*, not yellow." Then shutting the electric window so fast the man almost had his fingers caught in it from where he'd grabbed hold

Time's Bloodied Gold

of the side of the car to stop himself sliding in the mud. There was just enough room to turn the car here by the gate where the lane widened briefly, and Bill made sure that he flung the big car around so that the wheels were spraying mud in every direction, which caught the man full on several times during the middle pass of the three-point turn.

"I do hope there was cow shit in that," Morag said with a giggle, as they retreated up the lane.

"Well he's too busy hoicking mud out of his eyes to take our number," Bill said with a grin as he checked in his mirror.

"You think he might have a means to check it?"

"I don't know," Bill admitted as he took the car on towards Berrington, frequently checking behind them to make sure nobody had thought it a good idea to follow them. At Little Hereford and the main road he turned back to head towards Tenbury, but pulled over at the famous garden centre at Burford. "Time for a cuppa and a think," he declared and led the way into the cafe.

At this time of year it was quiet, so they managed to find a table away from the other customers, and tucked into their coffee and cake with gusto.

"I tell you what worries me, Morag. It's the English connection," Bill confessed. "It's whoever it was who rang in and made those arrangements to meet the welfare officer, or whoever. That someone passed as Danny, and it certainly wasn't those two thugs we saw in the pub. I briefly heard the one at the bar, and he had an accent thick enough to cut slices off. And that bloke we just spoke to was too much the foreign thug to have passed for him either. He's probably just some muscle brought down from the Black Country part of the gang to keep the locals at bay. I read somewhere in that heap of papers Charlie gave me, that the taskforce thought the gang had connections out that way because of there being plenty of old disused factory units to hide stuff and people in."

However Morag was wearing a smug grin. "Well when you handed the camera back to me I ran a few shots off, and kept doing it while you were turning the car. Look at these!"

She handed the digital SLR camera to Bill with the viewing screen on.

"Oh, Morag, you beauty!"

There, neatly framed in two of the shots were more of the people Danny had photographed. They were raking something up in the yard, but there was no mistaking the odd clothes and the looks of unconcealed terror on their faces as they looked up at the Citroen. And in another, once he zoomed in, Bill could see a man lurking in the shadows of the biggest barn clearly armed with some sort of assault rifle. It was too dark to make out the exactly make, although Bill would have guessed at an AK47 or AK74, both all too available to men like these in their own countries, whether that was Poland or one of the other former Eastern Bloc countries. What it definitely wasn't was just some farmer with a shotgun coming back from massacring the local rabbit population. Clearly the gatekeeper had had backup ready had he needed it.

"Now *that* is something we can use," Bill declared with satisfaction. "Whatever that is, is sure as hell isn't legal."

"Is there any way we can see anything from this side of the river? I know you well enough to know that you probably have binoculars in the car too."

"Sorry, gal, not a hope in hell. I already checked Google Earth, and the Teme is heavily wooded on both banks on this stretch. No doubt they took that into consideration. You'd think you'd be able to see across, wouldn't you? In terms of distance it's nothing at all. So maybe they played on that, expecting people to think that there couldn't be anything illegal going on because it would be in plain sight."

Morag took the last bite of her slice of Madeira cake. "I see what you mean about them being crafty." She looked around her in a vague sort of way as if trying to see beyond the cafe's walls. "It's a funny area, is this. It gets all of my highland blood tingling. Gives me the shivers in the same way that places like Glencoe do. I wonder how many times in the past this place was fought over?"

"This was all Marcher territory in the Middle Ages. You don't have to go too much further west to get to Mortimer's Cross, where one of the deciding battles of the Wars of the Roses was fought. And Clee Hill to the north is another of those Iron Age hill forts like on the Malverns."

Bill sighed and leaned back in his chair. "I had a weird case out this way by Clifton upon Teme last year, you know. There was a connection to an ancient Roman shrine, and it got very messy. The woman who did the killing is in Broadmore now. Mad as a box of frogs, but still crafty enough to hide a body in an old disused farmhouse nobody knew anything about. She damned near got away with it, as well, except that a bunch of archaeologists stumbled across her nasty little secret. Danny was with me on that one – Jeez, that was the last time we worked together now that I think on it – and I can't shake the feeling that this is going to turn out the same way."

"You do attract them," Morag teased, then saw that Bill wasn't smiling. That had been clearly been much more serious than she had heard. "Don't worry, Bill. We'll find him."

"Hmmm, but will it be in time? That's what worries me. Look, can you do something for me on Monday?"

"Of course, if I can."

"Well can you ring the inspector at Tenbury and ask them if they've had any reports of illegal workers in the area? Farmers saying that someone has pickers they shouldn't, that sort of thing."

"I can, but is this the time of the year for it?"

"Bollocks!" Bill saw what she meant immediately. At this start of the year it was the time to plough and sow, not be gathering in. The pickers would arrive in early summer and stay until the hop picking was done in the middle of September. Nobody would be hiring casual workers for the fields at this time of year. On the other hand that might work in their favour.

"Ask anyway," he said thoughtfully. "Farmers who might snap at the chance of some cheap labour at the busiest times might be more inclined to report dodgy goings on out of season, just in case they suddenly wake up and find a barn full of migrants they can't move on."

"Okay. ...You know, what I can't figure out is where these people are coming from? I mean, if they're coming in at Dover it's a bloody long way to drag them to get to here, isn't it? It's amazing that any of them survive after a long journey like that, because we know that mostly it's in sealed containers that they get through the port authorities."

Bill sat bolt upright. "That's it! You've hit the nail on the head!"

"Eh?"

"Come on, let's get back in the car so that I can talk more freely." They hurried back out to the car, at which point Bill elaborated, "I couldn't see how the different pieces came together. Why set fires hot enough to dispose of a body? In fact, what bodies? Where did they come from? But you've put your finger on it. They must have a ridiculous number of losses, and what do you do with them? You can hardly start digging mass graves. Okay, they can do that in the farm they're using at the moment. But I'd expect this lot to want the solution to be more permanent than that, because once they leave – and surely they will – then someone else could come in and in all innocence dig them up again."

"Oh, I get it now! Yes, but if you set a fire that's hot enough to disguise the corpses, and at the same time it gets you into places where you can nick other stuff to disguise your good pieces, then that makes more sense."

"And that would make a lot of sense of why there's not been anything surviving that might identify who was in there. Looking at these people, they've come from somewhere incredibly isolated. I doubt they've ever had any dental work done, there'd be nothing like pins in previously broken bones, in short, not a thing which would be likely to remain."

Morag was nodding gently. "And I've had another nasty thought. What if they've been doing both? What I'm saying is, they clearly haven't been setting the fires just to get rid of bodies. They've taken the time to select a target. So what if the bodies were already more than a little decomposed when they were incinerated?"

Bill gave her a shocked glance, but nodded. "I hadn't got that far, but yes, you're right. I wonder if they've been using lye to partially dissolve the bodies? It must be easy enough to get hold of drain clearer in the local farm suppliers, which is usually lye based if nothing else. Then they throw what remains into the fire. There's something niggling away in the back of my mind that says that in contact with aluminium, lye also becomes flammable – or at least something like the gasses it gives off do."

"Well wrapping the bodies in cooking foil would go some way to achieving that," Morag said with a shudder. "I don't think I'll see wrapping my chicken pieces in foil in quite the same way for a while."

Bill sighed, "And this is all stuff you could find out pretty easily. The hard part is finding the means to dispose of the residue, and they've cracked that one. On top of which, these are people who aren't missing, or at least not from this country. There's no missing person reports, no relatives jumping up and down demanding to know what's happened to them."

"And you only have to buy a copy of the *Big Issue* to see how many people still manage to go missing despite that. Illegals must be damned near invisible." She sighed heavily. "And on that cheery note, is there anywhere else you want to look at today?"

The light was fading fast, but that wasn't necessarily a bad thing, Bill thought. "Look, I stuck my wellies in the back of the car, and you don't have to do this if you don't want to, Mogs, but I can't do it alone. I want to walk down that track in the dark just far enough to see if there are lights on in that farmyard."

Morag gave him a stern look. "You, DI Scathlock, are doing no such thing! One slip on that mud and you'll never walk again. I'll take your wellies and go and have a look. You stay in the car and keep the engine running in case I come back in a hurry."

"Bloody hell, I wish you'd come back on the job," then saw her face and held up a placatory hand. "I know. I know all the reasons why you felt you couldn't stay, and I get them, truly I do. But it's a bloody waste of all of your talents. I'd have you back in a heartbeat."

"Thanks for the vote of confidence. If everyone was like you I'd never have left. Now stop dwelling on the past or we'll both end up snuffling into our tissues. Drive back and let's see what we can find."

Time's Bloodied Gold

By the time they got back to Kyrewood Graves it was fully dark, and Bill went just past the turning so that his headlights wouldn't be seen down the lane. Borrowing Bill's dark waterproof jacket as well as the wellies, Morag trotted as best she could back to the lane and peered down it. Bill saw her give him a thumbs up and then disappear. He had rarely felt so jittery sitting and waiting, and that came from his knowledge that he would be unable to do much to help her if she got into trouble.

He hadn't realised that he'd almost been holding his breath until he saw her emerge from the lane again. He also had a stiff neck from looking over his shoulder the whole time to watch for her.

"Anything?" he asked as she climbed in and he immediately drove off.

"Damned right," she answered brightly. "You owe me one of your curries for this, Scathlock," and she brandished the camera. "Wait until you see this! God bless digital where you can get the camera to stabilise the image for night shots. I got three clear mug shots. Not anything a pro' photographer would be proud of, but enough that we might get a facial recognition of them."

"Brilliant! I'll get Charlie on to it."

"What? Aren't you going to hand it on to the taskforce?"

"And say what? Christ, Mogs, I'd love to do nothing more, but when you get back to my place you can read those transcripts, and you'll get a sense of just how much nobody has believed a word Danny has said. I don't want to hand what I have so far on to them, only for it to be stuck in a 'pending' file on someone's desk and forgotten about. I want to be able to march into William's office, slap it down on his desk, and demand that he does something right now or I shall start screaming blue murder, and for him to know that his over-inflated career will go down in flames if he doesn't. Nothing less will save Danny, I'm afraid."

Chapter 6

Sunday

On Sunday morning Bill got up and decided to have another look at the photographs. Now that he'd got more of a feel for the area Danny had been in, he wanted to look and see if he could pinpoint some of the locations where they'd been taken. If necessary he'd go and get other shots of them, because some of the locations had been out of doors. Most had been inside, that was true, and he would have no chance of identifying them until he could get a raid on the farm at Kyrewood Graves, but that was no reason to stop trying.

It had been good to see Morag again, but he had the feeling that it would be a long time before they got to do it again. Jackie was due back later this afternoon, and Morag was determined to spend the morning licking the house into shape so that it didn't seem like she'd gone off the moment Jackie's back was turned. She had promised that she would ring the Tenbury inspector on Monday, though, and then see Bill on Tuesday. That wasn't doing much to quell Bill's rising anxiety over the full moon coming on Monday night, however, and that was what was pushing him on today.

However, his first job was to download and print off the photos they had got yesterday. Again he had to increase the exposure a bit to get more detail into them, but once blown up on A4 paper he could see quite a lot. Morag was right, the three villains she had caught under the farm's spotlights would be recognisable even if the shots weren't of the clearest. The harder part was trying to see if the two terrified victims she had caught appeared on any of Danny's photos.

For a couple of hours Bill persevered, finally coming to the conclusion that they might be two of the men in the January batch of photos. His biggest problem was that the victims all had longish hair and beards, which didn't give him much to work with. Jaw lines were all obscured and eyebrows weren't always that clear either.

Taking a break he decided he'd done as much as he could with this unless he could get a better image of someone. What he had realised, though, was that there was more background detail than he'd expected in some of Danny's shots. These photos he'd copied into a separate file as he went along so that he didn't have to plough through them all again to find the ones he wanted. Half a dozen in particular he wanted to see what he could bring out of with Photoshop, because there was something in the shadows that looked distinctive.

For all that he'd had no reason to get up early, he'd nonetheless been unable to fully switch off, so he'd been up with the dawn and even now it was only mid-morning. If he could find something in those backgrounds, he still had the afternoon to go out and look at stuff. So, fortified by a large bacon sandwich, he set to his task again. Three shots in particular merited some serious poking around at, and after a couple of failures and some referring back to his reference book on how to do stuff, Bill got the images to reveal their secrets.

The first thing which came out was that the building in the background was a church. It was a small place, without tower or spire, and inside he was sure it would be a single chambered place, or one with just a very simple apse. A couple of years past the same Robbie whose job had been

Time's Bloodied Gold

taken over by Charlie had taken a bunch of them who enjoyed country walks out to Kilpeck, and had shown them the wonderful ancient church there, so Bill had at least some idea of what he was looking at. This place would be unlikely to have the lovely apse and chancel arch that Kilpeck had, but the nave looked like it would be similar. He also recalled the archaeologists on that odd case last year talking about the church they'd found in the farmyard back then, and that it would have had a simple altar at the east end, without much separation from the nave in terms of stonework.

Scratching his chin, Bill sat back and stared at the enhanced image on his laptop screen. Yes, it definitely had the look of such a place. But what was that dark mass at the side? Saving and printing what he had, he started again, knowing that he was going to burn out some of the other details as he tried to see what it was. Yet all he could get was that it looked like stone.

Then suddenly he had a bright idea. What had been the name of that senior archaeologist he'd met on that case? Nick, ah yes, Dr Nick Robbins! Now did he still have his phone number anywhere? Some frantic rummaging turned up his notebook from that time and the number. And there was another reason he suddenly wanted to talk to Nick – he'd seen something so bizarre in that previous case that he would be the most open-minded person Bill could get to talk to at the moment, and that was something he wanted badly, because he still had a desperate feeling that he was missing something vital. The dred-locked, part-Jamaican archaeologist was also someone who looked as far from a fellow cop as Bill could imagine, and again he was thinking he would be someone who would never be suspected if spotted by the gang.

Keeping everything crossed he dialled the number and let it ring. When the answer-phone kicked in he left a message and his number, and went back to sit looking in frustration at the image he had printed off. Yet to his amazement his phone rang only minutes later.

"DI Scathlock? It's Nick Robbins. Sorry I didn't pick up straight away, I was just empting the bins. What can I do for you?"

"Look, I know this is more than a bit of a presumption to ask for your help, and I have to make it clear that this time I'm very much off-duty, but a friend of mine is in trouble and needs my help."

"Okay, that sounds mysterious. I'm intrigued! What can I do?"

"Well if I'm not disrupting your weekend...?"

"Oh, far from it! My husband, Richard, is up in Edinburgh doing his medical training. I was supposed to be joining him back in September, but it's proved a lot harder for me to find work up there, and our finances hardly allow me to be the unemployed house-husband. So I'm still down here and sitting feeling sorry for myself with too much weekend on my hands."

Somehow Bill couldn't imagine Nick as the moody type, but he took the explanation as a hint that Nick would be only too happy to have some distraction.

"Right, in that case, would you like to come over here to my place and look at some photos of an old place I could do with identifying? I can't come to you because I really don't want this stuff to leave my place for reasons you'll understand when I tell you more."

"Fine. Give me your address and I'll be over."

Bill told Nick his address and was relieved to hear Nick say, "Oh, you're only just down the road from me. We're in St John's too. I'll be with you in about half an hour."

Time's Bloodied Gold

By the time Nick appeared, Bill had hidden some of the more sensitive stuff away and had spread his photos out so that they made a something of a sequence. Inviting Nick in, Bill offered him a drink, poured him the preferred coffee, and then sat him down and told him an edited version of events so far. He avoided the police politics, but made much of Danny being an old friend whose disappearance hadn't been given nearly enough attention.

"You understand that I can't elaborate on the operational stuff," Bill wound up with, "but you can see why I'm worried about Danny. The more I look at this stuff, the more I'm convinced that this is nothing the major taskforce is looking into, and because of that, if something happens to Danny they aren't likely to hear about it."

Nick was already sitting forward eagerly. "These poor migrants ...let's have a look at what they're wearing, then."

Bill beckoned him to where they were spread out on the floor by the big window. "What do you think?"

"Anglo-Saxon or Viking era," Nick answered immediately. "That's where this stuff originates from ...well in influence, I mean." Then gave Bill a wry grin. "Unless you've found another place like Cold Hunger Farm?"

"Jesus, I hope not! That was enough weirdness for one career! Thank God that place has been sold and refurbished out of all recognition."

"I miss Pip," Nick confessed. "It's hard knowing I'll never see her again. She was a good friend, and having her around would have made this enforced separation from Richard easier to bear."

"Then do you fancy giving me a hand with this?" Bill asked sympathetically. "Could you find out where in this world someone might be still wearing this kind of stuff?"

However Nick instantly answered, "I can't think of anywhere that untouched by modern civilisation. I'd say it's more likely that whoever took them dressed them in this stuff to make them less traceable."

"Really?"

Nick looked sympathetically at Bill. "Well, I'm sure there *are* places this divorced from modernity. But you're talking about tribes in the Amazon basin, or some of the islands in Indonesia, or even the wilds of Russia in Mongolia or Siberia. These guys ...they're white! Quite resolutely Anglo-Saxon white, to be frank. They haven't fallen out of any ancient tribal society that I can think of."

And now he said it, Bill could see it too, but it had taken someone more sensitive to the issue of people of colour to see it clearly.

"Bugger! I should have spotted that a lot sooner. I have to say that I'd been thinking about it too much in terms of the trafficking trade. The top places where people who end up in Britain get trafficked from are Nigeria and Uganda of the African countries – and this lot clearly aren't from there – or from Romania and Albania of the central European countries, and Lithuania, Latvia and Slovakia in the north. But overriding all of them, when it comes to male workers, it's Poland that's the real trouble spot at the moment. So I'd been looking maybe too hard in those directions and thinking of remote parts of Poland or somewhere near there. But then I couldn't square that with their appearances."

"Well that's understandable," Nick conceded. "You came at it from a police point of view, whereas I'm looking at it anthropologically. I mean, maybe they're from the northern European countries, but you won't prove anything from what they're wearing in that respect."

"You're right," Bill declared without hesitation. "I reckon these poor sods have been trafficked from a lot closer to home once you look at them from your point of view. On the other hand that almost makes it worse, because to get those expressions of complete confusion it has to mean that they're what we would class as vulnerable people."

"That's nasty," Nick agreed. "I've heard of the odd case on the news of mentally disabled men being used as virtual slave labour on farms, but never of anything on this scale."

"Me neither," Bill admitted, "and it's worrying that they've not been missed more. I mean look at them. There have to be four or five men in this one shot of Danny's. How did five men who ought to have been in care, just up and vanish from wherever it was that they were being looked after? Because these aren't just someone's son who's walked away from home and not been seen again. They're not a collection of random men who've been scooped up and thrown together, this is a group. Look at the way in this sequence that they all keep looking at one another. They know each other. They aren't strangers."

"That's very disturbing."

"Very! But you'll understand why I called you when you look at these shots where I've managed to drag the background out a bit more. Do you have any idea where in this, or the surrounding counties, this place might be?"

Nick jumped in shock. "Shit! I mean, yes! In fact there's only one place it can be."

"Really?"

"Oh yes. That's St Michael's at Brimfield Wood."

"Bloody hell, I didn't expect you to be able to finger the place just like that."

Nick smile ruefully. "Well that's not because I'm such an amazing expert, but because the place is unique in these western counties. I can only think of another place anything like it, and that's in Scotland – oh, and this place isn't it.

What you've pulled out of this photo is a great big standing stone which is in the churchyard."

"Oh, that's what it is! It didn't look like a gravestone, but I couldn't think what else it could be."

By now Nick was grinning, thoroughly on his home territory. "I can understand why, because the Midland shires in general are very short on anything in the way of standing stones, let alone stone circles. In part, it's a simple case of survival. A farmer has a great big rock stuck in the middle of his field and pulls it out. Oh, and that's not modern vandalism, by the way. I reckon many of our megaliths and stuff must have been gone by the end of the seventeenth century, because the people back then wouldn't have had a clue what they were.

"You see more over in Wales, because there's less arable farming, while Scotland is positively overflowing with them – terrible though the Highland Clearances were, they did archaeology quite a service when they turned so much land over to sheep. There are vast tracts of land up there that have never seen modern heavy ploughing. And to be honest that's where I've seen all the best examples. If you went up to Kilmartin Glen in Argyll, for example, you'd see a whole complex system of stones. There are some which look like gateways. There's a lovely small stone circle with a cyst burial in the middle of it, and some wonderful burial mounds which are still pretty much intact. As for Orkney, well there's more archaeology per square mile up there than anywhere else – it's an archaeologists dream! It's no coincidence that several universities have ongoing digs up there, because it's a brilliant spot to train folks."

"You've obviously been there."

"Oh, many times! And that's really what's made me have some theories about this place you've got here. It's a bit of a pet project of mine to be honest. Every so often I try to get the Church – which still owns the land even if the church itself is never used – to let me dig around it."

"I'm guessing by your expression that they haven't."

"No. I can only think that somewhere in their archives there are records of something a bit shifty going on there, because the few graves they might have there ought not to be an obstacle to a properly supervised dig. I know they're never keen on you digging up bodies, but I wanted to dig round the walls of the circular churchyard to look for evidence of more stones."

"What? You mean you could tell if big stones like this had been there, even if they're gone now?"

"Yes, as long as the ground hasn't been turned over. You see they would have had to have cut a pretty big hole in the first place to drop the bottom part of the stone into. We're not talking about local lumps of rock here, Bill. Sometimes they dragged these monsters for miles to get them where they wanted them. You'll have heard about Stonehenge, of course, and that's unique in the distance the stones were brought, but it doesn't mean that other place simply used a natural rocky outcrop. These are carefully planned objects, placed in the landscape in very specific locations and patterns. You can tell that by the number of times they turn out to be lined up with sunrise at the winter solstice or the summer one. No way is that coincidental."

"Fascinating," Bill murmured, then looked questioningly at Nick. "So are you saying that you think that this was just such a planned landscape?"

"On a small scale, yes. You're up on the top of a moderate hill where this is, although a lot of that is obscured by woodland these days, so it's harder to tell when you're up there. And a mile or two away, further along the hillside there's a nice little earthworks."

"Like British Camp on the Malverns?"

"Exactly – although if you think of that one as the home of a local tribal lord, this is more like just a major family's place."

"Well I never. So why put a church there?"

Nick chuckled. "Oh never underestimate the Church's connivances to make sure people turn up! Back in the days when the early Anglo-Saxons were being converted to Christianity the man on the ground, so to speak, was St Augustine, and he had a letter from the pope of the day quite specifically telling him to convert pagan sacred places to churches."

"Good grief! So instead of getting folks to come to a new church built on new land, he put the church where the people already went to?"

"Precisely. That's why you often find really old churches have wells or springs by, or sometimes actually in, their churchyards. I could take you to a church not that far away where there's a glorious big yew tree which is far older than the church whose graveyard it now sits in. Very pragmatic were your converting priests!" and he winked mischievously.

Bill's mind was now racing. "Right, so if you have a stone circle..."

"...Or in this case I'm more inclined to two pairs of standing stones which might have been used as processional gateways at key astronomical times..."

"...and then that it was already a place for people to congregate, hence the church there. ...How old is this church, do you reckon?"

"What's standing now is Norman. I'd say it was built in that same wave of piety that got places like Kilpeck and Kempley built, which is something like 1130 to 1150. But I've found a small patch of herringbone stonework in the one wall, and that, my friend, usually screams 'Anglo-Saxon'. So I'd be inclined to say that there might well have been a church there well before the Conquest."

"So pre-1066?"

"Definitely. There are enough surviving fragments in other churches in this area for that to be more than possible. It would be by no means unique. Do you want to go and have a look at it?"

"God, yes! And if for no other reason than to see if the area around it looks far too trampled to be just from a few keen visitors to old sites."

"Then in that case I think we'll go in my Land Rover. You don't want to be taking that hire car over the rough track up to St Michael's."

With the assurance of having gone there many times, Nick took a different route to the one Bill had used to Tenbury, going through Bromyard and then turning off on narrow lanes before they reached Leominster.

"The National Trust's Berrington Hall is over to our left by a couple of miles or so," Nick informed Bill, as they crossed the main Tenbury-Leominster road and took to narrow tracks again, "but that's positively modern on the scale we're talking about. Very nice, but eighteenth century. Croft Castle, which is further west goes back to the Conquest, but it's the churches in this part of the world which go right back into the first millennium."

A little further on he pointed to where they had a glimpse of a church tower through the trees. "Middleton-on-the-Hill. Thirteenth century, so not that much later than the one we're heading for, but a considerable step up on the social ladder, if that makes sense. It had a lord with a bit more cash to spend on it, because these churches were most often built on the back of a generous bequest by some local lord who wanted assurances that his bloodthirsty acts in this life weren't going to catch up with him in the next."

Bill laughed. "There's a few big wigs in this life I know who'd behave like that if they had any faith in the first place."

Nick sniffed disparagingly. "I wouldn't call what those Norman lords had as faith in any form we'd recognise. What you have to remember, Bill, is that they had no science to explain why things happened. Why did people seem to die for no reason, for instance? If the plague was in town, then that could seem like the act of a very pissed-off God, and in the wake of the Black Death an awful lot of churches got serious upgrades. But on a personal level, how would you explain someone having a heart attack, for instance?"

"Hmm, I see what you mean. No outward signs, their heart just stops beating. That must have seemed pretty much like the hand of God if you didn't know about things like hereditary defects, or high cholesterol or high blood pressure."

"And that was enough to create a healthy fear of the unknown even into men who otherwise thought nothing of trampling over those they saw as beneath them. So when a bunch of zealous priests turn up telling them that what happens in the beyond can be influenced by them playing nicely with the Church, at which point the holy men – for a suitably large donation – would wear out their knees interceding for the said man, it tended to have the effect of opening their purses. And what better place to offer them to build their church, or chapel, on than the place that the locals were already superstitious of?"

Bill sighed and shook his head. "Politics – it always comes back to that, doesn't it?"

Time's Bloodied Gold

"I think it's more like human nature."

"And now another bunch of avaricious bastards are using the place to take advantage of some other poor sods."

"Avaricious bastards with Land Rovers," Nick declared, pointing to a patch of ground that was well churned up by tyres. "This is where we have to stop and get out and walk, but it wasn't anything like this much of a mess the last time I came here."

"When was that? And why do you say Land Rovers?"

Nick thought for a second. "I reckon I came here last Easter, and back then that muddy mess was a wide patch of grass. It's taken quite a bit of traffic to make it that bad, not just a couple of random tourists spinning the wheels of their nice MPVs. As for the Land Rovers, when you get out, look at my tyres and the width of the wheelbase. You're the expert, but I'd say those marks are pretty much an exact match."

Bill had already changed into stout walking boots, and got down with care. When he'd first come out of hospital he'd briefly had two crutches, soon going down to one, but now he had the two of them. Slipping on mud or rough terrain was something he really didn't want to do, even with a knee brace on. So with care he squelched round to the front of Nick's vehicle and then looked at the tracks.

"If you ever get fed up with archaeology I reckon I could find you a place in forensics," he complimented Nick. "I'd say you're spot on, and that fits with what we've seen our bad lads driving as well," and he paused to take several photographs of the tracks. "God knows when I'll be able to use these, but the more evidence I can get, the better chance I have of getting someone to act to rescue Danny."

"Let's go up over on this side of the track," Nick suggested, leading the way onto the less churned right-hand side of the space. "The one thing that might help you is that with all of this being so overhung by trees, even if we have a deluge, I don't think too much evidence will get washed away. And if we have a dry spell those ruts could dry out nicely."

Nick opened a small gate and went through, holding it for Bill, who saw that it led through the small belt of woodland they had pulled up on the edge of. Only a short way further on it became a track, fenced on both sides by a wire field-fence clearly meant to keep the grazing sheep in one field from straying too far. The track was clear and showing signs of regular traffic, and that was something else Nick commented on.

"This wasn't anything like as trampled before. When I came last it had been raining, and it was a good job I had my boots and over-trousers on, because the grass was knee-high most of the way, and I'd have got soaked. I think the farmer comes and strims it down a couple of times during the summer, if only to stop people trying to find what they think is an easier way to the church across his fields. Some twit always leaves a gate open in those cases. But even when he's done it, the grass isn't that short, whereas this is worn bald."

"I may need you to testify to that if we find something significant," Bill warned him, but Nick simply shrugged easily, clearly not bothered by the idea, for which Bill was relieved. Another professional, albeit in a different field, prepared to back him up could only be a good thing.

Then they emerged onto the close-cropped grass around the church via another gate, having climbed gently to the top of a rise so that the full view of the church was only now revealed.

Time's Bloodied Gold

"Bloody hell!" Bill gasped.

The golden sandstone of the small church was glowing in the watery late afternoon sun, but every bit as tall as the eaves of the low building were the two huge stones in the south. A simple metal fence formed a circle around the church where the churchyard must once have been, the entrance to which was in the south-easterly direction they were approaching from.

"The door is south facing, "Nick explained. "There was an old superstition that the Devil entered through north doors, so you don't often find them, and when you do they're often blocked up."

"I think devils of a very human kind have been entering here without the help of any north door," Bill declared dryly.

"Messy devils," Nick added, pointing to a scattering of cigarette ends clustered by the fence to the south of the stones, as if they had been watching the church door between them.

"I'll take that evidence, thank you very much," said Bill with a grateful grin. "Can't beat a good bit of solid DNA to prove that some nasty little urk was where you say he was when he's denying the hell out of it," and handing Nick some gloves and evidence bags, asked, "Would you gather me some nice random samples, please? Bending over isn't my strongest skill just at the moment. One end to a bag, so that we don't mix up the DNA."

"My pleasure. God knows what else this shower would do given half a chance. I don't like my ancient monuments getting mucked up."

Nick worked a lot quicker than Bill could have while hanging on to a crutch, and soon had a nice collection of samples. "I've tried to pick ones that look like they might have come from different brands, but one thing I can tell you is that some of these are not English brands. I've worked with enough archaeologists from around Europe, who light up at every opportunity, to know the look of some of the rough stuff they used to smoke. But even you probably know that this pair of ends comes from Black Russian cigarettes. They're pretty distinctive – slim with white tips and black papers, and if you get it analysed I'm sure they'll be Sobranie tobacco inside."

"I was thinking the same. Not the stuff you're average tourist puffs away on," Bill agreed, checking the photos he'd just taken of the scattering of ends and of Nick taking the samples. He wanted everything documented to the absolute best of what he had available so that they could be no question of where things had come from.

"Bill!"

The urgent tone in Nick's voice made him look up.

"I think you might want to photograph this as well," and Nick pointed to the ground between the two huge stones.

There, neatly imprinted in the soft mud were footprints, but not any made by modern shoes. These had every indication of being impressions made by the soft shoes Danny had photographed the refugees wearing. It had been fairly dry of late, with only occasional showers, and not enough to fully wash these away, because they were certainly older than the last few days.

"If either of us needed any convincing that we're in the right place, I think we just got it," Nick said in a voice where anger and sadness were fighting for control, as Bill ran off another batch of shots.

"We'll get them," Bill reassured him. "Whatever happens, what Danny's started I'm going to finish."

Chapter 7

Sunday – Monday

Together, Bill and Nick made their way around to the church door, carefully avoiding walking between the stones and leaving tracks of their own.

"Let's have a walk around the outside first," Bill suggested. "I want to get a sense of whether their activity is focused on that one area, or whether they've been traipsing all over the place."

Taking their time in case they spotted any other evidence, they made their way around to the northern side of the church. On a less than warm day it was downright cold on this side out of the sun. Another dense line of trees lay very close to the edge of the churchyard fence, making it even gloomier as they blocked what little light there was.

"Err... Nick, is that one of your other stones?" Bill suddenly said, nodding at the wall of the church.

The low winter light was casting some odd shadows, and revealing other shapes which would have been less obvious in bright light.

The way that Nick stopped in his tracks and stood open-mouthed looking at where Bill was pointing, said that it probably was.

"Looks to me as though they're embedded into the wall," Bill said thoughtfully, carefully making his way up to the wall.

"Jeez!" Nick breathed, "That's why I didn't see them before. Some of the other stones are overlapping them. You can't see a straight face or line."

"But that old mortar has crumbled away," Bill added, pointing to a spot where some of the horizontal mortar had fallen away, revealing that it had been merely smoothing out a deep indentation in the stone, rather than bonding two stones as it still looked like on either side of the break. Someone had obviously thought it was necessary to make the infill because otherwise rain could have got in behind the other, smaller stones at the point where the big stone had something close to a hollow in it.

Nick was almost reverently probing the stone, feeling his way up its edges, but standing back a little Bill was looking to either side to see if he could spot where the second stone of a pair might be.

"Is this its mate, Nick?" he asked, pointing to a slimmer stone which looked as though its true height had similarly been masked by ancient mortar.

Nick's eyes were shining with excitement as he came and probed the second stone, but nodding as he did so.

"So is this one of those blocked northern doorways you were talking about?" Bill asked, but Nick immediately shook his head.

"No, this is too close to the east end. On the other hand, when they built this place I think you can't discount the possibility that they thought that it was better to block off the northern pair of stones so that people couldn't walk through them. I don't know how far back the folk legend about north doors goes, but it could be a fair way. I do know that in some instances they were left open during christenings so that the Devil could leave by his door."

"Hmm, only it looks like a space for a hinge was cut into this one at some point."

Nick peered at it, then puffed his cheeks. "I'm going to start taking you on digs if you keep this up. That was part of what made me miss the other stone. I thought this had been used as the post for an early north door, and then some repairs had been done and the stone moved."

"Does that happen?"

"If you're talking about something close to a rebuild, yes it does, and this is the side of the church with the herringbone masonry on it."

"The Anglo-Saxon stuff?"

"Yes, look down there to the right. See? Herringbone patterned masonry. So you see there's evidence for a rebuild on this wall. It's quite likely that the first church had its north wall on this lie, and then it was partly demolished and the stone used as the foundations for the newer and almost certainly larger Norman church – this one."

"So should we be able to see them on the inside too?"

"Stones this big? God, yes! And now we know where they are, they should be all the more visible."

They went on round to the door and went in. The poor old place looked like it needed a fair bit of love and care, Bill thought. The interior walls had been coated with whitewash at some point, but now it was peeling and flaking, giving the place an air of dilapidation. There were no mighty tombs of the local great and good, no lovely stained glass, and even the floor was of humble tiles which had seen better days. Yet there was an air of tranquillity about the place too. At the east end, a tiny window let just enough light in to show a large but humble wooden cross standing on the floor, but no altar. To the south of the chancel area another small window let in crossing shafts of light to show that the floor of the chancel was a little higher than the nave, but only by the depth of a single step. Nick had left the door open to let some much needed light in, and there was a larger window in the south side of the nave which he said was fifteenth century, but without these it would have been very gloomy inside.

Together they headed for where the chancel area started on the north side.

"That's some thickness of wall," Bill observed, but Nick's face had broken into a wide grin.

"It's behind this brickwork!" he exclaimed, pointing to where the corner of the very simple chancel arch had been blocked off diagonally with bricks. "The big stone you spotted is behind these – that's why I never found it! These are very old bricks. You can tell by the way they're not very deep. Travelling brick makers used to move around making just enough for one job at a time up until the industrial age really got going, and these are just such handmade bricks. There was probably some attempt at a bit of fancy plasterwork here at one time, probably behind what passed for a pulpit, and maybe with the intention of making it a little grander. I'd guess it happened at the point when there was also the money to put the big window in, which might mean that there was a wall painting on it. If they had a leaky roof at some point, that probably got wet and collapsed, but the bricks remain and our big stone is behind them."

"I'm with you, now," Bill said, going to the opposite side of the chancel arch and tapping it. "This side goes back and forms a proper corner." Then he went on into the chancel. "So where do you think the stone with the door hinge is? It ought to be here ...shouldn't it?" He moved back to stand beside the small window and stared at the wall. "Is it my imagination, or is this wall not square on to the arch?"

Nick joined him. "No, you're right. I reckon maybe at some point they thought the wall was leaning – which also happens on some of these simple churches – and so they built a sort of buttress to support it, but on the inside. It's not elegant, but in a humble church like this you'd hardly be relying on the expertise of the local architect. It would be a simple stonemason and the local farm lads doing the labouring out of fear of the priest – although not the poor chap who tended a small flock like this, but probably the bishop's representative who came round and told them to get it sorted."

However, Bill had another question bothering him. "I'm no geographer, but if the east end is indeed facing east, then aren't these stones a bit off for true south and north?" He was turning round and trying to line the stones they now knew were in the wall with the ones outside, and by his reckoning they weren't exactly at right angles to the church. Nick, on the other hand, wasn't bothered by that.

"You have to remember that the position of north does change over the years if you're measuring it by the sun and stars, and it's going to be three thousand or so since those stones were erected, if not more. The earth does wobble on its orbit, so there will be changes. Not huge ones to be sure, but enough that you don't expect perfect alignment. There was a huge dig at an important church up at Wigtown in Dumfries and Galloway, and there, even within different phases of Christian burials there were some shifts in orientation. And sometimes medieval church builders had to be a bit pragmatic when it came to the sites they had to work with. Not every church faces perfectly east."

"Ah, so maybe here the overriding need was to cover up the stones?"

"Quite possibly. You may find it odd, but I'd put my money more on the creators of the stone gateways to have aligned them perfectly with the solstices than the later church builders."

"Amazing," Bill sighed in awe. "All those thousands of years ago and yet they did something as incredible as that.

You have to admire the sheer ingenuity and effort they put into it."

However he now pulled a hefty torch out of his coat pocket and began shining it around on the floor, questing about for any piece of evidence which might help them. Nothing seemed to have been dropped beside mud, but he still had the torch on when they left the church, and as Nick was making sure the door was firmly latched to keep bats and birds out, the beam caught something on the simple timber porch.

"Danny!" Bill yelped, making Nick spin around.

"Where?"

"Sorry, not him ...not actually here at any rate. Look at this, though," and Bill shone the torch on a small piece of graffiti.

A funny little cartoon face had been scrawled onto the bottom of the frame of the ancient and decrepit notice board with a soft pencil.

"That's Danny," Bill said emphatically. "He used to drive me nuts scribbling that thing on the bottom of post-it notes and stuff. Every bloody note he left on my desk had the damned thing on. Half the time I don't think he even realised he was doing it, because sometimes it cropped up on reports and things. It was almost a subconscious doodle."

"Nothing subconscious about this one, though," Nick said thoughtfully. "It's not where his companions would necessarily notice it, and if they did, they'd probably think it was some kid, 'cause it's quite low down. But it's still where someone like you would spot it." He shivered involuntarily. "Feels a bit the act of desperation, don't you think?"

Bill nodded miserably, but then brightened. Delving into his pocket he pulled out his penknife. "Sorry about the desecration, Nick, but these are desperate times," and with the point he carefully scratched 'BS' into the wood beside the face, then rubbed part of one of the face's eyes out with the sleeve of his jacket until it looked as though it was now winking.

"That should do it," Nick agreed. "Is there anything else you want to see here?"

Bill looked around. "Is there any way you could get up here by other means?"

"Why?"

"Well I'm worried sick about tomorrow night, to be frank. Ideally I'd like to get up here and go to ground if I could."

"Bill, you can hardly take this gang on in your condition!"

However Bill was already shaking his head. "I'm not that daft, Nick. That's why I said 'go to ground'. I'm thinking of positioning myself somewhere where I can stick the camera on the portable tripod I've got to avoid too much shake with night shots, and shoot off as many frames as I can manage. Two colleagues know I'm investigating, so if I tell them where I'm going and why, then there's the potential for others to follow if it all goes tits up. But like I said, I'm not aiming for confrontation."

"Well your best bet for a view of the church and stones would be that bit of wood back there where we came through," Nick suggested, "but you'll still have to come up the way we've come today." He gave a big sigh, then said, "I guess that means I'm coming with you again."

"I can't ask that of you," Bill remonstrated.

"No, but you were the one person who didn't brush Pip off as a nutcase last year, so let's call it pay-back. If I bring you up here early on and then take the Land Rover down the hill, there's a place I know where I can hide it out of sight. It'll take me a fraction of the time to hike back up than for us both to walk up."

Bill felt a huge sense of relief. Having someone else there as a witness was one side of it, but the other one was the thing he now put to Nick. "Okay, but you have to promise me something."

"What?"

"If we get made ...if it turns ugly ... then I want your word that you'll take off like a greyhound and leave me behind."

"No!"

"Yes! Because I'll give you some numbers to ring. I'll prepare my two co-conspirators, and you can ring them as well as the other number I'll give you. Between you, you can put a rocket under my colleagues and get help here as fast as it's every going to come around here. It might even be in time to save everyone concerned if they're dead set on clearing up so that there isn't any evidence left. I've taken a beating before, Nick. I know what I might be in for. I've been hauled out of more than one collapsed scrum as well. I'll survive."

Nick sighed, but looked faintly more reassured when Bill added,

"But that's all worst case scenario stuff. What I want more than anything is evidence that will get this bunch locked up for life, and confirmation that Danny is still alive. We've gone from fearing that he died at Christmas to knowing that he was alive a few weeks ago, so let's see if we can get confirmation that he's still with us. If he's survived this long then he can probably hang on a bit longer, especially if he knows someone's got his back."

"Let's go and look at this wood, then," Nick suggested, but took Bill on a loop back round past where they'd

Time's Bloodied Gold

parked, rather than leaving a track through the tall grass of the field in between it and the church.

Inside the wood it became clear that only one spot would give them anything like a decent view and still keep them out of sight. It was far from ideal, not least because Bill was going to have to stand to take the photos. Walking was one thing, but standing for long was still painful, and they decided that they would have to bring something to sit on while they waited to minimise the strain. It meant that Bill had a shopping list of things they would need for him to get tomorrow, and Nick agreed to leave work early so that they could get out here as fast as possible. For now, though, it was time to retire to a pub and a much earned hot meal.

Come Monday morning Bill was glad to sit with his leg up making phone calls first thing. He could tell that Morag was horribly torn between wanting to come with him and keeping Jackie happy.

"You're the cavalry, Mogs," he comforted her. "There's no point in us all getting nabbed. Someone has to be back at base to go and dance on Williams' toes if necessary."

She had been quick off the mark to make her calls to Tenbury, but had nothing positive to report back.

"Nobody's said anything about a sudden and mysterious glut of casual workers," she told him sorrowfully.

"Oh well, it was worth a try."

Charlie had rather better news on the speeding tickets, however.

"He was caught again – twice!"

"Brilliant news! Same roads?"

Charlie chuckled. "The crafty sod got tagged on the same camera on the M5 the first time, then on a camera in Leominster in the first batch. That was on the fifteenth of January, then the second lot were on the fifth of February, and this time he got tagged on the same Hereford camera that caught him the first time, but then on another one up by where the A49 meets the A456 by Brimfield. He's established a nice pattern, Bill. No smart arse defence lawyer will be able to dispute this evidence, and he was a bit earlier in the day on both of these times to the first ones we found, so you can see he's not alone in the car. Not who, sadly, but it's enough to prove that he wasn't just acting alone."

However, Charlie was no happier than Morag at the prospect of Bill's impending late night foray.

"You're taking a big risk," he told Bill worriedly.

"I know, but what else can I do? If we had a couple of weeks to try and bring others round to helping it would be a whole different kettle of fish, but having established that the full moon is tonight, I really don't think we can afford to let the chance go by without doing something. And to be honest, Charlie, I don't even know what I'm looking for. All we know is that the photos got taken on the full moon and that some of them were taken at St Michael's. What that signifies is anybody's guess, isn't it?

"So the next big step is to find out what the hell *does* go on up there at the full moon. Is it where they take delivery of these poor sods? And if so, where are they coming from? Because nobody's been camping out up there, that much is for sure. Nick and I saw no sign of anyone having spent any length of time in the church, and they certainly haven't been holding anyone for days in there. So why does the exchange take place up there? It's out of the way, but there must be a hundred and one other places that are as

Time's Bloodied Gold

remote but a damned-site easier to get vehicles up and down to, and without leaving such obvious tracks to follow. We need to know, Charlie, because if I can do nothing more than nail that bit of the investigation down, I'll have moved it on a sizable step, and that in turn might get the higher-ups to take Danny seriously again."

Charlie's sigh sounded as though it was coming up from the soles of his boots, but he relented. "You make sure you ring me when you get home, though, because otherwise I shall be gnawing my fingernails to the quick."

"I'll try to do better than that and ring you as soon as the coast is clear up at the site."

"I'd appreciate that, because I'll be sitting up waiting, but I've still got to get up and come into work tomorrow and I'm not the youngster I once was."

"Are any of us?" Bill sympathised.

A quick trip to a camping store got him the supplies, and then he spent the afternoon resting his knee until Nick knocked on his door. It took no time to move the stuff into Nick's Land Rover and then they were on the road. The nights were showing signs of getting shorter already, and with it being a bright enough day, they made it to the turning area with still a glimmer of light in the sky.

At this point Nick dumped Bill and the stuff just inside the wood, and then hurried off to hide the Land Rover while Bill took his time shifting the stuff to their hiding place. A small groundsheet had been the first item on the list so that they could put things down without them getting soaked, but Bill also staked it up at one end to act as a wind-break. Alongside that Bill had two folding chairs, a rucksack with all his camera stuff in, and another with two large flasks filled with hot soup, some rolls, and a couple of fleece blankets against the night chill. Both of them were wrapped up in heavy duty jackets and walking trousers as well as boots, and that would have to do. The only other thing Bill had brought with him was a small folding stool so that he could sit with his leg up while they waited, and he was comfortably ensconced by the time Nick reappeared.

The wait seemed to go for ever, and Bill had to force himself not to keep looking at his watch. It wouldn't make anything happen any faster. Neither could they really sit and chat. In the quiet of the countryside, even speaking softly the danger of their voices carrying to those they were stalking was too great.

However, two hours later there was the sound of engines approaching – two, possibly three, Land Rovers were coming up the hill. Then it was confirmed as Bill and Nick counted three sets of headlights flickering through the bare winter branches. Nick had chosen well, because while they could see the headlights, the lights never passed across where they were, and they remained hidden in the shadows.

What shocked Bill was that the men who got out were making no great effort to be quiet. The nearest farms were possibly a half to a full mile away, but to Bill it was confirmation that by now they had become so arrogantly confident that they were going to get away with what they were doing, that they would take few precautions. Doors were slammed shut, men called to, and then there was a procession of torches heading out along the track Bill and Nick had taken the day before.

One wag was shining the torch up onto his face and pulling horrible expressions, making the others laugh. *Do it Danny*, Bill found himself silently praying as he took a couple of shots of the man, *act the clown, you do it too*. And then he did! Danny's thin face was suddenly illuminated by his torch. The relief was so great that Bill was glad that he was using a cable release on the shutter, because his hand was suddenly shaking.

"Is that him?" Nick whispered very softly right in Bill's ear and got an equally soft, "Yes!" back.

At the churchyard the men all headed to the area where the cigarette butts were, but what astonished Bill and Nick was that they then set up a couple of bright car-battery-powered spotlights which illuminated the whole area, then stood around chatting noisily.

"God, they're brazen!" Nick breathed, taking infinitely more care to remain unheard than those they were watching.

"I know. I can believe they've got that much light. It's making my job so much easier."

For almost an hour nothing much seemed to be happening, but then someone's alarm went off on a mobile phone and the mood suddenly shift to much more serious. One of the men, whom Bill now realised hadn't been joining in the joking, took off his coat and pulled something out of a capacious bag on the floor at his feet. As he swirled it round him it was revealed as a heavy cloak embellished with all sorts of strange symbols.

"What the fuck?" Nick hissed. "What is this, some perverted version of a druids' meeting?"

The man disappeared into the church and now a bright light came on inside it. The next thing was that candles were lit. Bill and Nick couldn't see exactly how many, but at least two were put on the ledge of the big window and were visible from outside. A faint whiff of something pungent drifted across the field to them mixed in with the tobacco, something woody.

"Palo Santo wood," Nick whispered. "Very slow burning wood, comes from South America, supposed to be holy but gets used in all sorts of arcane rituals, originally it was shaman who used it. It's supposed to open a path to the Otherworld."

"Shit."

Both of them were thinking of the portal they had seen opening when they had first met. Neither had ever expected to encounter something like that again.

From within the church they could hear chanting beginning. Whoever the man was in there, he was whipping up a storm by the sound of it. What was also noticeable was the way that those outside had become very quiet. Whatever was about to happen it was profound enough to quell the arrogance of these thugs, and that all by itself told Bill that this was no mere pantomime.

"What language is that?" Bill risked whispering to Nick, who strained to listen harder before answering.

"Latin, I think," he breathed softly back, "but it's a very corrupt version, I thought I caught a couple of Spanish words in there." He listened hard again, then added, "I think part of it might be the mass, but it's hard to tell."

Across the fields a distant church clock faintly chimed midnight, but from within the church there came an enormous flash of light.

Bill and Nick both jumped, for an instant thinking that whatever was burning had exploded, but there was no sound, no calls of distress and nobody outside was making a move to rush inside and rescue anyone. Instead two of the men had produce the assault rifles Morag had caught on camera at the farm, and were loading them and bringing them up to a firing position, although they didn't look about to open up immediately. Then in the uncanny deep silence which followed the flash, from within the church someone – and it was probably the cloaked man – was calling out in a clear voice and someone else replied.

Time's Bloodied Gold

Bill turned to Nick to ask him what had been said only to find Nick standing open-mouthed in shock.

"What is it?" Bill hissed.

"Someone just spoke in Old English."

"Eh?"

"Old English. The language of the Anglo-Saxons ...not Shakespearian or even Chaucer's English..."

"It's okay, I know what Old English is, it's what Beowulf was written in, right?"

Visibly shaken, Nick nodded, then said,

"Oh, that man just replied and said, 'Come to me! Bring me your tithe.'"

"In Old English?"

"No, he's speaking Latin. There must be someone who can speak that too."

"What the fuck...?"

More screams were heard, but as if from a great distance, and then Bill saw Danny go into the church, but come out quickly and speak to the two holding the guns. Something didn't seem to be going quite right.

Suddenly there was the sound of a scuffle within the church and the two armed men ran in. There was the heavy chatter of a burst of automatic fire, some screams, and then a man in strange clothes staggered out of the church door, swinging a sword wildly and then collapsed in a heap to lie still. Two more of the men went forward, grabbed him by the arms, and dragged his limp form back into the church.

However, when they returned they were each pulling along a man, and again he was dressed in the strange clothes. Then someone called within the church, and Bill saw Danny go in and come out with a much younger man who looked terrified out of his wits. The lad's legs gave way in the porch and he went down, making one of the thugs outside call to Danny in what Bill presumed was Polish. He didn't need to speak it to know that Danny was being told to be brutal, but Danny said something and held up a placatory hand to the others, while pulling the lad over to the side by the notice board. He was obviously encouraging the lad to get up, but then Bill, looking through the zoomed in lens of his camera, saw Danny falter and look hard at the board just where Bill had carved his initials.

Risking all, but seeing that Danny was the only one looking out of the church not into it, Bill swiftly flicked the laser pointer on and off again which he had brought with him for just this eventuality. It was just a pinprick of red light, nothing beyond the tiniest of flickers playing on the notice board, but he saw Danny jump and then bolt round the church to throw up as the relief that he hadn't been abandoned hit him.

One of the other men called something derisory to Danny, who recovered himself enough to shout back in English,

"It's Piotr's bloody curry! That chicken was raw, I told you it was!"

What intrigued Bill was that the three who had appeared out of nowhere were being patted down by their guards. It couldn't be for weapons, so what was it? Then the light went out in the church and the strange leader came out holding a sword, but not the one the warrior had dropped outside. In the light of the lanterns the hilt suddenly glittered brightly.

"The best yet," the man crowed in heavily accented English, but beside Bill it was Nick's words which resonated more,

"Christ Almighty, it's another portal, only this time they're bringing artefacts from the past through! That's a pristine Anglo-Saxon sword hilt, it's priceless!"

Time's Bloodied Gold

Bill and Nick watched in stunned silence as the gang manhandled the three prisoners away from the church and back towards where the vehicles were.

"Do you think you could get close enough to see who goes in which cars?" Bill whispered to Nick and got a nod.

The archaeologist slipped quietly away back through the woods, and Bill began packing up their stuff, still being careful to be quiet even though the gang weren't. Within minutes the sounds of engines starting signalled the departure of the gang and then Nick was back.

"The creepy bloke went off on his own," he told Bill, relieved to be able to speak normally again. This cloak and dagger work was even more stressful than he'd imagined. "He was driving a Range Rover with Spanish plates." He handed Bill a tatty piece of paper on which the registration number was scribbled. "Hope you can read my writing? The rest of the gang went off in the two older Land Rovers. I can't be sure but I think your mate dropped something as he got into his."

"Really? Okay, then let's get this stuff back to the clearing and have a look."

Despite the fact that the strain and the cold were starting to get to his knee, Bill wasn't ready to give up yet, and at the clearing he switched on the brightest torch they had and began combing the area where Nick said Danny had been.

Suddenly he saw it. A scrap of paper torn from a small notebook. Easing himself down to peel it out from the mud, Bill very carefully flicked the mud off.

"It's a mobile number. Must be a new card Danny put in his phone. That would make sense. He wouldn't want Jane, or worse, Zoe, ringing his old number while he's with these monsters."

He pulled his own mobile out and switched it back on. Carefully he entered the new number into his addresses, then to Nick's amazement rang the number. However he didn't let it ring long and then switched off.

"He'll be able to cover that as a wrong number," he explained to Nick, "but Danny knows my mobile number off by heart, and that will tell him I got his."

Then he remembered his promises to Charlie and Morag and made quick phone calls to them both.

"I'm going to email you this registration number," he told Charlie. "See if you can find out who the hell it belongs to, because my feeling is that this bloke is at the heart of all of this." What he didn't tell either Charlie or Morag was the full truth of what they'd just seen. How on earth did you explain it to someone who hadn't been there without sounding a total idiot?

As Nick drove back, Bill began reviewing the photos on his camera, and his sighs alerted Nick to the fact that something was wrong.

"Did they not come out?" he asked worriedly.

"No, on the contrary, they've come out remarkably well. But that's the trouble. With all that light the gang set up it looks like the whole thing's been staged! Honestly, Nick, if you said these were taken by someone sneaking a peak at the filming of some spooky series, nobody would doubt it for a second. Looking at these I'm guessing that Danny might have tried to take some himself and come to the same conclusion and deleted them from the cards I've now got. Because in his shoes I'd probably do the same. Better to have some murky shots that the tech boys can pull something out of, however shaky and badly focused, than something like this which looks too clear to be true. I'll check these over again on my laptop, but to be honest, I can't see me taking these in to work tomorrow and dumping them on Williams' desk with a demand to get Danny out, because he'd laugh me out of the room."

"Shit! That's not good. The last thing you want is something counterproductive."

"No."

"And much as I didn't particularly like DI Savage when I met him with you, by the same token, I don't think he deserves what's happening to him now."

"He's not anymore."

"Not what?"

Bill sighed. "When you met us last year I was an acting DCI, and because of that Danny was an acting DI. But it was never formalised because of the whole restructuring thing. So I'm back as a DI, which I don't particularly mind because these days the DCIs are more managers than investigators in my eyes, and that's not me. All this started because Danny, on the other hand, was furious at being sent back to being a DS. He refused to believe that he couldn't stay as a DI even though I wasn't being promoted either."

"Oh dear, I begin to see the problem."

"There's more, unfortunately. He began kicking up a fuss, so much so that I thought he'd be better off away from me. He thought he was eternally in my shadow, and I thought that if he was with someone else, then he might see that it was just the way the police force is going these days. And then this came up and I mentioned that his surname was originally Sawaski and that he speaks Polish, and before you could blink he was being squirreled away on this thing."

"It's hardly your fault, though, Bill. He's a grown man. You hardly forced him to go."

"No, but just knowing that I'd turned the job down before him was one hell of an incentive for him to grab it without thinking it through."

"Oh bollocks!" Nick sighed heavily. "I'm beginning to see why you're so determined to put this right. God, I'm so sorry. What a mess!" He drove on for a while, then suggested. "Should we go back up there tomorrow evening?"

"Why do you say that?"

"Well the church might not be in use, but that doesn't mean it isn't cared for. I think the farmer's wife goes in and brooms the floor over once a month or so, and it does get checked over to make sure the roof isn't leaking, or birds have got in and started nesting, and stuff. Just because we didn't find evidence yesterday doesn't mean we won't find any tomorrow if the last lot got swept up as just the normal detritus of passing tourists since last month."

Bill brightened immediately. "Now that's a very good thought. In that case, if you don't mind giving up your evening again, yes please, I would very much like to go and have a poke around."

Chapter 8

Back in December

It was a source of considerable relief to Danny that he didn't have to spend all of his time at the farm, even though he recognised that at some point in the future he might have to, because his nerves were stretched to breaking point. What the fuck was the matter with everyone? His welfare office had long since vanished to who knew where with not so much as a 'kiss my arse', and with nobody taking over as far as Danny could see. So where were his contacts? Where were the men who he'd been told would be meeting him? Where had they gone to? Nobody seemed to be specifically looking at his part of the operation at all. And why did none of the contact methods work? Every time he left a message it seemed to be misunderstood or worse, lost! Why were the taskforce being so bloody slack about everything?

He had managed to convince the gang that he still needed to spend at least some time doing his 'proper job', even though he'd made a great play of losing several lucrative accounts to competitors to account for why he had increasingly more time on his hands, and also an urgent need for money. So he was usually able to retreat to the flat and to spend a precious day somewhere in the week there dithering as his fears got to him, under the pretext of making a few sales calls. One or two bits of evidence he'd managed to grab had been hidden in the flat, but after one of the gang had turned up there unexpectedly one night, he'd become even more careful about what he hid there and where. When he got to go there, he was inevitably given a list as he left the farm of things which needed getting from further afield than Tenbury, because the local shops there had their limits, but at least he was given the cash to pay for them, and the more often he did it without any problems the more he was trusted. But Danny was getting increasingly worried and jittery.

If there was one small mercy it was that Jerzy was in charge of the gang, not that total nutter Mikhail. Jerzy was as cold a fish as Danny had ever come across, and lacking in anything vaguely like human compassion, but at least with him it was all about the money. And because of that, Jerzy was smart enough to keep Mikhail on a very short leash. Nothing would bring them unwanted attention faster than Mikhail going off on one, and leaving a trail of blood straight back here. He was never let out on his own, for instance, nor was he left alone with the prisoners – Jerzy inevitably got Dymek or Stefan, or the other two who came across as passably human, Kazimierz and Piotr, to do things like handing out the food. Danny hadn't got quite far enough into Jerzy's trust yet to be allowed with the prisoners alone, but he wasn't pushing that, not least because from what the others had said, the stunned wrecks of people who stumbled out of the portal couldn't understand most of what was said to them anyway, let alone tell him where they'd come from.

Danny was still terribly cautious, though. He hadn't forgotten the horrible events which had taken place a few weeks back when he'd thought his end had come and he'd been uncovered as the spy in their midst.

The first had taken place early in the month and way too close to his undercover home for comfort. Already there had been a confusing message back in November from the taskforce asking for something to identify

Time's Bloodied Gold

Jerzy/'Boris' by, and Danny's guts still churned whenever he thought of what might have happened if he'd been caught with the handkerchief covered in Jerzy's blood from when he'd sliced a mole on his face when shaving. There was no possible reason for Danny to have the handkerchief, and it was distinctively Jerzy's.

That had had to go in the river when nobody had turned up after all. No way was Danny going back with that on him! But why ask for it and then not come? He felt at that point that he was just about keeping afloat in this mire of deception, so the chaos which came when he braced himself and then went back to find the gang on the third of December did nothing for his nerves.

When Jerzy let the gang off the leash for a night out it was never in Tenbury. That was too close to the base, and the pubs there were filled with people who knew everyone else. So with a designated driver they were allowed into Leominster, and after the first couple of times, Jerzy had decided that Danny could bring them back to the farm with him, since he was pretty much on hand and due to return anyway. As a result, whoever was one of those staying to watch the place would drive two or three others in during the late afternoon, then when Danny was supposedly home from work, he would join them in the *Eagle*, scoop them up, and bring them back.

It should have worked like a charm, and to be fair, when it was Dymek, Stefan and Kazimierz, it usually did. On that day, though, for some insane reason Jerzy had let Mikhail, Ulryk and Piotr in together, and by the time Danny had wandered into the bar in his faded suit, they were drunk as wasps in cider and every bit as dangerous.

"Hey, Danny! There's a friend of your here!" Ulryk had slurred snidely to him. Danny had kept to his own first name on the basis that he would be able to shrug off any chance encounters with someone he knew if they didn't surprise the gang by calling him by a name different to the one the gang knew him as.

Taken aback, all Danny had managed was, "Eh?"

"One of your rep friends," Mikhail had sniggered, tapping the side of his nose and winking. "We saw him come in. He's got a posh suitcase, why haven't you?"

"I'm not selling bloody stockings from a suitcase!" Danny had protested. "My customers order specialist technical items from a catalogue."

"So why haven't you got one, then?" Piotr had demanded belligerently. "Never seen you with a big book under your arm."

Danny had known right there and then that he had to nip this one in the bud. "That's because it's all on my laptop, you bunch of peasants! Get with the century, why don't you. It's technical stuff. It changes. The catalogue gets updated nearly every month online. Why the fuck would we print one out at that rate, eh? And before you ask, no, you can't look at it because I'm not bringing something that expensive within a mile of your clumsy fists!"

"Who you calling clumsy?" Mikhail had demanded, getting up of his barstool and then staggering badly. Then he'd sneered. "We'll show you. Come on Ulryk, let's go and get Danny's friend down from his room to talk to him!"

That had been the point when Danny had signalled the barmaid to ring the police, and he himself had gone to the other side of the room and made an urgent call to Jerzy. By the time he'd told him what he'd found, Jerzy was already calling for the others to lock up the prisoners and get to the Defenders immediately.

"Just do what you can to keep them out of trouble," he'd told Danny as he rang off, which was a lot easier said than done.

Time's Bloodied Gold

Luring Piotr outside to where the fresh air had hit him was the easy part. Calling him a few names under his breath had got the remaining and dumbest of the three up and staggering after him in no time. And as soon as he got to the smoking area and the cold air hit his vodka-soused stomach, Piotr had folded up like a string-less puppet, completely comatose, so Danny had left him there.

Hurrying back into the hotel he'd managed to say to the worried manager,

"They're only acquaintances, they're not my friends, but I've called someone to come and collect them. For God's sake ring whichever rep you have as a guest upstairs and tell him not to open the door to those two!"

Then he'd hurried to the stairs and been relieved to see that the drunken pair had only just made it to the landing. Following them he'd realised he would have to let them do some bawling and shouting at the bedroom door, if for no other reason than he needed to give the others time to get here. If he got these two outside, Ulryk might fold up too, but he suspected that Mikhail would still be capable of punching him out and then going on a smashing spree down the street. Someone beating the hell out of the window of Boots would be sure to get unwanted attention!

At the point when he feared that Mikhail might put his shoulder to the bedroom door, Danny finally called out to them, and taunting them horribly in Polish, had called them everything he could think off. Like a pair of enraged bulls, the pair had come careering back down the corridor towards him, bouncing off the walls like human billiard balls, but at least the ploy had worked. Now to get them outside, and Danny scampered downstairs and stood at the bottom making taunting gestures.

Luckily, Ulryk got two steps down the stairs and then took the rest head first, landing in a groaning heap at

Danny's feet. Before any of the staff could come out from the bar to see what was going on, Danny had grabbed Ulryk's coat collar and was dragging him out of the door beside the main reception desk. Ulryk was a big bloke and he weighed a ton, but Danny was fuelled by blind fury and panic, and he managed to get him outside. God forbid that the local plods should come along and decide to arrest them all. Nothing would blow his cover quicker than him being revealed as an undercover copper by some young and eager PC and his CSO, when they checked who he was and then thought to let him out while the others stayed in the cells.

Mikhail was following him now, as well, swearing like a trooper but mercifully incomprehensibly to the Herefordshire locals since his drunken brain could barely cope with Polish, let alone English. So Danny decided he had to get Ulryk round to Piotr in the hope that once outside, Mikhail would weave his drunken way round as well as he followed them. Shoving Ulryk up against the wall, and gradually manhandling him up to a point where he could get his arms around his own shoulders, Danny began trudging round to the rear of the hotel and its open area with Ulryk's dead weight like an oversized rucksack on his back, threatening to bring him to his knees at any moment. Thank God for it being a Monday night and with almost nobody about at this hour. The few who were had given them a wide berth and muttered darkly about the state of them, but hadn't interfered. Mikhail had nearly caught up with them a few times, but the bitterly cold air had finally got to his drink-filled head too, and he was barely staying on his own feet.

Another prayer of thanks went up that the *Eagle's* smoking area was out of sight in a corner of the car park beside the walkway through to Corn Street, and also that

Time's Bloodied Gold

the car park was almost empty. Piotr was slumped on the edge of one of the large barrels which, come the summer, would be full of bedding plants, and looking for all the world like an oversized snoozing garden gnome, and Danny made for him with Ulryk. He didn't get quite as far, but at least managed to dump Ulryk on a nearer barrel just in time to move sharply away from Mikhail as he blundered around the corner. Had the pub been anything like busy, and the car park full, there would have been car alarms going off left, right and centre, because Mikhail was all over the place and waving his fists about too. He was just about out of sight of the traffic on South Street, but Danny wanted him further out of view. Dare he lure him further? Mikhail was now getting very wobbly around the knees. Would he stand for much longer? Danny decided not and that he could now out-run him, so making one further taunt, he legged it out of the other side of the car park, tore through to Corn Street, round onto South Street, and then stood just by the entrance to the car park to keep watch for the others.

A squealing of tyres heralded the arrival of the Land Rovers, and Danny didn't want to think what kind of speeds they must have gone at down the country lanes to get here that fast. At the moment he was just glad to see them, and almost jumped up and down to wave them through to the car park. With speed the three drunks were thrown into the backs of the Defenders, while Danny was shoved into a front seat beside Jerzy, and the drive back was taken at a considerably more normal speed.

Nothing was said on the way back, although Danny had seen how furious Jerzy was, but the strange thing was that this incident seemed to have cemented his place within the gang. Far from being his undoing, from that point onwards he'd been treated with more respect by most of them, and Jerzy had made it plain in the bollocking of a lifetime to the drunken three the following morning, that without Danny they would have been arrested and deported. Never again were those three allowed out together, and Mikhail was banned from Leominster altogether.

The other heart-stopping moment he had in December had been at the end of the month, when they had gone up to Birmingham to meet Jerzy's cousin Tomek, who led the Birmingham and Walsall end of the gang. Danny hadn't wanted to go, fearful of walking into other members of the taskforce. He by no means knew his opposite numbers well enough to spot them instantly, and at this lengthy distance from his briefings he wasn't sure he could recall any of the names they were going by. What the hell would happen if he blundered into one of them? Because by now Danny had no faith in the taskforce whatsoever. They could have blackened his name something shocking for all he knew. And that could mean that his co-conspirator would be off to some place to make a private call on his mobile under cover of the milling shoppers, and the next thing Danny would know would be him being bundled into the back of some police van under whatever pretext they thought would get hold of him, as opposed to the rest of the gang.

It didn't help that for the last two weeks since the incident at the *Eagle*, Danny hadn't been let home to his flat. Jerzy kept saying that it was for his own good after the spectacle the trio had made.

"We don't want some nosy bastard remembering you were with them and calling the police," Jerzy had said with a wink and what he no doubt thought was a friendly slap on Danny's back.

"Oh I doubt that would happen," Danny had protested. "People have seen me walking back to my flat late on from the takeaway. Being out late was nothing unusual, and I don't drink in *The Eagle* on my own."

But Jerzy was having none of it. "No, I'm not taking any chances," he'd insisted, "you are useful to me. I don't want to lose you," and there was no changing his mind without Danny looking suspicious for not wanting to spend time with the gang.

Even his protest of, "I think I need to stay out of Mikhail's way for a bit," had cut no ice; and the one time Mikhail had grabbed hold of him in the farmyard, Jerzy had appeared out of nowhere, ripping into Mikhail with such a torrent of rapid and dialectic Polish that it was incomprehensible to Danny except in the overall impression that he was ripping Mikhail a new arsehole. Danny knew that from Jerzy's point of view he simply saw it as re-establishing his control over the most unpredictable member of the gang, but Danny also realised that now Mikhail hated his guts with a passion.

"You watch yourself," Dymek had warned him softly that same day. "Mikhail thinks you're deliberately making a fool of him and he's out to get you."

"I did nothing!" Danny had protested, but Dymek had shrugged and said,

"I know that, the others know that, but Mikhail thinks he's got God sitting on his bloody shoulder with all that crap de Arce is feeding him. To him you're interfering in his religious crusade – whatever that might be!"

De Arce was a strange Spanish priest attached to the gang who seemed to be the one who knew how things at the church worked, but who hid himself away in the empty old farmhouse up the lance, never associating with any of the gang except Jerzy and Mikhail. He was as crazy as Mikhail, if not more so, and just as dangerous, and he certainly didn't trust Danny either. And so December rolled on, with Danny stuck at the farm and endlessly skittering out of Mikhail's way, and yet with no means of putting real distance between them to allow things to cool off.

It was an even bitterer pill for Danny, because he'd not dared buy Zoe a Christmas present too early in case anyone came to the flat and asked who it was for. So he'd pinned all of his hopes on a last minute dash to the shops somewhere nicely anonymous, like Stratford-upon-Avon, where he could buy, wrap, and send the parcel all in one go. Therefore, by the time Christmas week came round, he was feeling like some giant rodent was gnawing its way through his heart and guts. Never had he missed a birthday or Christmas for Zoe, not even since he and Jane had been divorced, and what Jane would say to his letting Zoe down was for once nothing to what he was doing to himself.

So he was feeling downright sick when he was told by Jerzy he would be doing the driving into Birmingham. There was no getting round it, he would have to go.

"Your car is better for the city," Jerzy had declared. "The Land Rovers are good for the country, but bad for the towns. We use your car."

So on the morning of the twenty-first he got behind the wheel, found Jerzy in the front passenger seat, and Kazimierz and Stefan in the back seat with a sulking Ulryk in between them. The source of Ulryk's sulks was easy to guess – Ulryk was Tomek's own man within the gang and Jerzy was going to be reporting to Tomek that he'd damned near got them arrested, and everything that Danny had heard of Tomek led him to believe that his response would not be good.

"He's a hard man," Dymek had told him softly not long after the *Eagle* incident. "I heard Ulryk begging Jerzy not to say anything, and if *he's* worried about what Tomek will do, you don't need me to elaborate on how bad it could be."

"Just as long as it doesn't involve any corpses," had been Danny's response.

The prospect of driving back from Birmingham with Ulryk's rapidly cooling body in the back, right in the season when his motorway colleagues were at their most alert for anything amiss, was a thought which almost finished Danny off – especially as he had several days to stew over it from when he was told they were going.

Therefore he drove with even more care than normal up the M5 and took the Hagley Road into Birmingham city centre.

"We meet Tomek in Selfridges," Jerzy had said with a grin. "Nothing but the best for my cousin!"

That was some consolation for Danny. At least they weren't going to wherever the gang had their base in Birmingham, and that decreased his chances of colliding with someone he shouldn't. And there was something to be said for the heaving pre-Christmas traffic in that he had to concentrate so hard that he didn't have chance to fret. Parking was a nightmare, but at last he found a slot around the back of the Bull Ring complex in a side street near St Martin's church.

The gang were lost, he realised with amusement, as he led them with confidence to the back way into Selfridges. That was something worth remembering, because if he ever needed to lose them, up here in the city would be the place to do it.

"Mary, Mother of God," Stefan gasped as he had to shoulder his way through the crowds, including a bunch of burka-swathed, tall and muscular African mothers, so heavily covered that only a slit for their eyes showed, and towing an assortment of children with them.

"The joys of a multicultural city," Danny said to him with a wry smile.

"I've never been to a place like this," Stefan confessed. "This is how I imagined American cities to be," and he shuddered.

Kazimierz gave a dry laugh, informing Danny, "Stefan comes from a small market town about the size of Tenbury. He'd never been to a city until we left from Warsaw airport." Then his face fell and Danny heard him say softly, "But I'll take Krakow any day over this."

"You miss your home?" Danny asked sympathetically, adding, "This is all pretty normal for me. I grew up in a town much bigger than Leominster and spent a lot of my teens in Liverpool, so Birmingham just seems the same as what I've always known."

Kazimierz was so off-guard that for the first time he opened up to Danny, totally wrong-footed by another gaggle of Asian ladies surging around him, all screeching at their kids and wearing brightly patterned hijabs, appearing for all the world like a flock of vibrantly exotic and noisy birds swarming at them. "Krakow is more ...beautiful. Life is taken at a different pace." He glanced around him warily, trying to keep an eye on Ulryk and Jerzy in front, and the crowd at the same time. "Do you get many pick-pockets here?" and instinctively he put a hand to his underarm.

Oh Christ, he's armed! Danny thought in panic. Swallowing hard he answered, "Some, but they go for the soft targets – women with their bags open, or kids chatting on expensive phones and not looking where they're going. They're not likely to tackle a big bloke like you."

"Oh good!"

That was interesting, though. It sounded as though Kazimierz was as uncomfortable about carrying the weapon as Danny was about him having it. More and more the dark and handsome Kazimierz was revealing himself to be on what Danny thought of as the right side of the gang. He'd have no conscience about giving him, Stefan and Dymek the chance to make a run for it when it came to time for arrests. All three did their best to behave like decent human beings, and Danny was liking them more and more, but that wasn't helping his own health and temper either. He'd been warned of the dangers of sympathising with those he was going to mix with, but he'd expected them all to be guilty to a greater or lesser extent, whereas he couldn't think of any time when any of these three had done something he would have slapped the cuffs on them for.

No sure what to expect, Danny was surprised when they met Tomek in the men's-wear department. He'd thought it possible that they might meet in the cafe, but then realised that at this time of year finding a seat for all of them would be nigh on impossible, whereas Tomek could easily kill time trying on suits while his two minders stood watch.

"What you think?" Tomek asked Jerzy in heavily accented English as he preened himself in the full-length mirror.

If he thought he was blending in by speaking English not Polish he was sadly mistaken. Danny could see several shoppers giving them as wide a berth as possible in the crush, and while three other men were all trying to get a glimpse in the next full-length mirror, nobody was crowding Tomek. Possibly that had to do with his crushed nose and cauliflower ears, but mostly it was the cold, dead eyes. One look from them and people scuttled away like terrified crabs from a seagull's beak.

"Very handsome, cousin," Jerzy flattered.

"I think so too." Tomek disappeared back into the changing rooms, came out with the suit over his arm and handed it to one of the minders. "Pay for that. And this tie too." The tie was a ghastly cacophony of garish colours that even Mondrian would have drawn the line at, but clearly Tomek thought he would be the cat's whiskers in the outfit, and no-one was going to argue.

As the one thug moved away to go and stand in the long line at the tills, Tomek clicked his fingers and headed off for the exit. With them all in his wake, the Polish gangster led the way out of the store and into the shopping centre, then out to where the food court was. As they swept into the bar facing St Martin's, a group of young lads about to pounce on a newly vacated table suddenly thought the better of it, and Tomek plonked himself down on a chair and flicked his fingers at the other mountain of a man with him.

"Get drinks," he ordered. "Vodka!"

"Err, just a soft drink for me, please," Danny asked, hoping he didn't sound too much the wimp. "I'm the driver and I don't want to get stopped."

Tomek gave him a cold stare, but then his look softened a little and he nodded. "Sensible. I like a man who knows how to stay out of trouble. Get him a coke."

The minder lumbered off to the bar, and Jerzy and Ulryk sat down, however the way Tomek's eyebrows went up instantly had Ulryk squirming.

"I hear you've been a cunt," Tomek declared, reverting to Polish now that he wanted nobody to listen in. "Mikhail, he's a religious twat, but you, Ulryk, I thought you knew better."

Ulryk's head dropped and Danny knew that there would be some kind of punishment coming.

"If it hadn't been for Danny, here," Jerzy said with a nod in Danny's direction and a withering glance at Ulryk,

Time's Bloodied Gold

"it would have all gone belly up fast. He managed to get them out of the hotel before they caused any damage."

"And what were the three of them doing in town together?" Tomek asked icily.

"They weren't supposed to be in town together," Jerzy responded immediately, which hinted to Danny that Tomek was trying to find out if Jerzy had been partly to blame in the first place. "I only gave Ulryk and Piotr the night off. I was working in the office, and when I came out and saw Mikhail wasn't there, I thought he was at the big house with the priest. He wears out his knees in prayer up there often enough, it would hardly have been unusual. It was only when I took Danny's call that I knew where he had gone. And the reason I don't let Mikhail out very often is because it always gets into a drinking contest between him and Ulryk! Piotr can be let out to the local pub with Mikhail once in a while because we know how long it takes them to get pissed, and if they're not back when I say so, it's easy to drive down and drag them out. It should have been Piotr and Kazimierz anyway who went that night, but Kazimierz wasn't bothered about going and so when Ulryk asked I relented. That won't happen again!"

Tomek had been nodding slowly at Jerzy's words.

"I understand. You have to let the men out sometime or they go crazy."

"Exactly!" Jerzy replied, with considerable relief that Tomek got that, Danny thought. "And at some point you have to hope they won't behave like total fuckwits."

"But your trust was betrayed," Tomek declared. It was a pronouncement, not a question and Danny saw Ulryk shudder. "Can you give us a few minutes Danny? Go look at the pretty girls shopping!"

Trying not to look too delighted to be out of the rapidly deteriorating atmosphere, Danny managed a casual nod and turned to walk back into the Bull Ring. Once inside though he sprinted off and through the centre out to the main shopping streets. Just outside the centre he knew there was an internet cafe and if he was lucky there was time to get an email off. In the end he didn't quite get everything typed down that he wanted to. His phone rang and Jerzy demanded that he got himself back inside to the men's toilets on the upper level by Debenhams. Swearing under his breath, Danny just sent off what he'd got and sprinted back. He dared not be too long getting to them in case they wondered just how far he'd gone. Luckily pounding up the stairs accounted for his breathlessness when he got there.

What he wasn't expecting was to find a very nervous Stefan and Kazimierz blocking any members of the public from going into the loos.

"Someone being very ill in there," Stefan said to one elderly man who headed their way.

"The office party got a bit out of hand," Danny offered. "Silly bugger mixed his drinks and then finished it off with some wacky-baccy. Trust me, you don't want to go in there."

The old man tutted, but tottered off to go to the ones a floor lower down.

"What's going on?" Danny asked softly as soon as he could, but before either of them could answer the door opened and Tomek came out with his pair of guard dogs, shooting his cuffs and a sneer on his face.

"Go in, your boss needs you," were his parting words, and then the three of them disappeared into the Christmas shoppers, just three more men doing some last minute present buying. However Danny had seen Tomek's freshly washed knuckles, and knew he'd delivered one hell of a beating to someone.

Time's Bloodied Gold

Dashing in, the three of them found Jerzy standing over Ulryk, who was on the floor writhing in agony.

"Jesus!" Danny gulped. "We need to get him to A&E!"

"No," Jerzy said firmly. "We get him to the car and take him home."

"But he could be bleeding internally!" Danny protested.

"It's his own fault," was Jerzy's callous response. It reminded Danny that however much Jerzy was treating himself decently at the moment, this was a man with next to no conscience. If he was worried, then it was probably caused in part by what Tomek would do if a body was discovered by the authorities having been so professionally worked over. Even Jerzy had to be afraid of something or someone, and it was looking very much as though that something was what his cousin would do when provoked.

For now, though, the problem was how to get Ulryk home. Tomek had been very clever with his violence. There wasn't a mark on Ulryk's face, and slung between Kazimierz and Stefan he could have been just another Christmas drunk.

"Get him down to the church!" Danny instructed them. "I'll run for the car and bring it up to you," and before Jerzy could argue he took off.

When he got to the VW he was half tempted to just clear off and make a call to Steelhouse Lane central police station. The reason he didn't was because of how things would go down for Stefan and Kazimierz. Who would believe them when they said they'd had not part in the attack? No, it was Tomek he wanted to be brought in for this job, and the only way he could think of to do that was to get Ulryk home as fast as possible, and then take some swabs off him and hope that Tomek's DNA was all over him.

And so he screeched the car to a halt outside of the Bull Ring – where it was caught on the CCTV – allowed the others to bundle Ulryk in, and then took off as fast as he dared. Only when he was on the M5 and heading south again did he start to breathe more easily.

"Your cousin has some temper," he risked observing to Jerzy.

"That he does. His first kill was his own father, you know. The old man tried to beat him once too often and he never did it again."

"Christ!" What else could you say to something like that? Presumably that was why Tomek was over here? The Polish police must have fancied him for that murder, although given that Tomek was in his forties at least, the murder must have been a long time ago.

"The police in our town changed," Jerzy revealed, obviously anticipating another question from Danny. "The old head of police was, shall we say, amenable. The new man was connected in a different sort of way, and Tomek was too useful to be allowed to disappear off the scene. He swapped places with the man who was here and not doing a good enough job."

That explained a lot. The old gang leader hadn't been turning enough of a profit by the sound of it, but probably hadn't been such a violent, loose cannon either. No wonder the taskforce had been formed in response to what must have been perceived as a sudden new escalation in violence.

Back at the farm Ulryk was in such a state that he had to be carried from the car. There wasn't much they could do for him medically, and Danny wouldn't have wanted to dose him with anything even if they'd had any drugs for fear of him going under and never coming out of it. What did surprise him was that it was Kazimierz who stayed with him to help get Ulryk undressed and into bed. Stefan left as

Time's Bloodied Gold

soon as he could, and none of the others bothered to come and see what they were doing, not even Piotr, and Danny had thought he and Ulryk were as close as any.

"I think he's got several cracked ribs if not broken ones," Danny sighed. "Are there any bandages around here, because I think we ought to strap him up."

Kazimierz nodded and disappeared out of the room to find some. That gave Danny his chance and he pulled the couple of evidence bags he'd got tucked into his inside jacket pocket out, then used a few of the cotton wool buds from the packet on Ulryk's rickety bedside cupboard to take wipes from under his nails. If there was any proof it would be there, because his fingers looked bloody, as if he'd put his hands up to try and protect himself. That had to be the blood from Tomek's knuckles, because the cuts to Ulryk's body had been soaked up by his clothing.

He was so absorbed in what he was doing that he suddenly realised that Kazimierz was back in the room. Jesus, had he seen him taking the swabs? Kazimierz's expression was inscrutable, Danny could tell nothing from it, and he spirited the bags with the buds inside into his pocket on the side away from the other man. Yet he could have sworn he saw just a flicker of a smile play over Kazimierz's face as they worked together to bind Ulryk's ribs. What did that mean? Was Kazimierz going to tell Jerzy the moment he got the chance? And if not, then why not? God this tightrope walking was fraying on the nerves!

Chapter 9

Friday 28th December

Danny laced up his heavy walking boots and hoped his despair wasn't written all over his face. Here he was, heading back into the lion's den again – so to speak – and not a sodding back-up in sight. What an idiot he'd been to piss Bill Scathlock off. Just at the moment he'd weep with relief to see his big bear of a former boss coming over the horizon with a bunch of uniforms in tow. Instead he'd got this messy situation which was continuing in a downwards spiral as far as he could see, which was not what he'd signed up for, but then nothing about this assignment was.

The first time he'd seen that portal open back in October he'd damned near shit himself. Bizarre didn't even come near to describing that experience. Had it not been for Ulryk laughing nastily and saying in Polish,

"Fucking priest knows his voodoo, eh? Gave me the shits the first time too! Never thought the Pope had a hotline to the past, did you?" Danny might have thought he'd been covertly doped and was tripping wildly. But all of the gang had more than a touch of edginess to them when that crow of a priest started his freaky incantations and the light started to go all strange – some more than others, depending on their faith, it was true – but none of them were blasé about it.

It was Mikhail, the absolute sadist of the bunch, who was the one most committed to the lunatic priest and the most accepting of the portal, and that didn't bode well for the priest's intentions. Danny had seen Mikhail fingering

Time's Bloodied Gold

his crucifix and saying his rosary nightly, and guessed that he was a man who used the confessional quite callously to absolve himself of his sins so that he could go out and commit them over and over again, and thought that's what true faith was. There was something about Mikhail that really made Danny's flesh creep, and it was quite aside from his unpredictability and bloodthirstiness which varied very little whether he was drunk or sober. Sometimes when they were inside in the farmhouse, and Mikhail had his jacket off and only an army surplus sweater on like the rest of them, Danny was sure he'd seen signs of blood seeping through on his back.

Dymek, the sanest of the gang along with Stefan, had said that Mikhail practiced self-flagellation, believing that mortification of his flesh would make God look more kindly on him despite his many sins. And the fact that these two otherwise very devout Catholics sometimes couldn't restrain their shudders at Mikhail, told Danny that he wasn't the only one revolted by the man and his strange allegiances. But he was like the priest's Rottweiler, always alert and on guard and with a crazy glint in his eyes when the man appeared on these nights, as if he saw it as his chance of personal redemption; and that reason all by itself made him the most dangerous of the gang in Danny's eyes.

And now tonight they were heading for the tiny church again, and with Danny fearing what the hell would happen this time. Quite aside from the deaths here, in November a man had stumbled through the portal, had taken one look at the men around him and had keeled over with either a stroke or a heart attack. Nobody had batted an eyelid, though. Ulryk and Mikhail had stripped him naked, bundled his clothes up in the corner, and then when the priest had signalled that no others were coming their way, they had picked the poor soul up by his arms and legs, swung him a few times and then launched him back the way he had come.

The screams which had echoed through the portal in its closing seconds were ones Danny would remember for the rest of his life. Absolute terror was upper most, but also he was sure he'd heard a woman's voice scream a name. That man had been someone's husband, of that he was sure, and he was equally sure that the man had died. None of them looked well when they staggered into the here and now, and Danny couldn't believe that they were all sickening that badly back in their own place – wherever that was. The portal took its own toll on them in a way he couldn't begin to understand.

Nor was he sure why they seemed to inevitably sicken and die once they were back at the farm. He'd managed to make some progress with most of the gang when it came to the food the prisoners were given, reasoning with them that if they gave these displaced souls something at least nourishing, then maybe they wouldn't have the wretched job of getting rid of corpses all the time. Unfortunately his good intentions didn't seem to have made any difference. Despite Dymek, Stefan and himself buying plenty of vegetables and brewing up some good stews, which the prisoners ate with considerably more gusto than the pizzas and curry's they'd been given up to now, they were still dropping like flies. Maybe he'd have better luck with the next lot, because Jerzy had twigged to the fact that it was significantly cheaper to let Danny brew up the stews than keep sending one of the others into town for extras of the takeaways which the rest of them still existed on. So the prisoners got healthy stews, even though most of the others still went around perpetually reeking of curry. If ever it came to that lot being chased by tracker dogs, Danny's sympathies would be with the dogs, who'd probably go nose-blind after snorting that lot.

At least Danny had managed to put a stop to incinerating the bodies in the workshops and storage units the gang broke into. But what on earth he was going to get them to do with the three who were currently sickening out in the farm's barn was another matter. The only thing he could think of to suggest was that they dumped them out where rough sleepers might go, and hope that they were taken as tramps who'd fallen prey to the winter temperatures. Maybe that disused subway in Worcester would be a spot? By the time they were found the gang would be far away, but there at least his old colleagues would sit up and take notice of three mouldering corpses.

The three men from the October delivery had all died that week within days of one another from what seemed to be nothing more than a normal cold, and Danny, Dymek and Stefan had had the grim job of burying them in a shallow grave at the farm.

Danny had done his best to try to get Jerzy to allow him and the other two to take them into Worcester to the subway there and then.

"It's nothing out of the ordinary at this time of the year for a bunch of blokes to be carrying half of them home in the early hours," he'd tried to insist to Jerzy, but the big Pole hadn't been convinced.

"No. It's too busy," he'd argued back. "After New Year, that's when we dump them. I bet the police check that place for drunks at New Year. We don't want them found too soon."

That had been the very reason why Danny had wanted them dumped sooner than later, but he could hardly say so. The faster those three ended up on the coroner's slab, and the anomalies showed up, the faster an investigation would start. He'd even planned to whizz fast past the speed camera on Tybridge Street after they dropped the corpses off to leave another heavy hint, and that would be easier to do in the festive season, where he would be one of many drivers doing daft things on the road late at night. Afterwards and on an empty street, whoever he took with him would wonder what the hell he was up to if he did something like that.

What was worse, all attempts to get the taskforce to take notice seemed to have fallen on deaf ears, and Danny had lost all faith in them ever acting on anything he sent them. Please let it be Bill who found this trio, he prayed, because his old boss wouldn't drop the ball even if the rest did. Bill would see the anomaly with them being supposed tramps, of that he was sure. He'd even stolen one of Mikhail's many religious medallions to dump with a body to offer a pointer, but he couldn't dwell on that tonight. Instead his mind returned unbidden time and again to why the taskforce had lost interest, because had they listened, tonight they could have mopped up the operation and he could have gone home to something more like sanity.

Why, for instance, had they not acted when he'd sent them that text at the beginning of November telling them that he had more on Jerzy – codenamed 'Boris' for the purposes of identifying the man who was the leader of the gang? Surely they ought to have been interested in what Danny had found out? And it was pertinent to their cases, because Danny's discovery was that despite Jerzy being the younger second-cousin of Tomek, he seemed to be in business wholly for himself.

One night when he'd had a few vodkas too many, Jerzy had implied that he'd found this lucrative sideline all by himself, laughing that his cousin would have to back down when he showed him just how much money he'd accumulated. Tomek might have sent Ulryk to keep a watch on Jerzy, but the reality was that Ulryk was far too slow to keep tabs on a man as sharp as Jerzy. Nor did Jerzy have any intention of putting any of his earnings into the family pot. If his cousin wanted to expand his call-girl ring he'd be doing it with his own cash, not Jerzy's. But surely the taskforce would want to know about these divided loyalties? Danny was baffled by their indifference.

And only a couple of days ago he'd overheard an argument between Jerzy and Mikhail where Jerzy had made a reference to Mikhail being 'family'. That made sense of a lot, because you wouldn't want an unpredictable monster like Mikhail around unless there was some pressing reason to keep him. And equally as provocative had been Mikhail's spat response of,

"You wouldn't have any of this if it wasn't for me! I found him, remember? I found the bishop! I found Obispo de Arce! If I hadn't joined Opus Dei when I came here I would never have been in the right place to greet him when he came to us for help. All of this would have gone straight back into the Church's hands, because without me to look out for him he would have been whisked away to somewhere quiet until they could check him out. I was the one who saw what this could do for us! I was the one who listened to him. You mock my faith, but you're quick enough to use it when it brings you money, Jerzy, so just show me some respect or you might find out what else the bishop can do. God is with him!"

Danny had slunk away and looked up that odd word 'obispo' on his i-phone, because it wasn't more of de Arce's proper name of that he was sure, then discovering that it was Spanish for 'bishop'. That made a kind of sense and reinforced the word for bishop he'd heard in Polish; and at least it explained why a religious nut like Mikhail would be so in awe of someone who was hardly all there sanity-wise in Danny's eyes. But now Danny wanted to pass that on to someone on the outside as a matter of urgency, because what the hell was a Spanish bishop doing involved in all of this? Was he some bloody defrocked paedophile, for instance? He surely couldn't be the genuine article and still in office, because bishops didn't just clear off and get involved with trafficking gangs for months on end without someone noticing they'd gone AWOL from their proper duties. De Arce had to be dodgy, but to be able to pull the wool over Mikhail's eyes the strong probability was that, at the very least, he was a real priest – and that meant he must have attended some sort of seminary, which meant he was in somebody's system somewhere and was traceable.

And Danny might not be religious himself, but even he'd heard of Opus Dei, if only through Dan Brown's famous *Da Vinci Code* and the film of it. When he'd risked looking Opus Dei up on his i-phone when he was back at his Leominster flat, he'd been surprised to find out how modern it was as an organisation. Only started in 1928, it hadn't really got that much of a footing in Poland as yet, despite the strength of the Catholic Church there and the organisation getting some kind of endorsement by the late Polish pope, John-Paul II. So that, at least, made sense of Mikhail's declaration of getting involved with it only after he'd come to England.

But what confused Danny was that most of the web pages he looked at implied that the vast majority of people who belonged to it were lay people. It seemed to have a direct link to the Vatican, if he'd read things correctly, but was not included within the wider church system. It certainly didn't seem to figure highly amongst the priesthood, so what was the bishop's connection to the organisation? Did he even have one? Again he wished he had someone he could ask to do the background checks on this, because there was a huge difference between a rogue priest masquerading as a bishop indulging in strange practices with the aid of a few religious loonies, and quite another if it was something the Catholic Church itself was involved in and hushing up – that was something he couldn't hope to take on by himself.

Sighing to himself, Danny pulled on his battered waxed jacket and went to join Kazimierz, Piotr and Stefan in the second Defender. The first one with Jerzy in the driving seat was already pulling out of the farmyard, and the others were waiting only for him jump in and slam the Defender's back door shut before they were off too. The men from the previous delivery were chained up in the barn where they slept, and were unlikely to affect an escape, yet Danny was constantly amazed at how brazen the gang were about leaving the farm unguarded. Admittedly it was already approaching midnight and most of the local farming community would be tucked in their beds long ago, but they would also be rising with the sun too. Had nobody ever wondered what was going on at the old farm when nobody seemed to be doing any real farming there? And how long would it be before one of the locals decided to come down the track on their quad bike and, seeing the gate propped open for a change and nobody about, go into the farmyard and discover the farm's dark secret?

"You okay, Danny?" Stefan asked softly as the growling of the Land Rover's ancient engine masked his words from the two in the front.

"This isn't what I expected," Danny allowed himself the momentary confession. How Stefan chose to interpret that was up to him – he certainly wouldn't guess the truth of what Danny meant.

"Me neither," came back Stefan's surprising admission. "I had no choice about joining Jerzy – no jobs back home, and my family need someone bringing money in from somewhere – but this?" and he shook his head.

"It's the deaths," Danny ventured, leaving the words hanging and waiting to see what response they brought.

"Exactly," Stefan said so softly Danny barely heard him.

It was a strange relief to Danny to hear him say that so much from the heart, because if things turned really nasty that implied that Stefan still had some hold on a morality that drew the line at killing. And by the sound of it he'd been dragged into this by misfortune rather than anything else, which made him the polar opposite to Mikhail.

Danny made no further attempt to talk to Stefan on the drive over to St Michael's. At the moment they were conspirators in their joint discomfort, and Danny didn't want Stefan to think that he was being pumped to see if he would be disloyal to the gang. Much better to let him act as his conscience dictated when the time came, now that Danny knew he had one. Was it worth sounding out Dymek to see if he felt the same? If he got the same response then he'd even risk a few words with Kazimierz, because although he was another strange one, Danny had no sense of menace off him in the way he did with Mikhail, but also with Piotr and Ulryk. Those three he'd be delighted to the honours with when it came to slapping a set of handcuffs on them.

At the turning space they parked up and then squelched along the soggy track to the church, lugging the heavy bags with the spotlights and guns in them. Danny really didn't like those guns. They belonged in a war zone, not an English shire, and the thought of the damage they

Time's Bloodied Gold

could do if one of the gang went on the rampage gave him nightmares. Why had the taskforce not responded when he'd sent the makes and quantities of them? Even in Birmingham AK74s were hardly what the local thugs were totting! So surely getting them off the streets was a priority?

Sighing, and then covering it with a huff as he put his bag down and massaged his shoulder where the strap had been, Danny resigned himself to another wretched night.

"Danny," Jerzy called to him. "You and Dymek go and check the perimeter."

Dymek jerked his head for Danny to follow him, and together they started walking the perimeter of the ancient graveyard, scouring the trees for signs of watchers.

As they got behind the church and away from the ears of Jerzy and Mikhail, Danny took a deep breath and said softly,

"God, I hope nobody dies tonight."

Dymek looked almost relieved at that. "Ah, that's what's bothering you."

"That poor bastard last time ...that was horrible."

"Not even a few words for his immortal soul," Dymek responded with a sad shake of his head. "Made me think, too. What if it had been one of us? Would we have been thrown through un-absolved as well?"

So that was the way to Dymek! That was another step forward for Danny, and he built on it, saying,

"Bloody funny attitude for a priest. You'd think he'd at least go through the motions. Didn't even make the sign of the cross over him."

Dymek nodded and gave a shudder. "He's a powerful priest, that one, but not a good one I fear. All that he says to Mikhail about the West Indies ...makes me wonder if he's into some voodoo thing."

"Christ, I hope not!" Danny responded, crossing himself and getting an approving look for it from Dymek.

There was no chance to talk further because they were coming round into view again, but at least Danny felt a bit better for knowing that this wasn't going down well with at least two of the gang. If Mikhail got violent, maybe these two would back him up if he was the one who stood up first and said 'enough'?

From down the track there came the growling of another engine, and then the priest, de Arce, appeared, striding along the path with his black robes flowing around him like dark wings, and all banter dried up as if shrivelled to dust by his mere presence. Jerzy went to speak to him, but as on the other nights, Danny noticed how everyone else aside from Mikhail hung as far back as possible. Hard as nails though the gang might be, they had enough animal instinct to know that here was one more dangerous than them, and one who might turn on them at a moment's notice.

Not tonight, though. Tonight it was all business as usual, if anything about this could be described as usual. De Arce went into the church, and through the open door Danny could see him lighting his candles and then preparing the arc around where the portal would appear. Sooner or later someone was going to notice that, because the charcoal that de Arce was sprinkling in the arc to light and throw incense on was starting to scorch the old tiles. And the incense itself was hardly the stuff sold in the average New Age shop either. Danny had once dated a fellow student very into her incense, and consequently had a shrewd idea that the base was frankincense, but there was something which smelt faintly Indian in there somewhere as well as some dried herbs. If pressed he would have said sandalwood with something like wormwood, and possibly

Time's Bloodied Gold

star anise, all of which another internet trawl had revealed as the sort of thing you'd want to burn if you wanted to contact the dead.

The trouble with that, as far as Danny could see, was that while these people might be dead in the sense of living in the far distant past, they were far from dead when they came through the portal. These weren't ghosts, they were flesh and blood people, and they suffered like normal people too. So was de Arce's 'spell' doing something nasty to them by maybe trying to both pull them through the portal as the living, and at the same time trying to resurrect them in this era? Danny would have loved to have even a short conversation with one of his old colleagues, who had retired and gone into the Church, because even if Alf had never had anything to do with something as freaky as this, he'd still know ten times more about things spiritual than Danny did. But in the meantime how the hell could he protect these folk in any way? If what he'd seen so far was anything to go on, sending them straight back was likely to kill them as swiftly, if not quicker, than living in the twenty-first century did.

Desperately trying not to sigh too much again, Danny backed away from the church door and tried to put as much distance between him and it as possible. If there was nothing he could do to stop anything this time, at least he didn't have to force himself to witness the worst of it. After all, who on earth would believe him? Who could he go to and say, 'oh, by the way, the way they get hold of the artefacts is by opening a portal through time'? Williams would have him signed off as mentally unstable before you could sneeze, and in truth Danny would hardly blame him in this instance. Whatever he managed to throw at the gang had to be stuff he could offer proof of in the cold, hard light of scientific evidence which could be presented in court. A few bodies would be a good thing in that respect, because even if they were never identified, their very presence in the city morgue was a damned-site more tangible than him standing in the dock talking about a mad priest and time travel. And the artefacts themselves would stand up to scrutiny – that was something he was also mentally hanging onto – so he didn't need to witness the worst of this when he would never have to testify to it.

Somewhere an alarm on a phone rang, and Danny realised he had been dozing on his feet as the night had worn on. However now everything was happening, and fast. De Arce lit the charcoal and once it was glowing, walked along it trickling the incense onto it, and waving a smouldering stick of Palo Santo wood about him as he chanted in Latin. Wreathed in the smoke he looked like some vision from Hell in the flickering candle light. What he was saying Danny had no idea, and for once was glad that he'd not had such a privileged education that he understood Latin and therefore what was being said – he didn't want to know! If de Arce was saying the mass backwards, or whatever you did to summon the past into the present, then for once ignorance was bliss, because Danny hoped that nobody else would ever say those words, and if they never got recorded to be reused then that was all to the good.

"Mary, Mother of God, in your mercy, hear our prayer," Danny heard Dymek mutter, and turned in time to see him and Stefan crossing themselves and followed suit, then was surprised to see Kazimierz doing the same. So there were four of them now. That was good.

However a great flash of light made them all gasp, knowing as they did that the portal had just opened again.

Time's Bloodied Gold

"*He cymþ...*" an oddly distant voice cried out in fear in the language Danny couldn't figure out.

"*Ðes bið fealu stede,*" another voice said, but sounding closer, then de Arce's voice rang out threateningly in Latin, "*Affer mihi decimas tuas!*"

That, Danny knew from talking to the others, meant 'bring me your tithes'. De Arce was essentially demanding the Church's tenth of all income through time, even those these unfortunate souls had no doubt already paid up to the Church in their own era.

"*Domine, chi populus meus non possunt adducere aurum,*" a voice protested.

"What's he saying?" Danny heard Jerzy demand.

The accented voice of de Arce laughed nastily, "He's the priest. He says his people cannot keep bringing me gold." He switched back to Latin and snarled. "*Os Chi dona, die chi yn. Yn mittere ira Dei. Yn qui potest perdere lat.* ...I just told him if he doesn't he will die, and I will send the wrath of God to destroy them all, ha!"

Behind Danny he heard Stefan whisper to Dymek, "And if he can do *this* it's no wonder they believe him!"

The priest must have relayed that back to his flock, because it was followed by weeping and wailing coming through the portal.

"*Festina usque!*" de Arce snapped, which Danny guessed was something like 'hurry up'.

It certainly did the trick because moments later a man came through at the run, plunging through so fast in his terror that he collided with the church door and was then staggering like a drunkard towards Danny and the others.

Knowing that the only way to save the man from a beating from Mikhail or Ulryk was to intercept him, Danny hurried forward and caught him.

"Steady, mate," he said in his most reassuring tone. The man was shivering in fear, and his eyes were wide and staring. "Can you understand me? I won't hurt you, but you have to come with me now."

"*Ðær eom ic?*" the man whispered, and Danny didn't need to know any more of the language to know he was asking, 'where am I?'

"This is England. Worcestershire."

"*Angel lond? Ðær bið þæt?*"

"Oh God!" because Danny guessed he'd said 'where's that?' If these poor buggers didn't even know what England was, then where were they from? Then a bit of common sense kicked in and he remembered what the West Mercia Police Force was named after. "Mercia," he said carefully. "This is Mercia."

The man stared around him in disbelief, eyes sliding over the electric lights and the guns. "*Mierce? Na, ðis nis Mierce!*"

Danny followed his glances and sighed. "No mate, I suppose to you this isn't. This is more like Hell."

Chapter 10

Tuesday - January

The next day Bill got up and spruced himself up for a visit to work. He didn't have to fake needing to use two crutches today, because he really wanted to give his leg as much rest as possible after so much exercise yesterday. So he limped in and said his farewells to Terry, getting much sympathy in the process, including some he would rather not have had from Williams.

"Do you think you'll be able to resume active service?" he asked Bill with false concern.

"I'm bloody determined I will!" Bill said vehemently, and saw the flicker of disappointment in Williams' eyes. As the superintendent turned and walked away, Charlie's voice said from behind,

"You're too old school, that's your trouble. You will bloody insist on doing a proper job. I don't know, Bill, you really must stop poking that bugger's conscience," and winked as Bill turned to face him.

Both of them laughed.

"Did you see the latest in the local rag?" Charlie asked as he led Bill away from the massed gathering, referring to the headline on yesterday's newspaper. "Apparently we're going to get tough on the local drug dealers. The big boss said so."

"Did he, now? With what?"

Charlie snorted in disgust. "Who knows. Probably going to draft in penguins from Dudley Zoo! They're in black and white. Give 'em a helmet and a tazer and they'll be fine. Nothing like a mutant ninja penguin to put the crappers up a drug lord, 'cause God knows there aren't enough of us to go tooling round the estates on the off-chance of catching a deal in progress. I hate it when they do that, you know. Raise everyone's expectations that we're going to do something we blatantly can't with what we've got. And it's the few poor sods out on the streets who get the backlash when we don't deliver – them and the call centre operators."

Bill gave a grunt of disgust. "Comes of bringing in managers who've never spent any time on the beat, or if they have, then far too little. I've never been a fan of fast-tracking people, in our field or any other. It doesn't work, and seeing some useless twerp with a degree in basket-weaving in Bukhara, or something equally irrelevant, getting promoted does nothing but set up the kind of dissatisfaction that got Danny in such a knot."

"And talking of Danny," said Charlie, opening a door and ushering Bill in. "This is my office, so we shouldn't be disturbed in here, because I've got those tapes – or at least the few we have here. I did have a poke around to see if I could access what the taskforce lads have, but that's not going to happen any time soon."

As Charlie was getting things set up there was a tap on the door and then Morag slid in to the broom-cupboard sized space too.

"You were very cryptic last night," she remarked to Bill. "I got the feeling you weren't telling me the half of it."

Bill felt his heart sink into his boots. How on earth was he going to explain what he'd seen without sounding like he'd over done it on the pain killers and had been half hallucinating?

"The problem with the shots I've got is that this gang is so brazen they've got the place lit up like a night shoot on a film," he started off with. "Honestly, Mogs, I looked at what I'd got and I could have wept. It just looks so staged."

"But is there any reason why they should be using such an odd location?" she pressed him with.

Bill couldn't help himself from groaning out loud, which brought surprised looks from Morag and Charlie.

"Okay, first of all, did you have any success with that number plate I sent you?" he asked Charlie.

"That? Oh, yes," and Charlie ferreted around on his desk and pulled out his note pad. "It's registered to a Ramón José de Arce y Rebollar." Then Charlie shuffled in his seat and looked uncomfortable.

"There's a problem with that?" Morag asked in all innocence, but Bill was already suspecting what was coming.

"Well the only Ramón José de Arce y Rebollar we can find any trace of supposedly died in exile in Paris in 1844."

Morag's face was a picture, but Charlie was sharp enough to register that Bill wasn't as surprised as he ought to have been.

"Does this mean anything to you, Bill? Because this bloke was one of the last Grand Inquisitors of the Spanish Inquisition, and while I know you read avidly, I can't imagine that that's one of those facts you just happen to have squirreled away to amaze people with on drunken nights out."

However Bill wasn't to be drawn that easily.

"First of all, tell me what you've clearly found out about this Ramón – because you have, haven't you?"

Charlie gave Bill a gimlet stare, but humoured him. "Okay, it doesn't take long to tell. Ramón José de Arce y Rebollar was appointed as Archbishop of Burgos *and* as the Grand Inquisitor of Spain at the same time, on the eighteenth of December, 1797. That's a bit unusual. In fact I think he's the only one of the Inquisitors who gets that kind of promotion within the Spanish Church at the same time as coming to office. You'd have thought that they'd have chosen someone already of high rank, but I've not delved into the political shenanigans of that. What's also interesting is that he was then appointed as Patriarch of the West Indies only nine years later in August 1806."

"He was quite the player, wasn't he?" Morag observed. "In those days having power in the West Indies must have come with quite a bit of money attached to it when you think of the slave trade, and cotton and sugar. I don't remember much of my school history, but I do recall that during the Napoleonic Wars there was a big incentive to keep hold of the British territories in the West Indies because of how lucrative they were."

"Funny you should mention that," Charlie said, "because in 1808 the Spanish lost out to Napoleon in Spain, and de Arce was thought to have preached pro-French sermons. As a consequence, he was booted out when the Spanish – with a bit of help from our own Wellington – got Spain back, and the standard biography of him is that he had to go into exile in Paris and lived there until he died in 1844."

"Wow, that's quite a long exile," Morag observed. "Thirty-six years of living to stew over the cost of backing the wrong side, and only two years after getting his mitts on the West Indies' money. He can't have died a happy man."

Charlie grimaced in agreement. "And with all those high flown titles you can bet he'd got use to a certain lifestyle, and it wasn't a poor one. That was one spectacular fall from grace. ...But this can't have anything to do with your man, Bill, surely?"

Time's Bloodied Gold

Bracing himself for their scepticism, Bill nevertheless answered, "Actually it all fits rather too well. ...Okay, now I know this is going to sound bats, but hear me out first, will you? The man I saw last night had a pronounced Spanish accent, for a start off. And somebody went into that church and started saying the mass in Latin. Nick Robbins said that was what it was, and as he knows his stuff in this sort of respect, I believe him."

"But it's a far cry from some bloke saying the mass in Latin to..." Charlie started to object, but was halted by Bill holding up an admonishing finger. "Okay, I'll hear you out."

"I know it sounds far-fetched said like this in the cold, hard light of day," Bill conceded. "If I were you I know I'd have trouble believing me too. But I tell you this: there was nobody in that church when we got there to start watching. I'd swear to that in court. Nick and I checked that church over from front to back on Sunday, and no-one else had been up there when we got up there again on Monday night. You can't get to the church any other way than over the fields – in which case you'd trample the grass flat, and it wasn't – and what's more we watched that damned place for hours before the gang turned up, and there wasn't a mouse squeaking in there. And I'm telling you, those people who came out were not there willingly! They wouldn't have been keeping quiet unless they were very well guarded, and if that was the case, then why didn't those guards come out and speak to the gang? Because like us they were hanging around for quite a while waiting for midnight to come, and they were right outside the church door all that time. That I do have the photographs to prove!

"Now something very weird happened at midnight when that priest started whipping up a storm. I didn't expect it, and I wasn't looking for it. I was expecting someone to come along in something like a farm vehicle with the refugees in a trailer, not a bloody great flash of light inside the church, and then folks appearing as if out of thin air. And while every grain of common sense I possess is telling me that it can't have happened like that, on the other hand I have seen this once before. That's why I turned to Nick for help – because he was involved the last time."

"Not to throw aspersions too hard at this guy, Nick," Morag said cautiously, "but is there a coincidence that he been around both times?"

Bill shook his head. "No. He'd never have got involved in this if it wasn't for me asking him. And the last time we met he lost a very dear friend as a consequence. It's nothing he's set up or connected to. But what *is* similar is that that time it was someone who thought to get rich by using invested money from the past, and I think this time it's someone who has caught on to the value of antique items and is getting rich in the here and now by using the past."

Charlie winced. "Could you make it a bit clearer? Because that just isn't making sense to me. How are they getting hold of this stuff?"

Bill took a deep breath. "Okay, now to the massively weird bit. I think ...my suspicion is ... that this Ramón José de Arce y Rebollar somehow fell through into our time. ...I know ...it sounds bloody stupid just said like that! Please ...bear with me. I'm going to say that it must have been some weird accident, because if with all of our science these days we can't do that, then I don't imagine that some Georgian era Inquisitor would have known how to purposely do it.

"Now I can't even begin to tell you how such a thing might work, but to give you something more tangible: Nick was very quick to point out how rare St Michael's church is. Again, that's something very well recorded and real you can hang onto. If I've got him right, there's just one other example like it in the UK, and that's in the wilds of Aberdeenshire, so if we think of it as being just as rare to have a church encircled by standing stones in France or Spain, then he must have stumbled on such a place quite by accident. Nick says that there are some ancient stones in places like Brittany, so maybe de Arce went there trying to get to the coast and a ship to the West Indies, who knows?

"What I think we can say is that he didn't get to be what he was in his own time without a hefty dollop of cunning and an eye to the main chance. So however much of a shock it was to come through time, if it was initially to somewhere well out in the wilds of Brittany, for instance, then he wouldn't have fallen right into the middle of twenty-first century culture. He'd have had time to adapt, and if anyone was going to adapt, then it would be some amoral manipulator like him.

"I doubt we shall ever know how he came to move to England. He could even have fallen into the hands of traffickers in France. Given the number plate, maybe he even went to Northern Spain in the hope of getting somewhere and ended up coming here on one of the normal ferries? Who knows? He'd have been on the right stretches of coast to come across the bastards trying to smuggle people across to here. But what I don't doubt is that he saw the chance to live well again in this time on immoral earnings. He may even have originally tried to do what he's been doing here back at the place he came through at. But again, I think we have to make an assumption, and it's that for whatever reason, at that location it wasn't lucrative enough if indeed he could get it to work again.

"Now Nick was telling me that at the moment there's a very lively market in Anglo-Saxon artefacts thanks to the publicity surrounding the Staffordshire Hoard; and that little church at Brimfield Wood we were at is on a site which had an earlier church there of the right period. He also thinks that both phases of churches were very purposely built to disrupt the energy of the ancient stones. ...Don't look at me like that Charlie. Just because we live in an age where faith plays next to no part in people's day to day life, you can't argue with the depths of the beliefs which had ancient people building places like Stonehenge and Avebury, or those who built places like Worcester Cathedral. This is about what they believed, not us. Nick was telling me about how they had to dig deep to anchor those stones, and that was after dragging them for miles to get them to the right spot, so you have to conclude that they had some incredibly deep significance to them, even if we don't fully know what that was. Consequently, the stones and the church are intertwined in terms of continued worship on that site, and for all we know there could have been something like a spring or a sacred oak there in a middle phase that we know nothing about.

"So that's the place. As for what they're bringing through it, again it's nothing you would expect, is it? Who thinks of Anglo-Saxon gold and jewelled brooches and sword handles as worth millions on the black antiques market? We'd look for drugs or internet banking scams, and even for somebody like Nick it came as a shock. You should have seen his face when that priest started waving the sword around. I think Nick was even more stunned than me, because he instantly knew what it was and the value of it. And we decided on the way home that the reason why the gang were patting the men down was because other stuff has been stitched into their clothing.

Time's Bloodied Gold

"I hate the idea, but I suspect the strain on the bodies of their victims is sometimes too much and they die in the process. Well they aren't going to risk them dropping the stuff on the way through, are they? They'd want a way to make sure that the artefacts come through regardless of whether someone's grip fails."

Morag was looking very dubious. "I'm struggling to believe this, truly I am Bill, and if it was anyone but you, I'd be telling them to get stuffed for yanking my chain like this. But if I go along with this daft notion for a moment – and I will because of those poor souls I saw with you at the farm – then where are the others? The ones from the previous 'deliveries'?"

"That had been bothering the hell out of me too," Bill immediately agreed with her. "But Charlie bringing up this Inquisitor bloke has given me a nasty thought. The Spanish took some awful diseases to the New World with them when it was first discovered, things like pneumonia and measles which the natives had no immunity to whatsoever. Well the same would apply to someone coming from the distant past to here, wouldn't it? De Arce himself was probably not too badly off, because he'd only come a couple of centuries forwards, and from a time when there was already an increase in things like industrial air pollution. If you could survive Paris in the 1820s and 30s with its lack of sanitation and stuff, you must have been pretty hardy. But if you were coming from more than a thousand years ago, how much have things even like the common cold mutated since then? They'd have absolutely no defence against them, would they?"

"But why dispose of the bodies in fires, then?" Morag confronted him with. "There'd be no point."

However, Bill was suddenly struck by that. "The fires! There haven't been any for a couple of months! You're a genius, Mogs!"

"Eh? Why?"

"Well we said we thought the fires served two purposes, didn't we? The first was to get other artefacts which the gang could either test the water with new buyers with, or use to bulk up their cache to make it look less dodgy. Well surely they must have enough by now? Because experience says that if the buyers were discerning, then they would have only wanted the high quality items."

"Oh!" Morag exclaimed, catching on. "So the likelihood is that they've still got most of that stuff left over to use again."

"Exactly. And the other use they were putting it to was to dispose of the bodies, yes? But what if someone pointed out that they didn't need to do that? That actually they were taking a pointless risk putting bodies in the fire when they'd just died of natural causes?"

Charlie gasped. "And that person was Danny? Because he would know that if whole bodies turned up then we'd start looking harder if we had something to work with, instead of just a pile of ash that might, or might not, contain a corpse."

Bill nodded. "The shift away from the fires has come since Danny's been with them, so I think we are seeing his hand in this. And if we ever get this to a state where we can go to someone higher up, I think we can point out that it would be very in character for Danny to have been worried sick that one day those fires were going to claim an accidental victim in the form of someone working late at one of those places. He'll be doing what he can to exercise some kind of damage limitation, and the fires had to have been a priority because with that heat they must have been bloody unpredictable."

Morag puffed out her cheeks and leaned back in her

Time's Bloodied Gold

chair. "It's a tall story, Bill, but bugger it, it fits together."

He grunted. "And you now see why I wish what I photographed last night looked less like it fell out of a *Dr Who* episode. A bit more of the normal furtive scurrying around would have been a godsend. There wasn't a bloody balaclava in sight, and why would there be when they don't expect their victims to live long enough to escape, or to even know what a police force is to report them to if they did? De Arce may be focused on getting money to live the high life with, and be cocky enough to think that he's outside of our attention as the man from another time, but you can bet that one of those men Danny's with is the actual gang leader, and he'll be set on never doing time for what he's done. But even he must think he's fallen on to the Holy Grail with this one. No site director is going to get up and start wailing over how that lovely thing in the auctioneer's hand is his prize find from two years ago. This stuff can disappear into private collections, and even if a collector wants it authenticated, it's going to pass the physical tests, isn't it? If I recall what Nick's told me in the past, they measure things like radioactivity to tell when something was made. Well that sword handle, for instance, will pass with flying colours because until last night it had never existed in a time post-Hiroshima and Chernobyl."

"Why use his own name with the car?" Charlie asked, with the air of someone getting the grandfather of all headaches.

"Why not?" Bill laughed. "What's going to happen? Just what happened here. You tell me the name and then apologise because the only man you can find of that name died over a hundred and fifty years ago in a different country. The bastard's hardly traceable, is he? He's fallen into our world a fully grown and mature adult. There'll be no school records, no hospital records, and even if we pick up his fingerprints, that won't tell us anything except be something to start a new file with. He's the invisible man.

"And I'll tell you something else: I bet that the first time they went to do this portal opening thing, those thugs he's got hanging on his tailcoats were laughing like drains at the funny man with his barmy tales right up until he got the portal to work. That would be the point when he would have had something to negotiate with them with. The first time he quite literally put the fear of God into some unfortunate in the past, and got them to hand him a piece of gold, was the time when he became equal partners with the gang instead of their victim. Because everything about that lot screams to me that they aren't the sharpest knives in the drawer. De Arce needs them to do the dirty work and to handle the modern day stuff, but I bet he's the one with a master plan. They're just scooping up their share, and thinking it's money for old rope sitting and watching a bunch of terrified people slowly dying of the twenty-first century."

"That's nasty," Charlie said disgustedly, "but sadly I can see what you mean, Bill. I'm not saying I fully buy into this thing with time travel. But I think you're right that this de Arce bloke is the one with the plan for shifting the stuff, and the Poles are just the muscle."

Morag was nodding. "Like Charlie, I'm struggling with the time shift thing, but I do think that whoever this de Arce man is, he's the man with the plan. And the other thing I can easily believe is that he's doing it in the name of religion and is something senior within the Catholic Church. I was brought up Catholic, you know, but I see a vast difference between lovely old Father Thomas at mum and dad's church, and the monsters who get drawn into the Church – Catholic or Protestant – because they see it as a way to gain access to the vulnerable. As a copper, I'm

Time's Bloodied Gold

totally suspicious of the way the Vatican refuses to allow access to its archives. There must be some truly dreadful things buried in there if they think that even centuries later it would rock the foundations of the modern Church. Not long ago I came across this website which was trying to say that the Inquisition wasn't nasty at all. That things like the *auto de fé* were just encouragements to people to profess their faith, not burning people alive – which is what's well recorded outside of the Church."

"When did the Inquisition end?" Bill asked. "I mean, I know it's not around now, but when was its final gasp?"

Morag pulled a face. "That I remember from Sunday school with the bloody nuns! As late as 1908, would you believe? Well the Italian version, anyway. What right-minded person would still be believing in such things, eh? For God's sake, Newton and Darwin had lived and done their work by then, yet you still had these nutcases living in the Middle Ages and wanting to keep control of people by terrifying them to death. Unbelievable!"

"The Spanish Inquisition ended in 1834," Charlie offered, looking up from his screen where he'd done a quick search.

However Bill had a different thought. "You said de Arce supposedly died in 1844, didn't you Charlie? Well if the Spanish Inquisition was disbanded ten years earlier than that, if you were the ones who were supposed to be keeping an eye on one of the last Grand Masters, you wouldn't want to be making it public knowledge that he wasn't where you said he was in something like ...oh say, 1836, would you?"

Charlie flicked through his notes. "Hmm. See what you mean. And this is interesting. De Arce was forced into exile in 1808 and it sounds as though the Inquisition in Spain was put on hold until the end of the Napoleonic Wars. So de Arce didn't have an immediate successor, but then the Spanish branch of the Inquisition was reactivated in 1814 and a bishop called Francisco Javier Mier Campillo, who was bishop of Almeira, took on the job until he died only four years later in 1818. The next chap to be offered the job actually turned it down, and then the bishop of Tarazona, Gerónimo Castillón y Salas, took the job on from 1818 until 1820 when the Spanish side of the Inquisition got shut down in terms of any activity. So it only got revived for six years before being knocked on the head. However Salsa died around the time the Spanish Inquisition was officially abolished, as I said, in 1834.

"So de Arce was the only one of them who survived the abolition of the Spanish Inquisition; and really that was the end of the Inquisition in anywhere except Italy, where they were protected by the pope. It says here that there was an infamous case in 1858 against a Jewish family in Bologna, but that sort of backfired on them, because it fuelled Italian nationalism; it was something which drove the people on to the capture of Rome in 1870 when Italy became unified, and it was an international scandal. So really by the 1850s even the Roman Inquisition was finding it hard to operate in a modern society. De Arce must have been a very bitter man by the time he died, because by the mid-1840s the writing must have been on the wall if you were within the Inquisition, and knew how its claws had been cut from what it was like back when it was founded four centuries before."

"I wonder if he had any kids?" Morag mused. "Even the popes were known to have illegitimate offspring – so much for the celibacy bollocks! A mentally unstable great-grandson, for instance, could well be enthralled by the tales and be trying to live the life his ancestor did, adopting his

Time's Bloodied Gold

identity and stuff. Wouldn't be the first time something like that's happened."

"Could be," Bill conceded, knowing that he couldn't push this any further unless they actually saw with their own eyes the ritual he had seen. If them believing that the Spaniard he was chasing was the barmy offspring of the Inquisitor, and would keep them on side, then it was worth letting them believe that. He himself had no doubts, though. However impossible it might seem, this was de Arce himself pulling the strings.

"Okay, so let's have a listen to these tapes," he said, changing the subject. "What have you got for me, Charlie?"

Chapter 11

Tuesday

"Right," Charlie said as he brought the recordings up on his computer, "these are the only ones I found here of Danny ringing in. So the first one I have is for the meeting on the tenth of November, not the ninth as Danny said he'd arranged, and comes with an attached query as to whether anyone here set up this meeting with Danny."

He turned the speakers on that were attached to his computer and then clicked on the 'play' icon on the file.

"I need to meet," the disembodied voice said quite clearly. "Come on the tenth to the *Fox & Goose* at Tenbury. I have something for you!"

The recording ended and Bill turned in astonishment to Charlie.

"Is that it? Is that all they had to go on?"

Charlie grimaced and brought up on screen the attached email, which read,

```
Is this your chap? Rang
taskforce on 8th arranging this
meeting. Two officers from
taskforce went to the pub but
saw nobody who looked as though
he was waiting for them.
```

"Christ Almighty," Bill breathed, "they didn't even know what Danny looked like."

"But that's not Danny on the phone," Morag declared without hesitation. "The way he says 'come' just isn't

Time's Bloodied Gold

Danny. Danny has an almost Merseyside intonation on words like that."

Bill nodded, "And that's largely because he spent his latter teens in Liverpool. You're right, Morag, that's not Danny, whoever he is. But he's proof that someone arranged a meeting on the tenth. What I want to know is, what happened to Danny's message to meet on the ninth? Who did that go to? And why wasn't it acted upon? There's more than one mystery here."

Charlie was nodding. "I see what you mean. Danny clearly arranged a meeting for the ninth by some other means, and you have to ask how? Did he text in? Did he speak to someone in person, and if so why the need for an extra meeting?"

"I can't believe he asked for it in person," Bill said with a sigh. "Like you say, Charlie, if he thought he was meeting his welfare officer, or some other trusted member of the taskforce, surely he would have jumped at the opportunity to get rid of whatever evidence he had there and then? It makes no sense for him to have hung onto it for a later meet, not least because *any* meeting like that had to be prearranged, so he'd have known to take evidence with him. Danny's not daft enough to hang onto something that would incriminate him with such dangerous men any longer than absolutely necessary. No, he must have asked for it by some form of message, whether by a phone call to an answer phone, a text message, or an email – some means whereby he didn't speak directly to someone. And for the reasons we discussed before, I don't believe he risked a phone call when he could be overheard, which might mean if he did call it was to leave a message late at night when he was finally alone. That would explain why he had to just leave a brief message, wouldn't it? And for me the big question is *when* did he ask for that meeting on the ninth? I think it had to be well before the eighth."

Morag agreed. "It has to be before then so that someone somewhere in all of this mess would think it plausible that he was rearranging it for the tenth."

"Or..." Charlie said with a heavy pause, "...someone on the taskforce quite deliberately ignored or erased the first message from Danny."

Morag shivered. "I don't like the sound of that. That means that one of our own is dirty."

"Could be a civilian?" Bill proposed. "It doesn't have to be one of the actual officers on the taskforce."

"Yes, but surely they'd have been checked before being let loose on something big like the human trafficking taskforce?" Morag protested. "In which case, it still means that somebody who was thought to be trustful wasn't."

Bill puffed his cheeks in dismay. "God, what a mess! Okay, Charlie, let's hear the next one."

Charlie was also looking worried. "Well there's nothing relating to the message on the thirteenth, but then Danny wasn't asking for a meeting then. The next one is on the first of December requesting a meeting on the third. This again is one where Danny later rants by message about not having made any arrangement for that day."

He started the recording, and again they heard the voice from the previous message saying,

"If you want to know what this is all about you need to meet me in Leominster at the *Eagle* on the third. I'll have the evidence for you."

The three of them looked at one another in disbelief.

"What kind of idiot did they think Danny was?" Morag asked, mystified. "He'd never ask for something like that! And what's worse, that message tells them nothing, not what it is he's bringing or how much."

Time's Bloodied Gold

"Was any sort of incident reported at the *Eagle* on the third?" Bill wondered.

"Good point," Charlie muttered, already tapping away on his keyboard to check reported incidents. "Ah, now this is interesting. There was a phone call from the *Eagle* asking for officers to come by on the third. They said that there had been an altercation between a guest and two men who seemed to be the worse for drink, who insisted that he had invited them to his room when he said that he hadn't."

"Who was the guest?" Bill asked.

"A Mr Anthony Redman. A rep for a giftware company who'd been doing his rounds in the area the previous day as well, so it was his second night at the hotel, and he was moving on to Kent the next day. The staff at the *Eagle* reported to the patrol car which called in at midnight that all was quiet and the men had gone away."

"Okay. Charlie, can you ring this Mr Redman and do the concerned copper bit? You know, follow up call to make sure he hasn't had any further harassment from these guys."

"That should be easy enough."

"And when you do, can you ask him if they were the only ones who came to his room that night?"

"Sure, but why?"

Bill scratched his jaw absent-mindedly. "Because otherwise it doesn't make sense. Think about it. The bad guys in the gang think they have a mole in their midst – that's one thing. Yet somehow they find the precise phone number that gets them not just to a normal operator, but to someone in the very station where the taskforce is. Do you see? This call isn't one that got filtered through the vast mire of prank calls and lost cats that come into the main phone lines. This got *very* close to home without going through a host of channels, and that makes me suspicious.

"Now on top of that, just think about the meeting itself. If you want to lure the mole into your trap, where would *you* be?"

Morag's eyes went wide. "Oh my God! You'd be *in* the room, wouldn't you?"

"Exactly! Now I can well understand that, with the *Eagle* being a perfectly legitimate business, they may have let the room to a genuine guest in all innocence, and that buggered up the gang's plans. But even so, where would you be? You'd ask for a room on the same corridor, wouldn't you? You'd want to be in a position to see who came to that room, surely? The one thing you *wouldn't* do would be to send a pair of pissed-up Poles to blunder around outside of the very room you'd set the trap in!"

"Bloody hell!" Charlie breathed in disbelief. "It just doesn't add up, does it?"

"No, it doesn't. So who was setting a trap for whom? And that's why I want you to talk to this Mr Redman, Charlie. I want to know if someone else came to that room before the pair of drunks, because if it was a real trap, then someone ought to have gone there. It might have been someone who looked very like another guest who had just got the wrong room number. Someone who was polite and apologetic, and as a result of that was someone Mr Redman didn't think to mention to the staff, or any officer who happened to speak to him."

Morag's face was creased into a frown. "But I still don't understand why the Poles went there at all. If the gang set the trap, then the only person or persons inside that room would have been their own. There would have been no need for them to try and force their way in."

Bill was nodding. "It doesn't add up, does it? If our Mr Redman takes the room in all innocence – and it seems likely he did, because why else would he complain to the

Time's Bloodied Gold

hotel – then whoever from amongst the gang was supposed to be in that room would surely have reported back that the plan had gone base up to the others, and primed them to come to another room, if indeed there was ever an intention of needing an extra couple of pairs of hands to subdue someone. Nothing about this makes sense at the moment."

Morag was sat back, tapping at a tooth with a nail, deep in thought. "I tell you something else that's odd," she said pensively. "That first tape we listened to... In that case someone went to a meeting the day *after* the one Danny arranged, but this time the meeting was *before* the one Danny set up. Now the first one I can understand – a second message comes in and however wrongly, somebody assumes that it's Danny putting back his meeting. But this one? Danny wasn't expecting to meet anyone until the sixth – and don't forget that Danny said that someone called him and asked for that meeting, he wasn't the one who arranged it – yet Mr Redman gets his unexpected visitors on the third. How far in advance would someone from the taskforce have communicated with Danny to have set up such a meeting, do you think? Because unless it was before that fake message from the pretend-Danny on the first, a whole six days in advance of our real Danny's meet, then they almost look as though it's a horrible coincidence that they are only three days apart. Do you see what I mean? Was one side of the team setting up Danny to meet on the sixth practically on the day another had set the fake one up? It's crazy."

Bill looked at the transcript of Danny's subsequent message on the sixth,

"And Danny sounds so desperate there, doesn't he? That bit about having to ditch evidence in the Teme ...that doesn't sound right for something he'd been hanging on to for six days beforehand. I reckon he only got his hands on that a day or two beforehand, and was probably sweating buckets that wherever he had it stashed didn't get found, because I can't believe he was carting it around on his person even for that short a time. And did he risk that at all because someone had specifically asked him to bring whatever it was? Someone senior within the taskforce? Because that's even worse! If that's the case, then no wonder he was wound as tight as a clockwork monkey and screaming blue murder, because I'd have been doing the same in his place."

All three of them looked dismayed at that. Danny had been right out on a limb there, and with no safety net.

"I don't know that the third message is any better," Charlie sighed a moment later. "It's asking for a meeting in Bromyard again on the ninth of December, and the call came in on the seventh – and again, Morag, your point stands about how close these damned things are coming to one another."

Again the same voice was on the phone. "I need you to meet me in Bromyard in the car park by the swimming pool. There's nothing of importance happening with this gang. I can't stand the strain much longer, I want to go back to my old job."

The three looked at one another in disbelief, not least because of the tone of the speaker's voice.

"He sounds stoned!" Morag gasped. "Jesus! No wonder Danny's name is mud if others think that's him."

Bill was shaking his head in despair. "If anyone senior heard this, then read Danny's next message, they must have been wondering what the hell was going on with him. To them, one minute he's saying there's nothing to be got out of this investigation, and the next he's talking about centres of operations and things being moved around. Oh God,

Time's Bloodied Gold

what's happened here?"

"And it's happened again," Morag added. "Danny requests a meeting *after* the false caller sets one up, so why didn't anyone question the second call? Surely to God there was already a record of both and you'd at the very least wonder why Danny's asking for two totally different ones?" She suddenly grimaced. "*Hmph*, unless they were thinking he was so off his face on something the gang is peddling that he didn't know if it was Christmas or last week."

Charlie's printer suddenly started coughing out paper. "Here, this is the paperwork attached to these phone calls. Let's put our heads together and look at the paper trail. There must be *something* in all of this that will give us a clue."

They passed the printouts around between them, reading in silence as they scrutinised every little detail.

"Charlie, give me back that one you've got!" Morag suddenly exclaimed. She took the paper off him and peered intently at it.

"What is it, Mogs?" Bill asked softly, not wanting to jolt her train of thought.

"The officer who took these calls, the one whose number is on these records of the calls, it's the same person! Look at the others. There are random people receiving Danny's messages and putting them into the system, which you'd expect given that different people would be on different shifts. But the three dodgy calls are all taken by the same person even though they've come in late in the evening every time. Who is this person? Can we find out?"

"Leave it with me," Charlie said confidently. "I'll squirrel away and track this bugger down. I think we want a word with whoever this is and soon."

"And I think I want a word with Joe Connolly," Bill

said with dangerous softness, and reached for Charlie's phone. Having got through to the taskforce's office and effectively told the person on the other end of the phone that he would come up and sit on their doorstep every day for the next six months until he found Joe, he was told that Joe would be there the following day at the end of his shift, which in this case meant late morning.

"You tell him Bill Scathlock wants a very personal word with him," Bill concluded and rang off with a growl of disgust. "I hate these bloody taskforces! They give some folks the idea that they're above the rest of us. Pompous little shit-bag there was trying to tell me I wasn't senior enough to talk to Joe."

Morag couldn't help but chuckle. "Given the way you demanded to know their rank and then bawled down the phone how many years you've been a DI, I'm guessing that they were a bolshie DC?"

Bill snorted angrily. "Not even that! Bloody clerk, that's all! Cheeky little shit! I'll be having words with the senior man there about that too."

"Watch out Harborne," Charlie said under his breath, but with a wink at Morag. Bill on the rampage and with good cause to be angry could be an awesome experience for those who'd never come across him before.

However there really wasn't much more they could do just at the moment. Charlie promised to get others from Bill's team to come by and testify that it wasn't Danny on the phone, because the more serving officers right here who knew Danny and who turned round and said it wasn't him, the more those above them would have to take it seriously. Morag scurried back to her office, but with promises of helping Charlie if he needed it, and Bill went home to rest his leg before another evening with Nick.

Time's Bloodied Gold

"I think at work they think I've got another man on the sly," Nick teased as Bill climbed into the Land Rover. "A couple have remarked on the fact that I've gone from staying as late as I can to avoid the empty house, to suddenly rushing off as early as possible."

"Tell them you've met a bear," Bill chuckled, knowing from times he'd met some of Morag's gay male friends that that was how they'd described him.

Nick hooted with laughter. "That would set the cat amongst the pigeons! I'd better warn Richard, though, just in case some bright spark thinks to call him to warn him. It'll be all the better if he's in on the joke."

What fascinated Nick was the information about de Arce. "A bloody Inquisitor, no less! Well that explains why he knew how to put the frighteners on people, he'd had plenty of practice. And the Latin mass hadn't changed that much over the years, you know. If anything his Latin would have probably been better that that of the priests of the Anglo-Saxon times, because there were often lamentations in the chronicles back then about how poorly educated a lot of priests were. Alfred the Great actually instigated a program to improve clerical literacy, you know, because some priests were so poorly educated they couldn't read the bible or sacred texts. So, if this man came across as very learned, he would be treated by them with considerable awe, and that would have added to the potency of whatever he told them.

"And there's something else I can add to what you know in terms of context. De Arce wouldn't have been some poor peasant's son who rose through the ranks of the Church. He'd have come from a pretty good family to start off with, and so your colleague was completely on the ball when they said he was used to a certain lifestyle. De Arce's would have begun in childhood and grown from there, so life as a refugee in Paris would have been ten times worse than if he'd just been some zealot of a local priest who got booted out of Spain. He'd see a wealthy life-style as his right, and he'd be doing everything he could to get it back, quite aside from stumbling over the portal. He must have already had plans within plans, and I think your guesses of him wanting to reach the West Indies, where he must have had something stashed away, are probably spot on too."

As they headed out on the now familiar lanes Bill observed, "You know, it's a damned good thing I am off on sick leave. It would have been next to impossible to do this much chasing up on things if I was handling my normal workload. I'm usually knackered by the time I get home these days – comes of having fewer and fewer people to get the job done with. I don't know how I'd have done a couple of late nights like this, if I'd even been free on the right nights. And I'm really grateful for your help, Nick. This would have all taken so much longer if I'd been trying to track St Michael's down by myself. It's hardly the kind of thing we have databases on in the force. And knowing how to get to this place," he said as Nick turned up what looked like the track to a farm, but which led to the church, "would have taken me several goes and a detailed map, and I'd still have probably missed this turn."

Despite the twilight, it was clear that nobody had been here since yesterday, because now they spotted a carelessly dropped cigarette packet right at the first gate, which couldn't have failed to be spotted if anyone had come back to clear up.

"Polish," Bill said with satisfaction, looking at the writing on it, as he picked it up and put it another of the evidence bags he had stocked up on earlier at work. "Not exactly rare, but still pretty unusual out in the sticks like this, especially when there are no temporary pickers around on the farms at the moment."

They took their time walking the path, using torches, even though it wasn't really dark yet, so that they could peer into shaded areas. There was nothing on the path until they got to right by the church, and then Nick's torch caught a flicker of something bright.

"Bill!"

He pointed to the tuft of grass, and then when Bill was standing over him, bent down and with great care extracted a beautiful small gold cross. It was a tiny thing, but the workmanship on it was stunning. Serpentine shapes had been delicately chased on its almost tissue-thin surface, and Bill didn't need Nick to tell him that this wasn't something the average farm worker would have possessed.

"Who would have owned such a thing?" he asked as Nick straightened up, holding the cross reverently in his gloved hand.

The archaeologist shrugged. "Could have been any number of people. Maybe a wealthy churchman – and you have to understand that the church even back then was the career of choice for second or third sons of the nobility who were unlikely to inherit much of anything. They would still have wanted to keep some of the trappings of their earlier life and they could do that in the Church. But equally this could have belonged to just a regular member of a high-status family, man or woman. And if you're thinking of trying to track exactly which family this might have belonged to, I have to tell you that you won't. We know next to nothing about these people as individuals once you get down below the ranks who made it into history. Your best bet would be Domesday Book, actually. It's later, but it tends to give the names of the Anglo-Saxon families who got ousted by the Normans."

"Is that something hard to get hold of?"

"God, no! I have a nice modern translation at home. We can have a look when we go back. I'm just saying, don't expect it to get you anywhere. I get used to giving these warnings out to people trying to trace their family history, you see. They come in quite determined to trace their family back to some Roman emperor, then get all disheartened when they find that most folk can't get back much beyond 1800. One of the oldest families in England are the Berkeleys who own Berkeley Castle in Gloucestershire. They can actually go back to the Conquest, but there are very few others who can, even amongst the top drawer of nobility let alone lower down."

However Bill was looking at a different aspect. "What I'm really after is some sense of whether this is people being scared by that bloody priest into robbing one particular wealthy family – because if that's the case then they're going to eventually run out of stuff to bring through, aren't they? Or is this a response to something on a wider scale? What kind of upheavals are we looking at out here? It's hardly likely to be the Vikings, is it? They were more east coast."

But Nick was already shaking his head. "No, actually Bill, there's something called the *Anglo-Saxon Chronicle* which gives an interesting insight into where and when the Vikings were around. Yes, the main raids were east coast, as you say. But the *Chronicle* has several versions, depending on which monastery it was copied out in, and there's one which looks very much at Mercia, which is the old kingdom we're in at the moment. You won't be surprised to learn that it was the one written at Worcester, but it has a nice passage which is fairly famous amongst us specialists for the year 914, where it describes Vikings coming from Brittany and attacking up the Severn estuary, even going so far as to capture the bishop of an area known as

Time's Bloodied Gold

Archenfield, which today is the area around the Wye south of Hereford. It's only twelve miles from Hereford to Leominster, and another ten or less to Tenbury, so we're not that far here from where those raids were.

"Now under the command of an amazing woman called Æthelflæd, Lady of the Mercians – who by the way, was the daughter of Alfred the Great, and whose brother Edward was the king of Wessex – the men of Hereford managed to repulse the raiders. But you have to remember that the Vikings also managed to raid a long way down the River Dee from Chester, so folk here must have sometimes wondered which direction the dreaded raiders were going to come at them from, the south or the north. And then to add insult to injury, we know that in the summer of 916, Æthelflæd had to go and bring the Welsh prince who held the area around Brecon to heel, because he'd basically been fraternising with the enemy and giving them a sly helping hand."

Bill was astonished. "Well I never. So if we think of a time between 910 and 920, would this lovely little cross fit with that timescale?"

"Absolutely! There's been a lot of speculation about the Hoard, you know, with some people saying it's early and others that it's later. And the argument is largely focused on whether you think it was hidden very close to the time when a lot of the pieces were created; or whether you think that they had become almost valuable heirlooms that represented a family's accumulated wealth, and only got hidden at some time of crisis – and one of those times could have been when Mercia became vulnerable to Viking attacks."

"What's your take on it?"

Nick pulled a face. "I think it's stretching the imagination to think that things like the sword hilts were ripped off either in the heat of battle, or very close afterwards, and then buried almost immediately close to a battle site. I just don't see it. Blood and guts everywhere, and you stop to do a bit of pilfering in that much detail? No, I think such things were taken just as they were from the battle field, complete, and then the really valuable stuff was taken off them when there was time to do it properly, because these decorations were worth a fortune even at that time."

"I see what you mean. It'd be like someone nicking a Faberge egg and then stamping on it to make it flat enough to hide. What would be the point? You'd just have destroyed half of the value of it."

"Exactly! And by the way, I think that's why de Arce was so excited to get hold of the whole sword – it gives the hilt provenance and makes it all the more valuable. The stuff beloved of fantasy films and books about swords having names comes from that time, you know. A sword made by a master of the art was incredibly valuable, not just for the precious metals, but because of the legends that surrounded it. The battles won with it were like a validation of the man who wielded it, so if you took such a thing off a leading warrior from an opposing kingdom, by then destroying it – or at least separating the hilt from the blade – you were in effect breaking its lineage."

"You broke the mystique around it, and that could be as potent as killing the person who had it?"

"Yes. I mean, this is just a hypothetical situation, but if you were a Viking, and you had the hilt of the king of Northumberland, for instance, you had one of the symbols of his authority. Because to the Northumbrians that might be the very sword he had defeated the Scots with and won against the Mercians with. It showed he was the kind of king who could defend his people against all comers, and part of the job of a king in those days was to be the defender of his people in a very real and physical way; and success at that was something which would attract the right kind of warriors to his side so that he could be even more successful. A lost reputation could be disastrous in ways far beyond wounded pride."

"I wonder who that warrior was who we saw getting shot last night?"

Nick shrugged. "Probably a veteran warrior who had been given an estate – or a manor, as it would properly have been called – around here to act as a watchdog on what was a very fluid border with Wales. By that I mean that the border was fairly fixed, but people were constantly coming and going in raids across it. And when I say veteran, he could have been no older than his mid-thirties. The younger men would be in the army around the king, but the ones who proved themselves would become part of his cadre of advisors, called the duguth, and it was members of the duguth who would be the men to get manors as a reward for their services. So I think he'd have been one of those, even if we never get to know his name."

"Do you know what troubles me about that?" Bill sighed. "By killing him somebody just changed history. Who knows what else he might have gone on to do? What if he was the last man who managed to hold off a Viking raid, for instance? The repercussions could go far beyond just his own family. And I don't think there's *anyone* who really knows how dangerous that might be."

Nick sighed. "All I can say is that I don't think we'd be any the wiser. In an instant we'd have gone from the future we should have had to the one we have now, and it would seem equally as normal. The fact that you and I are still standing here talking to one another, though, probably means that nothing too awful has happened yet."

"And I don't bloody want it to!" Bill declared. "Let's go and see if there are any other clues inside the church."

The closer-cropped grass around the church showed nothing they hadn't found already, just more added to the collection of cigarette ends and the indentations in the grass where the lights had stood. When they got inside, though, this time Bill had brought some powerful hand-lamps of his own, and they flooded the little church with them.

"That looks remarkably like scorching on the tiles," Nick said, pointing to an arc of darker colour which curved round from just outside of where the stone on the nave side of the chancel arch lay, round and returning a foot or so east of the other stone in the chancel wall. "There's nothing historical which would account for that mark and anyway, it looks recent."

"That's good to know," said Bill as he ran off several shots of the marks using the flash on his camera to illuminate it well. "Could you use a couple of these swabs and see if you can pick up anything from the marks, please? I'd still be happier facing a jury with some good solid forensics on my side. I know I won't be able to prove what we saw, but deliberate desecration of a sacred site as an additional charge would be something I wouldn't turn down if it helped build a case against this lot."

Then he gave a small grunt of satisfaction.

"Found something?" Nick asked, and got a grim smile from Bill.

"Blood. Here on the floor. Looks like they dragged that warrior back to the portal and threw him through it." He took more shots, then when Nick came to him with the two samples from the burns, he handed him a different torch. "Shine that across the floor, would you?"

As Nick did so the torch shone an ultraviolet blue and the blood stains leapt out more clearly, making a track

Time's Bloodied Gold

straight back to the arc, where they disappeared.

"We may have to imply that the body was dragged onto a tarpaulin once there, and then carried out, to offer a palatable explanation," Bill warned him, "but no SOCO would dispute that someone bleeding badly was dragged across this floor ...and I'm really hoping I can get a proper team out here soon to get this properly recorded. ...Oh, and look at this..."

With great care, Bill eased himself down to the floor and, holding an evidence bag over his hand, teased something very gently out from between the floor tiles.

"Unless I'm mistaken, this is a fragment of human bone, and there's blood on it."

Nick shook his head in dismay. "Poor sod didn't stand a chance. I'm afraid his chances of surviving are next to none. Quite aside from whatever two trips in quick succession through that portal do to the human body, if the bullet cracked a bone, they won't have anything in his era to combat an infection getting into it. I know even in Roman times they knew to put a plaster of turpentine over an open fracture, and smother the wound underneath with honey to act as an antiseptic, but I don't think that would do the trick in this case."

Bill held out a hand for Nick to help him up again, but added, "It took some kind of courage for him to come belting through the portal like that. It must have seemed as though he was preparing to do battle in the very gates of Hell to someone of his time. And yet he came nevertheless to protect his people. I have to respect a man like that. What a waste of his life to be pitted against such overwhelming odds that he didn't stand a chance. You know, that only makes me want to get these bastards even more. They really are the scum of the earth!"

Chapter 12

Tuesday evening

They found nothing more of any consequence in the church, but Nick offered to trace whoever was responsible for looking after the church, and to throw his weight as a senior archaeologist with the county behind a request to avoid cleaning the church until further notice. If they could at least not have the evidence washed away by the efforts of a conscientious farmer's wife, it was a start.

Back at Nick's, it only took him a moment to haul his copy of the Domesday Book off the shelf.

"Right, let's have a look at the area," he said, gesturing Bill to the comfortable armchair by the fire, while he perched on the end of the sofa facing it.

"So, we're just nicely over the border into Herefordshire," Nick began, glancing at the road atlas which lay on the seat beside him. "Let's have a look in the index and see where the nearest entries are. Ah, Middleton-on-the-Hill is in. It originally belonged to Leominster which was a large manor held directly by the king – in this case that means Edward the Confessor. What's interesting is that the value of the land is not what it was, and that would imply that something has gone wrong somewhere, such as heavy raiding over the land affected. You usually find that when the value has gone down, that the land in question has been unfortunate enough to have been repeatedly raided, whether by Vikings or Welshmen, or as in the case of Yorkshire in Domesday, William the Conqueror himself."

Time's Bloodied Gold

He flicked back and forth between the atlas and the index a couple of times, muttering to himself, "Leysters ...no, not old enough to be in. ...Kimbolton ...no, that's not old enough either. ...Ah! Brimfield. Now Brimfield was held by Ralph de Mortimer of Wigmore in Domesday, and like all other major barons in these early days of the Conquest, he basically took over the land of an equally important Saxon lord, in this case someone called Alweard. The Mortimers are interesting in their own right, but not terribly relevant to this case. What I think this *is* telling us is that there was quite a bit of royal interest in this neck of the woods, and that whatever wasn't directly in the hands of the royal family was held by a lord of considerable standing who was perfectly able to hold his own in most instances. But in neither case would these high-born families have been living here. They were so far up the scale that they would have had their main houses closer to the political centre of the Anglo-Saxon world; and that means not only London but Winchester too, because that was the capital of Wessex, and the kings of Wessex had been the ones who brought about the unification of England."

"So no really big, flash manor houses round here where lots of sparkly goodies would have been lying around," Bill surmised, and got a nod from Nick, who added,

"And given who these land-holding people were – i.e. a king or Mercian nobleman of high rank – I think we're more likely looking at time when there was major disruption. A time when people might have had very real worries about whether the king would be able to protect them. That's the kind of time when lots of people with family heirlooms might have been looking to find a hideaway for them, which would lead those objects to be where they wouldn't normally have been."

"So does that mean we're still on for the 910s?"

Nick sat back and took a swig of his mug of coffee. "Well the other option is much earlier – and I really do mean a *lot* earlier. That would be when what we now think of as England was more fragmented. You see when the Anglo-Saxons first migrated our way they tended to be in something you'd think of as clans. Nothing much bigger. Then as time went by, the big man in the area got more control and became the king of a region about the size of our modern counties – which is where a lot of our shire boundaries originated, by the way. More fighting went on and those small kingdoms gradually coalesced into a handful of larger kingdoms – namely Northumbria, East Anglia, Mercia, Wessex and Kent. But for fighting between separate Anglo-Saxon kingdoms to be taking place in this area, I think you'd have to be looking at the time of King Penda of Mercia, and that means back in the first half of the seventh century, and that's a bit early to be finding things like that cross you spotted."

"They weren't Christian then?"

"Not uniformly, no. In fact one of the reasons why we even know about Penda at all was because he was a heathen king who made it into the annals because he was something of an opportunist. Sometimes he sided with the Christian kings, sometimes he fought against them. Now that doesn't mean that there weren't Christians within his kingdom because there most definitely were, but I just don't think there would have been the *volume* of high value stuff to have kept our gang going for this long. I think they'd have run out of things to demand be brought to them a couple of full-moons ago. There was an even more delicate cross found in the Staffordshire Hoard, incidentally, which is one of the objects academics argue over, because it's undoubtedly early in terms of manufacture. But is that

Time's Bloodied Gold

when it was buried? That's the million dollar question, and it applies just as much to what we've found. So in answer to your question, yes, I think the early tenth century is the right era for our poor trafficked peasants to be coming from."

Bill considered that for a moment, then asked,

"So is there anything I should be aware of about that particular era?"

Nick began to shake his head then stopped. "Oh bugger!"

"I don't like the sound of that. What have you remembered?"

His reply shocked Bill.

"In a word, slavery."

"Slavery? But I didn't think people were traded from Africa until much later than that?"

"That's because you, like most other people, think that slavery started with people being dragged from Africa to the Americas to work the plantations. But slavery is much older than that. The Egyptians had slaves brought from far afield, and of course Rome was notorious for its slaves. In this instance, though, the Welsh were feared by the Anglo-Saxons in these border areas to a very large extent because they would take captives. They would then ship them off down the River Severn where they were sold as slaves to the Vikings in the Bristol area, and then they were taken round the Welsh coast to make the crossing to Dublin."

"Dublin?"

"Yes, its origins are as a Viking trading port, you know. And what did the Vikings need in great measure? Slaves to man the oars of their galleys and to trade as commodities onwards. So if you were unfortunate enough to be an Anglo-Saxon foot soldier, and you got separated from your mates while fighting the Welsh, even though the Vikings hadn't necessarily raided as far as where you were, that didn't preclude you ending your days chained to the oars of a Viking galley, plundering up and down the coasts of what's now the UK. Because the Vikings were opportunists, and just because one Welsh prince had sold one band of them a nice group of slaves, that didn't mean that it brought him or any other Welsh prince security from another band of sea wolves, as they were frequently referred to as. The Vikings often operated as quite distinct and autonomous groups."

"Bloody hell!"

"Quite! So you see it's totally wrong to think that slavery is always a matter of colour. It isn't. In fact I think that's one of the problems with modern slavery – people think of it as always being white persecuting black, and therefore they don't see white people like the Poles, Latvians or Lithuanians as slaves, because they don't fit their preconceptions. If we could break that a bit more, you might find that more people would report cases to you guys, because they'd see it for what it is."

"That's a very disturbing analysis," Bill sighed, "but one I fear you're all too accurate with. ...Okay, let me ask you this, then. Do you think that because of those Welsh raids, the people who are on the other side of this portal are much more conditioned to think that they have no choice but to send people through with these goods? I guess I'm asking, are they likely to see this more in the light of having to permanently lose some of their community to pay for the rest to live in peace, rather than something we would see more as a hostage situation? In other words, a situation where they would be expecting to get their people back? Because that's been bothering me too. Why haven't they baulked at this before now if their local warrior, or whoever, who went through the last time with the goods hasn't come back yet? Why hasn't there been more resistance to de Arce's demands? Is that to do with their preconceptions of slavery?"

Nick considered his answer carefully. "I think there's a lot in that, to be sure. I don't think they would have our sensibilities over expecting to get someone back, the way we would over a ransom being paid. But I think you also have to be aware of the hold the Church had over people in that time, and how much their behaviour could be swayed by it to accept what was unpalatable. And by the way, that's another reason why I think we're talking about the later date. I don't think de Arce would have been able to gain quite such a strangle hold on the people of Penda's era. The Church hadn't got its hooks into people to the same all-encompassing extent back then. But by the time of Æthelflæd, the Church was well and truly embedded in English society, and with far more power than ever it had in much later times, such as the early Victorian era which you think that inquisitor came from. The nearest comparison I can give you is to think of Muslim countries nowadays, and the way that religion influences absolutely every aspect of life there. It's about how you act, how you dress, how you behave in public, even about what you eat and when. Well Christianity was every bit as controlling right up until long after the English Civil War, and that's many centuries in the future from these people. And a man like de Arce would know all the right things to say to prey on them to greatest effect."

"Hmmm... So between them feeling the pressure regarding the raiders, and de Arce putting the frighteners on them about the afterlife, that would account for why they've continued to go along with his demands?"

"Yes, I think that's a good summation. And maybe that's why this has turned out to be more lucrative, who knows? De Arce may have tried elsewhere, connected to a different time, and found the people less amenable to his threats. On the other hand he might just have got exceedingly lucky here first time round, and stumbled upon on a time that he can access when the people he's able to reach are both pious and frightened already."

Bill's grunt of disgust was more of a growl. "Bloody vampires, that's what this lot are! Feeding like vultures on people's fears – and I'm talking about both the folk in the past and the poor sods lined up at Calais thinking that once they get to this side of the Channel that they're coming to the land of milk and honey. Because my gut instinct is still telling me that the Polish gang have simply diversified from stealing from modern day refugees, to stealing from displaced people in the past. Bastards!"

Looking at Nick's huge collection of books, Bill suddenly thought of something he'd said earlier.

"Why did you say Bristol was the place where Vikings picked up slaves? I'd heard that much of its wealth came from the West Indies slave trade. Did it go back further than that?" He was remembering Danny's message about the house in Clifton and it having history, because even though Clifton would have been a village on its own back in the time they were talking about, it was still close enough to Bristol to be less than a mile from the city centre these days. So he was amazed when Nick immediately answered,

"Oh yes," and went and pulled a book off a shelf, and began flipping through it. "Remember when I was talking about those small tribal kingdoms that made up England in the early Anglo-Saxon era? Well in those days it wasn't unusual for prisoners of war to become enslaved by their captors, especially the ones who weren't worth ransoming. You could maybe see it as a hangover from Roman times, although it was pretty prevalent all over the place back then. You know about Roman slaves?"

"I knew they had them."

"Well sometimes it was no bad thing to be a Roman slave. It was pretty much part of the bargain that you had to be fed and kept well; and say for instance you were the slave of a craftsman who ended up going broke, well you would be sold on to someone else. That would guarantee that once again you would have a roof over your head and food in your belly. Whereas the craftsman's family would be turned out of their home and could well starve to death."

Bill sniffed. "Hmmm, I see what you mean. And I guess that there was no come back on you for whatever your master did, because you were considered to have been below being able to have influenced him?"

"Pretty much. Of course the slaves who had personal contact with the emperor were a different case altogether. Some of them had great influence and power, but I'm talking about the ones who were the equivalent to the Anglo-Saxon ones. Well here they weren't in quite such a fortunate position, but equally slavery wasn't quite the institution here as it was on the continent even after Rome fell, and within the shores of England internal trading in slaves was something that gradually faded away, especially once England was getting closer to becoming one united country.

"With regard to the Vikings, however, we come to something very different. Would you believe that it was the rampant progression of Islam across North Africa and parts of mainland Europe, like Spain, that created the market for slaves that the Vikings fulfilled?"

"Good grief!"

"Yes, an aggressive Islam created a market for

Christian slaves, and with the Vikings being initially pagan, they didn't give a shit who they traded to whom. And the one thing nobody disputes is that they were incredible seamen. Whether it was sailing the rivers of central Europe to found Kiev; or to go as far eastwards by sea and overland as the great court of the Byzantine emperors in what is now Istanbul; or down the western seaboard of the British Isles – what they did wherever they went was trade. And to be fair to them, all they did was fill the demand others created, although they weren't averse to using slaves themselves.

"Now here in England there were certain places we know had slave markets. London was one, as you might expect, and York, as the Viking HQ in England was another. Although York isn't coastal but on a major river, it was still the place where slaves were brought to who were going to be traded onwards to Scandinavia. But the one place which was downright notorious even by those standards was Bristol. One of the greatest opponents of slavery of the time was Bishop Wulfstan of Worcester, the only Anglo-Saxon bishop to retain his position after the Conquest, and that's key to this story. You see, he persuaded the man the Conqueror brought to England to be the archbishop of his new kingdom – a man called Lanfranc – to join him in pressing the new king to outlaw slavery. Even then, though, and with two such incredibly powerful advocates, it still took some doing because of the lucrative toll money the slave trade brought to the royal coffers.

"Now Wulfstan was so influential that he had his life written about by a monk who was a near contemporary, and that biography gives us some interesting insights into those times. The writer describes how the slave trade in Bristol was an 'ancient custom', which tells us that it had been going on for a very long time, and I would say it predated the Viking involvement, because the Vikings were a factor only from about 900AD onwards, and that would hardly qualify as an *ancient* custom in the mid-eleventh century."

Nick tapped the book in his hand. "And I've found the bit I was thinking of in here. Finally in 1102 the Council of Westminster completely outlawed slave trading in Britain, but Bristol remained a dangerous place to visit for at least half a century after that date because of Irish traders, who would seize the unwary and sail off with them!"

Bill blinked. "Good grief, so are we talking about something like happens off the African coast these days, where people are randomly seized?"

Nick gave a weary glance Bill's way. "Afraid so. Some things don't change, do they? By the way, for Irish read Vikings who had settled there – not the indigenous Celts – and were possibly second or third generation inhabitants, and who would take whoever they could if they couldn't buy slaves." He laughed wryly. "Orders had to be fulfilled by one means or another – they could give some of our dodgy traders a run for their money, I reckon."

"What about Clifton, then?" Bill asked, his curiosity building. "Was Clifton around in those days? Because Danny mentioned a house in Clifton in a couple of his reports and that a house there had 'history'. I only thought of it in the context of Georgian and Victorian slave traders, which didn't make much sense in the context, but this sounds like it could mean something a lot older."

Nick returned to his copy of Domesday Book and flicked through it again. "Well Clifton was certainly around then, and it's another of those places which was held directly by the king, although it says the man on the ground was the reeve who held Bristol, rather than someone like the sheriff of Somerset. It's quite a rich manor. Mind you," he turned to another page he'd been keeping marked with a finger, "Bristol itself paid a hundred and ten marks of silver directly to the king, which was a vast sum of money in those days, and also money to Bishop Geoffrey – not sure who he is without checking further because Geoffrey was an incredibly popular name at the time, but a good bet would be the bishop of Wells. That says that even though it hardly counted as a major city, Bristol wasn't some murky backwater, but a place of some consequence if it had to pay a tax like that. I couldn't say for certain, but some of that might have been assessed as what was due from those tolls from slavery I was talking about, because it's a *very* big sum to ask from just an agricultural manor. Domesday is, after all, a giant medieval tax assessment.

"But in answer to your question, yes, Clifton certainly goes back far enough. What I can say is that Clifton isn't mentioned as having a church, and that would be the one and only building in a small community which would be made of stone, and therefore likely to have lasted into the modern era. Anglo-Saxon houses just don't survive these days, that's something you can take as definite. One of the oldest houses in all of England is in Lincoln and that's late Norman and unique in its age. So I doubt we're talking about any standing structure in Clifton. Any connection is through the land the houses stand on. ...Want another coffee?"

Hobbling through to the kitchen behind Nick to get a refill, Bill was thinking furiously.

"I tell you what, Nick," he said, as they returned to the lounge with full mugs and a packet of digestive biscuits to dunk, "I don't like the coincidence of Bristol coming up in Danny's report. In fact, I don't think it's a coincidence at all. If you take it chronologically, you have the fact that

Time's Bloodied Gold

Bristol was a notorious slaving port even in Anglo-Saxon times, then by the time de Arce was living it would have been notorious as a focus for the West Indies trade – and with him having that link to the Indies it would be stretching credibility to think he didn't know of it. And then we have Danny telling us that something is being traded out of the Clifton area of Bristol."

He dunked his biscuit and munched thoughtfully for a moment.

"Would our Anglo-Saxons recognise the name of Bristol if they heard our gang mentioning it?"

Nick put down his coffee and looked at the Domesday index. "Says here it was known as *Bristou*. That's very little change at all. Some places' names have changed beyond recognition, and some names in Domesday we just can't place at all, but Bristol certainly isn't one of them."

"*Hmph*. So if it was that well known as a place you might go to and never come back, if de Arce said that someone had gone to Bristol, the people on the other side of the portal might think it no wonder that they never came back?"

"I see what you mean. Yes, it could be another contributory factor as to why they never questioned harder what had happened to their friends."

Bill nodded but added. "I was also thinking that if they've heard the word 'Bristol', recognised it, and believe that de Arce is hand in glove with those who are what you might call collaborators with the Vikings – in much the way that collaborators in France in World War Two were sometimes more dangerous than the Nazis themselves, because you didn't know who they were – they might be even more frightened of de Arce? Could they be thinking that he could get his 'friends' in Bristol to strike at them even if the Vikings weren't actually there at the time? Are you with me? They might be frightened that if they didn't do what he said, that this mystical priest with such magical powers – because that's what it must seem like to them – might come through this strange doorway and bring his Viking pals with him just when they weren't expecting it. Because I think in their place that portal would be frightening the crap out of me!"

Nick was nodding vigorously even before Bill had finished. "Oh I don't think there's much doubt about that. One of the hardest things to get across to students when I do some teaching is that there was no such thing as a non-believer in those times. You might find the occasional perverse thinker who batted for the opposition in the form of the Devil, but it was an age where everyone believed in things which these days most people would just laugh at. Nowadays the Church is at great pains to separate things like miracles from any hint of the magical, but in the medieval era the Church positively played on such things. The mystical pervaded the everyday to an extent that we in our science-filled era struggle to imagine, but it's there in the contemporary texts over and over again. And what else could they believe in? Even the simplest soul craves an explanation when something terrible happens, and if reality can't provide it then it looks like magic. So yes, in one way they would accept the appearance of the portal far more readily than someone like your colleagues can, but because of that belief, the potential of what harm it could do them would also be heightened.

"They might even think it was a way to Hell itself. I tell you, some of the medieval wall paintings showing the opening of Hell on Judgement Day are the stuff of nightmares! And these folk might not have been literate, but they would have been into church where such images would have been all over the walls. Forget the way old

Time's Bloodied Gold

churches and cathedrals these days are covered in whitewash. When they were built and in the centuries immediately afterwards they would have been filled with a riot of colour, and not just blocks of paint as we paint a blank wall. The walls would have been covered with biblical scenes, but also they could serve to pass on news if it was important enough.

"One of these days I'll take you to a lovely little church not far away where you can see the faded remains of what can only be an illustration of the murder of Thomas Becket. That was a momentous event, and of course he became a saint very quickly after his murder, so it's not surprising to find what became seen as his martyrdom on a church wall, but it was also very much a current event too. So the people looked to the painted walls of the church for illustrations of the Bible and current news. Beckett's murder was something which happened only a couple of centuries after the time we think we're connecting to, by the way, which is nothing compared to the millennium between then and now, so the comparison is valid and I think we can assume they would know what a Hell-mouth was."

Bill devoured another couple of biscuits, waving the last piece for emphasis as he said, "And I bet de Arce would know all of that!"

"Oh, no doubt about it at all! As an Inquisitor he would know about the Church's history, not least because there were some Christian sects that the Inquisition dealt with in a very bloody manner, because they were thought to be putting the wrong interpretation on Christian texts and leading their followers into paganism. The most famous of those were the Cathars, who most people know of through Dan Brown's books if nothing else."

"Thank you, Nick. You've joined up several of the dots I knew had to be important, but not how. I may never convince Charlie and Morag about the portal, but in my own mind I'm getting a much clearer picture of what Danny was trying to tell me."

"Do you think de Arce is the one who made the connection to Bristol?" Nick asked as Bill heaved himself to his feet and retrieved his coat. "I mean now, not with the Anglo-Saxons."

"I can't think the Polish traffickers would have," Bill replied. "They'd know about east coast places to land people, but not round in the west. And I have this gut feeling that the connection to the West Indies is important to de Arce, and he's found something which makes him think it's useful to him in the here and now. I just have to figure out what it is. Despite the history, they can't be sending slaves out of Bristol anymore, but there's some bloody connection going on there, because otherwise why has Danny made so many journeys to and from there?"

Chapter 13

January

The one thing Danny did better than any of the others in the gang was to drive with all the assurance of one who had done the police advanced driving course (although the gang knew nothing of the specific reason why Danny handled a car so well, of course), and because of the way he behaved on the Birmingham trip, Jerzy had subsequently made him the one to act as his driver when he went to Bristol. Nobody wanted de Arce to drive, that was certain – he was a danger to everyone! How the priest had managed to get the Land Rover from Spain to England without killing himself and countless others was a miracle which could have convinced the deepest sceptic of the existence of a God who looked after his own, because de Arce had a tendency to point the big beast in the right direction and expect everyone else to get out of his way. Granted, he'd had the vehicle acquired for him by the Church over there, who seemed also to have managed to get him his passport, but most of the gang thought those were acts of desperation to get rid of this extremist who constantly wittered on about resurrecting the Inquisition to combat the Muslim threat, and nobody believed he'd ever actually passed a driving test. Jerzy was amazed that he had never been stopped by the police as yet, for which reason none of the others were ever allowed to travel with de Arce, although only Mikhail was daft enough to want to.

So since he'd become the appointed driver, Danny had weaved his way around the city streets into Clifton twice a month, and then had been left kicking his heels in the parked car while the others had disappeared into a house. Not all of the gang to be sure. It was always Jerzy and de Arce, and the first time he'd driven to Bristol back in late November, Mikhail had come with them. However, when they had come back to the car that time, for once Mikhail was looking almost cowed, while Jerzy and de Arce were clearly furious. The fact that Mikhail was banished to the front passenger seat to continue wiping the blood off his knuckles while the other two conversed in the back of Danny's car, despite there being three seats back there, spoke of him losing it when he shouldn't have. Not that Danny was going to ask about it while driving. Mikhail going nuts at him and taking them off the road was not what he wanted.

Thereafter, for the following trips he had driven just the two of them, although for the first couple he'd been pretty sure that Jerzy had had a gun not far from his back the whole way there and back. The head of the gang was taking no chances of Danny betraying them while he was without the support of the rest. Not that Danny was going to do that. He wanted to know what the hell went on in that house in Clifton.

It was a tall, thin terraced house down by the suspension bridge, but it was Georgian and probably dated from the time when there was an attempt to revive the Hotwells area as a spa to rival Bath. There was no parking outside it, and at first Danny had wondered why anyone running a dodgy outfit would want the elegant five-storey building when it was nigh on impossible to get a vehicle close to the house. But then he realised that in a way that was an attraction. No rival was going to come hurtling up the drive and smash the door down – the van would end up on its nose, stuck in the three foot drop from the road

Time's Bloodied Gold

down to the strip of pavement in front of the house. And if you wanted pretensions of grandeur without forking out for one of the Grade II listed mansions up the hill, then this was as good as it got.

Something about the house gave him the shivers, though, and when he had commented to Jerzy that it looked a strange old house, the gang leader had simply laughed and said,

"It was built for a captain who made his money in the slave trade. It was built with blood money."

Danny had looked at the house and his imagination had inserted some poor slave girl looking out at the rain-soaked streets of Clifton and wondering whether she would ever see her home in Africa again. Yet he came to realise how wrong he'd been with that. Yes, the house and the rest of the terrace it was in had undoubtedly been built on the profits of the slave trade, but few slaves would ever have seen it. Listening in on a conversation between de Arce and Jerzy as he drove them back in early January, he was amazed to hear de Arce explain,

"No, my friend you have it all wrong. I know, because I invested some of my money into it. I knew of this place Clifton in my own time and long before I ever saw it, because they made gunpowder here. I paid for a ship to take guns made in Birmingham, and the powder from Bristol, to Africa. That's how we bought slaves from their own people. They wanted the means to silence their rivals permanently! Ha! Savages! Always it was kill or be killed. Trading their own people for profit, or to settle old vendettas. No finesse. Ha-ha! Then the ship went from Africa to my plantation in the Indies with slaves, and made its return journey to Bristol docks loaded with tobacco, sugar, rum and cotton."

His slimy laugh had sent a shudder down Danny's

spine as he added, "Ha-ha! A man could not fail to make money! So when it came to the time to promote a man of the Church in the Indies, the planters and merchants were only too glad to back the application of a bishop like myself who was also one of them. And of course, I had the right ...talents ...to ensure that the savages converted to the True Faith with suitable fervour, and knew the penalty for attacking good Catholics. ...A shame that those who bring us our goods to us now are useless to be traded as slaves."

"I told you that," Jerzy replied with some exasperation. "Girls who can be trained, yes, but there's no money in it otherwise. Kazimierz did his best to sell the farmer down the road a couple of workers, but these days it's all done by machines in this country. They only want fruit pickers for a few weeks a year. Don't you think I'd have found a market for them if there was? Before we met you, and we were running refugees in by boat, I'd already looked into it to see if we were missing a trick. I saw a news report about some farmer who'd kept a slave for years. Turned out, though, that it was only the one, and it was a really small farm, so they still did stuff by hand. The big farms who could afford to pay a good price just don't need labourers, though. They want men who can operate all the fancy equipment, not some idiot who only knows how to drive an ox-pulled plough in Somalia. There's no money in that.

"Now some tasty bit of Latvian pussy – *that* I can find you a market for! My cousin Tomek, ah, he has a girl who could make you weep with pleasure. For the right price I could arrange that for you, if you wanted? She's not too well-used as yet, and Tomek makes sure they stay clean when they're at the top end of his earners. The street-walkers are raddled, of course. You have to keep them at it all night to make anything, because who's going to pay top dollar for someone with more needle marks than my

Time's Bloodied Gold

mamma's lace tablecloth, eh?" and he dug de Arce with an elbow and winked at him.

Danny was glad he was on a straight stretch of motorway and it was quiet, because he had his eyes on the rear-view mirror more often than was truly safe just now, desperately wanting to read the men's reactions to one another by the motorway's lighting. But because of that he saw the look of absolute disgust on de Arce's face when Jerzy made him the offer. *You got that one all wrong*, Danny thought with grim satisfaction. *Whatever de Arce's fancies are, poking a prostitute isn't one of them*. Maybe the man was gay? It didn't seem likely, though. He'd shown no sign of interest in Kazimierz, and he was a good-looking chap he might have taken a second look at even if Kazimierz was never likely to respond to any advances. Nor had de Arce shown any of the signs of predatory interest Danny was tuned in to spot when it came to the young lad who'd been in the farm when Danny had first arrived. And grim thought though it was, if de Arce was a paedophile, why wouldn't he have taken advantage of the boy when everyone around him danced to his tune? Of course, the lad could have simply been too old for his tastes, but Danny thought it was more likely that sex just wasn't his thing.

"Suit yourself," Jerzy replied, shaking his head in mystification. Clearly one of the perks of working with his cousin was sampling the goods – something he wasn't getting here. And that made Danny think that he was earning serious money with de Arce. Certainly enough to keep him here, and away from the pleasures of working with the Walsall crew and the working girls, where it seemed he'd been close to the top and answerable only to Tomek, and virtually his own boss anyway.

Come on, Danny prayed, *give me some more, you bastards*.

He put the car radio on low and said casually to the

two in the back, "Just got this on for traffic reports, if that's okay? Coming down it looked like there was some hold up coming back this way."

The radio was on low enough for him to be able to hear them unless they whispered, but to his secret delight it must have convinced his passengers that he couldn't, because de Arce gave him a brief glance and then said,

"When I was with Mikhail at that other place, he contacted someone in the Indies for me – someone who can help me achieve my goal. Aaah, I feel such a connection with the Indies and with that river in Bristol. It calls to me! It makes my blood sing in my veins again and I know I am being called to do my work once again! You are a godless man, Jerzy, so you do not appreciate the ways you can control people by instilling a proper fear into them. I went there long ago, you know – the Indies. It was fascinating!" and Danny saw the tremor of pleasure that ran through de Arce now. "They have a more primal faith there. If only I'd had more time, oh the ecstasy to be had there!"

"You want drugs?" Jerzy sounded puzzled, and Danny knew he'd confused what de Arce had said with a request for the drug Ecstasy.

"No, fool!" de Arce snapped. "I am talking about the unrefined joy that comes of turning someone back to the path after extracting their demons. The *auto de fé* is a wondrous thing to behold."

Danny damned near took the car off the road at that. De Arce had just admitted to torture! Christ, when had that happened? Was that in the here and now, or back in whichever Godforsaken slot in time he had come from? If it was now, then where had he hidden the bodies? Because the one thing Danny knew about the *auto de fé* was that it was often lethal. It must even have rattled Jerzy a bit,

Time's Bloodied Gold

because Danny could have hugged him for asking the next question in appalled tones.

"Was *that* what you were doing in that last workshop with Mikhail while we were getting the extra goods, then? Saving that poor bastard's soul? Christ, surely he'd suffered enough already coming through the time gateway?"

De Arce gave a sniff of complete disdain. "He cursed me. No good Christian would curse a man of my station like that."

"Curse you? How did you know? You can't speak their language any more than we can! He could have been complaining about that fucking Thai fish curry Piotr keeps buying for all we know!"

"I knew," de Arce said in a voice dripping contempt, which dared Jerzy to argue with him. "I know the sound of a man who is cursing me, whatever his tongue."

Bloody hell, Danny thought, *that sounds like he's had enough practice!*

A similar thought must have crossed Jerzy's mind, because as Danny glanced into the mirror again, he saw Jerzy puff his cheeks out, exhaling heavily, and giving de Arce a wary look. His expression said that he thought de Arce was nuts, and on that Danny wouldn't have argued with him.

The drive continued in silence until they got back to the farm, but when de Arce had gone into the abandoned farmhouse up the track, and up to the first floor rooms that he had taken over for himself, Jerzy pulled Danny to one side. For a second Danny wondered what he'd done wrong and if he'd blown his cover. However that wasn't the problem.

"You're a smart guy," Jerzy said softly, "and I saw your face when that madman was talking about the *auto de fé*, and you knew what it was, just like me. So I'm asking you to not say anything about that to the others, okay?"

"Okay," Danny agreed, but his puzzlement must have sounded in his voice, because Jerzy sighed and explained,

"Mikhail is ...devout in strange ways. The other guys think he's odd as it is. If they find out that he helped de Arce torture someone because he didn't say his mass the right way, or whatever perverted reasons de Arce had for acting that way, there'll be bloodshed." He grunted and shook his head. "Mikhail I wouldn't weep over, even though getting rid of his body would be a pain in the arse – because he has a police record at home, and he *would* be identified. No, it's that he's a stone killer, and he'd be likely to take three or four of the others out with him, and I can't afford that. They're good lads. Piotr's as thick as the barn door, but he's a useful foot-soldier, and Ulryk's Tomek's as you know, so I'd have some explaining to do there if he ended up filleted by Mikhail – although I don't think he'd be one of the ones to go under. But Dymek and Stefan, they're good men and I know you like them, but they'd end up as dog meat in a fight with Mikhail. They're important to me because they're the calm heads. They're the ones I can send into town, like Kazimierz and you. You go, you get what we need, and you come back without causing any fuss. I have to have men like that on my team."

Danny could see what he meant. Even Stefan and Dymek had their limits to what they would put up with, and something they saw as dragging their faith through the mud might just be it.

"Fair enough, I see your point. I won't say anything," Danny agreed.

"Good! And for that reason I'm keeping you as the driver to go down to Bristol. You handle the traffic much better than the others anyway, but after tonight I don't want any of the others driving and de Arce coming out

Time's Bloodied Gold

with more of his weird comments!" It was a measure of Jerzy's relief that he continued without thinking about what he was revealing to Danny. "I wish we could keep him just for that bloody freaky stuff in the church. Unfortunately he's the one with the specialist contacts in the Dominican Republic – although he will insist on calling it Spanish Haiti for some bloody reason – confuses the fuck out of Tomek's contacts in Bristol and out there. But we need de Arce to arrange the sales of our 'goods' from there to the American antiques black market." He shook his head again. "Who knew the Catholic Church over there was so weird, eh? You'd have thought that they'd have some scruples about taking the money and laundering it into the drugs trade, but if the profit's right they're no better than the drug lords."

"Just a tick," Danny said, tapping furiously on his i-phone. "Here you go, what's now the Dominican Republic was known as Spanish Haiti from 1821 to 1865, and before that as Hispaniola – that was the whole island, because Haiti and the Dominican Republic are the two halves of one island, not two separate ones. God knows what it means, though, that de Arce calls it by its old name."

"Really? Oh well," and Jerzy shrugged, as bewildered as Danny as to de Arce's mental state.

However Danny had had another nasty thought. "You don't think he's got mixed up with the voodoo cults in Haiti, do you? I've got a funny feeling I read somewhere that voodoo arose out of African slaves being forcibly converted to Christianity – its origins are as a bastard mix of African tribal religions and the Catholic rites – and that in some places over there the Catholic churches have something of a relaxed attitude towards it. That's why I remembered the Spanish Haiti thing. If de Arce got exposed to that, that might have been what set him on the track of ferreting around in the past. You know, zombies, the living dead and all that crap."

Jerzy looked at Danny, appalled. "Mother of God! It would explain his contacts there. For the love of God, Danny, say nothing of this to the others! Let me deal with this ...but thank you for tonight! We're going back down on the fifteenth, because what we took down tonight should have reached the buyers by then, so be prepared for that." He sighed again. "I still wish I could leave him behind, but the computer with the bank codes and the Skype link to the West Indies are all in Clifton with bloody Reznik and his gang. Anyway, Reznik – who lives in that house, so we can't sneak in when he's not there – can only receive the bank transfer when de Arce speaks to some other fucking priest out there who has his hands on the cash. And that's another crazy man I'm not crossing!"

"The priest?"

"No! Reznik! ...What a fucking mess!"

As a result of that exchange, though, Danny was allowed some small measure of privacy for part of the next couple of weeks, and so he decided he'd go and scout around in Bristol. There was still more than a week to go to when he'd be needed to drive Jerzy back down there, and he thought he'd left it long enough that nobody would remember his car. It was a suitably anonymous big grey VW anyway, a typical rep's car and one of thousands of similar such cars on the road, and this time he intended to park it well away from the house.

Dressed very differently in trendy jeans and a brand-named fleece with a baseball cap to match, Danny looked more the tourist, and the compact camera swinging from a strap on his hand didn't look out of place. He wandered down the road past the house for the first time, and then paused to take photos of the suspension bridge. It all looked very innocent, and he made sure he walked on a way before turning and coming back. Now he started snapping away at the river and pretty much everything else, but getting several good shots of the house in the process. He'd spotted a generic mobile food cabin not far away, which was selling jacket potatoes with fillings, and had a small seating area of plastic chairs for those customers who weren't going back to work with their food. So he claimed a chair, ordered a jacket with grated cheese and a coffee, and sat back to watch the house.

With it being late lunchtime, the first batch of hot potatoes had gone and his meal took its time coming, which was just what Danny wanted. The house was certainly elegant, and somebody was keeping it in good order so that it didn't stand out amongst its neighbours. What was different, though, was that while the other houses looked quiet, except for a young woman coming back to one with a couple of very small children, the target house had men coming and going. Not all the time to be sure, but to Danny's experienced eye it looked very like the men who went out from there were probably dropping supplies of drugs off to the lowlifes who would be doing the actual pushing on the street. These men in the house wouldn't be getting their hands dirty in that sense, they were the ones doing the running for the boss man who undoubtedly lived in and owned the big house – i.e. Reznik.

However, the question Danny wanted answered most was, what was the drugs connection to Jerzy's gang? Because he'd have bet his next month's pay that it was drug dealing going on at that house. Jerzy himself seemed to take a dim view of drugs and pushers, so it was unlikely that they were trying to work their way into getting a slice of the business here. And it seemed even more unlikely that he would want to invest all of the money brought in by the antiquities' sales into drugs, even though he could no doubt turn a handsome profit. Jerzy seemed a touch too canny to be getting involved in something as precarious as drugs running. So what was the connection?

Looking around, Danny found a couple of places where he would be able to sneak round to get closer to the house, because if he didn't get invited in this time, then he was going to have to try and get in by himself. Presumably while the neighbours were coming and going the drug-runners went away to avoid awkward questions, so in the evening when Jerzy visited there shouldn't be too many men in the house, although no doubt they'd be back in the early hours to satiate the late-night revellers' needs for stimulation. All Danny could hope was that there'd be a way to get in through the kitchen or somewhere else at the back, because his foray only raised more questions than answers and he drove back to the farm, not needing to fake frustration when he arrived this time, even if his claims of a competitor stealing his client from under his nose wasn't quite the real reason for him wanting to grind his teeth.

15th January

On the Friday, Danny duly took the VW to the farm and picked up Jerzy and de Arce. Mikhail was giving him daggers glares again, but what that was all about Danny couldn't guess, not even when the big man said,

"One day Jerzy will find out your shit doesn't shine so bright. Then he'll know he should have trusted me all along."

Dymek and Stefan heard him and both shrugged when Danny caught their eyes, every bit as mystified as him as to what that meant, but then with Mikhail it could be almost anything. Mikhail hadn't been allowed back into Leominster again, so at least Danny was safe from him there, although Ulryk was still giving Danny filthy looks despite all his attempts to patch him up after Tomek's beating. There really was no winning with some people. And of course Piotr had gone into Leominster too, albeit with Stefan not Ulryk, but Danny also knew that on the last visit Piotr had gone off on his own for a hour or so – something Stefan was too shit scared to admit to Jerzy after what had happened with Ulryk, but he'd told Danny just in case Piotr had been causing mischief. Clearly Mikhail thought he'd got the drop on Danny somehow, though, and Danny knew he'd have to be extra observant for the next few weeks.

For now, however, Danny had to concentrate on getting down to Bristol and seeing if he could find anything more out about the house. So he couldn't believe his luck when he parked up and Jerzy said,

"This time you come in with me."

"I don't want him involved," de Arce complained, but for once Jerzy was having none of it.

"I don't bloody care. I want someone with some brains in there with me. You were fast to distract me the last time we came down to get paid, and I thought we got less than expected for that shipment, so I want someone to keep their eye on that computer who knows what it's doing." De Arce's blank expression said that he hadn't understood what Jerzy was talking about with regard to computers, but Danny did. "We're both in this for the money, priest, and that doesn't mean a chunk of my share going into your account instead, either."

"I am no priest," de Arce snapped, "I'm a bishop!"

"Good for you," Jerzy riposted. "Still doesn't mean you won't rob me, though."

Then as they were let into the house and all of them were patted down for weapons by a squint-eyed gorilla of a man, Jerzy said softly to Danny,

"I meant that. You get beside that desk and watch what happens when the transfer goes through. Something's going on and I don't know what it is yet. You and Kazimierz are the only ones with the brains to be able to help me figure it out, and you know why you're with me today," and his eyes flicked to de Arce.

They passed a door into the downstairs front room and then one to a kitchen at the back, although the kitchen alone was nearly as big as Danny's whole flat, and then were led upstairs. The living room of the house was on the first floor at the front and had three large windows which looked out to the river. The original decorative plasterwork was still in place, and Danny thought it was likely that this had always been the main reception room going by that and the elegant original fireplace which had a cheering coal fire burning away in it. It was also an excuse for Danny to go over to it and make like he was warming his hands after coming in from the freezing February evening, and under cover of that to observe when Jerzy went and greeted a portly older man.

So this was Reznik? Jerzy was definitely going through the motions of being deferential, even if Danny thought his body language said that he was only doing it because it was necessary to placate the other man's ego. And no doubt the vacuous but stunning peroxide blonde was Reznik's trophy wife. That was swiftly confirmed when she was sent to make coffee for them all and then told to leave them alone. Moments later they heard the sound of running water from upstairs and Reznik joked,

"Another bath! No wonder she never puts on any weight, she washes it all off every day, ha-ha!"

Time's Bloodied Gold

Personally, Danny would have put her rake-like skinniness down to whatever she was stuffing up her nose, but then no doubt Reznik thought it a good way to keep her quiet, and there would always be a replacement where she came from. Maybe she was even one of Tomek's girls originally?

Reznik waved them over to where an enormous desk sat close to one of the windows. It had more than one computer on it, and a bespectacled young man was sitting at a chair on the side open to the room, while Reznik himself went and lowered his considerable weight into a plush leather captain's chair on the other side.

"Are they ready?" he asked the youth and got a nod. "Very well. Would you like to speak to your man Mr de Arce?"

De Arce walked to where he could see a screen which suddenly flickered into life at the click of the assistant's mouse to show a man in clerical garb looking into it. As de Arce came into view Danny, who was looking around his shoulder, would have sworn he saw the other man flinch.

"Obispo de Arce," he said with some obsequiousness.

"Monsignor Montefiori," de Arce greeted him back, then launched into a string of fast Spanish.

However, although Danny's Spanish was next to nonexistent, even he could guess what 'Inquisición' meant.

What the implications were he couldn't figure out, though, except that de Arce was definitely giving the orders. Whoever Monsignor Montefiori was, and however senior he was in the Church over in the Dominican Republic, he was frightened enough by de Arce to be sweating profusely, and Danny knew damned well that it was winter over there as well as here, so it surely wasn't the heat of summer making his brow beaded like that. Was there some archaic branch of the Church out there that still wanted the Inquisition back? Or was it that they saw it as the only way to fight the rising tide of the curious and morbid who flocked to Haiti and its island neighbour in the wake of the current fad for zombie movies and TV series? Were the houngans and mambos, who acted as the voodoo priests, getting more than just the faithful of their own island under their charms? Danny could imagine the Vatican not being happy about that, and being willing to listen to even such a nutter as de Arce if they thought he could reverse the tide of good Catholics coming on holiday and going away less tied to Rome than they had been when they came.

He saw Jerzy watching him and nodded, moving himself into a position by the window. From here he could move one way and see the Skype link on one of the pair of laptops the geek was running, and the other and see the one Reznik was at.

"Are you ready to transfer the money, Monsignor?" Reznik cut across their conversation.

"Yes, I am," Montefiori answered in heavily accented English.

Reznik gestured for de Arce to come round to his side of the desk, which he did, but in the process blocked Jerzy's view of the screen. It was quite deliberately done, Danny could tell, because the obvious way for de Arce to have gone was past Danny and stay on the window side of the desk and Reznik, instead of which he'd gone the other way. However, because their focus was on Jerzy, whom they were now watching slyly, and the computer geek was oblivious to all except his screens, Danny was able to ease himself further into the corner of the room and get a good view of the screen. Bringing his phone out of his pocket he activated the camera, then held it cupped in his hand casually as if bored and playing a game on it. A couple of snatched glances down allowed him to angle it and focus it on the screen, and then it all started to happen.

A sum of money which almost made Danny gasp out loud came up on the screen, and then de Arce was leaning in and carefully putting in a password, when the assistant had put the cursor on the right spot, with the air of one who half expected the computer to spontaneously combust at any moment. It made Danny realise that whoever had set this up, it couldn't have been him. De Arce had no notion of how the computer worked, and his trust of it only extended to his acceptance that this was working to his advantage. Indeed he looked for all the world as if his greatest desire was to conduct an exorcism over its strange magic. Maybe Montefiori had done the set-up for him over there? Or even more likely he'd had some smart young kid who had fallen into the Church's hands do it for him. Danny did manage to get a shot of the screen, though, before it vanished with a click of the mouse in Reznik's podgy fingers to be replaced by another. The fat bastard had been logged in to these accounts already, Danny could see. There was no hanging about waiting for something to load or for him to log in. It was just click on another tabbed screen and go.

Together Reznik and de Arce watched the screen avidly and then as it flickered and refreshed to show a new balance, Reznik called out across the desk to the monitor with the Skype link, "Thank you, Monsignor!" then looked up at de Arce. "My payment for facilitating this if you please," he said with the look of a smug python contemplating an extra portion of tethered goat for lunch.

"Of course," de Arce said with condescension, and tapped in numbers to the highlighted box on the screen.

"Oh come now," Reznik purred, "I think this time we have something worth more like this?" and highlighted the sum and keyed in a new amount.

Jerzy's face was getting angrier and angrier, but Danny caught his eye and mouthed "ten percent," at which point Jerzy rolled his eyes but accepted it. Presumably this was the expected price of Reznik's help.

What Danny only just managed to capture on his phone was the way that Reznik brought up another screen and tapped in another amount, and at the most minute of nods from de Arce, another amount was transferred out to a wholly different account.

Danny's eyes flew open at that and Jerzy's signalled his question as to what it was. However, Danny frantically signalled to him not to ask now even as Reznik now looked up at Jerzy with a beaming smile, pointed to the substantially reduced amount he could now see on the geek's second laptop as de Arce moved out of the way, and said,

"There's your balance. Do we split it two ways between you like before?"

It was enough to have bought Danny everything he had ever wanted in life and more, and if Jerzy had been getting anything like this from each of the other transactions then he had to be a millionaire by now. De Arce wasn't a poor man even by modern standards, either, but then he was keeping all of his to himself, whereas Jerzy had the gang to give a share to. But what had robbed Danny of his breath had been where that other portion had gone to.

"Where? Who?" Jerzy hissed to him as they were shown out again, but even he stopped dead in his tracks when Danny whispered behind de Arce's back,

"Twenty percent straight into the Vatican!"

Chapter 14

full moon, Sunday 27th January

By the time the January full moon came around, Danny was a nervous wreck. The tension within the gang had reached snapping point, and some of it had come his way. For a start off, when he'd got back from Bristol with Jerzy, Kazimierz had pulled him to one side and said,

"Watch your back. I don't know what's gone on, but Ulryk went for the food this time and he was gone for far too long. But it was only later that it occurred to me that we didn't see Mikhail for that time too. I think he might have snuck out and gone wherever it was with Ulryk, and I think it concerns you. They came back very smug, and although Mikhail's not said anything, Ulryk couldn't resist gloating and saying that you'd come down a peg or two soon. When you get back to your flat, check around, because I think those two bastards have planted something there as a gift for what happened at the *Eagle*. I don't know if it's something that will get you in trouble with Jerzy, or with the police here – it could be either."

"Bloody hell," Danny groaned. "I didn't do anything! I just got them out of there before the police turned up. Would they have rather rotted in jail?"

Kazimierz shrugged. "You know that and we know that, but those two? Who knows? The way it looks to me, Mikhail is spitting blood because he thinks you made a fool of him in front of Jerzy. The fact that he didn't go tonight to him is proof of that, because he thought he was Jerzy's right-hand man. Not that he ever was, not even from long before you came. And if he's fallen from grace it's because of his own doing, no-one else's. Jerzy would have to be a fool not to see that Mikhail's becoming ever more unstable, and bloody de Arce is largely to blame for that. He draws Mikahil up to those rooms he's got in the old place and talks all sorts of crap to him, and Mikhail drinks it in."

Danny sighed. "Oh yes, and because none of the rest of us can stomach de Arce for long, we don't really know what he does say, do we?"

"No."

Then Danny decided to take a chance. "Look, stay clear of both Jerzy and Mikhail for a bit. I daren't say too much, but Jerzy's found out that de Arce has been taking more than his fair share and passing it on to a third party, a religious third party."

"Fucking hell!"

"I know. So there's one hell of a storm brewing and I for one don't want to get caught in the crossfire, but I might do because I witnessed stuff. But what I suspect is that Mikhail will take de Arce's side in this, and because of who it is, I don't know how some of the others will react. If it was just some drug dealer, or whoever, I know most of the others would back Jerzy, but this..."

Kazimierz's brow creased in a frown. "For the love of God, Danny, who is it? Tell me!"

Danny leaned in and whispered softly, "De Arce sent twenty percent of what we earned straight to the Vatican."

"Fuck me!"

"Quite! I don't know whether that's just the way he thinks – you know, some sort of obligatory donation he feels he has to make – or whether he's paying them for their silence or worse, but you should have heard Jerzy when he found out! Especially as it came out of the pot before it was divided up between us and de Arce. So you see, although I would normally say without reservation that someone like Dymek would back Jerzy, in this case I don't know who he'll support, because his faith is very strong."

"Then watch your back," Kazimierz cautioned, "because you'll be the one blamed for this if you're not careful."

Danny had escaped to the sanctuary of his flat as fast as he could after that, but in the morning he began a thorough inspection of it. The lock on the door wouldn't hold a professional like Ulryk back for long, so he accepted that he wouldn't be seeing obvious signs of a break in. However he was relieved to find that his secret stash of memory cards transferred from his phone were still in their place. That was good, because the gang would definitely be wondering why he'd been taking photos of the prisoners. What was far more worrying was the packet of cocaine he found in the toilet cistern. Where the hell had that come from? It was no small amount, and even if it wasn't the kind of amount a city dealer would get his hands one, it was still enough to send him down if he was caught with it.

On the other hand, was this Jerzy testing him again? Surely not after last night, but he couldn't be sure, in which case he'd better leave it where it was for a day or two. And the thought did occur to him that if all else failed then the packet must have Mikhail's fingerprints all over it, because he didn't credit him with the wits to wear gloves. So maybe he might need it to incriminate him if it looked like the gang were going to elude justice after all? After all the times he'd fretted about what would stand up in court when he could hardly talk about the portal, here was something which even the thickest juror would understand. Never in all his career to date had Danny considered planting evidence, but for what had been done to those poor people from the past he was prepared to make an exception, because the gang could never be put on trial for what they had really done.

In fairness he was increasingly of the opinion that Dymek and Stefan didn't deserve to go on trial for anything. Both of them had fallen into this by pure misfortune, and they had family back in Poland who would take the brunt of the gang's displeasure if they pulled out now. And both were decent men who tried to do the right thing, and they always treated the prisoners as kindly as they dared. Thinking back on it, Danny also realised that they were never the ones who handled the guns.

Funnily enough, Kazimierz did, but the way he behaved with a semi-automatic in his hands was more like a soldier. His actions were always calm and controlled, and Danny's gut feeling was that if ever he was to fire one it would be over the heads of people to frighten them, not in anger. Therefore Kazimierz was another one whom Danny had no desire to see locked away. He'd probably got sucked in to this when he came out of the army and couldn't get a job, because he certainly wasn't a mindless thug like Piotr or Ulryk. And his warning to Danny had showed him in a different light too, which had Danny thinking that there was definitely someone decent in there beneath the cold exterior, which was looking more and more like a shell put up to keep the likes of Ulryk at bay.

However, that warning had made Danny extra cautious, and he made sure that he was out of the flat for long periods on the days when he was supposed to be working, just in case Mikhail's gripes got to Jerzy and he came over to prove to Mikhail that Danny was what he said he was. And with that in mind, Danny went down to Cheltenham and Gloucester and bought some computer bits and pieces, which he then left mainly in the boot of his car, but took a few into the flat as well. He also

Time's Bloodied Gold

downloaded the complete catalogue of a real computer parts supplier so that if he needed to he had something on his laptop to show Jerzy. And as a final stop for his cover, he made sure he clocked up some serious mileage on the car. Until now he'd not bothered that much, but now he wanted his cover to be cast iron solid, not least because his gut feeling was that he was in this on his own and had been for some time.

With that in mind he'd taken to going up to Birmingham once a week and driving round the right areas in the hope of seeing someone from the taskforce. He didn't dare go into the station in Harborne that they were operating out of. It would be just his luck that someone from Tomek's lot would be in there being cautioned just at the wrong moment. But he did desperately want to get in touch with his team, and with that in mind he made a copy of the best of the photos and put them on another memory card. He put it in a thick envelope along with one of de Arce's black leather gloves which had been dropped one day in the farm yard, a couple of the spent cartridges from when he had to go out into the wilds with the gang and keep watch while those with the guns did some target practice, plus printouts of the computer screens from Bristol, and the whole lot went under the mat of the driving seat in the VW.

Jerzy had made Danny send those screen shots to him and then delete them, but not before Danny had managed to save them to a hidden file which he was then able to retrieve them from. So now he had plenty of proof, he just needed to give it to someone. With that in mind he had waited one evening to see who came out of the Harborne station, praying like mad that it would be Joe Connolly. Unfortunately the only one he saw whom he recognised from the taskforce was the young blonde DC, Rupert somebody or other. Danny had hardly ever said two words to him, but just at the moment he couldn't afford to be picky, especially as he'd been told that with only a few days to the next portal opening, once he got back he would have to stay at the farm, not at his flat, so this was a last opportunity in maybe weeks to hand something over. So he tailed Rupert from the station to where he saw him park up and head into a takeaway.

Tucking his own car into a dark spot on the next street, Danny hurried back and stood in the shadows on the corner watching the area around Rupert's car like a hawk for anyone who looked like they didn't belong there. Then when Rupert emerged with his takeaway, Danny slipped over to his car and came out of the shadows at him.

"Hey, Rupert!"

The DC jumped like he'd been shot. "Fuck me! Why'd you do that to me? Christ I nearly pissed myself!"

"Lad, you've got to get stronger nerves than that if you want to stay in this job," Danny said dryly. "Now listen, I can't get into the station, so give this to DCI Panesar. It's evidence, okay? There's a money trail to be followed, but I can't do that where I am."

He looked at the DC and thought he looked slightly glassy-eyed. How many hours had he been on the job to look like that? Bloody hell, the taskforce must have them working all hours up here. Mind you, these days he probably wasn't looking a lot better, and he was certainly starting to jump at shadows, so maybe he shouldn't be so hard on the lad.

"Look, I've got to go. I daren't risk being seen talking to you. But give that to Panesar as soon as you can, okay?"

He turned and walked away, not giving the DC chance to reply, but then what else was he going to do? He didn't start breathing easily until he was taking the back roads

Time's Bloodied Gold

down to the M5 and he was sure he hadn't been followed. It was a relief to have been able to hand something in at last, although a part of him was increasingly angry about the way this was being handled. Only last night he'd tried to ring in from his flat but had only been able to leave yet another message on an answer-phone. That was the trouble with keeping up this pretence of being a working rep on the road, his times when he could call in were all over the place and so desperately limited by the times he could get away from the farm, and it didn't help that the phone number he was supposed to call in to had been changed so many times. Out of nowhere he'd get a text telling him to ring a different number, and he wasn't best pleased about that, because whoever was sending those messages was being rather careless about how they phrased the requests. If one of the gang had read his phone over his shoulder he'd have had some explaining to do. As it was he was saving each new number under fake names and then deleting the messages as fast as he could. And what was worse was that those bloody numbers seemed to be unmanned for hours on end. What the hell was going on?

It was a relief to get rid of that glove and the casings, though, because the printout he could burn or flush away in an emergency, but not those, and the gang were like cats on hot tin roofs at the moment. His predictions that things would blow up into a massive row between Jerzy and Mikhail had been all too correct. The pair of them had gone at it hammer and tongs only a couple of days after they'd come back from Bristol, the only blessing being that Danny hadn't been there and had heard about it the day after from a very worried trio of Dymek, Stefan and Kazimierz.

"I've never seen Jerzy so angry," Dymek told him.

"We thought Mikhail was going to beat the crap out of him," Stefan added. "They were nose to nose and screaming. I honestly thought we were going to end up with Jerzy dead and Mikhail taking over the gang."

That was a legitimate fear, because the only other person whom de Arce would work with was Mikhail, so without him de Arce would pack his bags and head off to try and find someone else to work with. Or maybe he'd cut his losses and head for Haiti or wherever? That would be poor consolation for the gang, though.

"I don't want to go back to working for Tomek," Stefan confided to Danny. "This is bad enough, but what they do to those poor girls they bring over from Lithuania and Latvia just sickens me."

Kazimierz gave Danny a knowing look over Stefan's bowed head that indicated he sympathised with what had just been said, but went on with,

"It was quite an eye-opener, though. They started fighting, and like these two, I thought Mikhail would make mincemeat of Jerzy, but fuck me, that man's a fighter when he wants to be! Mikhail goes in and just starts slugging away, but Jerzy's got some moves. I wouldn't be surprised if he wasn't in some special combat team in the army, because he knows some very interesting techniques." Coming from a man who Danny thought had been a professional soldier himself, that was quite an assessment, and one he filed away under 'don't get into it with Jerzy!'

"The next thing we know, Mikhail is on the ground and Jerzy is giving him the kicking of a lifetime and reminding him about how he'd have been rotting in a Polish jail if not for him. I didn't know about that, and I don't think the others did either, except maybe Ulryk, but we all got what Jerzy thought of him for betraying his trust like that."

Dymek was nodding. "He left Mikhail all busted up on the floor and sent Ulryk to get de Arce, and right there in front of all of us he demanded to know what was going on with the money."

"Did he answer?" Danny wanted to know. That had been a shrewd move including all of the others. De Arce taking twenty percent off the top without telling anyone about it had robbed all of them, and they weren't so daft as to not know that. Limited intellectually in some ways they might be, but they weren't slow when it came to money.

Dymek shook his head in despair. "He stood there and told us that if we wanted God's help to get the jewels then he had to have his share. I tell you, I thought Jerzy was going to have a fit. He went nuts, screaming that God hadn't provided the means to find or get to that church with the big stones, nor had he used his contacts to find a way to sell the goods. That was all his – Jerzy's – work through his contacts with Tomek. He really tore into him, Danny, screaming at de Arce that he was so fucking stupid that he'd have taken the goods to the nearest dealer, and then wondered why he was locked up in some police cell somewhere."

"I guess Jerzy was the one who thought of salting other antiques with the good stuff?" Danny asked.

"Oh yes, that's all Jerzy. And Reznik is a contact of Tomek's, de Arce would never have got near him without Jerzy," Dymek replied, with Kazimierz adding,

"And without Reznik the stuff would never get to the West Indies. He already had the contacts and the routes mapped out to bring drugs in, so when his mules go back it was the simplest thing to have them take stuff with them..."

"...Because nobody was giving a second glance to someone going back to the Caribbean. Oh God, of course!" Danny groaned. "The customs and border forces wouldn't even be looking at them going that way except in the most cursory way. It's coming into the UK that they're worried about, because they know that they aren't moving drugs from here towards the USA."

Kazimierz gave a shiver and a terse nod. "I never wanted to get mixed up with the drugs cartels, Danny. That's way above my pay grade."

That was a funny way to put it, Danny immediately thought. The gang weren't getting paid in that sort of way, and then it hit him – what if Kazimierz was an undercover Polish cop? That would explain so much. He couldn't be operating here legally, but what if the poor sod had been in too deep to be able to bail out when they all came here? What if he'd been told to stay put for a while, just so that the gang didn't twig that they'd been infiltrated, and then been expected to slip away? Only stuck out here in the wilds of the Worcester-Hereford border there was never that chance? Christ, he had to find a way to drop the hint that he'd caught on, but nothing too explicit in case he was wholly wrong and Kazimierz was just an honest ex-army guy caught up in a nasty mess not of his making.

However no opportunity presented itself, and Thursday dragged on into Friday and then the weekend, and then Sunday came around and they were heading for the portal again. Danny was unhappy about another aspect of this on top of everything else – the first five full moons of this year were all in the early hours of the morning. Tonight de Arce had declared that he would try and open the portal at midnight, and he seemed confident that he could do it. But if he couldn't and it had to be at the astronomical full moon, then as far as Danny was concerned they were really in deep shit, because doing this at ten in the morning was just asking for someone to walk in on them. And some spooked tourist tearing off and dialling 999 to say that armed men were at a country church

Time's Bloodied Gold

would be bound to bring a full armed response team down on them, and Danny dreaded being caught in a fire-fight. So for the first time he found himself praying that de Arce succeeded.

Midnight came around and de Arce made his first moves, but Danny didn't see them. De Arce had made it plain that the only person he wanted in the church apart from Jerzy and himself was Mikhail.

"All of you, on the alert!" Jerzy had ordered in soft tones when he came over to let them know de Arce was ready. "Any hint of funny business and you come at my shout and fuck de Arce! And be prepared to take Mikhail on if he argues."

Yet the first arguments didn't come from their own but on the other side of the portal.

"*Auxilium nobis, placere!*" the priest's voice called.

"What did he say?" they heard Jerzy ask as they loitered right at the edge of the porch.

"He asked for help," sniffed de Arce, and demanded, "*Quid tibi opus est auxilium?*"

"*Qui sunt trans mare. Viri Bristou!*" the priest called back.

"He said the men from across the sea are coming, the men from Bristol," de Arce translated, then paused as another cry came from the other time. "He's asking if we sent them, ha-ha!"

"No, how could we?" was Jerzy's instant response, but de Arce was already saying,

"*Ita, Misi ergo ad eos vobis.*" They heard him saying with another of his nasty laughs, "I said yes I did. Well they're obviously scared of whoever it is, and if they think that was me too then they'll be more co-operative." Then they heard him call, "*Mitte mihi decimas obtulerunt.*"

Beside Danny, Stefan shifted uncomfortably. "I don't like this asking for tithes," he whispered. "Only the Church should ask for that, and de Arc isn't taking it for the Church. Why does he do that?"

"Because it works," Kazimierz answered sadly.

"And who are these men from Bristol?" Dymek asked worriedly. "Do they mean Bristol now? Is there someone down there asking for their cut too?"

"They hadn't fucking better be," Ulryk growled. "If they are, me and Mikhail will give them a kicking!"

However Danny was already shaking his head and rolling his eyes in disgust at Ulryk's instant resort to violence to sort every problem. "Oh come on, how would they do that, eh? Do you think they have another like de Arce? Jeez, Ulryk, one of him is bad enough, there can't be two! And do you think we'd be getting such a good price for what comes through if the markets were being flooded with antiques like these?"

It was the best he could come up with at short notice. What he'd wished he could say was, 'do you really think the British police are so thick that they wouldn't know about this if it was going on all over the place?' He couldn't, of course, but it was true. This had gone under the radar because the operation was so small and was taking place so far off the beaten track. If it was happening at one of the churches down in Clifton, for instance, it would be spotted in an instant. There were far too many people out and about at all hours.

"Good," Dymek said softly, but Danny had the feeling it was in relief that other poor souls weren't suffering, rather than being glad nobody was getting in the way of him getting his cut. Only Ulryk of the ones out here thought like that, and maybe Piotr, if he thought of anything at all.

What he didn't like was the way that de Arce was so smug when another four men had come staggering through the portal with their clothes weighted with precious pieces of jewellery.

"He said the north-men – whoever they are – have got as far as somewhere called Tamworth," the inquisitor said with an airy wave of his hand. "They asked for my protection. I told them to send whoever it is through and I will deal with them."

Danny couldn't help the "Eh?" that escaped from his lips.

De Arce gave him a look of superiority down his hawk-like nose. "They said these men are heathens, and *I* know how to bend a heathen to God's will." He saw the glint of a jewel in the torchlight and snatched the brooch from Ulryk's hand. "Give that to me. I will look after it until it goes to be sold," and stamped off towards the vehicles.

"What's wrong, Danny?" Jerzy asked waspishly, his temper already frayed from de Arce's haughtiness.

"Men from the north at Tamworth? Do you not know what that means?" Danny asked in disbelief, then remembered that these men hadn't had his British education, and as Jerzy's mouth tightened, added quickly, "No, sorry, of course you don't, you didn't get it in school like I did. The north men are the Vikings! No wonder these poor sods have been so quick to give de Arce their jewels. They think he's going to protect them when the Vikings come calling! Christ, I wonder if they've already had refugees coming their way fleeing westwards? Is that where these new jewels have come from?"

Jerzy blinked at the unexpected answer. "Did they get this far into England?"

"I don't fucking know!" Danny spluttered. "My history only gets as far as them at Tamworth, and I only know that because I've heard lately about Tamworth being the seat of the old kings of Mercia in the news about the Staffordshire Hoard; and what a catastrophe it was for them when the Danes took it. It's probably about the time of Alfred the Great, but it could be later because the Danes didn't just bugger off, they were here for decades even before Cnut became king. All I can tell you is that they were raiding up and down the coasts for ages. We can look on the net when we get back, but I have a feeling that they were in Dublin, so if we're talking about them coming up the River Severn right up to here, then I guess it's not impossible."

"Oh great," Jerzy fumed. "Bloody berserkers, as well, that's all we need! Next time, Kazimircz, make sure we have plenty of ammo', we may need it!"

Chapter 15

Wednesday

Bright and early, Bill got himself ready for the trip to Birmingham. He gave rather more thought to his appearance than he would normally have done just going into work, because although his work clothes were smart and serviceable, they had equally seen their share of crime scenes which had left their faded marks despite various dry cleaners' best efforts. Today he wanted to look every inch the DI in case he had to argue his way in to see Joe. He also wanted to go early, because although he had until after midday to wait to see Joe, Bill wanted to observe who was coming and going who might be related to the taskforce. If he saw a few familiar faces then it would be so much easier to express his fears and know he'd be taken seriously. On the other hand, if he hardly knew anyone even by sight, then he might well have more of a fight on his hands if Joe was barely involved anymore, or worse, had no influence at all with the group of officers Danny was involved with.

Moreover, he wanted to give himself plenty of time to get there. The M5 was notorious for getting snarled up by an accident at a moment's notice, and nothing would be worse than being stuck in a jam and missing his chance to speak to Joe. More and more Bill was thinking that there was another part to Danny's misfortune which had nothing to do with the gang and everything to do with something within the task force, and if anyone was going to be able to help him to straighten that out then it was Joe.

So he gave the morning rush of traffic chance to clear and then took the Citroen up the motorway to junction three, then weaved his way through the city streets to Harborne. The purpose-built modern police building was at odds with the Edwardian terraced houses across the narrow road from it, and there was clearly nowhere to park nearby. But that suited Bill. He would park at the station when he was actually going in, but for now he parked further away, got his crutches out and prepared to go for a walk. Because the one thing his knee operation did for him was give him an excuse to be apparently randomly walking, and if anyone saw him and asked why, he could quite legitimately answer that his consultant had told him he needed to have a daily walk and that he was choosing to do it now while he waited for Joe.

Taking it steady, he made his way around the block going slower on the road past the station. As he feared he saw nobody he knew nor even any familiar cars parked outside. This was going to be a tough day. He wouldn't be impressed with someone from another division coming in and casting aspersions against his own staff and mates, and he wasn't expecting these officers to be either. Yet he hoped that if he made his case clearly enough that they would understand why he was so concerned.

Taking himself off to the High Street, he went and got a coffee, then came back and this time drove into the station. It seemed a good start when the front desk folk were friendly and welcoming – a far cry from the person he had spoken to on the phone – and then Joe was walking down to meet him, smile on his face and hand outstretched.

"Bill! Good to see you. What can I do for you? It sounded urgent." Then he took in the crutch, blinked in surprise, and asked, "What the hell happened to you?"

Time's Bloodied Gold

"Oh this is just a knee replacement," Bill answered, keeping everything friendly and civil out here where others could hear. "It was going to go eventually but it just went sooner than I expected. Err ....what I'm here about is a little delicate, Joe. You see, officially I'm on sick leave until the knee heals, but I don't think this will wait much longer. Can we go and talk somewhere privately?"

Joe's mouth puckered in thought, then called across to one of the women behind the front desk, "Are any of the interview suites free, Carol?"

"Take your pick," Carol called back, and Bill was guided through by Joe to the inner workings of the station.

"Not exactly ideal, but if you want privacy, this about the best I can do, I'm afraid," Joe apologised. "I share an office with several others, and I'm getting the sense that you wouldn't want to talk there."

"No." Bill propped his crutches in the corner and eased himself into a chair which had seen better days. Cosmetic upgrades weren't budgeted for, so until a leg fell off or something equivalent, it would remain in use, but Bill lowered himself carefully onto it just in case it chose this moment to give up the fight.

"Okay, Joe, now I don't want you thinking I've come to sling mud at your lads, alright? But the first thing I have to ask you is this, have you heard anything about Danny?"

"Danny? No. Last I heard he was undercover down your way. Is he not still there?"

Picking his words carefully, Bill began with, "No he's not, and I think he's in awful trouble which for once isn't of his making. I know Danny can be an abrasive and annoying bugger when the mood takes him, however... I was contacted by one of my colleagues when I came out of hospital. He knew Danny well, too, and he had been contacted by Danny's ex-wife who was worried sick that

Danny had missed seeing their daughter. ...Yes, I know, he was undercover. But the thing is, Joe, even then Danny would have sent her a Christmas present, and he didn't – not so much as a card even, and he adores her. It might have been a crappy present, badly wrapped up in a hurry, but he'd have sent *something*.

"Well my mate started looking, at first just expecting to be able to find something he could happily relay onto Jane in a watered down form, allay her fears, and that would be that. What he found made his blood run cold, and when he came to me worried sick, it made me shudder too. So please, accept what I'm going to tell you in the spirit of the fact that I'm worried stiff, okay?"

Joe's face had creased into a worried frown, and he nodded. If Bill said it was something to be worried about it was hardly going to be a trifling matter.

Bill pulled a notebook out of his pocket, and in careful and concise stages, relayed Danny's series of contacts. "Now I know Danny," he said, pausing and looking up. "By the end one of these I can tell you that he's more scared than I've ever known him to be. And the other thing I can tell you, Joe, is that for all his faults, Danny's never been one to make mountains out of molehills. So I've been doing a bit of independent digging."

He sat back and watched Joe's reaction carefully. If he immediately got defensive then either he knew there was something amiss which he'd got drawn into, or he just plain didn't get why Bill was so concerned. To Bill's relief, though, Joe's first question was,

"Where's his welfare officer's reports? If you got this far then surely you've seen them?"

"Ah, the elusive John Taylor, you mean?"

"Why elusive?" Joe asked warily.

Time's Bloodied Gold

"Because some bright spark high up here decided that Taylor was very experienced, and therefore should be the welfare officer for a man going undercover with a rather nasty branch of the urban gang up here. Unfortunately someone also decided that Danny didn't need to have Taylor replaced," and he slid a sheet of photocopied paper across the desk to Joe which showed just the paragraphs concerning Danny. He had been careful to put blank paper across the rest before copying it at home so that anything which could be traced back to Charlie was masked.

"Oh my God!" Joe intoned as he read. "Jeez, Bill! ...Hold on a tick. Let me go and look in our files and see if there's anything here about this," and he dashed out of the door before Bill could object.

When he returned ten minutes later it was clutching a file.

"It says here that an email was supposed to be sent to you lot asking if someone at your end could take over as Danny's contact," he said, showing Bill a sheet of paper which looked like a printout of an email.

"We've got no record of having ever received that," Bill told him solemnly. "In a minute you might want to go and check your emails to double check that it got sent, because I've got more questions."

He could see Joe bristling a little at the implication that the blame lay squarely with his division, but didn't give him time to argue. He'd given careful thought as to how he would present what he knew, and so now he precisely laid out the anomalies he, Morag and Charlie had worked out, carefully keeping their two names out of it.

"So do you see why we've begun to think that wires have got seriously crossed?" he asked as he paused. "These dates and times just don't make sense as one sequence. It's like there are two separate conversations going on here, with someone playing silly bastards with Danny's life – because I can produce upwards of half a dozen officers who will all tell you that the voice on those phone calls you and we have recordings of is categorically *not* Danny's. I'm not blindly accusing your mates, Joe. We've dug through everything we've got at our end and there's just not enough for the problem to be of our making."

By now Joe was looking grim. "Bloody hell, Bill, you've uncovered a mess and a half. And I can see why you're thinking we've fucked up here, but can I just ask you one more thing? Has Danny actually found anything? I've got to question that, you understand, because the first thing my governor will wonder is whether this is a case of someone sent undercover for the first time who's found nothing, and therefore feels the need to justify himself by making a drama out of it all." He held up a hand to Bill as he saw his anger rising. "I know you said you know Danny, and that he's genuinely scared, but that just your word, and while it's good enough for me..."

He left the rest unsaid, but Bill knew what he meant. This was something he'd been braced for, and he'd known all along that he was going to have to be careful what he said here – one mention of portals through time and Joe would be thinking he'd taken one morphine tablet too many, and instantly dismiss all of what Bill had brought to him.

"I'm not sure what sort of trafficking you're investigating, you understand," Bill began cautiously, "but Danny got some photos of people who've been trafficked as agricultural labourers. I don't know that they're from abroad, but I think he was right to say that mentally they're not all there. Possibly we're looking at the enslavement of vulnerable British men who aren't capable of fending for themselves, not foreigners."

Time's Bloodied Gold

He wasn't about to say that he'd broken into Danny's temporary flat, so the only way to cover that was to say, "We have a few murky photos that show some very dazed and confused people in what looks like a farm setting."

Joe didn't immediately question that, so he hurried on with,

"What he did successfully uncover was a trade in stolen ancient artefacts. I hesitate to say antiques, because that tends to give the wrong idea. In this instance we're talking about things like Roman coins and Anglo-Saxon jewellery – small items which can be sewn into coat hems and the like. He made the link between some arson attacks in our patch as the cover for small antique dealers' units being broken into, and it looks very much like a bunch of Polish rogues who are behind it. Again, I don't know if they're part of the bigger trafficking gang you're investigating, or an independent bunch, and I'm not sure if Danny did either. I think that's why he was so eager to get evidence to you so that it could be cross-referenced.

"I'm afraid I rather went out on a limb and paid a visit to the pub in Tenbury Wells where some of the gang seem to hang out, and I can tell you that they look a nasty bunch. No great shakes intellectually. The implications are that there seems to be one bloke who comes and goes who looks like he's the brains behind all of it, while the Poles are the hired muscle – but if this is Danny's 'Boris', nobody else on our patch has actually seen him yet. We need Danny's evidence, and if we could only find Danny we might have enough evidence to arrest the lot of them."

Joe say bolt upright. "If you could *find* Danny? What the fuck do you mean by that?"

Bill gave him a steely look. "Exactly what I said. We have evidence of a car hired by Danny caught on speed cameras on several occasions, but where he himself is is a mystery. And *that*, mate, is why I'm worried fucking sick! These Poles are an evil crew who wouldn't think twice about slitting his throat if they thought he'd ratted them out, let alone being a copper. That would have been bloody dangerous even if he'd been in regular contact with someone ...*anyone* would have been nice! But now it's downright lethal. Since your lot dropped the ball, this scabby bunch of emails and messages is all we have to track down one of our own lost in the field for *months*."

"Christ!" Joe had gone pale, and Bill pressed his advantage with,

"So now you're on the same page as me when I say that I want to find out what the hell has been going on with these messages," and now he dropped the bombshell. "Look at the copies of the transcripts we received. Who is this person whose personal number appears as the one who took these calls? Because strangely enough, it's the same one every time – and in a station as busy as this, you'll forgive me for thinking that it's a bit too much of a coincidence that this person would happen to be on shift every time."

As he put the highlighted copies on the desk in front of Joe, he thought to take a second look at the email copy Joe had shown him purporting to have informed them of the removal of Taylor, and the need for Danny to be allocated a new welfare officer.

"Oh look, and here he – or she – is again," Bill said with withering sarcasm, tapping the email. "What a coincidence that they should have been sending us information, and it's the very stuff that never arrived." He paused for a second, then asked innocently, "Any idea who this might be?" although the way Joe's expression had darkened it was clear that he did.

Time's Bloodied Gold

"Fucking Rupert Godden!" Joe spluttered almost beside himself with anger.

"Clearly a favourite of yours?" Bill asked with a sarcastic quirk of an eyebrow.

Joe's growl was almost on a par with Bill's best. "Rupert Godden is a spoilt little bastard! Daddy is – or was – something very high up in the Navy. High enough up to be able to ask favours and expect them to be listened to. Rupert was treated to the best private schools money could buy, family holiday home in the Isles of Scilly and endless trips to Europe's finest hot spots, and an expectation that he only has to stamp his overindulged foot and life will be handed to him on a plate. Unfortunately he's hardly the brightest cadet that ever passed out, and so his expectation of reaching chief constable is more than a little unrealistic – and most of us who know him say thank God for that! If he ever got any real power he'd be bloody unbearable, because he has no grasp of what life for normal people is like.

"His latest whinge was about Susie, who's a DC who has the misfortune to have to work with him. She's had to have time off because her middle kid has been seriously ill. The poor little mite had meningitis, but shit-head-Godden felt he had the right to complain when he was asked to cover one of her shifts. The dozy prat was gobbing off to a few others that he couldn't see why the kiddie couldn't be left with his nanny now he's out of hospital – and he didn't mean a grandmother, either! Carol – who you met on your way in – had a real go back at him, forcefully pointed out to him that Susie has to depend on her mum for child care since her husband's job shifted to Wokingham, and he's away from home from Monday to Friday. But to cap it all, Godden then went and complained to the Super' about the way Carol had spoken to him."

Bill shook his head in dismay. "Don't tell me: the Super' had to give Carol a rap on the knuckles for inappropriate language even though Godden had provoked it and there were witnesses to prove it."

Joe nodded with a shudder of loathing. "Godden just about failed to say anything which would warrant him having a tongue lashing off the Super' as well to go onto his record, and now the little shit's going around all smug. If what you've shown me here is proof that he's fucked up mightily, it would give me great pleasure to escort him off the premises and give him a boot enema to help him on his way."

"Then what say you that we go and check a few rotas?" Bill suggested. "If he was working on those occasions, it will add weight to the accusations. He won't be able to say that it was someone who had it in for him using his identity. I have to say I wouldn't blame someone if they had, given how he's obviously loathed, if it wasn't for the fact that someone's put Danny's life in danger."

Joe led the way and took Bill up to an office where several officers were beavering away. The DC called Susie turned out to be a pleasant woman in her late thirties who was able to immediately call up the rota for the relevant times because she'd been on the same shift. Then when Joe gave her a brief and very edited reason for why he was checking up on Rupert she volunteered without any prompting,

"Oh God, that was another favourite gripe of his! He thought he should have been given the chance to do undercover." She rolled her eyes in exasperation. "Honestly, he's only been on the job five minutes and he thinks he's bloody Don Johnson or Colin Farrell! Give him half a chance and he'd be doing a *Miami Vice* round Birmingham, *tsk*! Thinks he's so bloody cool with his

Time's Bloodied Gold

designer haircut, his sodding Rolex, and the way he brags about where he's been and what he's done. Stupid shit thinks poverty automatically equates to being bent. I hope to God he never has to break bad news to some poor innocent soul in a rundown bedsit, because by the time he's done with them they'll be throwing themselves out of the nearest window."

"You say he was envious of Danny Sawaski?" Bill asked Susie in all innocence.

"Envious? He was as green as the Incredible Hulk! I did try to tell the Gov' that making him deal with the routine side of undercover work wouldn't be a good idea – I wouldn't let him within miles of anything that sensitive myself – but he said that Godden needed to get hands-on experience of what the reality was like. I did my best to keep an eye on him, but I couldn't be there at every turn. To be frank, I didn't like the way he kept wittering on about how Sawaski didn't seem to be getting any results, and that he would have got far more by then."

Joe's face had been getting darker with anger by the minute, and now he turned to Bill and said softly,

"You get out of here right now. This will go down better coming from one of us," and he gestured to the door and the stairs beyond.

Once they were out of the office and heading down to the way out, he declared, "I won't let this rest, Bill. Godden's overstepped the mark by a long way this time. I'll take this upstairs right now, have no fear."

Bill nodded, wishing that he could shadow Joe, but knowing what he meant about it being counter-productive. Nobody liked having an outsider slinging shit around, and his being there could end up with the taskforce closing ranks in self-defence. Far better that Joe should take over and get a fair hearing from his superiors.

"I could go home, but as a friend of Danny's you'll appreciate that I'd rather like to hear what happens," he said to Joe as he walked out to the car with Bill. "How do you feel about me going off to a local pub and you joining me for something to eat when you've done?"

Joe sniffed disgustedly. "This is doing nothing for my appetite, but in your shoes I'd be feeling the same. If you go to the end of the High Street there's a big pub called *The Green Man*. It's open all day and they do good food. Go and get yourself something. If I can join you any time soon I'll give you a text. But if you get fed up with waiting, text me and I'll call you when you get home."

The Green Man was easy to find, and Bill was soon tucked up in a small corner seat with the first pint in several weeks in front of him – at least there was that consolation since he was off the antibiotics now, and he was unlikely to be driving for several hours. In one way he was glad that the culprit had turned out to be someone known to be a pain in the arse. Joe would have far less trouble convincing his superiors of Godden's guilt than someone with an otherwise spotless record. And Bill knew the misery the Goddens of this world could cause. They cropped up in every walk of life – people who thought the world owed them something for walking on it. Mostly they were folk who'd been spoilt rotten in childhood, and had never quite worked out that the adult world wasn't going to fall to its knees in front of them in the way their parents had. The dangerous ones were the few like Godden, who had parents wealthy enough to either continue indulging their brat's adult fantasies, or the connections to ensure that the beloved child got much further than their own limited talents would otherwise have allowed.

He wasn't expecting instant results. There were channels to be gone through as in any job, and this wasn't a straight forward case such as Godden being caught thieving. That would have been an instant crash landing. Moreover, Bill had the feeling that Godden was crafty enough to have not done anything which he thought would get him thrown straight off the force. Going by what Bill had seen, there was a crafty, cunning mind at work here, but if Joe could tell him that at least people here were taking Danny's situation seriously again, that would be a major step forward.

It was three hours later when Bill's mobile pinged with a message from Joe, during which time he had demolished a large steak pie and chips, and was starting to consider whether he might fit in a pudding before driving home.

Where are you? Joe's text asked, and Bill immediately replied, with the result that ten minutes later Joe was coming in from the front door and scouring the pub for Bill.

"Over here, mate. ...Let me get you one," Bill said gesturing to the bar.

"I'll have a large Highland Park," Joe said with the air of a man who'd had a very hard day. "I can walk home from here and I need it."

Bill ordered the drink, got himself a tonic water, and led Joe to his table. "Okay, how did it go?"

Joe puffed his cheeks. "Well, aside from really setting the cat amongst the pigeons, about as good as we could ask for."

"Really? That's good isn't it?"

Joe took a sip of the single malt and held it in his mouth a moment, favouring it. "God, that's good! ...Err, yes it is good. I just meant that I don't think it's going to help Danny in the immediate future."

However, Bill was quick to reassure Joe, "Look, I didn't come here expecting miracles. What I wanted to happen was for people to start taking Danny seriously again. Because of this cock-up Williams is even starting to think of Danny as a bent copper."

"Oh Christ!"

"Yes. So if I can now go back to him and tell him that there's been a horrible misunderstanding, and that you guys are taking it seriously that Danny was trying to pass good information to you, but it all went wrong, then maybe he'll review how he's been seeing him. If I can get that far, then we can start looking for Danny in earnest without the poor bastard getting arrested for real."

Joe nodded and took another long sip of the malt. "In that case I can tell you that my immediate governor nearly produced kittens on the spot when I told him of our suspicions about Godden. DCI Panesar is as straight as a die. He's a tough boss but as fair as they come."

"Panesar? Does that mean he's a Sikh?"

Joe grinned. "Yes. Jamari Singh Panesar. And before you say it, yes, I do think Godden was put on his team for a reason, and that reason is that he couldn't just go slinging shit at him willy-nilly without looking like a racist prat – and Godden's got enough self-preservation to know not to do that. He knows how racism's viewed these days. And in this case, it's all the more so because Panesar is genuinely good, and he's going to go higher because of sheer ability, not just because those at the top want to balance their ethnic quotas.

"I managed to catch Panesar and said I needed an urgent word. He's bright enough to catch on quick, and the next thing I knew I was in his office with the door firmly shut and laying out those papers. He pretty much grasped that someone from outside had been involved straight away, but he also respects the fact that you've come to us to clear our mess up, and not just kicked up a fuss from

Time's Bloodied Gold

Worcester. He's heard of you, by the way, and in a good way, so that helped.

"So the situation at the moment is that Panesar is taking this upstairs because of the seriousness of the situation. When I told him about how long Danny's been lost for, and without any contact, I don't think I've ever seen him go quite that pale. He's a bright lad, Bill, and he's got the imagination to fill in the potential situations there might have been for Danny to come to some serious harm. And he's also able to see how it would look if Danny turned up as an unidentified corpse on someone else's patch, and then it comes out in the press that this was an undercover copper the force failed with honours."

Bill gave a grim smile. "Oh I well believe that that would cross a few minds. That's one of the PR department's worst nightmares. Makes us look like total idiots. So what's likely to happen?"

Joe leaned in confidentially. "I think Panesar and the Super' are likely to be having very strong words with DC Godden within the hour."

"Within the hour? That's faster than I expected."

"Oh this taskforce has been getting very mixed results, so the thought that Danny might have been trying to pass them good stuff which they've missed the boat to act upon has gone down like a lead welly. Both of them know how time-sensitive information can be when it comes to trafficking. It's no use going to a drop-off point even the day after and expecting to get much of anything useful. That makes it a bloody nightmare to pin down. And I'll tell you something else: Panesar is broad-minded enough to see the value in stopping a rural trafficking outfit, even if it's totally unconnected to the main operation. He's canny enough to see that as getting two for one out of the resources, and to know that always looks good, but in a better way than your Williams does. So he's taken it rather personally that Godden has both dragged his unit's name through the mud, *and* deprived them of some much needed kudos, just to satisfy his warped little ego."

Bill scratched his chin thoughtfully. "I suppose it's too much to expect Godden to be thrown off the force?"

Joe sighed. "Much as I wish I could say he's on his way out, I suspect he's just within the boundaries to stay. What does give me a heap of quiet pleasure is the knowledge that he's heading for one hell of a disciplinary, and he'll be back in uniform at the lowliest level faster than you can say knife – and he's probably only going to get that because this has been kept quiet so far, and because his daddy and several of our most senior are chums."

Bill sighed. "If it wouldn't both endanger Danny further, and drag a lot of good officers through the mud with him, it would almost be worth leaking it to the *Mail* and the *Post*," referring to the two main Birmingham papers.

However, Joe had a different thought on the matter. "It wouldn't surprise me if our great and good didn't have a quiet word in daddy's ear and tactfully suggest that his little Rupert might benefit from a change of career. They don't like being trapped between a rock and a hard place anymore than we do. And I bet that his dad is no fool and picks up on what's being hinted at." He sighed. "If Godden was a different lad, you'd almost feel sorry for him. His dad's footsteps are awfully big to have to follow in, and that's never easy. But he's such a thoroughly evil little tyke, any sympathy you might have had for him goes within minutes of him opening his self-opinionated gob."

"He'll wriggle like a worm on a hook, you know that, don't you?" Bill warned. "His sort always does. So I'd be prepared to wade in in Susie's defence, because he's already marked her as a target."

"Oh don't worry, Susie's covered! On one of those shifts at the last minute she was at home because of her kids having a tummy bug – wasn't even in the building. And on another occasion she was downstairs with a DS, because there was a woman brought in who tries to accuse every bloke in the station of sexual misconduct, and it just happened that Susie was the only woman available to go in with him. She's on camera as being down there at the crucial moment and an hour either side. Godden will only look all the guiltier if he tries to pass the blame onto her."

"Karma's a wonderful thing," Bill said with a mischievous grin as he chinked his glass against Joe's.

"Funny …I heard Panesar saying much the same under his breath as I left him!"

"What it is to be so popular," Bill quipped, and they both laughed.

Chapter 16

Thursday

For Bill the next question was whether he should pre-empt any contact by Joe's superiors and go and see Williams himself. There was something to be said for the tactic of letting those higher up just argue it out between themselves, but the downside was how long it might take for anything to happen. The next full moon was due in the early hours of Wednesday the twenty-seventh of March, and by that point Bill wanted to have de Arce well and truly locked up and beyond doing anyone any harm, much less opening up that damned portal – because Bill had a nasty feeling that something that de Arce was doing was key to getting the cursed thing to open. If not, then why hadn't it been spotted before? That was another question which had started to plague Bill.

St Michael's church had stood on that spot for centuries, as Nick had attested, so if the church was sufficient all by itself for the portal to open, then why hadn't it done so before? Surely there must have been points in nearly a thousand years of its history for some evening services to have coincided with a full moon? And he couldn't imagine the stolid farming folk of the Tudor or Georgian eras just accepting someone walking out of the walls without considerable excitement, and more like outright panic. So something had changed of late, and that had to be to do with de Arce.

Somehow he didn't think the Polish members of the gang had any ability to influence such a thing one way or

Time's Bloodied Gold

the other. They were undoubtedly a force to be reckoned with in the here and now, but were they likely to have caused the portal to open? Bill thought not. And part of that was because of the clear wariness he had seen on the faces of the gang on Monday night. They weren't going to look this gift horse in the mouth, but there had been visible discomfort there too, as if they were tolerating this because of the profit, but had there been another way to get rich quick they would have taken it in a heartbeat and dumped de Arce with speed.

As for Danny, Bill could only see one way of getting him home safely, and that was getting this bloody gang locked up. But if arresting all of them and pulling Danny out once they were at a station was the only option, then Bill had to be very sure that Danny would be recognised as one of their own. And that meant that he had to clear Danny's name as a priority.

Therefore the next morning he dug the decent suit he'd been wearing yesterday back out and prepared for the next round of the battle. And if he had used both his crutches for effect yesterday, then today he would use one and try to make out that he was close to discarding that one too, because if Williams thought he was well on the way to coming back, that was all to the good. Bill was under no illusions that if Williams thought he was likely to be off for months to come, then there would be a lot of platitudes designed to get Bill out of the office and not rocking the boat, but no real action until confirmation of Godden's guilt appeared on his desk and in triplicate. No, Williams had to be made to think that Bill would be back in the building within weeks and likely to muddy the waters if he found nothing had been done, because one of the biggest differences between the two men was that Bill didn't give a stuff about getting promoted, especially if it got the right result in something like this, whereas Williams still had aspirations to rise even higher.

At Williams' office Bill knocked on the door and then let himself in at the called, "Come!"

"Ah, Bill, how are you?" Williams asked, not getting up and holding his pen poised over the papers on his desk, making it clear to Bill that he was interrupting and should make it short.

"I'd give up on that for now," Bill said tactlessly and saw Williams' minute flinch around the eyes. "Sorry if this is going to piss all over things for you, but you need to know this," and sparing none of the details, Bill told Williams what had happened with Rupert Godden.

If he'd been a vengeful man, Bill would have got his fill that day as he watched Williams' jaw drop, then him turn pale as the implications sank in of each new disaster.

The moment Bill stopped talking, Williams pounced on his computer and his emails. Given that the screen was at an angle on the desk, and Bill had quite deliberately taken the seat which gave him the best view of it, he saw that three new ones were in the inbox – one from Panesar and two from his superiors in the West Midlands force. He couldn't quite read them, but the expressions tearing across Williams' face told of a disaster unfolding in which Williams was seeing his next promotion heading towards the sewers at speed.

With wide eyes and an unaccustomed pallor, Williams turned to Bill.

"Oh God! Oh bloody hell! This is terrible, it's appalling!"

Bill gave a snort of disgust. "It's that and more. Danny's been left hanging in the wind just because that obnoxious little shit thought he should have been the one to go undercover."

Time's Bloodied Gold

However Williams was already shaking his head, for once too horrified to stop and think about whether someone with Bill's tendency to tell the truth and shame the Devil was the right man to share this with.

"It's worse than that, far worse."

"How 'worse'?" Bill growled, feeling his gut twisting. If it was so bad as to percolate through Williams' thick skin then it was pretty bloody awful.

"It seems that DCI Panesar has had people going through the computers all night. They've found that Godden not only arranged those meetings that never took place, he actually sent instructions to Danny in Panesar's name."

"*What?*"

Williams stabbed an accusatory finger at the computer screen. "It says here that Godden sent texts to Danny telling him to ring in on other numbers. He made sure that Danny used numbers he could control so that Danny didn't have any contact with the taskforce except for those he arranged to get through. Everything that's come or gone to Danny since late November or early December has either gone through Godden or been filtered through him with arrangements being altered."

"Jesus! How extensive has that been?"

Williams dragged his hands across his face as if he could wash the dismay away. "Well there's the changed numbers for a start. ...Dear God, he's been indiscreet! If anyone read those messages on Danny's phone I dread to think what the outcome would be, because Godden openly referred to the taskforce. Only a total fool would fail to realise that Danny's an undercover cop reading those."

Bill had to ask the next question, "So did you ever get the email telling us that we needed to get a welfare officer for Danny from our own division?"

Williams shook his head but again made a vague stabbing finger at the screen. "It says that Panesar has looked into that, and that Godden altered just one letter in the email address to here. A tiny thing, but it guaranteed that the email would show up as sent, but would then bounce back. The techies had to dig for it because he erased the bounce-back message, and so Panesar and his superiors thought it had been sent..."

"...Because without scrutinising the email, who would check something like its addressee? It was in the right box as 'sent' mail, and it hardly required a major reply. If they heard nothing back it was hardly the end of the world, was it? They'd just assume we were acting on it."

"Exactly," Williams sighed in appalled tones. "He's a bastard, but he's a clever little shit, too." He looked down at his desk and gave another deep sigh. "I know the force is better off this way, but this is one of the rare times when I understand why the old coppers had a bottle of scotch in the desk drawer, 'cause if I had one I'd be pouring a very stiff one right now because it gets worse."

"Worse? Oh crap, what else has Godden done?"

"He got rid of evidence."

"*No!*" Bill was horrified. "How stupid is this twat? How the hell did he get onto the force in the first place? ...No, you don't need to answer that, I know only too well how. But what evidence did he ditch?"

Williams swallowed hard and changed back to a previous email. "This is from my opposite number up there. He says that they've wrung it out of Godden that Danny caught up with him one evening a week or so back and gave him an envelope. He told Godden that he didn't dare go into the station to drop the evidence off in person in case he was spotted, because he doesn't know all of this Tomek's crew up there. But apparently it contained images which show where the money was going from and to, plus a glove from one of the gang which might give DNA evidence. The trouble is, Godden just took it back to his flat and chucked it into the bin."

"Why, in God's name? And if he binned it how do they know? Did the fuckwit look at it and still bin it?"

"They know because they made a dash for Godden's home and raided the bins in the early hours when someone pointed out that the refuse collection would be today. Thank Christ we've gone to fortnightly refuse collections," Williams sighed mournfully, "never thought I'd be glad for that. Godden never gave it a second glance, so the envelope was easy to find since it was still sealed, but he's even less popular now that his co-workers have had to plough through two weeks of old curry containers to get to it. In his arrogance he assumed that Danny couldn't possibly have gathered anything important.

"Up until he clammed up and asked for legal representation he was still determinedly saying that Danny was just fucking about and getting nothing. Panesar is convinced that everything Godden has done has stemmed from that premise – that Danny is an idiot who couldn't find his own arse with both hands, and that he could have done so much better. He has no appreciation of how long some of these operations take to bear fruit. He thinks it should be as simple as arresting someone for shoplifting. In fairness to Panesar, he'd already been asking for Godden to be moved away from the taskforce, saying that he needed more experience elsewhere before returning to *any* sort of undercover operation. And he's taking little pleasure in being proved so horribly right."

"I bet his superiors are squirming at not having listened more closely to him," Bill said with a poor attempt to not sound sarcastic. What applied to those above Panesar applied equally to Danny's superiors here, and that most definitely included Williams. Yes, Williams was squirming alright! And so he damned-well should, Bill thought. He hadn't played fair with Danny at any point in this fiasco, expecting him to run a secondary investigation at the same time as the main one, just to feed Williams' ego and desire to look like he could make impossible budgets and timetables work, when everyone else knew that they couldn't possibly.

And in that moment Bill knew that he had to prod Williams hard right now while he was vulnerable. Give him time and he would be covering his arse with speed, and retreating behind an impregnable wall of platitudes until he knew which way the blame would fall, and that wouldn't do at all. Danny needed help right now, not in a month's time.

"What's Danny's status right now?" Bill demanded.

"Danny's status? What do you mean?"

Bill leaned in and gave Williams a steely glare. "I *mean*, is Danny's name out there as a suspected dirty cop? Because if any aspersion has been cast on him, *anything* that might make a uniform officer think he's gone bad, for instance, or is acting with the gang instead of against them, then it needs to be rescinded right now! ...Doesn't it? Right now! ...Because although we haven't the foggiest idea of why things are happening at the full moon," well he did, but he could hardly say so to Williams, "then we have a very short time to re-establish contact with Danny before it all starts happening again. And if we've got to find the poor bastard before we can even start the mopping up operation, then everyone out on the streets who might just spot him needs to know that Danny is clean and is an officer in terrible danger, not someone they just slap the cuffs on and drag in regardless."

Time's Bloodied Gold

Williams swallowed reflexively. He knew what Bill was leaving unsaid, and that he was also implying that he'd happily dob Williams in the shit at the first opportunity if he failed to act now.

"Right now," he said with a sickly hint of a smile.

"Right now!" Bill growled. "Maybe a good start would be the officers who are here in this building? And then a few phone calls to the stations? Not emails – too easily overlooked." That made Williams go pale again. Quite what his own emails read like was something Bill wasn't sure he wanted to find out. It might do nothing for his health and temper, and it wouldn't help Danny any if he ended up being escorted off the premises after decking Williams. That they would include an awful lot of covering of William's arse was in no doubt in Bill's mind, but they could be a whole heap worse too.

"I'll go and round up the troops, shall I?" Bill said waspishly, and levered himself out of the seat. "Downstairs in fifteen?"

"Fifteen," Williams sighed, realising that Bill wasn't leaving him time to ring his own superiors and wriggle out of anything, because those were going to be lengthy conversations.

"You'll come out of this better if you've been seen to act the moment you were told something was wrong," was Bill's parting shot as he left the office, and saw it strike home. Well it was about time that Williams realised that the higher you got up the tree the more shit you were supposed to be capable of dealing with. The extra salary wasn't handed out like doggy treats for good behaviour but as compensation for when the shit started flying.

By the time he eventually got back to his flat, Bill felt as wrung out as an old dishcloth. He'd stood right behind

Williams, practically breathing on the back of his neck as he'd told the assembled senior officers what had happened to Danny. The fact that Williams was already shifting the blame onto the West Mids lads without reservation made Bill's blood boil, because somebody here – and that was almost certainly Williams – had made the assumption that Danny wasn't coming back when he advertised Danny's position. So why hadn't he checked on Danny's status then? The simplest of phone calls would have revealed the discrepancy between the taskforce thinking that his own division had Danny's back, and Williams thinking that they had. Action could, and should, have been taken right there and then, and Bill knew he was standing in front of his old mates with a face like a thunderhead as the thoughts refused to leave him alone.

As he limped towards the door as everyone dissipated he saw Charlie standing in the shadows grinning like an idiot.

"What?" Bill demanded, too wound up to be patient.

"Your face," Charlie chortled, "I don't think a single person there was in any doubt as to why Williams was standing there wriggling like a worm on a hook. You didn't have to say a word for them to know that your boot just went up his arse bootlace deep. Christ, Bill, you looked as though you would have smote him with biblical wrath if he'd said a word wrong! I've already seen Sean and Jason leaving, alternately swearing like fishwives at Danny's predicament, and yet giggling like schoolboys at the way Williams has had to eat humble pie. They all know you did it! It'll be across the division by tea-time, you know. You don't need to worry about the word being spread. A better-liked man than Williams might have had some people feeling a bit sorry for him and being a bit slow to pass the word onwards, but not him."

Time's Bloodied Gold

"But Danny wasn't the best liked bloke, either, when he was here," Bill sighed.

Charlie puffed in dismissal. "Nah, in comparison to Williams, Danny was Mr Popularity. Don't forget, people might have thought Danny was an irritating shit, but he was bloody good at his job – that's not what most folks think of Williams. And while those who are lower down the ranks from the ones who were just in there with you might not have got it, every bloke in there was experienced enough to grasp how badly Danny's been let down, and more than a few will be thinking, 'thank God that wasn't me!'"

His words were proven within minutes as men approached Bill as he tried to leave, all offering help and wanting to know more of what had happened. Then Sean hurried up,

"I phoned Leominster and the PC there now tells me that a farmer came in reporting that somebody tried to get him to take on two workers back in September. He says he sorry, he thought when Morag rang that she was asking about new cases since then, because they reported it back to here as a matter of course. But you know how short-handed they are, so when they were told to keep an eye open and then let us know if there were any other offers, that was as far as it got, because the gang don't seem to have approached anyone else. He's saying now, though, that the farmer said that the man who approached him was foreign. At first the farmer thought he was offering men for casual work, and told him to come back in season, but then the bloke said something about the man being his all the time. Well the farmer had visions of being stuck with some illegal immigrant who'd be eating him out of house and home even when there was no work, so he told what I assume was one of the Poles to piss off, but just in case, he reported him to us. I reckon this has to be the ones

Danny's with because the nearest town to that farm is Tenbury Wells."

"That's the one," Bill sighed. He pulled the memory cards from Danny's flat out of his pocket in their protective bags. "Now that you all believe me, will someone please get the geeks to do their stuff on these?"

"Fucking hell, Bill, where did those come from?" Sean asked, astonished and not a little worried.

"The flat Danny rented in Leominster," Bill said with a sad shake of his head. "I went there trying to find him. He wasn't there but those were, hidden away. I've not touched them, but I haven't dared bring them in until today because I feared they'd just vanish into the backlog of work never to be seen again until it was far too late, because they're not attached to a specific case."

"Give them here," Sean declared firmly. "I'll take them over personally and breathe fire over the geeks to make sure they take this job as a priority. Jeez, Bill, how long have you known about this?"

"Only since last Thursday," Bill said truthfully, because that was when he'd started taking the documents apart in his flat.

Sean blinked in surprise. "You didn't waste time, did you? Well done, mate! I don't think I want to know how you found out, but you certainly haven't let the moss grow on this one."

Bill decided to squash any speculation right away. "It was Charlie who alerted me," he told Sean and the cluster who had gathered around them. "He ended up fielding a worried phone call from Jane. Danny missed Zoe's Christmas present. It was as simple as that, and if Williams had been doing his job, her call would never have got as far as Charlie and something would have been done the first time she rang. It was Charlie getting worried at how many times she'd called in and been brushed off that started things rolling, and he got straight on to me. It was nothing more sinister than that."

Well he could hardly say that Charlie had got further into Williams' files than he had any right to, could he? It hadn't been quite that simple, but it was believable enough, because already someone behind him was saying,

"Danny worshipped his kid, he'd never have let her down," and others were agreeing with him.

And so it was heading into the late afternoon by the time Bill got free and managed to drive home to a much needed mug of tea. What he wasn't expecting was to have the doorbell ring and to find Nick on his doorstep.

"I come bearing pizza," Nick said, holding up a large flat box, "and some more information, if you want it."

"I'll take anything you've got," Bill said gratefully, and told Nick of how his day had gone so far.

"Well while you've been bearding lions in their dens, I had a few questions of my own I wanted answering," Nick began.

"Like what?"

"Well of all the churches in this area, why should it be St Michael's that this happened at? Oh I know there are the stones," he said, holding up a hand for Bill to let him finish, "but even so, I was wondering why de Arce thought his tricks would work there? Because, like you, I was wondering why it hadn't happened before if it was just the church and stones combination, and I was remembering what happened with Pip, you see, and the way that blood had an effect on that portal. Why, I wanted to know, did the portal open to the Anglo-Saxon era and not to the time when the stones were put there? You'd expect that, wouldn't you? If the power is in the stones, then why didn't the portal connect to the time when they were at their most potent – for want of a better way of putting it? We have a pretty good idea that these ancient sacred sites often had blood sacrifices made at them, so why didn't the portal go to then?"

Bill blinked in surprise. "That's a damned good point. Yes, I see what you mean. It can't be the current church building, can it, because that was built after the time when those people are coming through from? ...You are still thinking about the early 900s, aren't you?"

"Oh yes, and before you ask, by the 1140s when the current church was being built, the language even of ordinary people was starting to move towards what we know as Middle English. It was still very identifiable as Old English in origin, but what those folk we heard were speaking wasn't what we call Transitional English, it was definitely Anglo-Saxon, which in my books backs up our previous deductions."

"So what have you found?"

Nick grinned. "There are some bonuses to working in the archives. I started digging backwards, because I had a funny feeling that just because we haven't been allowed to dig in the last century or so, that doesn't mean that some keen Victorian or Georgian gentleman didn't. There were a lot of those men of means who weren't stinking rich, but who had enough money to be able to pursue their enthusiasms without the need to hold down a job, and because of the sheer amount of time and focus they could bring to things, quite often their results haven't been bettered. Oh we interpret them differently nowadays, but the initial research is often decades of painstaking work – no academic can do that in the current climate."

"Are these those antiquarians you've referred to before now?"

Time's Bloodied Gold

"Those are the guys. Well there are advantages to living and working in the city with the oldest continuously produced newspaper in existence! *The Berrow's Journal* goes back to 1753, you know, and its direct predecessor to before that. I found a tiny reference in 1755 to the vicar of St Michael's, one Reverend Obadiah Farr, having found mutilated bones in the churchyard while they were clearing the ground to allow the carriages of the local worthies to get closer to the church door. Now St Michael's is a small church, and even in those days it wasn't important enough to be allowed to bury the locals in its own graveyard. You see, right from back in the days of the earliest conversions to Christianity, the Church wanted payments for people to be buried on sacred ground, and while rich landowners could stump up the cash to have a chapel built on their land, and pay for a priest to come and say mass there, the local mother church kept its hands firmly on the burial rights."

"Mother church?"

"Yes. It would have been the local big church and it would have had strong ties with the local bishop, although we're not talking exclusively about cathedrals, you understand. A good example round here is Ledbury's main church. That's the kind of place I'm talking about – an imposing church that covered a large area beyond its modern parish. Now they would be the ones to send out someone to officiate at any smaller churches in the area set up by the local big families, and they would keep control of things like burials and baptisms which they could charge for. Nowadays they're usually the parish churches, although some of our current parish churches aren't as old and date from times when the population expanded and there was a real need for the church to grow with them. But the ancient mother churches are all really venerable in origins, even if their buildings have had multiple upgrades as architectural fashions changed. St Martin's in the Bull Ring in the heart of Birmingham is a classic case – gothic style with what's standing, but going back centuries before then.

"That's where Mother's Day originates from, by the way. It's got nothing to do with anyone's mum – that's just a modern reassignment. It was the day in the year when everyone had to go to their mother church so that the priests there knew how many people they had under their thumbs, and who they could expect payments from, even if on other Sundays they went to whichever church or chapel was nearest. Also, there are some fascinating old lanes still in existence which were known as corpse roads for the same reason – they were the ways that everyone took to the nearest church that was actually allowed to bury the dead, not just hold services in. And all of this is relevant to what we've been doing because I've checked all the old maps and there's not a corpse road in sight around St Michael's. Nor has St Michael's ever been allowed to bury the dead there. That circle around the church is more a token of respect for the place, and most likely for the stones which were there before it, it has no specific Christian ritual function.

"So you can imagine when old Obadiah suddenly turns up shrieking that he's got corpses at the church, there was quite a kerfuffle because they shouldn't have been there. That's all there is in the *Journal*, but I went to the cathedral library and had a chat with a mate of mine who helps in there, and together we went digging. The bishop of the time, one Isaac Maddocks, and a man who must have been possessed of quite a brain because he was a member of the Royal Society, no less, ordered the matter to be investigated. Now what seems to have been kept very quiet is that a total of seven bodies of badly hacked about men were discovered. Without the benefits of modern forensics it must have been quite hard to tell when they had been buried, and you have to appreciate that finding men with the rusted remains of swords could easily have been thought to have been from any one of the religious upheavals that the country had experienced in the preceding centuries.

"I mean, they'd only just had the centenary of Charles I getting his head chopped off by Cromwell, so you can see why they'd be a bit touchy about things like that. On top of that, there were still a lot of people who were very uncomfortable about having a Hanoverian king, and who would have welcomed the Stuarts back in – and if you think you don't know anything about that, we're talking Bonnie Prince Charlie, here! He came remarkably close to taking the throne back in 1745, which is only ten years before these bodies turned up at St Michael's, and his army got down as far as the Midlands, you know. So you begin to see why it would be worrying to have dead soldiers appearing where none were supposed to be."

"So who did they think they were?" Bill asked curiously. "And are these bodies the ones you think provided the link to the portal?"

"I think they are," said Nick emphatically. "At the time they were discovered you're definitely coming into the time when science started being the way to interpret things, but it's still a long way off from any time when people can date bodies accurately. And these guys didn't have any grave goods with them, by which I mean inevitably something metallic which survived intact enough to show a style or design, which would have been the primary way that dating would have been done back then once things like clothes had decomposed. The swords looked just like any utilitarian sword – a basic blade with a hilt, and if that was wood, even if it got bound with wire for a better grip, that wood would still have rotted away. Only the best swords had the kind of ornate metal hilt you and I saw that man brandishing. The ordinary troops didn't have anything that good.

"So I think that what they found were the bodies of Viking raiders who somewhere along the line got separated from the main band, or maybe they just decided to do a bit of raping and pillaging on their own? The chronicles of the time don't report any big bands of Vikings coming this way, but that doesn't preclude a small cadre of men ending up there, and that's why I think the portal is at St Michael's. It's not just the stones, it's the fact that there was major bloodshed at the stones. Quite possibly one of more of them bled out against one or more of those stones, and because of that it's the Viking era that has called this hole in time to it."

Bill finished his slice of pizza and sat back with a huff of contentment. "That's actually quite a relief. I'd been wondering where else that portal might connect to, but from what you've just told me, this is a one-way thing."

"I think it is."

"But de Arce surely didn't know about the Vikings?"

Now Nick was shaking his head emphatically. "No, not a chance. Their existence was carefully buried in the bishop's records, safe from prying eyes. No, I think we can safely say that what de Arce aimed for was a church with standing stones right close to it. That's what he could have asked someone in this time to look for and hope to find with a reasonable internet search, not specialist knowledge."

"I'd love to know where that bastard came from – in our time, I mean," Bill sighed. "We don't want another like him turning up, do we?"

Time's Bloodied Gold

Nick rocked a hand in doubt. "Naah, I don't think that's likely, and I'll tell you why. Again, I've been thinking the same as you, and so I did some digging around with regard to French or Spanish connections for stone circles and churches. Now the obvious place to look was Carnac in Brittany, because that has the most amazing stone circles, and there is a big Benedictine monastery not far away these days. However, when I dug deeper, that monastery is far too recent – it was only founded in 1898."

Bill nodded. "I see where you're going with this. De Arce must have had help, and a religious house would be an excellent contender, but I'm assuming from your expression that there wasn't anything in this place you're talking about at the right time?"

"No. And it's not the right area to have seen fighting in the Napoleonic Wars, either, because again, I'm on the trail for bloodshed. Carnac has been well known for a very long time, and any sort of major bloodletting there would definitely have made the newspapers, even in the 1830s or 40s."

"So where else is there?"

Nick's face broke into a grin. "Compostela!"

"Compostela? Where's that?"

"Northern coast of Spain!" Nick declared triumphantly. "And the pilgrimage route to Santiago de Compostela – which is St. James to you – has been a major route for centuries. Truly Bill, you can't overemphasise the importance of Santiago. It was the place medieval pilgrims in the West made for if they couldn't make it all the way to Rome, or Jerusalem. The Camino, as the pilgrimage is called, still goes on today, and consists of a prescribed route from many major cities in Western Europe all the way to the great church of St James itself. London and Paris were key starting points, with what you might think of as other branches of a tree joining up to make a trunk which then went over the Pyrenees to Spain.

"Now there are two things which are swaying me this way. The first is that if de Arce told those he was with in Paris that he wanted to make the pilgrimage to Santiago, they would have let him. I can't imagine any but the worst circumstances when he would have been denied that, and there might well have been brothers within the Church who would have readily agreed to go with him, so he wouldn't have gone alone. We may see de Arce as a murdering bastard, but to his fellow Catholics of his own time he would have looked like a man of God who just backed the wrong politician. What's more, when he set out the Italian Inquisition was still definitely in operation, and therefore he could have commanded a lot of deference. It's hard for us to step into the shoes of the people of the time when it comes to this, but those who were around in the middle of the nineteenth century had lived with the reputation of the Inquisition since time immemorial as far as they were concerned. It wouldn't have been at all hard for de Arce to intimidate people, even if his own Inquisition was fading."

"And the other reason?"

"Blood! Sodding buckets of the stuff! Honestly, Bill, the things people do in the name of religion! I could have kicked myself when I caught on to this, because I'd been thinking of blood in the sense of someone having to die, but the Camino must have the blood of millions on every damned step. And the closer to Sanitago you get, the worse it gets. People go the last miles on their knees, or barefoot over jagged stones ...you name it, people do it to prove their faith!"

"Christ!"

"Precisely! The things people do to themselves in his name sometimes defy belief. Now there are markers along the way, and I wouldn't be remotely surprised if one or more of them turned out to be an old standing stone, because that tip of northern Spain was thought to be the end of the known world going back into Roman times and beyond. It's a truly ancient landscape down there. We know that there's an ancient Celtic altar to the sun down at Cape Finisterre, for instance, just a few miles beyond Compostela. So what if de Arce either bled himself or a couple of his fellow pilgrims at an ancient stone already soaked in blood and on the full moon? There still needed to be some freak other ingredient involved that we'll probably never discover, I'd guess, but this is the closest I can get to where he came from."

Bill was nodding thoughtfully. "And a place so filled with people who are already expecting miracles – and I'm thinking of the modern day pilgrims now – would give de Arce a reception committee who would probably be amongst the few these days who wouldn't question too hard the appearance of a self-proclaimed Inquisitor from the past. Good grief, that makes sense, doesn't it? They must get more than their share of nutters claiming something like that anyway, quite aside from the genuinely devout – although I have to say that my own feeling regarding that is that the Church is taking advantage of people desperate for something to help them cope with life."

"You and me," Nick said with a sad shake of his head. "The people making the pilgrimage I have sympathy for, but the ones I regard as preying on them ...they're something else. And I think de Arce must have impressed even them, because that Spanish registered Range Rover came from somewhere, and who richer than the Church at one of the greatest pilgrimage sites in the world? I'm not saying that they endorsed everything de Arce said, but if he tweaked their whiskers, then they are the ones who would have been able to get him what he needed to move on."

"Yes, that Spanish registration bothered me," Bill admitted. "I couldn't figure out how de Arce would have known that he needed the vehicle registered in his own name if he wasn't conversant with modern society, but if it was bought for him, then that makes more sense."

Nick nodded. "And I tell you something else. I bet if you dig around you'll find that he was booked onto a cruise ship heading for the West Indies and his other old seat of power – because that's another reason why northern Spain makes sense. He could get a ferry from Santander to Portsmouth, and from there onto a transatlantic crossing. If he didn't know that, then I bet whoever did the booking for him did."

Bill gave a grunt of satisfaction. "Agreed. And do you know what? I doubt he even got to Compostela itself for two reasons. I reckon once he was over the French border in his own time he'd have wanted his watchdogs gone; and then because, if he turned up at some Church-run hostel along the way and started preaching, I bet whoever was in charge even in his own time wanted him moved on and kept well away from the main pilgrimage site. As you said, they were only a few years out from the hell that had been the Napoleonic Wars – they wouldn't have wanted some twat fomenting dissent or outright rebellion, would they? He may have only had to turn back a few miles from his passage point into our time, once he'd met up with churchmen in the modern day, to be shoved onto the ferry, and it wouldn't surprise me at all if the Polish gang didn't have contacts on the northern Spanish coast who were instrumental in all of this."

Nick was nodding thoughtfully. "I agree with all of that. Yes, I think you're right. But now I have one for you,

Time's Bloodied Gold

Bill. Back at Cold Hunger Farm, when I first met you, that shrine had to have blood on it in the present as well as the past. So I think you need to get your mates to start looking really hard at missing persons..."

"...Oh crap! Because someone died here to complete the circle, and we don't know who, do we?"

Chapter 17

February

The time between the January visit and their return in February was fraught to say the least, and Danny found himself worried by the escalating tension within the gang. What was worse, although he'd taken the three bodies into Worcester with Stefan and Dymek immediately after the January portal opened, and they'd been found, nothing was appearing in the news about them after that first report. Whenever it was safe to do so, Danny was checking the local paper's online reports, praying for something like a police appeal to help with identifying these strange men. Yet nothing happened.

Maybe he'd been wrong to place all his hopes in Bill getting those cases and it had gone to someone else? Not that he thought anybody in his division was that slack as to mess things up. But what if someone new had come in? Even if it was someone on secondment, it could be somebody who wasn't quite up to the standard of the others and who'd dropped the ball again. What the hell did it take for his colleagues to sit up and take notice, for pity's sake?

About the only good thing to happen was that he got to have a private conversation with Kazimierz.

"Jerzy let slip that Mikhail's got quite the record with the police back in Poland," Danny began casually, as they stood in the kitchen one evening while the others played cards in the other room. "I can't help wondering why the

Time's Bloodied Gold

Polish police never tried to infiltrate the gang? They must have had enough cause."

"Oh I think they had cause," Kazimiercz said with equally studied casualness. "I think the difference might have been between suspecting and proving. Jerzy might not like Mikhail, but he dearly loved his grandmother, and she was the one who brought Mikhail up when his father killed his mother. It would have been the end of the old lady if he'd been locked up too. So Jerzy went to great lengths to cover Mikhail's trails back home. Bleach to mask forensic evidence and stuff like that." As he was talking Kazimiercz's voice and tone were becoming less of the off-hand ones of a casual criminal, and more like another copper's.

"Ah," Danny said, turning to lean casually against the big old ceramic sink while he nursed his coffee mug, so that if anyone looked through from the other room it was just two blokes chatting, but also so that he could see the others coming if need be. "But now Mikhail is in another country...?"

"...And the old lady died a couple of months ago," Kazimiercz supplied with a hint of a twinkle in his eye.

"Ah! Things have changed!"

"That they have. ...And I can't help wondering how come the British police haven't taken more notice of Tomek's activities. He's upped the violence considerably since he took over, and you'd expect them to notice that."

"Oh I think you can safely say that they've noticed," Danny said, keeping an expression of studied innocence on his face. "I wonder if that's why Jerzy is glad to keep out of the way down here? He doesn't strike me as a fool. However much he enjoys sampling the wares, he surely knows that Tomek's days are numbered?" Then a thought occurred. "Who arrived here first, Tomek or Jerzy?"

"Oh, Jerzy," Kazimiercz declared without hesitation. "He served old Wojtek for a few months before Tomek arrived, but what's interesting is that Mikhail and Ulryk didn't come over here until Tomek came."

"That is interesting. Do you think Jerzy came over here voluntarily so that he actually *couldn't* be held responsible for Mikhail? If so, he can't be happy that his albatross followed him to hang around his neck again like some bloody Ancient Mariner."

"No, especially as it was Mikhail and Ulryk whom the Polish police were watching, not him particularly."

"Hmm. I had wondered how deeply Jerzy was involved with the original gang."

"Pretty deep if you mean the business end, but Jerzy's always been careful to keep his hands clean, and it would be hard to make much stick to him. His value would, I suspect, be as someone whom the police would hope to turn as an informant in return for a shorter sentence, because he could finger a lot of people."

"Good to know," Danny said with a nod and a smile to Kazimiercz, then with the minutest of winks, "Nice to know that Jerzy is as keen to stay out of trouble as I am."

"I've been praying for a peaceful resolution," was Kazimiercz's response, to which Danny said,

"I'm sure that can be arranged."

Not much doubt there then, he thought as he scooped up the food for the prisoners and signalled to the others that he was taking it over to them. Kazimiercz was either another undercover cop or the best actor he'd ever met in the flesh, and it was enough so that Danny would risk sticking his neck out to help him if the chance came. Although in truth, these days Danny was as worried about how the hell he was going to extract himself, let alone anyone else. Because he'd come to the same conclusion as

Time's Bloodied Gold

Kazimiercz's colleagues, that nothing much was going to stick to Jerzy. However morally wrong he might be, when it came to the letter of the law, Jerzy hadn't ever handled the guns as far as Danny could tell; he'd not killed anyone except by neglect; and the only charge of GBH Danny could have brought against him was his beating up of Mikhail – which was never going to go anywhere since the victim might hate Jerzy's guts, but was too much the career thug not to just clam up and say nothing the moment he saw the inside of a police station.

So in terms of a prosecution, why was he staying? It was those unfortunates in the stable who were keeping him here, that was all, because someone had to take some responsibility for them, and if not him then who? But how was he going to leave? If he was really lucky this lot would be the last ones to come through, and then he might just be able to make an escape, but what his reception would be from his old colleagues was another huge worry.

What was unexpected was Jerzy coming to find Danny earlier than before, on the fifteenth, for him to drive down to Bristol.

"Reznik says his contact in Florida has got in touch with him. A private collector bought the whole of the last shipment we took down on the fifth - it hasn't had to be distributed through the auction houses."

"Isn't that bit suspicious?" Danny wondered. Well someone had to say it! Jerzy wasn't daft, and better he thought Danny was on the ball. He had to know that a bulk sale like that vastly increased their chances of being caught, but Danny desperately wanted to know which way the gangster was going to react.

Jerzy gave him a tight-lipped smile of approval. "I knew you'd see it too. I think Reznik's getting sloppy, that's for sure! I have little choice but to use his smuggling boats to get the articles into the States, but given the bits he's told me about what happens over there, I understood that our pieces were being stored in a Florida church in return for the Latino boys of the parish being left alone by the gangs Resnik's connected to – or at least the worst of them, because I doubt anyone has full control over all of the street gangs. It also made it easier for the seller to collect them, because an innocent visit to take mass by an antiques dealer was far less suspicious than visiting the haunts of known cartel members."

Danny felt he wasn't going to blow any American operation by musing out loud, "Maybe Montefiori had a visit from his cardinal? He looked like a man on edge to me, so I wonder if he spilled his guts in the confessional? If so, perhaps his superior had a word with his oppo' on the US mainland? Something to the effect of 'get your man to stop this nonsense now, before he drags the Church's reputation through the mud'?"

"That's much what I thought," Jerzy agreed. "And if he confessed that a cut has been going to Rome, that's not the same as just some daft priest, who's on an island where they still slit cockerel's throats as offerings, going a bit native, is it? One man they could deny, say he'd fallen prey to some mambo's sexual charms and gone off his rocker. But even the faintest hint of a provable money trail back to the Vatican must have had them shitting bricks, even if it was received without fully realising where it came from."

"Did Reznik suspect nothing?" Danny asked, puzzled.

However Jerzy shrugged. "You have to remember that he's only the courier. And he has to alter his routes all the time because of the US Coastguard and the ATF federal agents. This is just a sideline for him. The money that he earns from me goes into a separate account to his regular

Time's Bloodied Gold

trade. It's his little nest egg in a Swiss bank, so if it sits there for another twenty years just gaining interest and attracting no curiosity, he's lost nothing and is still set to gain hugely. Nor is he going to bring anything down onto his boss with any of this. And his men over there have noses like bloodhounds for even a whiff of a cop. They see anyone lurking around the church they just dump the goods and fuck off. We lose out but they won't risk getting caught."

That wasn't what Danny wanted to hear and he wished he could get a message out. Someone should prime the Americans to be careful around the church, but also that they might catch some couriers if they did. That wasn't going to happen, though, was it?

"I guess you can't question Reznik too hard?" Danny asked sympathetically.

Jerzy shook his head. "No. But I have already told him that there might only be another couple of deliveries to be made. I told him that things were getting more violent from where we were taking the stuff, because he thinks we're nicking it from Spanish museums. I told him we'd run into some Basque separatists the last time, and that there was a danger of it getting into a fire-fight if they were there the next time. He's sharp enough to know that that wouldn't be good, because even out in the wilds of the Pyrenees the police will draw the line at a Wild West shoot out."

That had been a smart excuse, Danny thought, and assured Jerzy, "I'll keep that in mind when we go down in case someone says something to me," which had Jerzy giving him an approving pat on the back.

The drive down in the car was tense, though. De Arce wasn't in a good mood.

"There is more to be got out of these people, I'm telling you," he insisted.

"Look, there's only so far we can push this," Jerzy

remonstrated.

"But I need more money!" de Arce snapped. "Reznik has told me what it will cost to buy a new headquarters for the Inquisition, even on Spanish Haiti, and to keep the men I will need to guard it."

"Has he, how very considerate of him," Jerzy replied with withering sarcasm, but it was lost on de Arce, who simply ploughed on outlining his lunatic plans to recruit a whole new generation of inquisitors from the ranks of the islanders, who would then go out and bring order to the world.

By the time they pulled up by the River Avon in Clifton, for once Danny found himself wholly in agreement with Jerzy, who declared, "For Christ's sake, put the radio on loud going back or I'm going to kill him! He's total lost the plot."

There was also a heated exchange between Jerzy and Reznik in Polish, which effectively cut de Arce out, but not Danny.

"When were you going to tell me about the cut going to the Vatican?" Jerzy demanded.

"Why are you so upset?" Reznik asked smoothly. "Are you not a good Catholic? I thought your grandmother brought you up right?"

"You keep her name out of this," Jerzy whipped back, "and since when have you been so religious? You were quick enough to rob old churches back home! And with a Polish pope on the holy throne then, too! Your conscience wasn't pricking you back then, was it?"

"I've been shown the error of my ways," Reznik declared with false piety, but a man close to Danny whispered to him,

"He wants heirs to his empire!" and rolled his eyes in disgust. "The skinny bitch isn't fertile."

Time's Bloodied Gold

Danny gave the man a conspiratorial wink. "Perhaps to do with what she's snorting?" and was gratified to see the man's flicker of a smile as he added,

"Any poor mite she had would be doing cold turkey the moment it came out, 'cause she's got one hell of a habit."

"Probably for the best, then?"

"Oh yes. Anyway, the old man's losing his touch. Reckon he's got until the end of the year at most before something goes dreadfully wrong and he costs Mr Oczkowski money. There'll be a new boss then, you mark my words."

"Gentlemen," de Arce broke into the conversations, "I believe it's time."

And so again the same process was gone through, but to Danny's eyes Montefiori looked even more stressed than before.

As they left and Danny got the car back onto the M5 heading north again, Jerzy asked him softly, "Did the same happen as before?"

"Yes, twenty percent to the Vatican."

"Bastard! I asked Reznik to ask me first, but he didn't, did he?" Jerzy hissed softly and looking in the vanity mirror back at de Arce, who was staring out of the window as if he hadn't a care in the world. It said a lot that this time Jerzy was riding in the front and not in the back as when they'd come and on previous trips. There was a distinct shift in their relationship, and Jerzy seemed to want to put a physical distance between himself and de Arce as well as the operational one.

"There's something else," Danny admitted and told Jerzy what Reznik's thug had said.

"I don't like the sound of that," Jerzy said with feeling. "Good work, Danny. Time we started thinking about leaving, I reckon, with or without him in the back there."

What Danny hadn't told Jerzy yet was that, while he'd pretended to be fiddling around with his phone playing some game, he'd actually made a note of the passwords both de Arce and Reznik were using. What he was less sure about was how he was going to use that information. Because those words about Reznik's impending forced retirement had jolted him into thinking about what was going to happen to himself when all this ended. If the taskforce had hung him out to dry, or worse, he was now so mistrusted that he was in danger of being hauled in as a dirty cop, then how was he going to live for the rest of his life? He'd always presumed that he would get his police pension, but that would vanish if he got thrown out, or worse, prosecuted and sent down. And what would happen then? It went against everything he'd held dear in the past to think about shifting a chunk out of Reznik's private slush fund into one for himself, but reality was nipping his heels here.

What shook him even more was the fact that he caught himself thinking that he didn't want to rob men like Dymek and Stefan of their shares of the cash either. They would need it for their families. Moreover, this money had come from men who were stinking rich and could afford to amass private art collections without a second thought. They wouldn't be hurt by it, nor had this come from some public fund to save an important piece for the nation either. The only one being robbed was the money laundering Reznik, and he was another who was hardly poor.

And when push came to shove, who would have his back now? It was more likely to be Stefan, Dymek and Kazimierz who saved his skin if Mikhail decided to give him a working over. They'd be the ones who at least would drive him to where he could stagger into an A&E ward, it wouldn't be his fellow officers. So who did he owe the greatest allegiance to? That he was even wondering this disturbed him to the core, and what added to his misery was knowing that he couldn't just walk away right now, because if he did then Mikhail and Ulryk would without a doubt kill their prisoners, and might just have the means to frame him for that act. An anonymous call to the police, and his flat could be being searched before he could get back there and get rid of those drugs, and why wouldn't they say he was a killer too to guarantee his arrest the moment he walked in through his front door? They, on the other hand, could be long gone by the time he'd convinced anyone to come looking at the farm, and if all they found were bodies, who would look guiltier?

So by the time they left for the February opening the tension within the gang was getting worse by the day, because de Arce had clearly said something to Mikhail and Ulryk after the Bristol visit, and they'd gone around verbally prodding and poking everyone, as if trying to find something out, although nobody else had a clue as to what. Maybe because of that, there was a brittle edge to everyone which resulted in some goofing around when they got to St Michael's. First Stefan and then Dymek were pulling faces in the torch lights, and Danny, glad of the chance to let off a little steam himself, gladly joined in. Ulryk and Mikhail just sniffed and tutted, but even Piotr joined with Kazimierz in laughing at them. That someone as thick as Piotr was feeling the strain said a lot. He wasn't happy that Jerzy and Mikhail were still sniping at one another, and what Danny found interesting was that Piotr was definitely siding with Jerzy, but even more so that he'd taken sides after it had been revealed that de Arce had sent money to the Vatican. Something had clearly happened to Piotr to give him a great mistrust of the Church, and he wasn't going anywhere near de Arce now.

As they stood around outside of St Michael's chatting, Danny decided to throw caution to the wind in one respect at least, and drew the three he was increasingly thinking of as his friends to one side, as Piotr and Ulryk chain-smoked by the stones.

"Have any of you heard Piotr talk about something that happened to him in the past?" Danny asked casually, and got puzzled glances in reply.

"How do you mean?" Stefan asked.

"Well, the way he reacted to de Arce shoving money the Vatican's way. I didn't expect him to be pleased about losing money, but I thought there was something more to his reaction. He really keeps his distance from de Arce now. I guess what I'm asking is, have you ever heard any hint that Piotr might have caught the attention of some priest who was a bit too fond of the choirboys, if you get my drift?"

Dymek and Stefan's eyes opened wide at that, but Kazimierz was already nodding thoughtfully, although it was Dymek who spoke first.

"Mary, Mother of God, that explains a lot! I asked Jerzy if there was a Catholic church around here we could go to sometime, and Piotr really shot me down in flames for asking. He said the Church was corrupt and I was a fool for 'feeding' corrupt priests. I just thought he was a staunch communist, but your take on it is far better."

Kazimierz added, "I never heard him say anything specific, but I can tell you that just before you joined us, when we had a couple of young boys come through the portal on the second time, he was always trying to tell them to stay away from de Arce. At the time it didn't register one way or the other, because I'd not really seen how he behaved towards the adults who'd arrived, but looking back now, he was definitely more protective of those lads. But why does that matter now, Danny?"

Danny grimaced. "Because I'm feeling that we're heading for a big fight, and if Piotr is with us lot, for whatever reason, then that only leaves Ulryk with Mikhail and de Arce, and that has to be good. If the fists start flying, then I can see Mikhail going after Jerzy to get even. That leaves Ulryk to pick on who he chooses first, but if Piotr had been with him then he could have taken a swing or two at you guys, Dymek and Stefan, and that would mean Kazimierz and me to take Ulryk down, which in a straight fight wouldn't be too bad. But what if he turns that bloody gun on us? Because he's daft enough to do it!"

The three looked worried as the permutations of such a fight sunk in, blissfully unaware that they were being caught on camera by Bill and Nick from the wood.

However, it was once the portal opened that things got ugly. De Arce did his usual performance with the incense and chanting while waving the smoking Palo Santo about, and as much as anything like this could have a normality it, seemed to be it. Yet no sooner had the portal fully opened then the priest from the village was there almost screaming in panic. Danny wasn't in the church as yet, but the tone in the man's voice made him look in.

For the first time he saw the portal fully open and it made him gasp. It was like looking through a fine veil of water, as if from behind a waterfall, but the land beyond it was as clear as anything and what he saw wasn't good. Smoke was rising from something burning and it looked horribly like it was the houses on the outskirts of the settlement.

"What's he saying?" Jerzy demanded for the second

time of de Arce.

"He says that the sea-wolves have come. Who are they?" He sniffed disparagingly. "He's no doubt lying to cheat us."

"You fucking idiot!" Jerzy snapped. "Look! Do you think they'd burn their own homes down just for us? Your reach might be long, de Arce, but even those poor fools don't think you're going to come through the portal at them."

"I told them God would smite them if they did not do my bidding," de Arce sneered, "and it looks as though he has."

Unable to bear it any longer, Danny stepped into the church saying, "You bloody idiot, they mean Vikings! This is a Viking raid! Close the damned thing down before we get twenty hairy-arsed marauders throwing themselves through it and trying to cut us down!"

"Get out!" de Arce screamed, and Danny retreated, but not before signalling Kazimierz forward.

"I'd get ready to fire that thing," he told him and Piotr, who had the other AK74. "Bloody de Arce won't close the portal and there's a Viking war-band in the village on the other side."

"How do you know?" Piotr demanded.

Hardly able to say that he'd read a lot to a man who'd never picked up a book in his life, Danny tutted and said, "I've been watching that new TV series *Vikings*, you dumb-arse! And that's what they get called, the Vikings that is – sea-wolves."

Insanely that satisfied Piotr. Clearly if it was on TV it must be true. Kazimierz on the other hand had taken one look at Danny's face and knew this was serious. He was enough of a realist to know that in the confines of the church, if the Viking warriors got in, then it would be hand

Time's Bloodied Gold

to hand fighting, because there would be no way they could use the guns without mowing down their own in the process.

The next thing was a call of alarm from Jerzy and the sound of a scuffle, at which Kazimierz and Piotr tore inside. Danny caught a glimpse of a man in leather and ring-mail, right there in the church, screaming at de Arce and trying to hack at him with a sword which looked as though it was lethally sharp. The word he kept shouting took a moment to catch, and then Danny realised he must be shouting, "murderer!" Well he'd got that right, if not necessarily for the right reasons, and Danny half hoped that he'd cleave de Arce in two right there and then. Certainly Jerzy was keeping the man at bay by dancing nimbly around him, and landing some serious unarmed-combat kicks and punches while dodging the sword blade, but he wasn't exactly defending de Arce either. However, Danny had the feeling that the warrior wasn't a Viking but one of the Anglo-Saxons, and he clearly thought that de Arce had summoned the Vikings to his village, and that he was cutting the head off the snake by killing what he no doubt thought of as the Devil's priest.

Then the watery veil parted and three men charged through screaming like they'd emerged from the depths of Hell, and also brandishing swords although much more rough and ready ones. Kazimierz and Piotr opened fire without hesitation, taking the three down, but another two were on their heels and one made it to just outside of the church door before one of Kazimierz's more controlled bursts took him down. Immediately Ulryk and Mikhail pounced on him and dragged him back inside, throwing him and the other corpses back through the portal even as Piotr sprayed it with another burst of bullets. Then as the Anglo-Saxon warrior faltered and almost tripped as he turned to try and see what had made the alien sound of the automatic fire, Mikhail was drawing a wicked knife and sliding it between the warrior's ribs with a practiced move that made Danny shudder. That wasn't the first time he'd done that for certain, and how often was he toting that damned knife about with him?

There was no time to think about that, though. Now, first one then another man came through the portal, clearly the villagers going by the now familiar poor clothing. Stefan and Dymek grabbed a man each and hauled him outside, and then Danny found himself looking at a poor lad who couldn't have been above fifteen.

"Come on, son," he said gently, putting a firm arm around the pitifully thin shoulders. "Let's get you out of here."

However the lad was almost out of his wits and shaking like a leaf, and by the church porch Danny paused, thinking to let him catch his breath now that he was far enough from the more violent members of the gang. It was as he looked down at the lad that his eye caught something. It had been right back on the first time he'd been here that he'd scribbled that doodle on the board, but now it was altered, and then he saw the B.S., a tiny prick of a red laser light flickered on and off, and suddenly his guts churned.

Belting around the porch and throwing up everything he'd eaten, it was all Danny could do not to weep in relief. Bill was here! Someone had finally answered his prayers! It didn't matter if it was only Bill on his own – and going by the fact that the cavalry wasn't piling in, he must be – just knowing that his old boss was out there and had his back made everything feel that bit better.

Letting the others pat down the three men and reassure de Arce that something was in their clothing, he was more concerned now to get the three refugees from the past back

Time's Bloodied Gold

to the farm and away from Mikhail and Ulryk, both of whom seemed horribly pumped up by the fight. At least it gave him the chance to scribble his mobile number on a scrap of paper and drop it not far from the cars, because he couldn't be sure, but he thought he saw someone moving in the woods. Not Bill, but surely someone with him?

Climbing into the Defender he was glad to see the back of de Arce, who was still crowing over having the Anglo-Saxon warrior's sword – something Danny found sickening. That man had been fighting valiantly to save his village and he hadn't deserved to die with Mikhail's knife in his back, even if his chances against the Vikings as one against seven had been thin. Nor had he deserved to be thrown back through the portal like a meat carcass with his enemies.

Being in the vehicle with Jerzy, Danny risked saying, "If we go back next month, I wouldn't expect anything, you know."

Jerzy gave a tight-lipped grimace. "No, I don't think there will. Fucking de Arce will want to try, though. I think we've bled those people white anyway, but you were right, Danny, those were homes burning."

Then Kazimierz spoke up from beside Danny. "Will it even open up if the church gets burned down? I don't remember much from school history, but that church through the other side always looked like it was mostly wood to me."

Danny agreed. "This church we go to is later – it says so on the notice board – so something happened to the original church."

Jerzy gave him a quick glance. "Does it? Hmmm. ...I may warn Reznik that this might be the last consignment." Then a wolfish grin spread across his face and Danny knew that he had just decided de Arce's fate.

Chapter 18

late February

Back at the farmhouse Danny's emotions were all over the place. One moment he'd be feeling huge surges of relief that someone was finally taking his part, and the next absolute grief at the fate of the poor folk back in that village through the portal. God only knew how they were going to survive now that the one man who looked like a professional fighter had been killed. Had they changed the fate of that village down through time, too, not just in that one period? That was an awful weight on Danny's conscience.

Luckily the saner ones of the group were not much better. Dymek and Stefan were far more solicitous towards the three they'd brought back with them, and Danny caught them furtively wiping the odd tear away; while in an unprecedented show of feeling, Piotr had stood shoulder to shoulder with Kazimierz and refused to let either Ulryk or Mikhail anywhere near them, blocking the way into the old stable where the refugees were held.

"You leave them be!" Piotr snarled at Mikhail. "This was supposed to be just about the money! I don't want some of what I've earned going to the fucking Vatican and I'm not letting some pervert priest anywhere near these either!"

"Stupid country boy!" Mikhail snapped back, but when he looked at Kazimierz something in his expression made him decide that caution was the better part of valour, and he stamped off to the old farmhouse and de Arce's company.

Coming to them from the smaller, more modern house that the gang used, Danny found himself feeling some sympathy for Piotr. Thick as two short planks he might be, but if he'd been brutalised as a child then it wasn't his fault that he was such a thug now.

"Good for you," Danny said to him softly, and was surprised to see Piotr's expression soften from his usual scowl.

"My grandfather was a priest when the Russians rolled over my country in World War Two, and the Church was outlawed under Communist rule," Piotr told him and spat on the yard in disgust. "Miserable coward forced himself onto my grandmother and had everyone in the village cover up for him. He fucked my uncles when they were small, and then when they and my mother had children, he did the same to us. Bastard! And everyone was too scared of him to tell on him. Even then he kept telling them that they'd rot in Hell if they defied a priest."

Piotr's thick rural accent made him hard to follow sometimes, but not now. He was spitting every word out clearly and with venom. "I only agreed to this because I was already with Jerzy when we found that fucking priest. ...Thought he was just some crazy man at first. So he knew the mass? So what? Must be millions of us all over Europe who still know the mass in Latin. But two nights ago Ulryk tells me that Mikhail and that fucker tortured that last poor bastard who survived a few months ago, and two more before then. Why, eh? No reason. We wasn't going to get any more money out of them. He did it just 'cause he could. Did it to get off on it, playing like a cat with a mouse. Bastard!"

This was music to Danny's ears. If they got the gang into custody, Piotr testifying to this could help no end. It didn't matter if anyone believed him about where they'd come from, if there was a scrap of forensic evidence that there'd been a body in that workshop that went up in smoke, then his testimony would stand.

"All I want now is my money," Piotr was saying. "I'm gonna find myself some nice place in the sun and drink myself silly. I ain't never going back to that bloody village, that's for sure. My cousins are all gone – except for the two who hung themselves. There's nobody back there I ever want to see again. I still got my fake passport. I'm on the next plane to the sun I can get on!"

Danny patted him on the arm and went past him into the stable.

"How are they?" he asked Stefan and was surprised to see his face more worried than ever.

"They're not bad, all things considering," he replied, "but this one's just said that three women and two girls came through as the portal was closing. They're still at the church!"

"Oh Christ!" Danny gasped. "Are you sure? Are they sure they survived?"

Stefan gave a shrugged. "He said the word 'wif'. I'm pretty sure he meant wife, and he's just mimed two small children."

"Bloody hell! Okay, you stay here with them, Dymek. Stefan, you come with me since you seem to have the best grasp of what they're saying of any of us." As he hurried out he told Piotr, "Can you stay here and keep a watch on these? Try to keep Ulryk and Mikhail away from them. I need Kazimierz to come with me to see Jerzy."

Time's Bloodied Gold

They found the gang leader in the kitchen going over the spoils. "How come we didn't bring the others with us?" Danny demanded without preamble.

Jerzy blinked in surprise. "What others?"

"Were you the last out of the church?"

"No, de Arce was as usual. What the fuck are you on about?"

Danny threw his hands in the air in exasperation. "He didn't tell you that three women followed through the portal?"

Jerzy jumped like he'd touched a bare electric wire. "Holy crap, no! Do you mean there are witnesses still up there?"

"From what Stefan just got out of them, yes," and Danny gestured to Stefan to repeat what he'd told him. "Can I take these two and go back and check? If we take the two Defenders we can put them in and bring them back here if they are there."

"Go!" Jerzy said with alacrity.

Kazimierz grabbed the Defenders' keys and threw a set to Danny, and the three of them ran out and piled into the two vehicles. With Kazimierz in the lead they tore through the hazy early morning back to St Michael's. They stopped a little further back than they had last night, and it gave Danny a chance to glance down to where he'd thrown the scrap of paper with his number on. It had gone! Furtively he checked his mobile and saw he'd had one missed call which must have come through when he hadn't heard it over the Defender's rattling engine, a call from a number he knew as well as his own – Bill had got the message!

At the church porch they found three women huddled together, wide-eyed with terror, and two little girls clinging to them, too stunned to even cry. They looked up at the three men with huge, blank eyes and began shuffling backwards into the corner of the porch, looking back to the interior of the church and then at the three men in equal fear.

"It's okay, we're not going to hurt you," Danny said gently, holding his hands out but keeping them low so that they would see that not only did he not have any weapons, but that he was unlikely to hit them either. He crouched down in front of them. "Your man ...oh bloody hell, Stefan, do you have any idea what husband might be in their language?"

Stefan shrugged, but said hopefully, "I think he said he was the father of the children. That word was 'fæder'. And I think he said another of the women was his sister. He certainly said 'broðer' and 'sweoster', and from the German I learned in school and my English, if these are Anglo-Saxons then I think the chances are that they mean brother and sister. If it's any help, 'husband' in German is 'mann'?"

Danny pointed to the two cowering little girls and said, "Fæder."

How did, 'your husband is here,' go in German?

"Ihr Mann ist hier," he said cautiously. Was that right? It seemed like they'd grasped something.

He held out a cautious hand. "Come!"

It was hardly subtle but he seemed to be getting through to them.

He waved a hand generally around and tried again, "Hier nicht gut. It's no good here, it's dangerous. Come!"

He stood up and backed away a little out of the porch. "Let's give them a bit of room, lads, but not enough that they can bolt for it."

Very slowly the three women came out, but keeping the girls huddled between them. With cautious steps they got along the path to the cars, but Danny knew getting them into the Defenders was going to be a nightmare.

Time's Bloodied Gold

"Kazimierz, can you go ahead and get the doors open? I think we're going to have to just herd them into one and take a risk on being spotted. We'll never get seatbelts on them whatever happens, and the way this is going, we won't be able to separate them into two vehicles either."

Kazimierz nodded. "I was thinking that, too. You take them and have Stefan with you in the front in case one of them tries to grab you while you're driving. I'll follow you in case one of them manages to get out and needs chasing." He took off with the keys and jogged ahead, and Danny heard the *clunk* of the Defenders' locks opening before they got to the clearing.

It took some persuading to get the women and girls into the Defender, including much getting in and out on Danny and Stefan's parts to prove that they could sit down and get out again. Kazimierz did whisper, though, "I've put the child locks on," which was probably a good idea. Them opening the doors whilst at speed just didn't bear thinking about.

Even shutting the doors as gently as they could nonetheless frightened their passengers, and when Danny started the engine one of the women fainted in terror.

"It's no good, I'm going to have to go round and get in the estate bit of the back," Stefan sighed. "I can't turn round enough in the passenger seat. I'm better off right in the back where I can lean over and catch hold of them if they look like making a grab for you," and he jumped out and round to the rear of the vehicle.

Opening the big rear door was a risk, but the sudden increase in noise from the exhaust spooked the women so much that the two remaining conscious ones shrank away from it, instead of trying to get out through it.

It was a nerve-wracking drive back to the farm, with Danny sweating at every turn that there would be a car passing who would look in and wonder why there was a man in the back of the Defender holding onto the shoulders of two women passengers. God help him if a patrol car should pass, because they'd be all over them in a shot for not wearing seat belts, and then everything else would come out. There were a few very early commuters on the roads, but they were all bleary-eyed and too busy sipping from their portable mugs of coffee to take much notice of anything except what was straight in front of them.

They actually managed to get back to the farm without any disasters, which Danny thought was little short of a miracle. On the last stretch of road coming back out of Tenbury he'd let Kazimierz overtake him, and by the time he reached the farmyard the gate was open and he could drive straight in, with Kazimierz shutting it behind him and then running to help get the women out. What didn't help was the appearance of Mikhail and de Arce from up the road. Whatever else the women were afraid of, he was certainly a significant terror they remembered seeing from the portal, and they immediately began screaming, which brought Jerzy tearing out of the house.

"Mother of God, you found them!" he gasped, then rounded on Mikhail and de Arce. "Will you two piss off! You're not helping. Get out of here, de Arce, before half the neighbourhood hears them!"

"If they are true Christians they have nothing to worry about from me," de Arce declared with a haughty sniff.

"*Everybody* has cause to be worried by *you*!" snapped Jerzy. "You're a fucking liability!"

"Without me you wouldn't have got the mon..."

"...We know! You're the fucking man with the mojo! But you're also the fuckwit who could get us all arrested. Now piss off!"

Time's Bloodied Gold

Mercifully all of the rest of them except for Ulryk had now formed a semi-circle around the women and children, and as if herding cows, they managed to shoo them into the stable where there were sudden wails of relief as the women found their men. De Arce and Mikhail stood like statues watching, but at least on the other side of the main yard gate, while Ulryk lounged insolently against the inner side of the metal five-barred barrier, almost defying Jerzy to demand that he help.

"Well done you three," Jerzy said when they had bolted the stable door, and all of those from the church were safely contained. "Christ, that was close! Come on, let's go inside, we've got coffee on the brew."

Yet at the door to the kitchen, Mikhail had come to stand in their way with an argumentative look on his face and with Ulryk at his elbow, clearly thinking he was showing the right sort of support. De Arce was gone, presumably back to his nest in the big house.

"Why did you bring them back?" Mikahil demanded, his jaw shoved out belligerently and a scowl on his face. "That's more bodies we've got to get rid of!"

Jerzy turned to him in fury, but Danny put a hand on his arm and stepped in front of him, coming nose to nose with Mikhail.

"I've just about had it with you. All you ever do is complain, but you don't *do* anything, do you? Who took those three stinking corpses into Worcester, eh? Wasn't you, was it? It was Stefan, Dymek and me. And has it been plastered all over the news? No it hasn't. Just a small note in the paper to say that the bodies of three tramps were found having died of the cold. So remind me again, who disposed of the bodies?"

He leaned in as if straining to hear Mikhail's reply, and then plunged on with,

"No? Wasn't you, was it! And that pervert up the road wants to go back to the church next month, doesn't he?" Mikhail was wrong-footed by the switch in subject, as he understood it.

"'Course he does!"

"Well then it might be an idea if it wasn't crawling with cops and forensic teams, wouldn't it, you dumb-arse! Those women weren't going anywhere fast, and sooner rather than later they'd have died of lack of water, never mind food. And you really think that *nobody* would go there in a whole month? Nobody? Not a solitary soul, not even the farmer checking on those sodding sheep in the field? Somebody who'd notice the stink of five bodies rotting in the church porch? It's lambing season you stupid knob! And those ewes were fat with lambs – even I know that, and I'm a townie!"

Mikhail's expression was going blacker by the second. He knew he'd made a fool of himself, but in his dim brain it was Danny making a fool of him again in front of Jerzy.

And now Jerzy spoke, the edge having been taken off his fury by Danny's words, but his voice had turned to icy anger. "You never fucking think, do you, Mikhail? Jesus, if they ever bring in brain transplants you'll be worth a fortune, because your bugger's never been used! All the others saw this – even Piotr." The big man had luckily gone on into the kitchen already, because that was hardly a compliment, and at the moment Danny was glad to have him on their side. "We'll do what we've always done – we keep them here and feed them, and if they survive, then we'll worry about what to do with them."

Mikhail turned on his heels and snarled over his shoulder, "You're a fool, Jerzy. You're letting these fools rule you. You're no leader. You should drown those five

Time's Bloodied Gold

like useless kittens and slit the men's throats, they've served their purpose."

Even by the gang's standards that was cold, and Danny was pleased to see the shock on all but Ulryk and Jerzy's faces, and although Ulryk plodded off in Mikhail's wake, even Jerzy had an expression of distaste curling his lips.

"Bloody animal," he muttered, then waved the others inside.

Clustered around the big old table, they all nursed mugs of coffee silently, until Jerzy cleared his throat.

"What I'm about to say never gets repeated to Ulryk or Mikahil, okay? If anyone feels they can't manage that, then go out now." Nobody moved. "Right ...you all know what happened last night. That monster, de Arce, thinks that if he stamps his foot hard enough that those people will still bring him stuff the next time. I think that's bollocks. I think Danny and Kazimierz are right – it'll be amazing if that damned thing even opens up next time, and if it does all we'll see is the ruins of that village. There'll be no jewels coming through. Any arguments with that?"

There was a general shaking of heads.

"Right, then I'm making this one the last consignment. I've called Resnik and told him that, and why – well as much as I could without him thinking I've gone crazy. In a couple of days' time I'm taking Danny and going down to Bristol again. Ideally I'd like you with me, Kazimierz, but I think I need you to be here more. I don't trust Mikhail anymore, and if he decides to go on a killing spree while I'm gone you have my permission to shoot the mad fucker. You're the best shot of all of us. You can do it with the least noise and mess. And then when we leave we're leaving the prisoners behind.

"What I'm *not* doing is leaving bodies behind with their throats cut or worse. It's one thing if they die of natural causes. There's nothing I can do about that. But I'm buggered if I'm rotting in a Polish jail for murder, because make no mistake, if we're accused of that we'll be sent back – it won't be an easy number in a British prison for us."

It was a pretty cold way of looking at things, Danny thought, but as long as it saved the prisoners' lives he wasn't about to object. With any luck he'd be able to get a message to Bill as soon as they left, and get Social Services up here within the day.

Come Friday, Danny was back behind the wheel of his VW and heading back down to Bristol, but with a significant change – this time Jerzy was sitting in the front on the way down, not just coming back as the last time, leaving de Arce smouldering in the back on his own. The goods, including the sword were in the boot, carefully wrapped up in blankets.

"That sword is an amazing thing," Danny said to make conversation, as they joined the stream of traffic snaking into Bristol. "The workmanship on it is unbelievable."

That brought a small smile to Jerzy's face. "Yes, it is, isn't it? Who'd have thought they could do such inlaying and chasing without modern tools? Those rubies must be worth a fortune all by themselves. I've had to tell Reznik several times over that the sword as a whole piece will be even more valuable. I don't want some clown prizing the jewels off it."

"It could be next to impossible to fly that into the States, though," Danny warned.

Jerzy nodded. "I'd thought of that. If we have to, it will go by sea to the West Indies in a yacht Reznik sometimes uses, and then into Florida by another boat. It might take some time to get the money through for that one, but it'll be worth the wait." Then he rolled his eyes back towards de

Time's Bloodied Gold

Arce, and Danny knew he'd probably had to explain this many times over to the inquisitor. But then Jerzy also winked, and that confused Danny. That implied that he had something up his sleeve.

When they got to the tall terraced house and got ushered into Reznik's presence, Danny knew something was up. De Arce might have taken Reznik's effusive greeting as nothing more than enthusiasm for the money this cache was going to earn him, but Danny sensed there was something more, and he knew there had been several calls to Bristol from Jerzy in the evenings. Unless he was so stressed he was wildly off the mark, there was some backroom deal going on here.

"My dear bishop," Reznik greeted him, "come, we have the link already set up."

Once more the worried face of Monsignor Montefiori appeared on the Skype link.

"Monsignor," Reznik greeted him. "We have a need to split this consignment."

"I really do not see this as necessary," de Arce protested, and got a fierce glare from Reznik.

"Really, my dear bishop, do you not? Have you been through our customs lately? No, of course you haven't, because your contacts liaised with us to get you into England by a back door that isn't watched. But I can most definitely assure you that you would not normally be allowed to walk through customs with a sword in your hands. It would be taken from you and you would not get it back. Not even I could get it back for you once it had gone that way, and you do not want that, do you?"

There was a gasp from Montefiori. "A sword? You mean a real one?"

"A real one with sharp edges," Jerzy said dryly.

"Obispo de Arce!" Montefiori gulped. "No! I cannot get a sword through to the States for you! It's impossible! They have metal detectors and all sorts of high tech equipment. It would be seized the moment it touched American soil. You do not understand how they fear the Muslim threat. Their security is getting tighter by the day. There is only so much I can do no matter how much you threaten me."

De Arce sneered. "And soon we will show them how to deal with that, Monsignor. With the money I have and the money we have sent to Rome there will be more than enough to start a crusade of our own."

Danny heard Jerzy's soft, "Fucking hell!" at the word 'crusade', and he felt the same. This man wasn't just crazy, he was dangerous.

However Reznik simply said with oily smoothness, "All in good time, my dear bishop. You can start your world war in your own good time. For now we need to get the finances sorted, and for that you need me, and I say that the sword will have to go by sea. There is no other way. I have I played you false yet?"

Grudgingly, de Arce shook his head.

"Good, then if I may...? Monsignor, you may expect a delivery by the usual means in a few days. If you can arrange for it to be taken across to the Bahamas as you have done before, my contacts will relieve you of the items and take them across to Florida. There are somewhat fewer than before, so they will be easier to make into a smaller package."

"That's good," Montefiori said with no attempt to disguise his relief. "The last lot were ...difficult!"

"But you get paid handsomely for your efforts," Reznik reminded him with the air of a weary parent with a child, then the shock on his face seemed totally genuine when Montefiori said witheringly,

"Paid? I haven't seen so much as a cent yet."

Reznik turned to de Arce, appalled. "Have you no idea at all of how to do business? You cannot expect your people to keep silent if they do not share in some of the rewards."

"His reward will come in the service of the Church," de Arce snapped. "And I will be over there soon to supervise what comes next, so if Monsignor Montefiori does not wish an experienced inquisitor to test his faith, he had better do as he is told."

Montefiori's shudder was visible to Reznik, Jerzy and Danny, who were all looking at the screen as de Arce turned haughtily away.

"Do not worry, Monsignor, this will soon be over," Reznik reassured the man far away, and again there was that wink.

Then they were making arrangements for how the courier would come to Montefiori, and Danny realised that the Haitian priest had no more idea of which flights these people were coming in on than he did. At least Reznik was security conscious that far, which ought to have been a relief to Danny that the world and his wife didn't know of their arrangements, but it wasn't. What he did see on the desk, though, was a pile of bank statements, and a quick glance and a snapped photo with his phone again got him an account number and the bank Reznik used. If he was going to help himself to a retirement fund, then it would be that much easier if he opened an account with the same bank as Reznik, because he knew how odd banks could be sometimes about shifting large amounts of cash out of their own accounts to one of their rival's. He must get a glimpse of which bank Jerzy was using, too. That could be helpful.

However, just now Danny was gestured to lead de Arce downstairs, but as he did so he heard Jerzy say to Reznik in Polish,

"You heard that. Do you see now why we have to resolve this ourselves?"

And then Reznik's reply of, "Oh indeed I do. Under other circumstance I would question doing ...*hmmm*, business ...in this way, but a man who would start wars is very bad for men in our position. I think your solution now is the best one, with the added proviso that we make some provision for the Monsignor to ensure his silence. *Tsk*! To not pay a man who is doing you such a service speaks of a man who thinks fear alone rules men's lives, but what do you do when a man feels he has nothing left to lose? It is not the subtle way to coerce someone, and all too often it backfires on you. Greed is so much simpler."

Chapter 19

Danny – Wednesday to Friday

At least his services to Jerzy allowed Danny to ask for, and get, the chance for a day at the flat. Looking forward to doing nothing more than falling into his own bed without having to have every nerve at full stretch, Danny was horrified to get to his front door and then realise it was unlocked. Oh Christ! What had happened?

Edging the door open nervously, he peered in and listened. Not a peep, so nobody was in there unless they were being very quiet. He slid in and shut the front door, realising that it was on the catch but that the lock was intact. No-one had broken it to get in, and there was almost a sense of someone taking care over it. That didn't ring true for a burglary. Then he looked in the bedroom and saw his clothes strewn about. Okay, so it certainly looked like a terrier had dug its way through his bedroom drawers, but something still felt just that bit off about it all? It almost wasn't messy enough.

Still moving with care, Danny went into the bathroom next and saw the cistern lid askew. Using a piece of toilet roll to handle the lid with, he looked in and sighed with relief to see the cocaine had gone. Had someone come to get it? Maybe, but then why the need to make things look like a burglary? They'd have been told where it was, come in, grabbed it and scarpered. There'd be no need to rough up the flat.

He moved on to the lounge, and it was when he turned around and looked at his empty bookcase that his face broke into a grin. Bill! It had to be Bill who'd been here. Only he would have known to take his favourite books away for safe keeping.

"Oh, you star!" Danny gasped out loud in relief.

He must have come here looking for him, and thought how to leave a sign only Danny himself would recognise. Well the books were like a shining beacon. And if Bill had found the cocaine then he'd dealt with it, and in that moment Danny knew what his old boss had meant him to understand. He'd faked the flat being turned over so that Danny had an excuse to present to the gang. Knowing Bill, he'd probably wondered whether Danny would come back alone or with one of the others, and had left the mess to convince them.

Then Danny had another thought and went to his secret stash in the bedroom. The SD cards were gone! But the cover had been carefully screwed back on, so could he assume that Bill had taken the evidence in? God, he hoped so! Had this come on the back of him sending stuff in with that dippy DC? If so then he was feeling better about this already. But then another thought hit him. Why had nobody messaged him if that was the case?

He checked his phone, then pulled his laptop out from under the divan bed and switched on. Yet there were no carefully worded emails waiting for him, and that made him sit back and stare into space as he thought frantically. If Bill had faith in him but no-one else did, then he was still in a terrible conundrum. Could he ever go back to his old job?

Had he known that at that very moment Bill was sitting talking with Joe at the *Green Man*, and that a rocket had been lit beneath the taskforce on his behalf, then he might have felt very differently. Instead he came to the conclusion that he should stick to his old plan – he would go into Gloucester to the German bank there that Resnik used and

Time's Bloodied Gold

open an account. That way, whatever happened, he was prepared.

Dumping stuff approximately back into the drawers, he fell into bed early and slept well for the first time in weeks. The next morning he drove down to Gloucester and presented himself at the bank. His cover was that his company was expanding into Germany, and he wanted to be able to access his own money more easily than he could with an English bank. He'd all but skinned out his true current account to get a decent sum together to deposit into the account, and even so the bank were a little wary when he couldn't produce a payslip to confirm that regular funds were going to be going into the account. In the end he sorted it by settling for a savings account, saying that he was primarily interested in being able to withdraw cash anyway, rather than using a card. At least he'd been at the Leominster flat for long enough to have things like utilities bills to the address with his name on, and he'd been provided with a driving license as Danny Sawaski, so proving his identity was easy enough.

What was less pleasant was then driving around looking for a place to dump two bodies, for the January men were sickening like all the others and two of them were already dead and decomposing in the old sheep pen at the farm, carefully covered by a heavy smothering of straw. Where the hell could he put these? Even a man as thick as Piotr would raise his eyebrows at sticking them in the subway like the previous three, because that was asking for someone to wonder why men kept turning up there in particular. He did wonder about the old riverside pump house down by Cripplegate Park in Worcester, but discounted that because it was now very securely locked up after someone had got in there while drunk and had drowned.

He was also in more of a quandary over whether he wanted them found so easily this time. If he was suspect, then maybe it would be better if the bodies didn't come to light until he'd found out how things stood a bit better? Of course, if he was just getting paranoid from being under strain for so long, then it would be a simple matter to bring others to where the bodies lay at a later point. But if his reception was a lot cooler, and he got the sense someone was just itching to find something to pin on him, well then the bodies would stay put until they came to light by other means. For all of his faith in Bill, equally he knew that his old boss' reach only went so far, and that protecting him from a murder charge wasn't possible.

However, it was no small matter to find a place where they could pull up one of the Defenders and haul two body bags out where few people would see them, and which was close to somewhere where there was the kind of place he was looking for. In the end he decided on the Powick roundabout. It was a big thing with trees on it and a hidden dip in the middle. What was better was that there was no need for any pedestrian to ever go onto it, and with the daytime traffic it handled, it would be downright dangerous for anyone to try. The only time anyone went there was when the local council cut the grass, and they were a long way away from then as yet. And if there were any strange smells then they might be blamed on the sewage works not far up the river from there. He knew only too well that that got smelly at times and could be smelled on the west side of the river when the wind was in the right direction. The only down side to this plan was the mobile food van which parked in one of the nearby lay-bys until the early hours. However, Danny thought a simple scouting mission would soon determine when the owner of that gave up and went home, and in all likelihood he wouldn't be out early in the week when there were no late-night revellers to call in and stop for a burger.

Therefore he returned to the farm on Thursday evening in a much better frame of mind and told Jerzy of his plan for the bodies.

"I think that sounds a good plan," Jerzy agreed. "If this place is so rarely visited by people it gives us plenty of time." Then he dropped the bombshell. "But I want you to do it tomorrow night."

"Tomorrow?" Danny was aghast. This fucked up all of his plans! "Why tomorrow night? Monday would be so much better. The food van won't be there for a start off. And on a Friday night there'll be more traffic than in the early part of the week."

However, Jerzy drew him further off to one side. "We don't have that much time. Something's wrong with Reznik. I can just feel it! He rang while you were away. Our consignment got seized along with his drug couriers when they arrived in Florida."

"Oh crap!"

"Crap, indeed, but Reznik is panicking. He should be keeping calm and simply rerouting the couriers who are here for the time being. I think what you were told at the house is right. He's on the way out. Well I'm not going down with him, that's for sure! One of my contacts within Tomek's gang texted me. He says that Reznik has been called down to London to meet Mr Oczkowski. That makes me think that he might not be coming back. Mr Oczkowski isn't known for his patience – actually he's an utter bastard. Reznik is likely to be drinking the dirty water of the Thames when he gets down there, and floating out to sea with the next tide, if I'm any judge of character. So I want us to be ready to pack up and leave at a moment's notice."

"What about the people we have here?" Danny protested.

"We leave them! Look Danny, as refugees they'll be looked after, and while we'll be on the wanted list, it's not the same as murder. But for that to happen and the UK cops to not hunt us as killers, there can't be any bodies about the place. So those two bodies have to go *now*! Even if the last of those three or any of the new lot dies before they're discovered, at worst it would be manslaughter if any of us were caught, but to me it's the intensity of the search that matters. I want time to get away!"

"Me too!" Danny admitted, feeling that it was an understandable enough emotion to confess to under the circumstances. Obviously he couldn't say that he didn't want to be done as a crooked copper, but even in his sales rep' guise he could be anxious to avoid jail.

Then an awful thought came to him and he had to ask, "How soon are you thinking of going?"

"Early next week," Jerzy said without hesitation. "Or at least that's when some of us will be going. Not de Arce. He can stay here and rot for all I care. Once Reznik is blown there's nothing he can give away, and I doubt he ever took notice of anything like an address even so. If they can get anything usable out of him I'll be amazed. Mikhail can take his pick. I'm done with shovelling him out of the shit all the time. If he thinks de Arce's God can save him, then he can get on with it. The same goes for Ulryk. He was wished onto me by Tomek, and he's been a bloody liability ever since. I'll give the rest of you chance to make your escape, though."

"What about you?" Danny had to ask.

Now Jerzy became serious and drew Danny into the kitchen away from the others. "I need you. Do you think you could get into Reznik's computers if we go down there?"

"In what way? I mean, I can open them up, but it depends on what you want me to look for?"

"The bank accounts. Can you access them?"

Now Danny was really torn. Dare he tell Jerzy that he had the passwords to both Resnik and de Arce's accounts? However his pause allowed Jerzy to add,

"If you can get me in, you can have your cut. I play fair with my men, and you've been an asset."

That really twisted the knife in Danny's guts. Here was Jerzy – supposedly the bad guy – offering to help him out, while his own team hadn't said a word to him in ages. Even Bill might be just being decent because that's what Bill was. It didn't mean that anyone else was backing him up.

Taking a deep breath, Danny said, "I've got Resnik's password. I've got the password to his bank account and the number, so I can track the bank's website from the computer's memory."

Jerzy's face broke into a broad smile. "I knew you were the right sort! Right, we get rid of those stinking corpses tomorrow night – and I'm sorry but you're going to have to go because you know where you're talking about – and then on Saturday you and I are going to Bristol."

He turned to go but Danny plucked at his sleeve. "I'm sorry, Jerzy, but I have to ask this: did you plant any cocaine at my flat?"

"What? Why would I do something like that?"

His obvious incredulity was proof enough for Danny. "I didn't think it was you, but I had to check," and he told Jerzy of Kazimierz's warning about Ulryk and Mikhail, and their apparent determination to get himself into deep trouble.

"The thing is," he concluded, "I got back to my flat

and it had been broken into. I think it was just a casual thing – those bloody doors wouldn't hold back a hamster let alone some teenager hoping to find something to sell so that he could get a fix. Well if he snorts all that was in the package I found he'll only do it once. He'll be found floating in the river or in a ditch somewhere. I don't think it was anyone more serious – such as whoever Ulryk got the drugs off coming to find their gear if he strong-armed it off some kid. I'm just glad it's gone!"

Jerzy scowled, glaring at the wall through to where Mikhail and Ulryk were sitting in the main room as if his looks could incinerate them on the spot. "Fucking idiots! Fucking *stupid* idiots! I told them right at the start: no drugs!" He saw Danny's blink of surprise. "The ones who deal never seem to be able to resist trying their own products," he said with a shudder. "Give me an old-fashioned criminal any day. You know where you are with them. Druggies are way too fucking unpredictable. You're always on your toes in case someone close to them decides to stick a knife through your slats to make a point, or to launch a takeover bid. And it's the cops' big target. Can't blame them for that. The low-lifes at the bottom end of the chain are a bloody nuisance with their endless petty crimes, and what they do when they're hyped up can be the stuff of nightmares. But if you want to do business they're a fucking liability, because they always attract the wrong sort of attention. I told this lot that right at the start. No drugs. No taking, no selling. You don't go near them while you're with me. Those two fuck-wits in there just broke the golden rule, and I don't care what excuses they try to cook up – although I believe what you've told me Danny. They've just forfeited any right to a cut of what's coming, and if they don't like it, that's tough."

Time's Bloodied Gold

Bill ~ Friday

Bill woke on the Friday morning finding it hard to believe that it was barely a week since this rollercoaster ride had begun. On the one hand he was beyond relieved that he'd been able to get Danny seen in a better light. If he came into contact with anyone from the force now he was far safer than he had been. On the other hand, Bill felt oddly deflated. What was he to do now? If he'd been at work he'd still have been rushing around wrapping the case up, preparing all the evidence ready for when it came to court, but none of the normal stuff applied here. Yet doing nothing today didn't feel right.

He'd managed to wring out of Williams a promise that a forensics team would be dispatched without delay up to the church, and he'd hissed perhaps harder than he should have at Williams as they'd stood in front of the assembled officers, so that Jason had been appointed to go out there today. Could he go too? He didn't want Jason to think that he was standing on his heels out there because he didn't trust him, but equally, maybe he could answer some questions straightaway? That pretty much decided it for him, and he got up and had a hurried breakfast.

At the main road below the church he found the team and Jason standing around the collection of vans and cars, all scratching their heads and peering at maps.

"It's a bugger to find," Bill called cheerily as he pulled the big Citroen up alongside them. "Get in and follow me." That was good – they'd needed him here even to find the church, so he could hardly be accused of interfering.

Just below the turning place Bill pulled in and got out, waving the others to park behind him.

"There's room to turn around up ahead," he told them,

"but only after you've swept the area. You'll get some good tyre prints of the vehicles up by the gate, and there might be other stuff up there too. I've only ever seen it in poor light."

Jason sidled up to him and asked with studied insouciance, "Came up here did you, Bill?"

However Bill was determined to be straight with his colleagues now. "I came up with an old friend on Monday night," he admitted. "It was the full moon, I'd talked it over with Charlie and Morag, and we all agreed that the chances of getting Williams to get folk out here at that point were nil. But at the same time, I was worried sick about Danny. His car had been seen after Christmas, but not him. If it was your DS," nodding towards the bonny Irish lass who worked with Jason, "would you have wanted to wait to see if you could find the right thing to get Williams moving?"

"Like fuck I would!" Jason admitted immediately. "If that had been Clara, what you've done would look like the patience of Buddha by comparison!"

Bill shrugged. "What you're calling patience was more to do with me having to start from scratch. Don't forget I was way out of the loop where Danny was concerned. I'd waved him off to the taskforce and thought that would be the last I saw of him for months until he came back covered in glory, and in a better frame of mind. So the fact that I hadn't seen him didn't mean much until Charlie called me up."

"Well bloody good for Charlie, that's all I can say!"

"Oh I'll second that! Now while we're out here, away from flapping ears who might get the wrong idea, I can tell you that he found a vehicle registration for me. I was up here last Monday with one of the county archaeologists, because he identified the church for me, and also he can move a bit faster than me at the moment. He got a look at a registration plate and when Charlie put it through the system it turned out to be some sort of Spanish priest who owns it. This is it," he said, handing Jason a slip of paper. "So can you get things moving for the lads to keep an eye open for this one as well as Danny's hire car?"

"Sure can. ...So what did you see up here?"

This was where things got tricky. Bill could hardly tell the whole truth on this and hope to be believed. "Well Nick and I got up here and set up in the woods over there. It's about the only place where you can see much of anything and still stay hidden. I'm not daft enough to try and take on a gang on my own, and what Williams said about them being armed and dangerous is all too true. They had a couple of what I think were AK74s, for God's sake! I was worried, not suicidal, so we stayed out of sight."

"Show me."

So while the rest of the team gathered evidence at the turning space, Bill led Jason off to where he and Nick had been.

"Hmm, I see what you mean," Jason agreed as they stood looking out at the church. "You can't see the back of it, can you?"

"No, not at all, and I think somebody was inside the church itself. There are signs of some kind of ritual going on in there, Jas', but don't ask me what. We saw men hanging around by those two big standing stones, and then the people they're trafficking just kind of appeared out of the night. Maybe they were back in the woods, I don't know. What we did see was the gang patting them down. I reckon they had the valuables sewn into their clothes, but Danny's the one who can shed light on where they were taken to. He mentioned Bristol in his texts to the taskforce, but we can hardly take the city apart brick by brick just based on that. We need Danny back and in one piece for more than just his sake, although that would be enough all by itself."

They went back and found that the team were already moving on to check the track up to the church.

"We've got some good tyre tracks," someone reported back to Jason, "and some cigarette butts. We should be able to do something with them."

When the SOCOs found the heap of cigarette butts by the stones they were positively joyful.

"How wonderfully considerate of them to leave us these," chuckled a white swathed girl, who looked barely old enough to be in senior school let alone a graduate. But she was fast enough in bagging up the samples and tagging them to go to be processed, and Bill knew this team would leave no stone unturned now they knew an officer's life might be hanging in the balance. These were good people and he had to trust them to do their jobs.

Inside the church they agreed that someone had been burning charcoal for incense at the scorch marks on the floor, but at that point Bill left them alone and took himself to perch on the most substantial of the railings out of the stiff breeze that was gusting up the small valley. He was going to be very careful not to prompt anyone too much, because if the time came when they were called upon to give expert testimony in court, they had to be able to say, "I found exhibit F," not be tied in knots by the defence team claiming that they had been directed to only look for specific evidence that pertained to their clients.

"Have you tried texting Danny?" Jason asked as he came over to tell Bill that the team had done as much as they could in the church.

"Not yet, although I haven't had the number he was using on this operation until a day or so back. And I must admit I was worried by the way he was never alone. I've

Time's Bloodied Gold

been trying to think of something to say that wouldn't endanger him. I have no idea what his cover is aside from the fact that he was posing as a computer parts and software rep', so I don't want him to have to explain my message just for getting it, if you see what I mean."

Jason considered that, then offered. "This is just a thought, but if he hasn't been blown by that dickhead Godden's messages, then I think you can safely say that he's managed to keep his phone semi-private. I'm not saying that he could take a call, but I reckon you could risk a text. Make it innocuous – you know, 'I hear things have been tough of late, fancy meeting for a pint?' That sort of thing. The kind of message any bloke might get from a mate."

Bill perked up at that. "That's a bloody good idea! I couldn't do it when I first started digging and I'd sort of forgotten that there might be a way now that I have a contact number for him." He didn't tell Jason how he'd got it. Let him think it was one of the things Joe had supplied up in Birmingham.

Pulling out his phone he keyed in, *Hi Danny, it's been a while, hear things have been tough for you? Fancy meeting up for a pint? Leave it you to say where and when. Bill.*

That should do it. Danny could cover that any way he wanted – a text from a colleague or a mate, or even another criminal.

To his amazement it was only a couple of moments until his phone pinged to let him know a text had come in.

Would love to! it read. *Things a bit complicated here, so won't get away this weekend. Early next week any good?*

Immediately Bill texted back, *Absolutely! Name your time and place.*

Great, came back as fast, *will let you know after Sunday. Thanks for the books, by the way.*

That brought a smile to Bill's face.

"Good news?" Jason asked.

"Yes. He's realised it was me who went into his flat last week. That was where I got those SD cards. I went hoping to find some clue of where he was, but got only them. I did scoop up the copies of his favourite books, though, and took them back to my place for safe keeping. The thing was, I didn't even know if Danny was dead or alive at that point, and I couldn't bear the thought of his stuff just being toss into a skip by the landlord when the rent ran out. But he's just made reference to them, so he knows I went there and that has to be good."

Jason grinned, "Then maybe we can work on extracting him when he comes to meet you? That would be the obvious thing to do, wouldn't it? The gang will expect him to be gone for a few hours anyway, so by the time they come looking for him he'll be safe and sound."

Bill puffed in relief. "God, yes, that would be good, wouldn't it?"

However a nasty thought intruded on his moment of optimism. "Jas', have you or Sean heard whether someone's actually been appointed to Danny's old job?"

"Eh?" Jason was clearly surprised by the question.

"Didn't you know? Morag told me that Danny's job within the division has been advertised as a vacancy."

"Holy crap! No, I didn't know that, and I don't think many others did either."

"But you see where I'm going with this, don't you? If someone is already promised Danny's job, then where's Danny going? This undercover job was always envisaged as a several months' worth of secondment, and we all know the trouble with secondments – you might be guaranteed a job at the end of them, but it isn't necessarily the one you left."

Time's Bloodied Gold

They were interrupted by one of the forensic team coming to tell Jason that they were done here and were heading back.

"One last thing," Bill said, hoping he sounded as though he was just making a suggestion. "Did you find any blood on any of those big stones? I only ask because my archaeologist friend suggested that back in the ancient times the people would have made blood sacrifices at them, and I don't want any nasty surprises of that sort of murder having been done up here. I know you've checked the church, but would you check the two stones outside too? You know, just to be on the safe side?"

The woman was a touch startled, but called to her colleagues to check the stones, and Bill saw them playing the blue lights over them, and then them taking some swabs of something.

"We've found blood, but whether it's human or sheep is anyone's guess," the SOCO reported back, "because it's fairly low down. Could just be a badly hurt sheep from the barbed wire. We'll only know when we've analysed it."

"Off you go, then," Jason told them. "Thanks for all your hard work."

He let them all disappear off, then turned to Bill and said,

"I'm heading back to base now, so do you want to come with me? I think we need to ask around about this bloody job business, don't you?"

And so Bill tailed Jason back and parked in his normal spot, joining Jason at the main doors. Up at their normal working area, Jason crooked a finger at Sean, and his DS called Pete who was part of the same bunch who all tended to congregate at the coffee machines together.

"Where's Williams?" Jason asked Sean quietly as they loitered by the gents.

"Been called to the presence," Sean announced with a mischievous grin and a finger pointing upwards. "Didn't look as though his toast was sitting very comfortably this morning, for some reason."

"Charlie's office," Bill declared, and when they were all wedged into Charlie's shoebox of a space, he told them why they were worried. "If the bloke's already started they can hardly send him back, can they?" he concluded. "It's not the fault of whoever it is, is it? And because I think Williams will be spitting tin tacks over this he'll not be kindly disposed towards Danny. His shiny career has been too tarnished by this. So, if he can legitimately shunt Danny sideways to somewhere else, he will, and that's why we need to know if anyone's actually been appointed."

Pete gave a snort of disgust. "Poor Danny! Talk about getting crapped on. It's not his fault all of this has gone wrong, is it?"

"No it isn't," Charlie agreed, "but I'm afraid the bad news is that someone called Dennis from the Warwickshire lads is due to start a week on Monday. He'd been on secondment somewhere else and returned to find his chair wasn't his anymore, so he's been kicking his heels and applying for everything in sight – just like it looks as though Danny will have to do."

"He'll never stand for that," Bill said without hesitation. "He took this job on the clear understanding that it would enhance his career, not leave it dead in the water."

"You think he'd leave the force?" Sean asked worriedly. "But what would he do?"

Bill shook his head sadly. "I don't know, but I know Danny all too well. He was disenchanted as it was. When you factor in the way he's been treated, even when he was doing a bloody good job under horrendous circumstances, to come back to no regular job would be the last straw. He'll quit because he'll never believe another word anyone senior tells him ever again."

"And there's not a damned thing any of us can do about that, is there?" Pete said dejectedly. "We can do everything possible to clear his name and make these cases stick, but the decision about Danny's place on our team is way above our grades."

"Oh crap," Sean sighed. "The only thing that might save this is us mopping up the gang Danny's with, and at speed. Can we do that, do you think, Bill?"

Bill regarded them all solemnly. "Only if you are prepared to come in and do some of this for free. We'll never get paid overtime approved in time. It's Friday afternoon, Williams is busy covering his arse and will probably go home afterwards to lick his wounds. Is there even anyone of rank we could call on to help?"

"I think Tony Bracegirdle is on duty," Charlie said from behind the computer, referring to the uniforms' superintendent.

"No we can't drag him into this," Bill immediately declared. "He'd be crossing a pretty big boundary by interfering in a CID case – not that Tony wouldn't given the circumstances, because he's a good bloke. But I'd like to be saving jobs, not wrecking them if at all possible. I think the farmhouse is the key place. Anyone up for a recc'y tomorrow? We could at least see if the guys with guns are still on the prowl? We won't be able to actually do anything, but we can make sure they're still where we can get to them."

"I'm on duty tomorrow," Jason said, "but Clara can handle the pro' we were going to go and question. She doesn't need my help for that. If you come with me, then at least you've got someone who is officially on duty – it's a bit thin, I know, but then it doesn't look like we've gone completely off the reservation on this one."

"I'm with you too," Sean said, "if you can make it an afternoon job. I'll be pretty much wrapped up by then."

"For this, I'm free too," Pete declared. "Sal will understand. We were heading for the garden centre, but we can go on Sunday instead. She'd want this if it was me in Danny's place."

Charlie chuckled. "Three DIs and a DS. Talk about the heavy squad going in!"

Bill had the grace to look a little sheepish, but they all knew what was at stake. "Okay, then, everyone bugger off and we'll meet back here at noon tomorrow if that suits everyone? We can hang around for you Sean if you get held up, but if we're all ready to go the moment you turn up that would be great."

Chapter 20

Danny – Friday to Saturday

Danny had never been so grateful for a wet and miserable Friday night. He'd got Bill's text, and it was another sign that Bill was on the case, but it was too late to be able to set anything up with him for what they had to do tonight. And in truth Danny was thinking that he would have to make some decisions tomorrow without being any the wiser about how things stood back at his old HQ, because he wasn't quite ready to openly ask Bill such things, if only because Bill would have to make the reply call to his own phone, and that made it vulnerable to being grabbed by one of those he didn't trust. Indeed, with Kazimierz being the only one who had a clue as to who he really was, it would be pushing it with even Stefan or Dymek if they got a whiff of him being a copper.

So tonight was going to have to be played as for real, and that meant no eye-witnesses and many thanks for the weather. Luckily, tonight any late-night party animals would be scampering home to continue their overindulging in the warm, not loitering around fast food vans in the open. The owner of the burger van had obviously thought much the same, because by the time Danny and his helpers did what they thought would be their first cruise by, all was in darkness.

"Thank God for that!" Kazimierz said from the heart. The inside of the Defender was getting more rank by the minute, and even with the heat on low and the windows partly open, despite it being a cold night for the time of year, the smell was still bloody awful.

"You try being here in the back!" Stefan retorted. He and Dymek both had their faces pressed to the window gaps in a desperate attempt to avoid the worst of the stench.

"I'm going to pull over by the burger van," Danny told them. "If anyone drives past, the car parked there won't be suspicious. People seem to dump cars here all the time and then come back for them later. There's so little traffic we'll be able to get across the road on foot without any trouble. It's way less conspicuous than a car on the turf over in the middle of the road."

He slid the Defender into the cover of the trees overhanging part of the pull-in and left the windows down. The four of them lifted the two black tarpaulins out of the back and rested them briefly on the ground while Danny nipped up to the road and scouted for them.

"Clear to go!" he called softly, running back to grab his end of the wrapped corpse Kazimierz had the other end of. "I can't even hear an engine or see any distant lights on the by-pass, so don't try to run, guys. We've got time get across safely. If we rush we might shake something loose! We don't want to be leaving stray hands or feet in the road!"

Nonetheless they found themselves going at the nearest to a trot that they could manage across what in only a few hours would be solid traffic. Once up on the roundabout Danny didn't need to give any directions. It was blindingly obvious where the natural hollow was, and the four of them manhandled the corpses around low-hanging tree branches to the top of the dip.

"Let's just cut the string and let them roll!" Dymek said, his face turned away from his stinking cargo.

"No! Carry them down!" Danny said. "If anyone

comes looking then, it will seem as if they walked down here and just died where they were. If you roll them in the state they're in, there'll be all sorts of evidence that they were dumped because there'll be bits of them sticking to every blade of grass."

"*Euw*," Stefan gulped, swallowing hard, hawking and then spitting onto the wet grass. That wasn't the best thing to have done, Danny thought, but he wasn't going to search for the gobbet in the dark on the off-chance that some smart techie found it and extracted Stefan's DNA. Friendship only went so far under these circumstances.

Dymek and Stefan turned and ran back up the slope as fast as they could the moment they'd dropped their load, but Danny stayed and cut the cords, pulling the string out and arranging things to look as though a couple of derelicts had nicked some tarpaulin to give them a ground sheet each.

"Danny?" Kazimierz said questioningly. He looked pointedly to where Dymek and Stefan were now long out of hearing anything, then back at Danny. "You really want these guys not to be found?"

It was the first time that Kazimierz had as good as admitted that he was also a cop, so Danny felt he had to honest with him.

"Look, mate, I'm not sure of my own position, let alone anyone else's," he confessed. "I haven't had contact with the people I should have had in far too long, if you get my meaning. So I want these poor bastards to lie undisturbed until I can figure out who and how to tell about them. Oh, make no mistake, they'll be discovered sooner than later! But there aren't that many places in the English countryside where you can just dump a body and it not be found pretty quickly. We're too small a country for that. Every inch belongs to somebody or other. And to be frank we've got more control over things here than in a field somewhere – there'd be way too much danger of a farmer coming along on his quad bike with his sheep dogs the next bloody morning and all hell breaking loose! I want to have some control over this, not be second guessing my bosses as well as bloody de Arce and Mikhail."

"Amen to that," Kazimierz agreed.

"So what the fuck happened to you, mate? How did you get to be stuck out here on your own?"

"Ah," Kazimierz sighed. "I was supposed to stay with them only as far as the ship up on the Baltic and then slip away at the quay. Trouble was, we didn't go that way. The goods did, and they got seized, but we went by train into Germany and then by road down to here. I rang in when I could, but it never seemed to be the right time to speak to someone senior enough to make a decision."

"God, I know that feeling," Danny sympathised, and Kazimierz smiled wanly,

"I'm sure you do. I got that feeling about you."

"Likewise. Look, we need to get back to the car or those two will wonder what the hell we're up to, but I need to tell you this: Jerzy told me yesterday that Reznik's operation has been blown in the States. He's pulling out, but I don't think it includes taking us with him. I've got to go with him to Bristol tomorrow to Reznik's and I'll know more when I get back, but I've been trying to think of a way to get you and those two out before the world crashes in on us. Us lot and the prisoners, that is."

Kazimierz nodded. "You think Dymek and Stefan are okay, then?"

"I certainly don't think they're here by choice, and unless you tell me otherwise, I can't think of a single time when they've done something truly illegal. Belonging to a gang is stupid, but I can't imagine you'd get a prosecution to stick just on that. I think they were caught between a rock and a hard place back at home, joined the gang because it was the only way to get money to support their families, and then found out too late how deep they were into something truly awful."

"That was my assessment, too."

"Great. Then get thinking about a way that we can get out, because I have the nastiest feeling that Jerzy is going to bolt and leave the rest of us to take our chances."

All too early the next morning Danny was back in the VW with Jerzy, although the journey was infinitely more pleasant without de Arce's fulminations from the back seat. He'd left Kazimierz in the early hours with a promise to try and get Stefan and Dymek on their own at some point during the day and pre-warn them that something was happening, but until he got back he couldn't tell them what the worst might be.

When they pulled up to the tall terrace, this time Jerzy motioned Danny to the back entrance.

At the kitchen door Jerzy produced a set of picks and proceeded to pick the lock with professional ease. His eyebrows went up when Danny handed him a pair of latex gloves, but then grinned. "You are bright."

"I have the sense to not want to leave evidence," Danny pointed out dryly, and got another grin of approval.

The house was uncannily quiet when they walked in. Whatever trade normally went on had clearly been temporarily suspended, which seemed odd.

"No dealing on a Saturday?" Danny queried to Jerzy. "Seems odd. Even if there's a change in the guard coming, you'd expect the foot soldiers to be carrying on business, and just wait for the new boss to arrive."

"Something's gone very wrong here," Jerzy declared

and Danny thought he looked genuinely worried. "Let's search this place before we get down to business – don't want any nasty surprises, do we?"

However the nasty surprise was waiting for them. The anorexic blonde was lying on a vast bed covered in tacky purple satin bedding, her empty eyes staring up at the ceiling and very dead. The man's tie still around her neck meant Danny hardly needed a coroner to tell him what had happened. Reznik was running and leaving no witnesses. What was less expected was seeing the young computer geek naked on the bed beside her and equally as dead.

"That's staged," Jerzy said with a sniff of disgust. "He wouldn't have touched her."

"A healthy fear of Reznik?"

"No, he liked the big buxom types. Resnik came up to see Tomek and his lads had their pick of the girls. This lad went for the biggest black girl Tomek had around that night, and she was *big*! I wouldn't have gone near her – you couldn't tell which roll of flesh was which – but this lad looked like he'd won the jackpot as she all but dragged him off to a room."

"None so strange as folk," Danny said philosophically. "My guess would be that this one knew too much about Reznik's finances."

"Mine too. Let's go and find those fucking computers."

In the lounge the big desk had been emptied and for a moment Danny thought that they'd struck out, because there wasn't a computer to be seen. Yet as Jerzy began swearing fluently and continuously in Polish, Danny spotted a hint of a cable beneath one of the sofas.

"Hold on. What have we got here?"

He got down on his hands and knees and groped beneath the sofa, coming out with a laptop in his hands.

Time's Bloodied Gold

"Looks like the geek got the last laugh after all," he said to Jerzy and powered it up.

"Any good?" Jerzy asked almost straight away, but had to be content to wait while the machine warmed up and connected to the internet.

With care, Danny began ferreting around on the laptop and then gave a quiet yip of triumph. "I've got Reznik's account up!"

"And I've got the sword," Jerzy said triumphantly from the other side of the room, turning round with a long thin bundle in his arms. "Reznik didn't believe me when I told him what it was worth. He's obviously left it here as being of no value. What a dickhead! Well this is coming with me."

He strode over to where Danny was sitting at the desk. "So how much is there in Reznik's acco... Fuck me! The robbing bastard!"

The amount was huge and Danny thought it couldn't all have come from their operation alone. "Do you think he's been skimming the drugs money as well? I've never seen those accounts, so I have no idea myself."

Jerzy's face fell. "Bugger! If he has, then Mr Oczkowski will be wanting it back."

"But not all of it," Danny pointed out. "I would say that this," and he typed a number into a box on the screen, "is what he owes from our operation. Which account would you like it moved to?" It was still just about a six digit sum which would mean Jerzy would never have to work again.

Jerzy dug into an inside jacket pocket and pulled out a scruffy piece of paper. "This bank in the Cayman Islands will do nicely."

"Thank you very much, sir," Danny said in his best imitation of a bank clerk. "that's in your account right away. Always a pleasure doing business with you. And this is the account details for Mr Oczkowski, if you feel like sending them to him as a gesture of good will so that he leaves you alone?" He scribbled them on to a piece of paper from the notepad on the desk and handed it across.

Jerzy chuckled, then his face became serious and he hefted the sword experimentally in his hand. "And what guarantee do I have that you won't transfer that money back out as soon as my back's turned?"

Danny gave him a calm, disapproving look, even though his guts were churning at the thought of what that razor sharp blade could do to him. "Well for a start off, while I can transfer money *into* your account from this one I have the password to, I can't transfer it out of yours without *your* online password, and I've never seen that, have I? So I can't possibly know it, and therefore I couldn't do that even if I wanted to."

"True," Jerzy admitted, and the sword's point went down to the floor.

"And you've got the sword, which you can trade, but I'm hanging on to this laptop," Danny said with a wink. "Don't forget, de Arce's details are on here."

"You cunning bastard!" Jerzy said with clear admiration, and guffawed. "For sheer bloody nerve I'm going to let you get away with that one!"

"And you have my word that I'll cut it with Stefan, Dymek and Kazimierz," Danny added. "It's like Reznik said about de Arce, your people deserve to have their share, and those three lads have done everything you've asked of them – and those bodies last night were on a whole extra level of asking, I can tell you."

Jerzy took the hint – he could keep the enormous sum he'd just acquired without even paying off the others if he let Danny do as he was proposing, and Jerzy wasn't daft enough to turn down an offer like that.

Time's Bloodied Gold

"Right, let's get out of this place before anyone comes looking," he said, and as soon as Danny had the laptop closed down they were heading back out of the back door.

It wasn't a moment too soon. They were already pulling away in the car when they saw three men go up to the front door and start knocking on it. When nobody came straight away they started looking in at the ground floor windows and calling through the letterbox.

"Nicely timed," Jerzy observed. "Something tells me that the oh-so-nice neighbours are in for a nasty shock this weekend."

When Danny and Jerzy got back to the farmhouse, Jerzy marched into the kitchen where everyone was congregated with coffee and announced,

"That's it, we're shutting this down as of right now."

"No! You can't!" Mikhail shouted. "Obispo de Arce wants to go back to the church next month. He needs to go!"

Jerzy looked at Mikhail coldly. "Well then I guess you'll be doing that without me, then. But if you do then you'd better be sure that he's going to pay you your cut."

"What do you mean? I earned mine!"

"Yes you, did, and you also forfeited it, Mikhail. I told you at the start, no drugs, but what did you get and leave at Danny's? No, don't pull faces at him. He came straight out and asked me if it had been a test from me. I told him, 'that's not my style', but I know whose it is – it's yours, isn't it? So where did all that cocaine come from Ulryk?" Jerzy's change of direction caught the other man off guard. "It had to be you who got it for him, because Mikhail's not been let out. He's not had the chance to go searching for street dealers."

"Wasn't me!" Ulryk spluttered. "It was him!" and he

stabbed a finger at Piotr. "He went and got the cocaine!"

"But *you* sent me!" Piotr protested. "*You* said Jerzy was going to test Danny! I brought it back here to you, *I* didn't go to Danny's flat!" And that was the thing about Piotr – he was too thick to be able to lie convincingly or on the spur of the moment. Challenged like this you got an honest reaction from him, and Jerzy knew it.

"You did this in my name?" he in dangerous, soft tones, turning back to Ulryk and Mikahil. "I don't ask for much from you, just loyalty, and this is how you repay me? Well I hope for your sakes that the mad priest is feeling generous, because I'm not. The rest of these lads will get their cut, but not you two."

"You can't do that!" Ulryk snarled, fists bunched by his sides and spoiling for a fight.

"Actually I can and I have," Jerzy declared coldly.

He turned to go, but spun on the balls of his feet as Ulryk snarled again and began to thrown a punch towards the back of Jerzy's head. The blow never landed. Instead it was Ulryk who was thrown off his feet backwards into Mikhail, who had been coming up off his seat to join in the beating. The two of them went down in a heap, Mikhail cracking his head hard against the wooden arm of the ancient sofa hard enough that he was slow to get back up.

Now Danny saw the fighter Jerzy was. He almost danced in and delivered a series of vicious jabs, first to Ulryk, who went down again, grunting in pain before he'd fully regained his feet, and then to Mikhail while he was still on the carpet.

"Still feel like arguing?" Jerzy demanded, and when he only got groans, turned and marched out, calling over his shoulder, "Everyone get packed up! We're leaving tomorrow!"

Time's Bloodied Gold

Bill – Saturday

The four detectives wedged themselves into Jason's silver BMW, chosen because it had the option of lights and sirens.

"Won't do much against an AK74 if we see something we have to act upon there and then," Jason admitted, "but sometimes just turning up in style makes the bastards pause."

Under Bill's directions they found the right road out of Tenbury and cruised gently up to the Kyrewood Graves crossroad. Passing a farm which fronted directly onto the road, they saw a young lad eying them suspiciously from the other side of the farm gate, a wall-eyed collie slinking at his heels and just itching for a chance to start snapping at them.

Jason pulled in and Sean got out and strolled up to the lad. The collie immediately started a high-pitched yipping, but he ignored it, instead producing his warrant card for the lad to see.

"We've had reports of suspicious activities out here," Sean began, keeping his words deliberately vague. "Any idea what that's about?"

The lad looked him up and down and said insolently, "You took your bloody time getting here, didn't you? Dad went in and told you lot about down the road months ago. Fucking foreigners! We should come out of the EU. They wouldn't be able to come over then."

The three in the car saw Sean's shoulders move as he took a deep breath. Sometimes dealing with the public was like spending a day being dipped in slurry.

"Fascinating though your political rhetoric is," Sean said dryly, "do you think you could just tell me what's been going on and where?"

"Fucking Poles! They're in the old Peterson farm down the next lane."

"Doesn't anyone live there anymore?"

"*Naah*. Old man Peterson died last year. His son, Clive, wanted to sell up years ago, so the moment the old man went he put the place up on the market. Only trouble, was, Clive then went and had a stroke and then another one and died too. His ex-wife was already arguing the toss about how much she could get of what was left to Clive – not that she had a claim to much of anything. Clive's two sons don't want to farm, but his daughter married a lad from out Church Stretton way, and they want to sell up their smallholding and come and take over the farm. So it's all tied up with the lawyers at the moment."

"So there's a lot of money at stake?"

"Not in cash there ain't. But there's the big old Georgian house – that'll go for a mint, 'cause there's room to make it into several executive apartments. Cheryl – the daughter – is prepared to let her brothers have that if she can have the modern farm house, but they think there's more to be had out of selling all of it. Fuckin' knobs! Those tatty farm buildings ain't worth much of anything! And Cheryl wants to sell the outlying fields to my dad anyway, 'cause they're more his thing. We're mostly arable, but she wants to farm rare breeds, see? So the top fields that plough well dad'll pay a good price for, and she don't mind keeping the ones on the river slope for the sheep."

"And how do the Poles come into this?" Sean asked with fading patience.

"Well some o' them are in the big old house, ain't they? They've got to be squatting! Cheryl just put the modern house up to let short-term to keep some money coming in, but I don't think she knows what them lot down there are doing either."

"And you didn't think to ring her and tell her?"

"Can't! The brothers got suspicious that Cheryl was doing deals with me dad behind their backs, so they got a court order preventing us from talking directly to one another. Everything has to go through the solicitors, see?"

"Bloody marvellous," Sean sighed. "So you're saying that you think there are Poles squatting illegally in the big house, and more in the farmhouse who may or may not be there legally?"

"S'pose," the lad said sullenly.

"Can you tell me how many there are in all?"

The lad screwed his face up as he thought, which was obviously a painful process. "Seven or eight? They seem to come and go. And there are some weird blokes they seem to have labouring for them. I spoke to one of them over the fence the one day. Stupid fucker didn't understand English, though."

Sean thanked him, then when he was back in the car and pulling away, said, "If our Kevin turns out like that I'll bloody drown him, no matter what his mother says!"

From the back seat beside Bill, Pete chuckled, "He won't mate, not a chance. You have to be inbred for generations to be like that. Half of these folk have probably never lived beyond this valley."

"True," Sean conceded with a sigh. "It just pisses me off that they're happy enough to have illegal pickers when the season comes – not a chance of them shopping them to us then, oh no! – but they won't pay our own folk a proper wage to do the work. It's easy to take advantage of the migrants – they only come for a few months and they don't have to afford our living costs – yet they don't want them living on their doorsteps all year round. God forbid that!"

Jason had pulled up only a short way down the road as

Bill tapped him on the shoulder and said, "Just here. This is the track down to the farm."

They were beyond the entrance to the single track lane down to the farm, so the car was well out of sight, and all four of them got out and approached it with caution.

"I'll go down," Bill volunteered.

"Don't be bloody daft!" Pete remonstrated. "You can't run with that leg!"

But Bill taped his crutch. "And they won't think some poor old crippled bugger will be a threat, either. But Danny will spot me in a heartbeat. That's what I'm hoping for. That Danny will find a way to come out and speak to me."

It happened that Sean and Jason had come into the police from the army, and some skills never quite left. For all that they weren't armed, as Bill exaggerated his limp and went down the more open left-hand side of the lane, Sean and Jason hugged the straggly conifer hedge on the right and went skirmish-style along it as they kept pace with Bill. It was no cover from the big old house, and so Pete was a little way behind them all but with his eyes scouring the large windows of the old place searching for any hint of watchers behind them.

As the lane bent round to the right towards the farm yard, and the collection of various buildings within it, Bill must have caught someone's attention, because there was the sound of someone calling out to others. Then a familiar voice called back, and although Bill couldn't hear what Danny had said, he knew he'd been spotted.

"I'm sorry, mate, you can't walk here," Danny's voice then came more clearly, and Sean and Jason saw Bill stop and adopt an air of puzzlement, then there was the squeal of hinges in need of oiling and Danny appeared out on the track. He jogged up to Bill calling out,

"Sorry but this is private property. We've got a

Time's Bloodied Gold

suspected outbreak of foot and mouth, so we can't let anyone walk over the land."

Then Danny was up to Bill and saying softly,

"Make it look like you're arguing the toss with me!"

So Bill punctuated his conversation with random arm waving and gesturing as if he was saying he was trying to connect with other footpaths.

"What the fuck happened to you?" was Danny's first question, looking at the crutch.

"The knee gave out. Replacement job." Bill said tersely. "Officially I'm on sick leave but that's why I've been able to try and find you. Are you okay?"

"Been better," Danny admitted. "Look, this lot are about to decamp. If the taskforce are going to raid this place it's got to be tonight!"

"Ah mate, that's not going to happen," Bill said sympathetically. "This is Sean, Jason, Pete and me doing stuff off the books to find you. Williams has finally caught up, but nothing's going to happen until Monday at the earliest, that I can tell you."

"Bollocks! All this for nothing!"

"Something went really wrong," Bill said sympathetically. "Tell you all about it when you're safe and sound. Can we get you out soon?"

Danny threw his hands up in exasperation. "I'll be able to walk out before then, and whatever evidence I can grab will be useless because they'll all be gone. The best you can do is to get Social Services to come up here first thing on Monday. There are civilians here who need help. Look I've got to get back, but there are two bodies on Powick roundabout, okay? They'll look like tramps."

"Like the three in the underpass?" Bill managed to ask without shouting as Danny turned back.

"Yes," Danny called back over his shoulder, but then

he was walking back and not giving Bill a backwards glance.

Left with little choice, Bill turned and exaggeratedly limped back up the track until he was out of sight of the farm.

"What did he say?" Jason demanded.

"They're pulling out this weekend. Bugger! That gives us no time to do anything! The only good thing about it is that it sounds as though at that point Danny will be able to walk away from them. I don't get the sense that he'll be forced to move on with them."

Sean gave a sniff of disapproval. "That's not saying a lot, though, is it? Not wishing to worry you or anything, Bill, but have they given him that impression because he's destined for a bullet in the back of the head? I really don't want to roll up here on Monday afternoon to find Danny's body."

Bill sighed miserably and gestured around them. "But what can we do? Even if we took it in shifts to stake this place out, any car parked up here will stick out like a sore thumb. There isn't a bloody hiding place along here at all. Not so much as a useful field gateway where we could drive in through and hide a car behind a hedge. The best we could hope for is to ask that other farmer if we could park in his yard and keep watch on foot, but I've got to tell you, lads, that standing for ages on this leg isn't an option for me at the moment."

"And I wouldn't trust that kid not to be on Facebook in seconds broadcasting it far and wide that his dad had coppers in his yard," Sean added mournfully. "We'd be more likely to have local teenagers all over us thinking they can come and watch. We'd never get away with it."

"I guess it's back to base then?" Jason asked and got a frustrated grunt of agreement from the others.

Chapter 21

Bill – Sunday

Having got up feeling utterly disillusioned, and despairing of how they were going to make anything positive out of the mess surrounding Danny, the last thing Bill was expecting was a phone call from Joe Connolly.

"Not disturbing anything, am I?" the voice on the other end of the phone said. "No luscious blonde stopping the night after a moment of wild passion?"

"Oh piss off, Joe! A chance would be a fine thing!" Bill had to laugh. "Honestly, when do I ever get chance to meet luscious blondes, eh?"

Joe was also laughing. "I was hoping you'd say yes and that she had a sister. Bugger, that's my date nights down the chute for another couple of years. Never mind."

"You daft sod! What has you ringing me on a day off?"

"Ah! News I think you'll want, although whether it will make you happy or not is another matter."

Bill immediately moved towards the coffee table and the A4 pad and pen he had there. "Go on, tell me the worst."

"Well the first thing concerns that tosser Godden. It's probably a good thing I was only observing the interview with him, because if I'd been in the room with him I'd have probably have strangled the little bastard."

"Oh God, that bad?"

"Uh-hmm! Panesar and his boss were taking Godden through everything piece by piece yesterday, and they got to the third of December. I remembered you saying that that was one hell of a muddle, what with the supposed meeting in the hotel room and all of that, so I'd primed them to dig on that one. Well you wouldn't credit what Godden did."

"Crap! This is bad, isn't it?"

"It is, but I have to say that everyone concerned has said that if Danny managed to get out of that – and believe me we're all amazed that he's in one piece still – then he was doing one hell of a job on his cover story. It turns out that Godden's squirrely brain had picked up on the fact that Danny was the *Eagle* a lot of the time with the gang, although mercifully he's too fucking thick to have really grasped what was happening there. So the dippy sod only went and left a message with the hotel reception for Danny."

"Jesus Christ!"

"I know. Un-bloody-believable! Well the receptionist thought at first that it must be message for the rep they had staying there."

"Anthony Redman?"

"Aye, him. Panesar rang the hotel as a matter of urgency yesterday to check on what happened. He must have made an impression, because by the time I saw him again at the end of the day, he was able to tell me that he'd spoken to the girl who was on duty on that day. The day had made quite an impression on her, because she said she gave Redman the message as he came in and the Poles were in the bar and already drinking hard. She said they were quick to butt in and say that Danny was a rep too, and to start badgering Redman to see if Danny was a friend of his when he said that the message wasn't his.

"I think everyone in the hotel must have held their breath later on when the Poles went blundering up to Redman's room and started hammering on his door. Let's face it, out there they must know only too well how long the response time is for a car to get to them, and how long they might have to be handling these violent drunks. So it's no surprise that they were more than grateful when Danny lured the Poles outside. As far as they're concerned that was the end of it, because the drunks went without causing any damage and never came back, but they've seen Danny a few times since and said they thanked him for calling someone to come and pick the troublemakers up.

"God knows what Danny did, Bill, but he got the situation under control very quickly. What amazes me is that it didn't all backfire on him. We can only think that the men concerned were known to be trouble within the gang, but until we can talk it over with Danny, I doubt we'll ever know why they were let loose in town in that case."

Bill could feel his heart thumping. What a narrow escape! "Please tell me that Godden didn't identify himself in the message as a copper? I can't imagine any possible way that Danny could have got around that."

Joe's terse laugh was lacking any humour. "Sheer bloody luck, nothing more! His message was sent in Panesar's name, but he didn't give his rank or anything that would mark him as a DCI, or any other kind of policeman. He just referred to Panesar by name or as 'the boss'. But get this – the girl thinks Danny never actually got the message! Of course on the night it was chaos. Being early in the week there were very few staff on, and she was doubling up in the bar as well as on reception even before the trouble, so she says she tucked the note with the message on into the diary and just carried on rushing around. Apparently she found it again after the Christmas rush when they were tidying things up. They looked through the guest book, couldn't find Danny's name, and binned the message as something somebody left for a diner rather than a staying guest, but she remembered his name when prompted because of the Poles."

"Holy-screaming-crap! ...Fuck!..." For a moment Bill was mentally paralysed at the thought of what had nearly happened. "So do we presume that these ...how many Poles?"

"Three."

"...that these three Poles were actually so pissed up that they probably couldn't remember what happened in any detail the next day? That it was that, and nothing else, that saved Danny's bacon?"

Joe sounded as dismayed as Bill felt. "We think so. Terrifying, isn't it?"

"I think that's an understatement! So what's happening with Godden now?"

"That's above my pay grade, but Panesar hinted that at the moment they're working out what prosecutions can be brought against him. With this level of disaster I don't think there's any chance of him staying within the force – for which a great many people are saying 'thank God'! I can't imagine anyone who would want to work with him after this.

"I've also been asked to privately pass on the thanks of my bosses to you. The potentials for what could have happened if this unholy cock-up had gone on for longer aren't lost on them, and the fact that you came to me and it's been able to be sorted out in-house has been deeply appreciated. A suitably worded letter will be going to your boss to the effect that anything that might have been said to you for digging away on this while off-duty should be squashed with speed. From our end what you've done has been seen as an almighty blessing, and nobody wants to see you getting a black mark against your name for it. If

Williams has the brains he was born with, he'll go along with it."

This time Bill was genuinely amused. "Oh, I don't know that he has any of those! But pass back my thanks to your guys, because if their letter goes to those above Williams he won't rock the boat. I've heard nothing directly, you understand, but I wouldn't be at all surprised if someone hadn't asked him how the hell we managed to lose Danny to the extent of filling his place in the team, yet without knowing what had happened to him."

"They did *what*?" Now it was Joe's turn to be appalled. "So the poor bastard doesn't even have his job to go back to?"

"Doesn't look like it. Honestly, Joe, I don't see him staying with the force. And in that context, the fact that we're unlikely to get much out of this operation perhaps matters less to other people than it should."

"Why wouldn't you get anything out of it?"

Bill briefly explained his unofficial foray to the farm the previous day. "So if they're packing up, and possibly splitting up, unless we can make an arrest this weekend it's all been for nothing from our end."

Joe's groan of despair was enough without words. There was a pause, then a deep sigh before he continued,

"And I've got some more news for you. We've been liaising with our colleagues down in Bristol for some time, because one of the lads on the inside up here noticed that a nasty piece of work called Anatol Reznik seemed to be coming up and speaking to the head honcho up here, who's another charmer by the name of Tomek Miskiewicz. Now given what you've just said about what Danny managed to tell you, I have to tell you that I'm going to pass that back to my lot as soon as I get off the phone to you, because the Bristol lads rang us this morning to tell us that something has gone seriously base up at the Bristol end of the operation.

"Apparently Reznik's neighbours phoned them when there was a right old kerfuffle going on at the house with people trying to make those inside hear. Of course, those bad lads vanished into thin air the moment the patrol car pulled up, but because of the address being on the list of those to watch, Bristol CID were hot on their heels. It didn't take long to gain access to the house through an open back door, and inside they found two bodies. The one is Reznik's mistress, and the other one of the hired helps. Some genius within the gang probably thought they were making the crime scene look as though the lad did for the mistress then topped himself. Well nobody needed the pathologist to arrive to see that that hadn't happened, but Reznik seems to have vanished into thin air."

"Can I presume that with two bodies in the place, nobody was protesting when it got taken apart all the way down to the floor boards being lifted?"

"Give the man a gold star. Yep, you're right, they dug deep."

"And did they find anything?"

"Well lots for the drugs' squad to get stuck into, because the dead lad looks as though he was their tame computer geek, but not a total fool, and he's left memory cards hidden under his bed with copies of all sorts of files on them. The chap who rang us said the drugs' taskforce's DCI practically did a 'happy dance' on the spot when he saw what they'd got."

"I'm glad someone's got something out of this."

"Oh, that's not the end of it! The peroxide, anorexic mistress wasn't quite the fool Reznik took her for either. She might not have been the brightest, but he earned her eternal hatred when he let someone use her sister for some

Time's Bloodied Gold

strange ritual. The lads emailed us copies of letters written in Latvian – they hadn't had chance to translate them but thought something in there might relate to us, and so sent scanned copies up a.s.a.p. It looks as though she knew her days were always going to be numbered, so she wrote letters for her parents which she hoped would one day find their way back to them. God knows if we'll ever let them have the full letters, because the translator said they make harrowing reading. My mate Tony was sitting in with him last night while he worked, and he said the poor bloke had to keep stopping when it all got to him.

"She very explicitly tells of the violence she and her sisters were subjected to – and I mean in graphic detail. There's one part, Tony said, where she says her oldest sister said she must do this letter writing thing, and he thinks the oldest one had some glimmer of what either the Polish police or us would need to nail Reznik."

"What happened to the oldest one?"

"Hang on," there was a rustling of paper down the phone. "That would be Agnese. The one they found was called Kristine and the youngest Elizabete. Looks like their surname was Dukurs, since the letters were addressed to a Mr & Mrs Dukurs. Agnese was the one who always defied Reznik, and one day he gave her the beating of a lifetime. Kristine's letter says that the last she saw of Agnese she was being carried out of the house and she looked dead. That same night Reznik sent Elizabete away with some strange man who Kristine refers to as a priest. I doubt that's right..."

"...But it is!" Bill all but yelped. "He's the weirdo who's been egging the lot over here on! He's a total freak. When did this happen, Joe? The date is really important!"

"Really? Blimey, hang on a tick. ...Sorry, Bill, I don't have it here but I can find out for you."

"If you could and let my lot know. Look, I know this is going to sound beyond bonkers, but from what we've dug up here, this bloke is called de Arce and he fancies himself as a latter day Spanish Inquisitor."

"Fuckin' hell! That is weird."

"Oh he is. And I've been talking to one of our local archaeologists who I know from a previous case, because he knows more about this historical stuff than ever I will, and we came to conclusion that de Arce would think that he needed some kind of blood sacrifice to..." Oh crap, how to explain this without sounding like he was losing the plot too? "...to in some freaky way validate what he was going to do. We think the way he got to the poor buggers being trafficked – how he got them under his spell, if you like – was that he said he was acting in the name of God, you see. It might sound nuts to us, but I guess if you come from a rural community out in the wilds of Latvia or Poland or wherever, where the Church still has quite a hold, you might well fall for it. He's totally off his rocker, Joe, so don't look for logic in any of this, but he's been another reason I've been worried sick about Danny. De Arce is the one who's come up with the sicker stuff and he's with the Poles out in the sticks, and this Inquisition stuff means he thinks everything has to be blessed with blood."

"Shit! So Kristine was probably right to think that Agnese and Elizabete are both dead?"

"I think the only thing left to do is find their bodies, mate, and if I'm right and they vanished back in say July or August of last year, then they were de Arce's grand gesture at the start of the whole trafficking thing. I can't be more specific because neither my friend nor Danny really knows what crazy ritual de Arce thinks he's undertaking, although Nick – my historical buddy – did mention the possibility of de Arce trying to resurrect the *auto da fé*, and that involves

Time's Bloodied Gold

blood and fire as a ritual penance before being executed."

"Oh, those poor girls," Joe gasped. "What a way to go."

Bill agreed. "Bloody awful. I wouldn't discourage the Bristol lads from looking for their bodies, but I think I can guess where they might be. Unfortunately, though, we'll need someone up here with ground radar to comb the area to find them, so it'll take a while to get that set up. But the moment you said 'ritual' I had that kick-in-the-guts feeling that that's where they ended up."

"Can you give me any more than that?"

"It's out at an unused church that's famous for nothing except for having some standing stones built into the wall. By the sound of it they haven't held regular services there in decades. If you can even find a reference to it you'll be lucky. It's called St Michael's at Brimfield Wood right on the edge of Worcestershire. Pass it on if you want to, but I'll be prodding the lads up here to dig deeper there. They did a forensic sweep of the place on Friday, but the results won't be in yet and they didn't know they needed to look for graves maybe beyond the churchyard boundary, although I'm sure your lot and the Bristol team can be copied in on the results."

"I'd appreciate that. Let me know if you get Danny out, won't you? We're all rooting for him here."

There was little more to say, but Bill had hardly put the phone down before it rang again. This time it was Sean.

"We found the bodies on Powick roundabout!" he declared triumphantly. "It's a bloody good job it's a Sunday. The chaos that would have caused in the week doesn't bear thinking about."

"So what's the story there?" Bill asked, finding himself dreading that the answer might be something ambiguous enough to put Danny in danger of being prosecuted as an accessory.

Sean could be heard taking a deep breath. "Well it didn't take a genius to work out that they've only just been dumped there. They were on a couple of tarpaulins, and I'd say that they'd been wrapped up in them for some time, but the outside of the tarp's look as though they were buried for some time – possibly under straw as well as earth. Jeez, Bill, they were bloody rank! They were fair crawling with maggots. Even the pathologist went a bit pale at the smell. I don't think even he's seen many like this, but he did say straight away that they reminded him of the three dead tramps you found just before you went off sick."

"Now that is interesting! Danny hinted at that and I remember that we found some sort of religious medal on one of them that just didn't fit with rough sleepers. What's more, the autopsy said that it didn't look like they were from Poland, even though the medal was of a Polish saint."

"Did they, now? That's interesting," Sean mused. "Are you thinking what I'm thinking?"

"That these are some of the people the gang was trafficking?" Bill supplied. "And maybe Danny planted that medallion to make us sit up and take notice?"

"Yes. Shit, we should have chased that one harder, shouldn't we?"

"God, don't Sean, I'm feeling bad enough about this as it is! We certainly found evidence that the three in the underpass hadn't died there, and had been kept somewhere for some considerable time before being dumped there. With Danny telling me about this new pair, I don't think anybody's going to question that the five are all connected."

"I'll pass the word to get hold of the autopsy on your three to give us a head start on these two," declared Sean

Time's Bloodied Gold

with some satisfaction. "We won't be so slow this time, I'll make sure of that."

"I'd prepare the SOCOs to swoop in on Kyrewood Graves the moment we can, as well," Bill hinted. "My money is on us finding the original deposition site for all five there. Have you or Jason been able to get anywhere with getting a search warrant for that place?"

Sean groaned. "No. The trouble is, it's all down to Danny's word and what you and Charlie worked out. We brainstormed it yesterday after we dropped you off, but when you look hard at it we haven't got a scrap of physical evidence to go on. If something comes out of the autopsies on our two new bodies that implies that they've been kept in the vicinity of Kyrewood, and even better, on a farm, then we might be in with a chance, but not until then. We can't even tie what we found at St Michael's specifically to that farm. Yes, the Land Rovers we took the tyre casts of look like they've been on a farm, but that hardly narrows things down when you're out there! And hearsay about a bunch of Polish workers renting an old farmhouse isn't going to cut it either."

"What about the photographs of the people they have hidden there?"

There was another groan from Sean. "Hardly evidence, Bill, as you well know. They weren't tied up, no obvious signs of violence, and it's not a crime to have workers who aren't all there mentally when we have nothing like a witness statement to say that they've been seen being abused."

Bill knew Sean was right, but he was as frustrated as hell by it all. Danny was right, this bloody gang was going to get away with this scot-free. What was almost worse was that Jason and Sean seemed to now be tied up with this case in an official capacity, which meant that he couldn't really call upon them for unofficial forays without endangering any prosecutions which might result from their work. He was on his own again except for the moral support of Morag and Charlie, but the clock was now ticking for Danny even more than before.

Danny – Sunday

Having hardly slept at all, Danny was awake with the birds and down in the kitchen brewing up coffee when Jerzy emerged. The gang leader seemed surprised to see someone up and about at this hour.

"Leaving us?" Danny asked resignedly. He was sure he'd just seen Jerzy dump a holdall back out of sight when he'd spotted him.

Jerzy gave him a wry shrug.

"Then would you answer me something before you go?" Danny ventured. "What did de Arce do to make that portal thing open? Surely he didn't just go and say some magic word over it?"

Jerzy blinked and gave Danny a funny look. "Why does that matter now?"

With his voice becoming bitter, Danny threw back at him, "Because if you're buggering off and leaving de Arce behind, what are the chances of the police catching him once you've stopped covering his tracks, eh? And do you see him, with all of his arrogance and belief that God is sitting on his shoulder, keeping quiet under interrogation?" That made Jerzy stop whatever he was about to say or do and stare at Danny with a look of growing dismay, which softened Danny's tone a bit as he went on,

Time's Bloodied Gold

"Look, you were right when you said that we've done no actual harm to the people who came here. When their bodies are found there'll be no sign of foul play, nothing to hang any charges on. They weren't even kept short of food, and their autopsies will show that too. But I've been up all night thinking, and the one thing that really worries me is if there are some bodies out there that *do* have signs of a violent end written all over them. I know now that you wouldn't have done anything as stupid as that, but de Arce or Mikhail? Would they?"

For a moment Jerzy did nothing but swear long and hard, then he picked his holdall up, brought it into the kitchen and kicked it out of sight into the walk-in pantry.

"Fuck! I'd forgotten all about them," he fumed as he dumped some instant coffee into a mug and poured the remains of the kettle over them. Then he bumped Danny's arm with his fist, "But God Almighty, I'm glad you thought of that! We need to clear that up before we go or we'll be hounded for ever more."

"So there are bodies?"

"Oh yes! That mad man...!" And Jerzy puffed and shook his head. "For this you deserve the truth, my friend. You see, I was over here already. I'd been glad to get away from Mikhail and Tomek to be honest, and I never had any intention of stopping here that long. I just wanted to get enough money so that I could live in some comfort and then I was going to be gone. Find myself some nice little place on the Med' and grow olives." He sighed heavily again. "The world has got too complicated, Danny. There's so much science these days, so many ways you can get caught. You either have to be too stupid to care – like Ulryk – or very, very clever, and I know I'm not that good. I don't have the education to be able to deceive the science and the computers. I'm just an old-fashioned crook, and I don't like drugs either. Taking some fat cat to the cleaners is one thing, destroying whole families is another. I don't know, maybe my Catholic upbringing has stuck to me more than I like to think, but I have my limits as to what I'll do.

"So I was perfectly happy in Birmingham running part of the operation there until Tomek showed up. And then when he said that Mikhail had been over here for a couple of months already, having come looking for me, I ...well I went out and got as drunk as I've ever been, I can tell you. Talk about my worst nightmares turning up!"

"So where was Mikhail, then?" Danny knew he had to know about this. It could be something else that needed clearing up once he got away from here. However, Jerzy's reply reminded him of what he'd overheard, and he knew it wouldn't be that simple after all.

"Oh he's always been religious, has Mikhail, so I shouldn't have been surprised that he came here through some bunch of freaks as warped as he is. What I'd forgotten until we saw Reznik the last time is that he was the one who introduced Mikhail to them."

"Opus Dei?"

"Yes. I suspect that Reznik just thought they might be useful to him when he first made contact with them. I hadn't realised that they'd got to him for real until now, though."

"Okay, that's starting to make a bit more sense to me."

"Well I knew of Reznik by reputation, so when I got told that Mikhail was down there I thought I'd better go and check on what was happening. Mikhail has had a talent for dragging me into his messes ever since we were kids, and I knew that just because he was down with Reznik, while I was up in Birmingham, it wouldn't save me if he got caught."

Against all of his better judgement, Danny was feeling

Time's Bloodied Gold

increasing sympathy for Jerzy. Maybe he wasn't that bad after all? "God, you can't have been happy about that!"

"I wasn't. So I went down to Bristol to the house you've been to, and there was Mikhail with the man I came to know as de Arce. Reznik was away in London talking to his boss, and at that stage hadn't actually met de Arce, but Mikhail was already banging on about how the 'bishop' could make us all rich. However, the Opus Dei people over here had been contacted by some of their own in Spain wanting to arrange passage for de Arce to the West Indies, and they'd spoken to Reznik who'd got him on one of his boats that operates out of the north of Spain bringing refugees in. I don't like that trade, Danny. That robbing people of every last penny they have in the world. The only thing I can say for Reznik is that at least he has a high success rate of getting people here. He does actually do what he says he's going to, not like some who take the money then drown their passengers. It's a longer journey to come round and up the Bristol Channel, but it's less policed than around Calais."

"No doubt he charges more, though?" Danny said dryly.

"Oh yes! He only brings in people who can afford his services, or ones who will bring their bosses plenty of money like the best of the call girls."

"Another Bristol slave trader," Danny sighed and got no argument from Jerzy on that. "Some things never change, do they? So de Arce got brought into the UK by Reznik's people - what then?"

Jerzy rolled his eyes. "Well he had something of a wait before there was a ship heading to the Caribbean. Luckily he'd been put in the same rooming house as Mikhail run by some others within Opus Dei, so at least he was off the streets. But once he started spouting his stuff, I think

Reznik – or rather his lieutenants at that stage – realised what a liability they'd had wished on them by their Spanish buddies. And apparently he was very insistent that it had to be the Dominican Republic or Haiti he went to. Try as they might to convince him, he just wouldn't have it that he could go to Jamaica or any of the other islands, and they could hardly book him on the next package holiday!"

The thought of de Arce rammed onto a plane full of British holiday makers thinking they were on their way to sun, sand and probably plenty of sex too was mind boggling.

"No, you definitely couldn't do that, even if his passport was in order," Danny agreed with a shudder. "So you were lumbered with him?"

"I wasn't – or not yet, at least – and even Reznik was getting worried, I can tell you, but Mikhail was still banging on about how this man could make us all rich, and money always did override sense with Reznik. To be frank, Danny, I thought they were the ramblings of a madman. I didn't set any credence to them at all. But somebody who knew their way around the internet found that church we go to, and the next thing I know, I'm getting a phone call from Reznik saying that Mikhail and de Arce are coming up to look at the place, and can I find them a place to stay? I thought he meant just for the night, so I met them in Worcester, we went to the church, and then I shoved them into the local Travelodge thinking that was the end of it.

"I'd not been back many nights when I got the call from Reznik that they were on their way up from Bristol to Worcester with two girls who'd been trouble for Reznik and needed taking care of. Then before I knew it, Tomek was sending me down to meet them with the guys you know from here to make sure that there was no trail of blood that could lead back to him or Reznik – they both

Time's Bloodied Gold

answer to the same boss, you see. It was then that I got asked to rent some place to stash de Arce until he could be got onto a boat and I got this place. Never thought I'd be here this long, though."

"Two girls?" Danny's blood ran cold. "Are we talking children here? Because Piotr thinks de Arce is a kiddie fiddler as well as a nut-job. He thinks he's a paedophile."

Jerzy's eyes flew wide. "Really? No, I saw nothing of that, and these were working girls, not children. I was pretty horrified to find out that one of them had got herself pregnant – and she was visibly pregnant – but that seemed to jazz de Arce up even more. He kept ranting on about three lives joined by blood being what he needed."

"Three?"

"The women were sisters."

"Bloody hell! So two sisters and one of them's unborn child?"

"Yes." Jerzy shook his head wearily. "I don't think any of us were happy about that except for Ulryk, Mikhail and de Arce. Ulryk was one of Tomek's enforcers with the working girls – liked knocking them about – and the other two I hardly need to explain about, do I?"

Danny sighed. "No you don't. ...So I'm guessing that you had no idea what de Arce was about at that point?"

"Not a clue. And when he started all of his hoodoo-voodoo stuff up at the church, we were all laughing up our sleeves." Jerzy gave a shudder. "Or at least we were until he went and grabbed the girls and carved them to pieces up against those two big stones. I've killed, Danny. I'm no saint. I'm probably going to rot in Hell when my time comes. But I swear to God I've never done anything like that. I've broken men's necks, I've slit their throats, but it's always been quick and clean. I'm not a fucking cat! I don't play with my prey.

"And I've only ever done it when I've had no other choice. That's not an apology. I don't pretend I was a victim just defending myself. I wasn't. But the ones I killed were men who were as bad as or worse than me. I've never killed a woman and I've never hurt a child. Like I say, I have my limits. But not de Arce. What he did that night sickened me to the pit of my stomach, and the only reason it's sort of gone to the back of my mind is because of what happened next."

"The portal opened?"

"What a fucking shock that was! Jesus Christ! I mean, you've seen it. It's not like watching some special effect on TV, it's bloody real. And there's de Arce ranting away in Latin and then someone actually answers him. What a shit-loosener that was! And we could hear people screaming and calling out in that other language, but we knew they weren't here with us 'cause we'd checked the place out beforehand."

Jerzy shook himself like a dog shedding water at the memory. "Mother of God, we've got used to it a bit more now, but that first time was in a whole different league to anything else any of us had ever experienced. We just stood there in shock, and then this bloke comes staggering through that hole in time and almost throws a gold chalice into de Arce's hands with some bits of jewellery. He turned and ran back, but his screams make me think he didn't arrive back in one piece."

"What happened to the girls' bodies?" Danny asked softly, not wanting to break the spell while Jerzy was spilling the beans like this. "Why didn't you send them through the portal? It would have got rid of the evidence."

With a shrug Jerzy told him. "At the time we were too shocked to think of it, to be honest. We were too paralysed by what we'd seen to be thinking much about anything, and

Time's Bloodied Gold

de Arce doesn't think about things like the consequences of his actions. I think he's always been used to having someone who mops up after him and being immune from prosecution. So before we knew it the opening had closed again. And then when we went outside and saw the bloody mess again, first off de Arce said that their bodies had to stay there – something about anchoring the spell – and then we thought, well what better place to hide bodies than in a graveyard, right?"

"So they're buried there? You did a good job. I never saw anything like disturbed ground that would make me think there was newly disturbed soil there."

Jerzy grimaced. "Oh we didn't bury them round the front. We managed to convince de Arce that even though the church looks like it doesn't get many visitors, even so, we couldn't just go around digging the place up. Round the back, though, it's much rougher. So we put them in the ground at the back of where that damned thing opened up. It looks like whoever mows the grass there dumps the cuttings out of sight round there, so we moved a heap of them, dug the holes and put the girls in, filled them in, and then put all the cuttings back on top. It seemed to work. Nobody's raised a stink about finding them as yet."

Then Jerzy looked hard at Danny. "But what you just said about de Arce in custody... Oh man, that opens up a whole new set of possibilities. If he starts bragging, thinking he's so above us all, he could drag us all down with him, 'cause who's to say whose hand was on the knife, eh? Those girls were so carved up it could have been more than one of us, and de Arce won't think twice about dumping us in it if he thinks it will get him out of jail and out to where he can start his new crusade. We've got to move that evidence, Danny, for all of our sakes!"

Chapter 22

Danny – Sunday

"Where do you want to move the bodies to?" Danny asked Jerzy.

"I really don't mind as long as they're not where de Arce can finger us for killing them," was the instant reply. "If you have any ideas...?"

However Danny was quick to point out, "Look, my ideas worked because we had men who could pass as derelicts, and they had no signs of violence on them. I'm guessing de Arce used a knife on the girls?"

"Yes, he did."

"Well then there are going to be cut marks on the bones even if the flesh has rotted down a lot by now." Then Danny thought he might be showing a touch too much knowledge about the state of corpses and quickly qualified it with, "My ex was glued to those bloody CSI programmes. Gory stuff, but she couldn't get enough of it, and I had to watch it with her. So while I guess some of what they do might not be possible in real life, I've got the feeling that stuff like that is, and if we're not exactly going to be dealing with a lot of gloop and rotting stuff after eight or nine months, there's still going to be a lot of evidence there. That means we can't just dump them like we've done the others."

Jerzy grunted in disgust and turned to begin pacing the kitchen as he slurped his coffee. After a couple of turns he stopped and gestured with his mug at Danny. "Reznik got

Time's Bloodied Gold

me into this mess, I think it's only fair that he gets the blame for this."

"Hang on, we can't go back to the house in Clifton," Danny protested. "The police will be crawling all over it by now!"

But Jerzy was shaking his head. "Not the house, no, but Reznik had other places. There's an old Victorian warehouse building close by the river – one of the few that hasn't been made into fancy apartments. Reznik rents the basement space, supposedly for storage."

"Supposedly?"

"That's what he tells his foot soldiers. Old boxes and car parts, that sort of thing, because the basement of the house has the stuff in it that he wanted to keep a close eye on, if you follow me. But I know he has a space where he hides people down in that warehouse behind the boxes. It's where he hid de Arce when he first arrived."

"Do you think it's been used since?"

"I doubt it."

Danny could feel a grin spreading across his face. "Then any DNA lingering down there will be his."

He saw Jerzy start to smile too. "I was only thinking that it's a place that hardly ever got used, so few of Reznik's men even knew it existed to go there and disturb it, but you've just hit on another good reason to use it. Right, let's get the shovels and some tarpaulin. This is just you and me, I don't want any of the others involved."

Danny agreed, but largely because he knew that the only other men Jerzy would allow on this were the three he himself least wanted compromised. However he did say, "Let me go and wake Kazimierz and tell him what we're doing. We're not likely to be back much before dark and we want a lid kept on this place. If Ulryk and Mikhail think we've just buggered off there's no telling what they might decide to do. We don't want to come back to more corpses do we? Better that they think you're coming back and staying for now."

Jerzy conceded the point and went to take his holdall back upstairs, while Danny went up to the room that Kazimierz shared with Dymek and Stefan, and where he'd had a camp bed on the nights he'd had to stay over. He didn't just wake Kazimierz, though, but carefully roused all of them and told them what was happening.

"Are you sure about this, Danny?" Kazimierz asked, and Danny knew there was a double meaning to his question.

"Very!" Danny answered. "You three mustn't be involved – the fewer of us the better. If any blame is going to fall for those girls' murders it has to be on the ones who really were guilty. That means de Arce and the two who are likely to stick up for him if he falls into the hands of the law. He can point the finger at them all he likes as far as I'm concerned, but if he starts crowing about his freaky rituals in some insane show of superiority under questioning, then we can't have easily found evidence at the church which would trigger a manhunt for everyone de Arce decides to name. Because once you're in the cells and under suspicion, getting out will be a lot harder if there's so much as a hint of being an accomplice to murder."

"I'll come downstairs with you," Kazimierz volunteered. "You two stay here and pretend you were asleep the whole time."

As Jerzy climbed into the Defender nearest the gate and started the engine, its rattling gave Danny the chance to hiss to Kazimierz, "Don't worry, the Bristol police will get a tip-off about those bodies soon enough. I just want to keep some last vestige of control over what happens and when."

Time's Bloodied Gold

At the church they had a moment's panic as they realised that it was Sunday morning, and if ever there was going to be an unwanted presence there it was going to be then. Happily the church was silent, and when they got to the door they found it was locked with a printed note on it saying that, due to vandalism, it would remain locked for the foreseeable future, but that if anyone wished to visit, a key could be got from Hilltop Farm. Privately Danny thought this might have something to do with what Bill had witnessed, and he noticed that the cigarette ends had gone from around the stones. Was that proof that the SOCOs had already been doing their thing here?

Yet with this being the first time that Danny had really been here in daylight, something else struck him.

"Err... Jerzy?"

"Yes?"

"I don't think this was quite the secure site you thought it was for bodies."

"Why?"

"Well I think this is a churchyard, not a graveyard."

The big Pole looked around, perplexed. "There's a difference?"

"I'm afraid so. Churchyards are the area around *any* church or chapel. Sort of a mark of respect by giving it its own space. But here in England there's a kind of hierarchy of church buildings, and little places like this often weren't licensed to bury people on their patch of land." He could hardly refer back to that case last year when they'd got mixed up with the archaeologists, and that shrine and chapel in the farm not that far from here as the crow flew, which was pretty much the extent of his knowledge of such things. "I don't see a single gravestone," he covered his story with, "And there weren't any tombs inside either, were there? You'd think that the bigwig who paid for this place to be built would at least have a few of his family buried inside if it was possible, wouldn't you?" Jerzy looked around as if seeing the place for the first time. "So I don't think there are any bodies here except ours."

Jerzy muttered darkly under his breath, then handed Danny a shovel and gestured for him to follow him. Together they went around to the back of the church to right by where Bill and Nick had found the other two stones in the wall. Without a word, Jerzy began digging, at first flinging the composted grass out of the way on one side.

"Put that stuff over there," he instructed Danny. "We'll have to make sure it goes back on top, and not the earth, or people will wonder what's gone on."

They worked as fast as they dared, but to Danny's barely concealed dismay, the girls weren't buried that deeply. How they'd never been discovered was little short of a miracle. Had nobody been here to wonder at the smell in those early days when they'd been relatively fresh corpses? Or was simply it that none of the few visitors went around the back of the church to the gloomy, overhung north side? There were signs that the local rats had had a field day too, and Danny felt the familiar tug at his emotions that two human beings could be reduced to vermin fodder and have no-one around to care about them. Fresh murder scenes were bad enough, but it was these aging corpses which always got to him the most.

"What's wrong?" Jerzy asked as he stood up and caught Danny's expression.

"These were somebody's daughters," Danny said quietly. "I've got a daughter. I can't imagine how I'd feel if she suddenly just vanished, and then I found out that something like this had happened to her."

Time's Bloodied Gold

Jerzy knuckle-bumped his arm. "You're a good man, Danny. You're better off out of this business. Leave such things to bastards like me."

Danny gave him a sideways look. "And even you have a conscience, Jerzy, you can't fool me anymore. You're not the mindless thug Ulryk is, who enjoys doing such things, let alone the nut-jobs Mikhail and de Arce are. Have you any family back in Poland?"

"A sister in Gdansk." He took a ragged breath. "Damn you, Danny…she has three little girls," and he looked down at the two bundles of rags and shook his head.

"Then let's do the right thing by these two," Danny said firmly. "Let's get them down to Bristol, and then when we're sure everyone has got clear, the police can have an anonymous tip-off about these two, eh? At least that way their parents will get them back and be able to bury them properly, even if it's a bit late."

Jerzy straightened up almost as if a weight had been taken off his shoulders. *Yes, you're not quite the hard man you try to make out you are, are you?* Danny thought. *You're not wholly beyond redemption yet.*

They carefully lifted the two bodies into their own tarpaulin, backfilled the hole and tried to make the place look as undisturbed as possible, and then carried the girls down to the Defender. For once Danny was glad that they wouldn't be making the run to Bristol in his car. He'd made sure he'd been flashed on enough speed cameras over these last months that his car would be spotted in an instant, and he didn't want any proof at all that he'd been involved in this. With that in mind he kept the Defender at a far lower speed, and given the way the older engine howled at anything over sixty m.p.h., Jerzy's curiosity wasn't aroused by the slower journey.

Driving into Bristol was far easier on a Sunday, and

once they got down the hill from Clifton proper to the Hotwells area by the River Avon, Jerzy gave Danny clear directions as to how to get to the old warehouse. It was an unremarkable building of the sort that could be found in any British city in an old industrial area – rows of arched windows rising like sightless eyes in the dirty bricks to watch over the water, most of them broken, even up on the third floor.

"Round the back," Jerzy directed, gesturing to what would once have been the warehouse yard, and Danny pulled the Defender in and stopped.

A short flight of badly worn brick steps with a protecting low wall led down from the yard to a padlocked door, which Jerzy made short work of. Danny saw him go inside and flick a light on, then he was back outside and helping Danny carry the tarpaulin inside.

"Over there," Jerzy said with a jerk of his head towards a pile of wooden packing crates of the sort furniture removers had once used. "Let's get them behind there and then you can go and lock up the car and close the door before we get spotted."

Yet as they began manoeuvring around the other bits of detritus scattered across the floor there came a slow hand-clapping behind them.

"How very enterprising," de Arce's voice said from the door.

They dropped the bodies and spun to face him. There was a manic glint in his eyes as he snarled,

"How dare you! How dare you disrupt my sacred space! You've ruined it! Now I shall have to begin all over again."

"You're a crazy man," Jerzy said with distaste. "Who do you think is going to help you this time, eh?"

"You wait 'til I tell Reznik what you've done, how

Time's Bloodied Gold

you've defied God!" de Arce ranted.

"You might have a problem doing that," was Jerzy wry response. "If he's still alive after Mr Oczkowski's finished with him, he'll be on the next plane back to Poland. Of course, if he's not, then he's probably floating face down in the lower reaches of the Thames by now."

"You lie!" de Arce shrieked.

"No." Jerzy said with complete calm. "If you doubt me, you try going to that house of his. Best of luck to you if you do, though, because my guess is that there'll be an unmarked police car watching it to see who turns up."

"Why would they be watching it?" Mikhail's voice said, and he loomed into view through the door too.

Danny sighed. This wasn't good, this wasn't good at all. "Because your pal Reznik went on a bit of killing spree. We came down here on Saturday because Reznik was being a twat about the sword. What we found was the house empty and two cold corpses – one of them that mistress of his. And the way his bag-men were banging on the front door as we came away, I wouldn't think it would have been long before one of the neighbours called the police. We're a bit funny like that here in England, you know. We see strange men banging around and we tend to call it in."

"Funny man," Mikhail snarled. "I've had enough of you," and his hand came up from behind his back to reveal one of the MK74s.

"Holy crap!" Danny gulped and dived for the floor with Jerzy almost on top of him as the first burst ripped through the packing cases.

"You fucking madman!" Jerzy screamed. "Do you want every cop in Bristol on us? Stop that!"

Then they both had to roll as another burst from the gun slammed into the floor where they had just been. Together they scrambled in a low crouch and dived behind a big piece of rusting old machinery, which was the most solid thing down there. Bullets ricocheted off it and they were gratified to hear a scream from one of their two assailants as they got caught on the rebound.

Risking a peek through a gap in the metal, Danny was able to mouth to Jerzy, "de Arce's been hit."

"Ever serve him right," Jerzy whispered back. "Where's Mikhail?"

Then there was a grunt and swearing from right by them as Mikhail stumbled over something unseen on the floor, and then he tripped into view around the machine. It saved Danny, but the random burst from the gun started over his head and swept down to hit Jerzy twice in the chest.

Something snapped inside of Danny. All the months of strain came apart in one go, and without even thinking about it he was up in a crouch and then launching himself at Mikhail. His head caught the other man full in the gut, driving the breath out of him. One of Bill's stylish tackles it wasn't, but it worked, and as Mikhail was thrown backwards the gun went off again as he tightened his grasp on it but flung his arm out.

From closer to the door there was a scream of agony and then, as Danny stumbled and managed to land a punch in Mikhail's groin, he saw de Arce keel over and slump to the floor. The random spray had hit him. And that was when things went very strange.

As Danny also fell and cracked his head hard against the old brick floor, seeing stars, he was nonetheless sure he saw other shapes. As the pool of blood around de Arce's body spread, Danny would swear for the rest of his life that he saw the faint shapes of people reaching up with ethereal hands to grasp at him, and an equally faint replica of de Arce separating from his solid body and desperately trying

Time's Bloodied Gold

to fight them off. This was another site where history lay very close beneath the surface, a place where the deeds of evil men were not forgotten by their enslaved victims.

When he came to, he realised that he'd lost consciousness for a moment. In the distance he could hear sirens, and that must have been what spooked Mikhail, that or the ghosts, because Danny heard another car starting up close by, a squeal of tyres, and the engine gunning as it faded away, but there was no sign of the man. The MK74 lay on the floor some feet away, wedged where it had fallen in a heap of rusting huge chain links, and Danny could only guess that Mikhail had tried to snatch it up only to wedge it all the harder, and then had panicked and fled without it.

Rolling over, Danny was horrified to see how badly Jerzy had already bled out. Moving him would only end things sooner, and no ambulance would get here fast enough to save him. Crawling over to him, Danny took his hand and squeezed it, shocked by the depth of his grief at the passing of this man whom he should have been glad was gone.

A vague bubbling noise alerted him to the fact that Jerzy was trying to speak and he leaned in closer. What he got was a string of letters and numbers, and suddenly he knew that what he was being given was the password to Jerzy's online account.

"I'll see your sister gets it, mate, I promise I will," Danny managed to wring out, and then Jerzy was gone.

Knowing the chances of him remembering the sequence later was nil, Danny grubbed around in his pocket, found his pen and tiny notebook and scribbled them down. Strangely the sirens had passed. Maybe they had been for something totally separate and nobody had noticed the commotion down here?

Looking around, Danny checked to make sure he

hadn't dropped anything, blessing the fact that he'd been wearing gloves. There was a bloody handprint beside Jerzy, and of course, had he not been wearing gloves, he'd have left his hand prints on Jerzy too, but so far he was in the clear. He got to his feet carefully and drew a deep breath. *Think!* he told himself sternly. *Come on, think!*

He looked around and realised that nothing here implicated him. Yes, there had been a struggle, but there were two bodies here, and the casings scattered across the floor told of a third man who had been the shooter, but nothing said there had to be a fourth man. Two men at least had to have carried the two girls' bodies in here, but there was nothing to say that three men hadn't come in here to do that and then had a falling out. He could walk out of here and nobody would be any the wiser. It just looked like a falling out within a gang, and it might even be read as Jerzy and de Arce fighting and the gun going off and killing them both.

Going to the door he peered out cautiously, and finding nobody about, he walked up the steps and had a quick look around. There were fresh black streaks of tyre rubber on the old concrete where Mikhail had taken off, and from them Danny could now see where Mikhail must have tucked de Arce's Range Rover into the shadows of the building at the side. But how the hell had they found out about what had gone on? Someone must have overheard him and Jerzy at the farmhouse, or maybe Kazimierz telling Dymek and Stefan? That was the only explanation, and that meant that he had to get back there fast in case Kazimierz was trying to hold off disaster on his own.

However there were a couple of things he needed to take care of first. He peeled off the bloody gloves along with his blood-drenched jacket, then got some clean gloves on from the packet in his jeans. Rolling the jacket around the handles of the spades from the Defender so that they were tied together as a loose bundle, he then went to the road and peered out. There wasn't a soul about, and Danny was careful to look across at the other side of the river too. Making a rapid dash out to the river's edge, he threw the bundle as far out into the river as he could. The jacket would probably come loose in no time, but it was also light enough to be taken at speed down the river to the Severn Estuary, and who was looking for the spades here? Hopefully they would sink into the silt and if they ever came to light would be taken as lost workman's tools.

Then he got into the Defender, started it up and set the heater on as high as it would go. It was still bloody cold to be going around in just shirt sleeves, but hopefully he would just be thought a poser trying to be tough and that the black latex gloves would be mistaken for leather ones by anyone who took notice of him. What was more, he knew which way he was going to go back this time, and it wasn't by the motorway. He eased his way out of Clifton and headed for the Severn Road Bridge, just one more motorist out for a Sunday afternoon drive through the pretty countryside of the Forest of Dean. He had to get back to the farm as fast as he could, but if Mikhail had got pulled over by a motorway patrol that was one incident Danny did not want to be passing. Mikhail screaming his 'accomplice's' guilt to those arresting him could result in a high speed chase that Danny wanted to avoid at all costs.

Bill – Sunday

By midday Bill was almost climbing the walls. Dare he ring Danny? Best not to, but he found himself looking at his phone every five minutes in case there had been a text. So when it rang for real, he almost jumped out of his skin having been concentrating so hard.

"Danny? Are you okay?"

"No, I'm not."

"Oh fuck, what's gone wrong?"

He heard the ragged gasp on the other end of the phone. "Bill, I need you to ring something in for me. There's been a shooting in Bristol. It's down at an old warehouse by the river that belongs to Reznik. There are two bodies down there. Well there are four actually, because two are girls de Arce killed back in the summer to do that weird fucking thing with the portal with, but they're wrapped in a tarpaulin. But there are two fresh ones. One is de Arce. He got caught when Mikhail stumbled with his finger still on the trigger."

"Christ! You mean he opened fire with one of those AK74s? Who else got hurt? Are you okay?"

"I am ...but Jerzy bought it."

"Jerzy?"

"The gang leader."

"Well he's no loss then," was Bill's automatic response, then was worried by Danny's silence and the hint of a sob down the phone. "Danny?"

"He wasn't all bad, Bill. Not like de Arce and that mad bastard Mikhail. Those two and Ulryk are just animals. Jerzy ...he was a hard man, but he'd had a hard life. And he had his own morality. There were limits to what he'd do, Bill. You know the sort – the old school villains who draw the line at women and kids getting hurt."

That really worried Bill. It sounded as though Danny had lost track of where his loyalties lay. Not so surprising, given what had happened, of course. That's why a welfare officer was supposed to have such close contact with an

Time's Bloodied Gold

undercover officer – to watch for such sympathies developing and to be there to reassure the undercover person that they were doing the right things. But Danny, he'd been left to form what alliances he could while at the same time, thanks to Rupert-fucking-Godden, being messed around from pillar to post by his own side.

"He died in my arms, Bill," was Danny's next gulping statement. "I've never had that happen. Not like that. You know, only the druggies and the ones we'd go into houses to find, and even then most of them were already dead, not dying. Not someone bleeding out over me."

Bill screwed his eyes up and pinched the bridge of his nose. Christ, what a cock-up! And he was hardly the best person to be handing out advice here. He'd never been involved in undercover work, not even as a handler, nor even in a fatal shooting at close quarters.

"Where are you now, Danny?"

"Driving back up to the farm."

"Is that wise? Is Mikhail likely to be there?"

"Yes, but I can't leave Kazimierz in his own to try and defend the others."

"Why not? Listen to me, Danny, they're crooks. They got themselves into this."

"No! No, they're not! And Kazimierz isn't a crook, he's a Polish undercover copper who got stuck like me. He was supposed to be got out long before they got here, but it all went wrong. I can't leave him there, Bill, I can't!"

"Okay, okay! Calm down, I hear what you're saying." Holy crap on a cracker! What next? A lost Polish copper in the mix as well. This was getting more hellish by the second. "Look, be careful, alright? What are you in, your car?"

"No, one of the Land Rover Defenders they have."

"Then leave it somewhere you can get to it. Don't take it into the farm and behind that gate. It'll be a lot easier for you and these others to leg it over the gate than trying to get a vehicle out." Why the hell was he saying that? God, his own morals were getting compromised now!

"That's a good thought. Thanks Bill." There was a pause. "I don't think I can come back."

"What do you mean?"

"I don't think I can go back to doing my old job, Bill. Not after being let down like this. Apart from you, I don't know who I can trust anymore. Especially not Williams. Him I'll never trust again. Not one word."

Bill felt his heart sinking even lower. "I know, I hear what you're saying. Look, Danny..." How much should he say with Danny in this state? Dare he say, 'you haven't got a job anyway'? No, that might tip Danny over the edge altogether. "Make sure you don't compromise yourself, eh? You know what I mean? Don't do anything that could be misinterpreted. I'm rebuilding fences for you as fast as I can, but they won't hold if you look suspect. Do you get what I mean?"

"I do." There was another long pause in which Bill could hear the Defender's elderly engine rattling away over the phone. "Remember to send Social Services up here tomorrow, won't you? I'll try to get the civilians to safety, and so will Kazimierz."

"How far are you from the farm?"

"About twenty minutes."

Bugger he was too close for Bill to intercept him. "I'm coming out, you need help!"

"No! No, I don't want you getting shot too. Just get the Bristol police out to the warehouse. They'll know where it is. It's on the riverside below where the house is in Clifton." Then the line went dead.

Time's Bloodied Gold

"Danny? ....Danny? ...Oh bollocks!"

Bill cleared the line and rang through to a number he knew either Sean or Jason was likely to pick up. He got Jason. In terse sentences he told him what had happened. "For fuck's sake get the lads down in Bristol moving before some little tyke gets in there and gets that AK74!" Bill pleaded.

"I'm on it. I'll call you back!"

Again the line went dead and Bill drew what felt like the first breath in several minutes. What could he do? It went against all of his instincts to just sit here like some spider in the centre of a web relaying messages back and forth. And what was worse, he wasn't sure where his own sympathies lay right now. Never in all his years had he questioned what to do the way he was doing at the moment. Procedures and protocols were all well and good, but they didn't cover eventualities like this, where someone he knew to be good at heart was in terrible trouble because the system had abjectly failed them. What the hell to do? Danny and this other abandoned copper could end up being taken in on murder charges if he did or said the wrong thing to someone. It was as bad a situation as he had ever known.

He made himself go and get ready to go out at a moment's notice, which filled a few minutes, then just as he was fingering his car keys and wondering whether he should just risk it and go, the phone rang again.

"Danny?"

"No, it's Sean. There was a patrol car close to the warehouse and they were there pretty much straight away. But there's a problem, Bill."

"A problem? What sort of problem? Is the gun missing?"

"No, the gun's there alright. It's the bodies. How many did you say there were?"

"Danny said there were two corpses of girls killed last summer wrapped in a tarp' and two fresh ones."

Sean's sigh was deep. "Well the lads down there haven't gone in yet for fear of disturbing the crime scene, but they're telling me that they can see one fresh body, and they can see the tarp, but there's and old and desiccated body right by the steps going in. There's a lot of blood around it like someone bled out there, but the body itself looks really old, like a century or so old. So someone' telling porkies. Did Danny say he actually saw this other guy getting shot?"

"Yes he did."

"And Danny himself isn't hurt?"

"Distressed, but if you mean has he been shot, then no, I don't think so."

"Then I hate to have to tell you this, Bill, but either Danny's the shooter or he's got the numbers wrong and there was another bloke there who carried the one who was bleeding out to the car and took him away. Although how the crusty old corpse then got dumped in the blood is something forensics will have to untangle. But there's no blood trail outside, which can only mean that someone is covered in a huge amount of blood that's not their own, because their clothes have to have absorbed one hell of a lot for there to be no drips."

Bill had a sinking feeling he knew what had happened. De Arce had reverted to the state he would have been in if he'd died in his own time. Who knew, maybe he had always had a limited amount of time he could remain functional in this one? It was hardly something Bill was expert in, and neither was anyone else. The only time he'd encountered anything like this was when he was back with Nick, and then the person coming into this time was returning to it having been in the past but born in the here and now, they weren't coming forwards to a point where they had never existed before. But none of this helped Danny, not least because it was hardly the kind of thing you could talk openly about and expect to be believed.

In the meantime he had to give Sean some kind of answer.

"Danny's not the shooter, Sean, but he was terribly shocked, and he did say that he hit his head pretty hard on the floor. He probably didn't see the other guy properly. He also said to me that this Mikhail bloke had a buddy called Ulryk who was another thoroughly nasty piece of work. He sounds as though he'd be quite capable of committing murder, and the two of them would probably cover for one another."

"Do you know where Danny is at the moment?"

"No." It wasn't totally a lie. Bill really didn't know if Danny was at the farm yet, and he knew that whatever instinct it was that had made him omit from telling Sean that Danny was heading for the farm had been the right one, just as he'd not yet told him about Kazimierz. "No, he was on his mobile and I could hear the car engine, so he was on the move, but he cut the call before I could get any more out of him."

Sean sighed again. "Okay, thanks, Bill. I'll try to keep you in the loop, but it looks like it's going to be a busy night."

The moment he rang off, Bill dialled Danny's number. "Bill?"

"Switch your mobile off *now*! You're about too be traced. They only found one body at Bristol!"

The line went dead.

Chapter 23

Sunday afternoon – evening
Bill

Bill hobbled at speed to the hire car and prayed that he wouldn't be too late. He had to get to the farm and try and get Danny and this Polish copper out of the way before all hell broke loose. Maybe it was a good thing that Danny didn't want to come back after all. The time it would take to sort this mess out would put a strain on all of them, and feeling under scrutiny by those who were once his close colleagues would be even worse than Williams' ineptitude and the indifference of the taskforce.

He took the road across country to Tenbury Wells as fast as he dared, and he was in Tenbury itself when he saw flickers of the flashing blue lights standing out through the falling light. The cars were just turning in over the bridge from the A456 as he pulled out of the B road at the other end of the main street. At least he wasn't in his instantly recognisable Mini, and so he put his foot down and flung the Citroen onto the car park at the *Fox & Goose* and killed the lights. Sure enough two patrol cars went past with an unmarked car behind them which was Jason's, lights flashing but sirens silent to avoid alerting the gang trouble was coming.

"Oh fuck!" Bill groaned, leaning his head onto the steering wheel. He was too late. They were ahead of him now and bound to get to the farm first.

Then he thought of the advice he'd given Danny. With any luck he would spot it, whereas to the others it would just be some parked up farmer's vehicle. So he pulled out and drove with more caution up the hill out of the town and along the twisting road towards Kyrewood Graves. Sure enough, there in a field gateway was a battered Defender, and Bill pulled the Citroen in beside it.

Easing himself out and slipping some gloves on, he went round to the driver's side and tried the door. Not only was the door unlocked but the keys were in the ignition. This had to be Danny's. But how to let him know that Bill had found it? Then he spied the almost empty bottle of water on the passenger seat. With care he opened it and wet a finger of his glove, then drew Danny's doodle in the muck and dust on the outside of the door, which couldn't have been cleaned in months. That ought to do it, but to be on the safe side, Bill took the water bottle with him – no point in leaving clues should his colleagues come driving back and think to check the vehicle. Danny must have been really badly shocked to leave potential DNA evidence like that lying around.

Then as he stood there he heard shots in the twilight. Not a shotgun. Not a farmer potting rabbits. This was the sound of something much more deadly than that and Bill's blood ran cold. Someone in that gang was using at least one other of those dreadful semi-automatics, and Bill prayed that it wasn't Danny in the firing line.

Danny

Tearing into Kyrewood Graves, Danny dumped the Defender in a gateway and set on foot over the last few fields towards the farm. He was still shaking over what had happened in Bristol, and all he could think of was getting to

Kazimierz, Stefan and Dymek before Mikhail turned the gun on them.

At the farmyard he slipped over the wall like a ghost and hugged the house's wall until he got to a lit window and could hear what was happening. There was an almighty row going on, and peeking in around the window frame he saw the remainder of the gang clustered together and shouting in one another's faces.

"You left him?" Kazimierz was screaming at Mikhail. "You left Danny?"

"He was dead," Mikhail snapped back. "Why do you keep coming back to him? He's no loss. De Arce is, though! And fucking Jerzy is dead and without paying us!"

"We have to go to Tomek!" Ulryk was shouting at the same time at Stefan and Dymek.

"I'm not going back to beating up working girls," Dymek snapped back at him, only to have Ulryk laugh in his face and taunt,

"And how are you going to live, eh? Who's going to pay you? Can't exactly go and get benefits can you when you're an illegal? British hospitality don't run that far!"

Then Mikhail's hand came out of his pocket with a pistol and fired a shot into the ceiling of the room.

Silence descended.

"I'm not fucking arguing," Mikhail snarled at them. "This is what we're doing, and anyone who argues can bite on one of these bullets, because I'm not pandering to you bunch of dancing nancies. I'm not going down in some British jail. And that means no witnesses, right?" He brought the pistol up and menacingly arced his arm around so that every one of the gang at some point came into the firing line. "Go and get your kit together *now*! Don't leave anything behind! Bring it down here."

"Then what?" Ulryk asked, clearly accepting Mikhail's

Time's Bloodied Gold

assumption of leadership without hesitation.

"Drown those fucking kids out there in the well. That should keep the parents quiet for a bit. Then we march them down to the river and into it, and I'll take care of them there. If the kids are already dead there'll be nothing for them to try any heroics for."

"And then?"

"Then we leave. Now *go*!"

Danny's mind was racing. Even Piotr was looking aghast at being told to drown the children, but what to do?

He looked up at the thick tangle of ivy that clung to the wall of the farmhouse and went up past the room he'd shared. Would it stand his weight? Only one way to find out.

He reached up, grabbed hold of the thick trunk and began scrambling up it.

At the window he glanced in, saw that only his friends were in there and tapped the window. Their faces were a picture as they saw him there, but Kazimierz recovered fastest and was opening the window and hauling him in before the others had caught their breath.

"Danny!" he gasped in relief. "We thought you were..."

"I know, I just heard. Look we have no time for me to tell you about Bristol. Listen! We have to get those kids away. I'm going to go and grab them and start running back towards Tenbury. I left the Defender by the side of the road back that way.

"What I need you to do is pretend to be searching when it gets discovered the kids are gone. Get Mikhail moving after the kids, not focusing on the parents! Stefan, can you offer to stay and guard them, and then when the others are out of the yard, let them go?"

"Yes."

"Good. As soon as they've gone, run like mad! If you

team up with Piotr, Dymek, I don't think you'll have any real trouble with him if you tell him it's a ruse once you're out in the fields. I saw his face downstairs. He doesn't want to do this."

He turned to Kazimierz. "I hate to ask this of you, but can you take Ulryk down? I don't mean kill him, but knock the bastard out cold or cripple him in some way so that he can't follow us. Mikhail's the random one. I have no idea what he'll do, but hopefully he'll come hunting us on his own. But if we can get him out in the open and without Ulryk backing him up at every turn, we might be able to get the jump on him. It can't be here, though, not with those poor sods in the stable close enough for him to threaten you with killing them if you don't do as he says."

Then he gave them the last vital piece of information. "The Defender I went in is parked in a farm gateway back along the road with the keys in it. Hopefully it's still there. Once you've got away from here pretending to search for me, get into that and drive into Worcester." He'd realised he couldn't tell them the twisting back ways. "Go over the bridge in Tenbury and take the main road but keep your speed down." He thrust some gloves at them. "Wear these! All of you! Don't leave any prints. Dump the Defender down under the railway arches by the river." He shoved a piece of paper and keys into Dymek's hands. "Go to this address, stay out of sight, and wait for me!"

"We're with you," Dymek said, as Kazimierz told Danny,

"Get back down there, then, and get a head start! Here, let us lower you down."

As soon as he dropped the last few feet to the yard, Danny was off and running in a low crouch to the stables. He didn't worry too much about leaving the outer door ajar, it was hardly that easy to tell from the farmhouse. But

Time's Bloodied Gold

it took ages to get the prisoners to realise that he had to take the two little girls. It was hearing Mikhail shouting something that finally got the second woman to release the smallest child, and then Danny was sweeping her into his arms, grasping the other one firmly by the wrist and heading out into the deepening darkness.

It helped no end that it was downhill towards the town, and soon Danny had a child on each hip as he plunged across the fields, always being careful to keep to the sides where the shadows lay heaviest. The moon might be waning from its height, but tonight it was still being treacherously bright, and a figure in the centre of an open field would stick out like a sore thumb. What was more, he could hear voices calling in Polish behind him, but if he had caught some of the more audible bits right, it was a couple of the lads making out that all of them were hunting him, but what that was about he couldn't begin to guess. Why hadn't they split up as planned?

Then behind him Danny heard the chatter of the remaining AK74. Dear God, what did that mean? Was one of his friends dead, or even the prisoners? He could feel himself starting to come apart inside. Why had nothing worked out right? Every plan he'd tried to make had gone to hell in a handcart, and he wished with all his heart that he had Bill's talent for picking the right path to follow.

"God, Bill, I'd give anything to see you now," he whispered to the skies, hoping that all of his prayers might be answered this night.

With a growing stitch in his side, Danny realised that he wasn't that far from the *Fox & Goose* by now. But dare he go into the town? No, not with Mikhail armed and dangerous, and as if some malevolent spirit had read his mind, there came another chatter of automatic gunfire in the distance. It sounded as though it was still at the farm, though. Christ, that wasn't good. Who was back there?

Then he caught the whiff of Russian tobacco and, keeping the girls quiet, risked looking out of the clump of hawthorns and wild cherries he was hidden by. There, still several yards away, were Dymek and Piotr, and it was Piotr who was dragging heavily on the cigarette. Also, neither of them was armed. That was good in one way, because it meant that the chances were that Kazimierz had got his hands on one of the remaining guns.

He plunged towards the river, knowing that if he could get to by the bridge, then he might just be able to flag down the Land Rover as it came past him as long as nobody was in hot pursuit. That had been the reason he'd not asked the others to wait for him. He knew these lanes like the back of his hand, and if he had to sneak back to the farm in the morning and get his car, then at least he knew the less patrolled roads to risk travelling on. The others didn't, and they needed to be out of sight by morning.

Then he heard a car coming down to by the bridge and stopping. It pulled into the narrow road which hugged the riverside for a short way, so it was off the road, but whoever it was had reversed it in to be able to drive out at speed. It wasn't a car he recognised, though. Dare he try and take it?

A much older engine noise suddenly echoed through the deserted streets, and to his relief Danny saw the Defender coming barrelling through the town and over the bridge. In it he could make out four figures, and that was definitely Kazimierz driving with Piotr in the front passenger seat, so hopefully it was Stefan and Dymek in the back. But how had Stefan got away so fast? That didn't bode well. What else had gone wrong at the farm?

What rocked him to the core was suddenly hearing a familiar voice speaking on a phone saying, "Armed

Response Unit? Blimey, Sean, that's heavy stuff! ...Two armed men making a siege of it? Jeez? Have you seen Danny? ...Oh Christ, I hope he's okay. ...Yes, I'll be sitting up. Ring my mobile, though. The house phone's batteries have gone dead. I must have not stuck it in the cradle right because it's as flat as a pancake at the moment. ...Okay, keep me in the loop."

For a moment there was silence, then Danny risked calling out softly, "Bill?"

"Danny?" There was nothing but relief in that word. "God, where are you?"

"Here," Danny said more loudly, scrambling to get the two girls up onto the road, and then seeing Bill's hand come out of the gloom to take one of them and pull her up, then reach back for the other.

"They were going to kill them," Danny said, his voice shaking badly as he almost collapsed against Bill. "I had to make a run for it."

Bill was already steering them towards the big gold car. "Get the kids in," he said calmly, as though this was nothing more than a routine matter. All by itself that was a balm to Danny's shattered soul. "You, in the front."

When Danny had climbed in and put his seatbelt on, Bill took off and headed for the 'B' road across country.

"Do you know what's happening at the farm?" he asked Danny. "What's this about an Armed Response Unit being needed?"

"I have no idea, truly I haven't," Danny replied honestly. "I heard you say two men. That can only be Mikhail and Ulryk making a fight of it, but who went out there?"

"Jason and a couple of patrol cars."

"Oh God! They're no match for those two killers!"

"Well Jas' didn't say that anyone's been hurt yet."

"Thank God for that!"

Bill risked taking a glance at Danny. He seemed totally genuine in that response, and that was what finally made up his mind. If two of the gang were likely to end up being carted out in body-bags, then there was no reason why Danny should get mixed up in this.

"Right, this is what we're going to do, okay? I'm going to drive straight up to the hospital and park up somewhere out of sight. Then you are going to walk in through the front doors of A&E and leave these two kiddies there with the nurses. I don't care how you do it, go in and come out. Then you're coming back to my place. At that point I'm going to ring Jason and tell him you're with me."

"No, Bill, I can't have you do that. You can't give me an alibi. I'm not having your career on my conscience."

"I wasn't giving you an option."

"No, I know you weren't, but listen: I'm not coming back. I'm never coming back!"

"Where the hell are you going, then? You'll be a hunted man, Danny!"

"No I won't. Not once they really investigate that place in Bristol."

"Danny, they only found one fresh corpse. De Arce's went back to what it would have been – it looks a hundred years old! That means they're looking for another man. A real man."

"And when they compare Mikhail's prints and DNA to what's down there they'll have him. I left nothing, Bill, nothing at all. The best they'll get is the muck of the farmyard from off my shoes, and any one of the gang could have left that. Please, let me disappear."

"To where?"

"I'm not sure. But the first thing I have to do is help Kazimierz go home. I don't think either of us trusts for him to get a fair hearing here, no more than I do. We've got access to some money – don't worry, it's not that dirty, it's not drugs or blood money. We'll go north and east, take the long way across to Europe." He didn't want to say that there would be more of the gang with them – even Bill could only be pushed so far.

There was a heavy sigh from the driver's seat. "What about Zoe? This all started because of her, you know."

Danny groaned. "I know, but maybe she's better off without me. Jane's seeing someone else and it's serious. He seems like a nice bloke. Steady job, nine to five, weekends off. He'll be there more than I ever could be. I'll get myself set up somewhere and send back what I can. It's for the best, Bill. None of you should have to take sides with me in some bloody awful trial. Even if I'm acquitted – and I haven't actually done anything wrong, so a prosecution ought to fall apart – I still fear Williams dragging me through the mud just to prove that his men did their duty and followed every clue. I can't face that. Those blokes I've been with were mostly just poor bastards who got dragged into this by mistake. I truly do not want to testify against them. But that means I have to either perjure myself or live with so much guilt for the rest of my life that it wouldn't be worth the living. I can't win in that situation."

Bill was silent for a while, but then his deep sigh presaged his agreement. "I get it. ...I'm so sorry, Danny, I should never have recommended you for that secondment."

"Don't be daft. I was as eager for it as anyone. I just never expected it to go so wrong."

"Ah, about that..." and Bill told him about Rupert

Godden. "So you see, that's why it was such a god-awful cock-up," Bill concluded over Danny's soft and fluent swearing. "I promise you, *I'll* deal with him for you! Don't you go take revenge on him. At the moment you're right, you've done nothing except be in the wrong place at the wrong time. Let's keep it like that, eh?"

By now they were into the outskirts of Worcester, and Bill steered his way through and out the other side up to the hospital. Tucking the car into a shadowy spot, Bill helped Danny get the two little girls out and walked them part of the way to the A&E entrance. However the moment it became better lit by the street lamps and security cameras, Bill stopped and let Danny go on alone.

It was a tense wait, but then Danny came jogging back to him, hugging the shadows of the trees which bordered the hospital car park.

"Are they okay?" Bill asked.

"I left them sitting between two families bringing kids in. They'll soon be spotted, and they seemed reassured by there being other children there. They're a good way from the door. They can't just wander out on their own."

"Good. Now where do you want to go if not to my place?"

"My old flat, please. I need to get my passport and some stuff."

"I'm not happy about this, Danny."

"I know you aren't, but this is for the best."

"You keep saying that, but is it?"

Danny leaned forwards and buried his head in his hands. "I think so. Maybe if you can tell me at some point that everything's been sorted out, then I might risk coming back. I've got your number – just don't go changing it!"

"I won't."

Time's Bloodied Gold

Danny

Outside his real home building, Bill dropped Danny off. It was hardly a major clue for anyone trying trace them since it was an enormous complex of apartments not far from the river and the local nightclubs, where a lot of young people lived and who tended to come and go at all hours. No-one would take a blind bit of notice of a car pulling in at this hour.

However, Danny knew that Bill would have made better time getting here than the others would, even allowing for the stop at the hospital, because they would be trying to find their way through unfamiliar streets, and so he loitered in the public foyer, watching for them. Sure enough, within minutes he saw them coming his way along the road known as The Butts, and opened the front door for them.

"Come on up," he said, and led them to his flat.

Inside, once the blinds were drawn and the lights were on, he could see how drawn and exhausted they all looked.

"What the hell happened at the farm?" he asked.

"Mikhail went nuts," Stefan said, then made a dash for the bathroom and could be heard being very ill.

"He went into the stable with the MK74," Kazimierz said with a shudder. "Poor Stefan saw him gun the prisoners down in cold blood."

"And you?"

"Me? I had a fight with Ulryk. Gave him a thump to the side of the head, but that bastard could get kicked in the head by a bull and it wouldn't stop him. He went down just long enough for me to run and grab Stefan, then together we were just about to jump the gate when we saw blue lights. So we dived off into the fields and ran like crazy for the Defender. We'd already arranged to grab Dymek with Piotr further down the lane." Kazimierz gave another shudder as a wan Stefan came out of the bathroom. "The next thing we hear, Mikhail must have opened up on those cops. Fucking lunatic!"

"Right, we stay locked up here for a few days," Danny declared. "Everyone will assume that we'll be making a run for it right away. So we stay here and rest and plan. Find yourselves somewhere comfortable and get some sleep."

"Where is this place?" Piotr asked warily.

"This is mine," Danny told him, "my flat." Then he remembered that none of the men here had been to the one in Leominster and that he could explain the two flats away quite easily. "The place in Leominster belongs to a mate of mine in the navy. He's away for months on end and I had the key to keep an eye on it, so I used it while I was with you." Another lie to add to the growing list. Better that, though, than confess to being a cop after what had gone down tonight.

Only when the others were all snoring mightily did he and Kazimierz slip into the kitchen for a quiet conversation.

"I think my bridges are burnt," Danny told him sadly, "how about yours? Can you go back to Poland?"

Kazimierz looked dejected. "I have a terrible feeling not." He turned and looked wistfully out of the window to the trees swaying in the wind by the river, visible even at night by the yellow light of the street lamps, but seeing none of it as he became lost in thought. "I tried to ring my parents a few times when I first got here. All I got was a rant about what a terrible son I was to bring such disgrace down on them. I couldn't get a word in. And my wife was very strange when I rang. I got the feeling she was trying to tell me either that there was someone in the apartment with her, or that she knew our phone was being tapped. And that makes me think that despite trying to leave message for my colleagues about how I was stuck with the gang, they didn't believe it.

"What was then worse was finding myself over here. My English has got better over the months we've been here, but I'm glad you speak Polish, because I still struggle with it a lot. I couldn't have even asked my way to the train station when I got here, you see, let alone come into a police station and try to make my situation understood – and I confess, I feared what might happen under those circumstances if I was misunderstood and taken for one of the gang. I certainly didn't think the English police would expend much effort getting in touch with my old force, or that they'd give me much of a reference if they did."

"Same here," Danny sympathised, "I don't anticipate much sympathy for me. What do you think the others will do?"

"Dymek and Stefan will want to go home no matter what," Kazimierz said without hesitation. "I think they'd rather do time in a jail at home, if that's the price they have to pay to go back, and at least have their families come to visit. Piotr…he's anyone's guess. Maybe he really does want that place in the sun? But it's all a bit academic, isn't it? Unless you can fund us a ticket on a ferry we're not getting out of England." Danny's growing smile clearly puzzled him. "What? Why are you grinning like that at me?"

"Because I have the codes to get into de Arce's bank account. He's dead, Kazimierz, and my contact in the force says his body crumbled away to what it ought to be by now. There's just a crusty corpse down in Bristol now. He's never going to try to claim that money and he's hardly going to have son or daughter appear out of the woodwork and prove they have a claim to it. Now it can sit in that bank account for ever more, earning interest but benefitting only the bank; or we split it between us and get something out of it."

Kazimierz looked at him in amazement. "You can access it? How?"

Danny chuckled. "It's an online banking service, mate. De Arce probably never had a clue as to how he could get at it. He was probably relying on somebody like Montefiori to help him get at it once he was in the West Indies. But the thing is, I've got the secure password and I know how to access the account. I'll do that before I ever try to transfer any money so that I make sure any other information is stuff that I've changed to things I can remember. They sometimes ask you for your mother's maiden name and stuff like that, you see.

"Now I know I've got to get away from here. My old boss has already helped me, but in all conscience I can't ask him to do more. The rest wouldn't believe me anymore, no matter what I said. So I'm heading for somewhere where I can lie low for a few years, and I was thinking of going to the Dominican Republic and seeing if I could find this Montefiori chap. De Arce never gave him a cent for his trouble, you know. So if he looks like he's genuine, and was just somebody else who was caught in de Arce's snare, then I don't mind transferring some of the money his way. I reckon for the stress he's had he's due it.

"Don't look at me like that, Kazimierz. This money came from very rich men who were happy to pay for ancient artefacts on the black market, artefacts that they still have – nobody's cheated them. And we can't give the artefacts back to the people back through time who originally had them, can we? So we've robbed nobody we could possibly compensate, and worse, if we gave this money in, who would believe us where it had come from, and it would just go to the government in the end. Well screw that! We've had a lifetime's worth of shit thrown at us, and if anyone has earned the right to live off the proceeds it's us for what we at least tried to do – and don't forget, neither you nor I will ever draw our professional pensions! What we have needs to see us into our old age."

The expression on Kazimierz's face said that he'd not thought of it in those terms before, and it was a rude awakening.

"Oh Mother of God!"

Danny gave a wry sniff. "Exactly, my old son. We either rely on her divine intervention, or we take a practical point of view. So are you with me on this? If you are, tomorrow while we sit here out of sight, I can go online and transfer money around and tell the others that they can go where they want. But I can't do that with you sitting there looking disapproving. They know and trust you far more than they do me, so if you start looking at me sideways, they're going to copy you."

Kazimierz gave a deep and sorrowful sigh. "We've been left no other choice, have we?"

"Not that I can see. I tell you no word of a lie, if someone told me this time last year that I'd be feeling this way and doing what I'm about to do, I'd have punched them out. I'd have taken it a slur against all that I've worked towards as a detective. Never in a million years would I have believed that I could feel the way I do about my old job now. But I've seen too much of the other side, and been too trapped there to ever be able to be as blinkered again."

He went and fetched the bottle of Highland Park he had in the top kitchen cupboard for special moments, and poured two generous measures out, then chinked his glass against the one he pushed towards Kazimierz and took an appreciative sip.

"My old boss, Bill, used to tell me that I needed to see things from the other bloke's viewpoint more often. God knows how, but he was always able to be broadminded. If it had been him in this situation, maybe he'd be able to go back, because it wouldn't have come as such a shock to his values and beliefs. And from where I stand now, I think he was always the better and more committed copper than I am – something I really want to be able to tell him sometime. He went into it with a far more 'eyes wide open' approach than me. I used to think I was rounding up the scum of the earth. I never saw them as people who maybe had very few choices. He warned me it would come back to bite me, but I don't think even he was prepared for how."

The following morning, having brewed up copious amounts of coffee and disabled the smoke alarm so that the others could smoke without ending up evacuating the block, he sat them down and broke the news of the money. As expected, Stefan and Dymek immediately asked to be able to go home. The surprise came when Danny announced that he was going to the Dominican Republic to try and find Montefiori.

"I'm going to come with you, then," Piotr announced. "It's hot and sunny there, you can live cheaply enough and the booze is decent, that'll suit me."

"Suppose I'd better come to, then," Kazimierz decided, his look at Danny saying that it might take both of them to get Piotr there without incident.

"Have you got your passports with you?" Danny asked the others and was pleasantly surprised to see them all pulling them out of inside pockets.

Time's Bloodied Gold

"I told them to keep them on them," Kazimierz said with a rueful smile. "Had a funny feeling that things might not go down as we hoped."

"I'm bloody glad you did," Danny said with relief. "Without them this next step would be so much harder."

He had already checked and found that at least they didn't need a visa to get into the D.R., and so the next step was to book them all onto holiday tour groups.

"Stefan and Dymek, I've booked you onto a holiday tour going to Krakow. If anyone asks you're two cousins going back, but once you are in the country you'd best tell the tour guide that you've had an offer to stay on with some family member and won't be returning with the rest of the party. Make it sound as normal as possible. Something like an elderly aunt being frailer than you thought and in her last days, that sort of thing. As long as you reassure them that you won't be asking for any refund, I doubt that they'll argue too hard.

"Kazimierz and Piotr, we're going on a holiday to the sun which we've won off our employers for hitting our targets. We've worked on an important building contract that's come in ahead of schedule. Don't worry too hard about the story – just smile and nod when I give you the wink if I'm talking to people, because you'll be on a plane full of British holiday-makers. We go as a last minute booking at the end of the week. You two others will go on Wednesday, so I'd better go and get you something that will pass as baggage, because nothing will look stranger than holiday makers with no cases – and anyway you'll need a change of clothes before then for all our sakes!"

What he did do was speak to Dymek and Stefan on one side under the pretext of getting their sizes for clothes.

"I promised Jerzy his sister would get his share," he told them. "Can you try and trace her in Gdansk? I'll give you a phone number to use to get to me. When you find her, ring me with her bank details and I'll send her the money."

"I thought you were splitting the money between us five?" Dymek asked worriedly.

"De Arce's money, yes I am," Danny answered with a grin. "But that's far more than Jerzy had in the account he had, because he was taking all the expense of renting the farmhouse and stuff. He gave me the code to his account as he died. It's that money that I'm splitting between his sister and Montefiori. Just don't tell Piotr, eh? Kazimierz knows already, but I don't know how Piotr would take the idea that Jerzy was going to clear off without having given him his cut at the last. Better to keep him calm for now.

"What I would say to you is that when you get home, move your families well away from where you used to live. Make sure you're not where anyone would expect to find you. I doubt that Tomek will come hunting in person, but he undoubtedly has connections, so make sure you're out of their reach."

They both assured him that they would, and three days later Danny was waving them off from Birmingham International Airport having taken them there by train. No way was he risking trying to hire a car or use his own. And then three days later he, Kazimierz and Piotr were on their way, and as the English countryside fell away beneath him, Danny felt a terrible pang of longing at whether he would ever see it again – this job had started as the answer to all of his prayers and had ended as his worst nightmare.

Chapter 24

March

The letter fell on Bill's mat the following Monday and he immediately recognised the handwriting. Tearing it open, two sets of keys fell out onto his carpet, one clearly car keys and the other house keys.

Dear Bill, it began, *by the time you read this I'll hopefully be on a plane and heading far from England. I have written to my building society and told them I am selling the flat. Would you do me one last favour and go round and empty it out for me? I can't see me coming back for a very long time and nothing will leave a clearer trail to me than continued payments on the mortgage from a foreign account. If there's anything left at the end it's to go to Zoe. As for the car, it's about time you had something a bit more modern, so feel free to use it if you want to, or give it to Jane. The forms are in the flat already signed, so it can all be transferred legally, but would you go round and explain to them both why I can't do this in person? After all that's happened, I find I can't bear the thought that they think any worse of me than they do already. I will try to find a way to be in touch with them, but warn them that it won't be for a few months until I'm sure I'm not bringing any trouble down on them.*

Over these last months, I've found myself wanting to tell you this more and more: you were right, about all of it! I saw things too black and white. That I've learned the hard way. And I now see that I only made things hard for myself by baiting people all the time to live up to standards no normal person ever could do – I certainly couldn't. My best didn't even come close to it, but I only realised that far too late. You're a far better man than I am, and I'm truly sorry for all the grief I've caused you, and for some of the stupid, thoughtless things I said to you in the past. You never deserved them, and I'm heartily ashamed of myself. I certainly don't deserve the way you've stuck by me in these last days, but I'm very grateful that you did.

I can't tell you more, but I'm going to try and live a better life and put right the wrong done to another person by de Arce, and maybe sometime in the future I'll be able to tell you all about it. I'll never be able to repay you for what you've done, but you have my eternal gratitude,
Danny

Bill found he had a lump in his throat by the time he got to the end. So the Danny he'd always believed in was still there after all. That was good to know. And then he noticed a phone number scribbled at the bottom of the note, with the added warning 'Do not try to use for three months! Won't be switched on until then!' Still being cautious then, and who could blame him?

He himself had spent the intervening week going in and out of work to answer questions. It was clear that Williams was seething at being outmanoeuvred, but was equally being restrained by those higher up from reprimanding Bill. That didn't bother Bill that much. There

Time's Bloodied Gold

wasn't that much Williams could do to him when he had no aspirations to rise any higher, and really wouldn't have been distraught at dropping down to DS again if Williams chose to push his luck and demote him. Far more important was trying to clear up the mess they'd found at the farm, not helped by the taskforce admitting through gritted teeth the degree to which Danny had tried to pass on warnings which had been buried by Godden.

Jason was in line for a commendation for the way he'd handled the situation he'd found out there on the Sunday night, for it had had the potential to be a total disaster. Luckily only two of the PCs had been hurt, and that only minorly by flying chips of stone off the track where Mikhail's bullets had flung them up. Nobody had died amongst their own, and that was little short of a miracle given what they had found in the stables once the Armed Response Unit had gone in and turned Mikhail and Ulryk into human sieves.

"Heaven know where these poor sods came from," the pathologist confided to Sean, and he in turn to Bill. "They don't seem to belong to anywhere I can pinpoint. I've never seen people so untouched by modern life. I can only hope to God they have no family waiting for them to come back, because I can't give you a single thing that would help you trace them. If we didn't have so many of them all the same, I'd be thinking one or two of them were cases of people kept as virtual prisoners from birth in some wild and remote place as the only explanation, and even that doesn't fit that well."

However, if there was a good side to all of this it was that having had such a dramatic shoot-out at the farm, there was no doubt in everyone's minds that these two were also responsible for the shootings in Bristol. Bill couldn't dig too deep, but Danny's name never even cropped up where those shootings were concerned, for which he was greatly relieved. That was another reason to hunt for Danny gone, and amen to that.

Joe Connolly had been one of those who had gone to break the news to Tomek that his cousin Jerzy was dead, and that so too were Mikhail and Ulryk who had been responsible for Jerzy's death.

"He didn't know what the hell to do or say," Joe told Bill as he joined him for a pint in the *Wheatsheaf* on the Sunday after it had all happened. "I think he was genuinely upset about his cousin, but he's such a dyed-in-the-wool gangster that he was tying himself in knots not to say anything that might imply that he knew anything about what had gone on. And the news that Reznik has vanished off the face of the earth really seemed to worry him. He wouldn't give us so much as a hint, but you could see that he was shit-scared that he was next, because the big man down in London has a nasty reputation even amongst that bunch of thugs. I took the greatest of pleasure in offering him protection if he'd come clean with us and seeing him squirm. He didn't take it, of course, but it was fun baiting him."

"He's a fool for not taking that offer," Bill said sagely. "He's made too many ripples in the water in Birmingham; his days have to be numbered within the gang. And speaking of numbered days, what of Godden?"

"Ah, can't say too much on that score to you, but don't be surprised if you aren't called to give a witness statement in court."

"Hint duly taken, and it couldn't happen to a more fitting person."

"What about Danny?" Joe asked carefully.

"He's taken to the hills."

"Is that wise, Bill?"

Time's Bloodied Gold

"Maybe not, but he wouldn't hear of coming in. That's how badly he feels let down, and I won't hesitate to make my thoughts on that very clear to anyone who asks me. We've lost a good man, Joe. A man who got so badly let down that he's past trusting anyone."

"Except you. I don't believe he's lost faith in you." Joe looked at Bill with squinted eyes. "I do believe you're keeping secrets young William! ...But if you are, then I understand why. Just practise that poker face for when you speak to the brass – you'll need it."

"Surely they aren't going to try and press any charges against Danny?" Bill asked, appalled.

However Joe immediately shook his head vigorously. "God, no! There's nothing they could make stick. And to be honest there's very little will from anyone at our end to work up what little we have into some half-baked, feeble case. If Danny's chosen to run it's terribly sad but we have no legal reason to drag him back, let alone ask for an extradition from wherever he's gone."

"No, that's pretty much what Sean and Jason were telling me about our end of things. It doesn't look good from any outsider's viewpoint that a gang with that much firepower was holed up on our patch and keeping people prisoners and we did nothing about it, to start with anyway. And for them to then go on a killing spree is something our great and good really don't want bandied about. They've managed to keep it down to one gunman and one casualty, who was a vulnerable man being kept on the farm as a worker. I'm told that the person who let the farm out, and the charming lad at the farm up the road, have both been told that talking to the press would not be one of their brighter ideas. The woman soon got the idea, because she needs to be able to sell the place. The other farmer and his son took a bit more leaning on, but once Sean had laid it on heavy about ghoulish visitors tramping all over their crops, they got the point.

"In amongst all of that, Danny's become something of a secondary consideration. He shouldn't have. Someone should be screaming blue murder to find out where he is as a priority for his own well-being, because he ought to be shoved the way of a bloody good shrink and given counselling for as long as he needs it on the force's budget. I think he needs it, Joe, I really do. We've failed him in a whole extra way by not picking up the pieces of the disaster we sent him into, and on a purely personal level I'm worried that he may never be the same again. But if he does come in, I don't think that's how he'll be treated, and that's why I'm keeping his secrets. Either he gets treated properly or not at all, because I, for one, am not prepared to bring him in for a witch hunt. I don't think he's always made the right decisions, but from where he was standing I doubt that a 'right' decision ever existed as anything more than wishful thinking."

Joe nodded thoughtfully. "I agree with every word. I tell you, I've told my bosses that I'm never getting involved with another operation like that again. I made it very clear that after what I've seen happen to Danny, there's no way I'm putting my neck on the line again. I don't think they liked it, but given the circumstances they could hardly argue with me either."

That had been the response of most of the people Bill had met in the course of the week, and so as he stood in his lounge looking down at the keys in his hands he thought it was time he went and paid Jane a visit. If anyone was camped on Jane's doorstep waiting for Danny to show up, a quiet word in their ear about how they might want their own mates to look out for their wives if the situation was reversed ought to do the trick. And who was to say that Bill

Time's Bloodied Gold

wasn't just there to offer his condolences? He'd just make sure that he had the relevant bit of the talk somewhere like the garden out of anybody's hearing.

And so he got into the Citroen, which he'd kept on for the next couple of weeks, and drove across the river to St Peter's where Jane and Zoe now lived. Luckily Zoe was at school and there was no sign of anyone parked outside of Jane's tiny modern house.

When she came to the door, Bill thought she looked downright ill with stress. Maybe there was still enough there that they could patch things up if Danny wasn't away all hours with the job?

"Bill! How lovely to see you!"

That wasn't forced. Jane was openly glad to see him, and so Bill went in and accepted the offer of coffee.

"Before I tell you anything," he began cautiously, "has anyone from the job been here of late?"

He quirked an eyebrow and looked at the phone, and was not surprised but disappointed when Jane said,

"Not recently," but nodded at the phone.

So there was a phone tap, was there? Whose idea was that? Williams still wanting his petty revenge on Danny for the almighty bollocking everyone knew he'd had, even though nothing had been announced publicly. You only had to look at the way he was behaving in the last week to know that somebody very senior had danced all over his toes.

"Let's go for a walk in the garden," Bill suggested. "Those daffodils look wonderful!"

Once outside in their coats and nursing hot coffees against the brisk early March wind, Bill did his best to bring Jane up to date.

"He's been treated appallingly," he concluded. "We both know that he's been unhappy with the job for a few years now, but nothing Danny ever did or said warranted what he's been through. I want you to be very clear on that Jane. I know that by the time you split up you could hardly have had much of anything good to say about Danny aside from the fact that he still adored Zoe, and in truth, that wasn't far from the situation with me. He'd pushed me and pushed me, and in those first weeks after he went to the taskforce I was heartily glad to have seen the back of him. But even those who couldn't stand him have been going around this last week or so muttering about how even he didn't deserve this."

"But what's he going to do?" Jane asked, appalled. "What's he going to live on if he has no job? Where's he gone? It's not about the money he pays to me, Bill. Tom and I have been talking about moving in together for months now. We're just waiting for Zoe, because she finishes junior school this summer and so she'd be moving school anyway. So we'll be living in Droitwich by August because Tom's house is much bigger – it's a proper family home. But Danny ...what's he going to do? You're right, at the break up I hated his guts, but now I'm just sad that what we had fell apart so badly, and you're right – the job was at least half of that. I couldn't cope with never knowing when he was coming home, and looking back now, I can see that he was finding it harder and harder to get anything out of it, and that's why he was such a bad-tempered sod all the time."

Bill took a deep breath. He really hoped Jane would understand what he was about to tell her.

"This is only a guess, okay? I have no proof of it at all. I think he's probably in the West Indies."

"The West Indies? How the hell did he get there?" Jane was clearly already getting ideas of Danny sunning himself

Time's Bloodied Gold

on a beach and drinking tequila while she'd been worried sick about him.

"Oh he'll only just have gone – in this last week, I mean. He was here and in great danger right up until that shoot-out at the farm last weekend. I know because I spoke to him on the phone and he was bloody terrified!" He wasn't going to say he'd actually seen Danny, because he knew Jane's instant response would be why hadn't he come to see her then? "But part of that fear was of what his own side were going to do to him. Truly, Jane, he's lost all faith in them.

"Now I want you to understand what I'm telling you here, okay? There was money the gang had that's not been found." He saw Jane's face settle into a frown and hastily continued. "We're not talking drugs' money or anything like that. This lot were trading artefacts, but we have no idea from where. They clearly came a very long way, and even if we could trace them to the dodgy collectors who have them, there's no way we could send them back to where they came from – it's probably some war-torn part of Syria or Iran! So the money that came from the collectors, while dubious, isn't actually stolen. These are genuinely stinking rich people who just happen to have a total lack of morals when it comes to getting some lovely shiny antique.

"So I think that those of the gang that got away found a way to get at this. Danny was very insistent that some of the men he was with were just poor blokes who'd been pressured into the gang back in Poland. Even in the reports that have been dug out of Godden's laptop, Danny's saying as far back as November that he felt that there were only a couple of the gang who were even criminals in the true sense of the word, let alone dangerous. And at the end he confessed to me that one of them was an undercover Polish cop who'd got stuck when they took off and came here, because presumably he had little or no English. He'll be in the exact same pickle as Danny – no job and no money, and certainly no pension – and that's why I think someone got into the bank account and redistributed the funds."

"But why the West Indies?" Jane demanded. "Couldn't he have just fucked off to the Costas or bloody Tunisia or somewhere?"

Bill sighed. "It's not to do with money, if that's what you're thinking. He's not living the high life, Jane – there was cash, but not that much once it was broken up. What makes me say the West Indies is because of what went on in the house in Bristol. It's like this nutcase de Arce filled the gang leader, Reznik's, head with ideas of being some latter-day slave trader – not bringing slaves across like they used to, mind. So they had these trafficked people bringing them the goods, but then the goods were being taken to Haiti and places by Reznik's drugs couriers when they went back, and from there the artefacts were being taken into America. Now Danny always said that West Indies link was really important, and I think that if he can't come back here, then he and that Polish copper have gone out to Haiti to make sure that some other victim isn't still being held with his family jewels in a vice by whatever remains of Reznik's network out there. I think he's trying to put something right, Jane."

He saw the tension drain out of her. "God, that would be so like Danny. Or at least the Danny I once thought I knew."

"I think so too," Bill agreed. "Especially as he sent me this letter," and he handed it over for Jane to read.

As she got to the end her hand went over her mouth and the tears began to flow. "Oh Danny, why did you have to be such bloody hard work?" she sobbed.

Time's Bloodied Gold

When she could speak again, she handed Bill the letter back. "Will you do that? Will you take care of things for him?"

"Yes. I have a big basement storage area under my place. I've got plenty of room to store things as long as I put stuff like his books into sealed plastic containers so that they don't get damp."

"I don't want that phone number," Jane said. "If I have it and Zoe finds it, it will only upset her."

Bill nodded. "Please tell her the truth about her dad, though, won't you? Tell her he was a bloody hero at the end. I can't tell you more about that bit specifically, but he did something very brave on the last day with the gang." Given that Bill himself hadn't dared to ask anyone to dig into two abandoned little girls at Worcester hospital, and wasn't back at his desk yet to check himself, he didn't dare say anything in case Jane got the wrong idea if anything came out in the press, like an appeal for the parents to come forward. "Do you want me to let you know if he does ring?"

Jane looked torn. Too many broken promises lay between her and Danny.

"In a year or two's time it might be possible for Zoe to go and visit her dad," Bill prompted. "You know, if he's settled somewhere." Jane looked balefully at him, making Bill add hurriedly. "He's never questioned that Zoe was better off living with you, Jane. He wouldn't get Zoe out of the country and then go on the run with her. Jeez, even you can't think that badly of him, surely?"

Jane huffed and then shook her head. "No, you're right, Bill, he wouldn't. And by then she'll be in her teens and not a little girl anymore. But if you can bear to do this, let's keep you as the go-between for now, eh? Probably better that I don't speak to him for a while."

Bill didn't argue with that, but as much because he feared that given the state Danny must be in mentally, having Jane throw accusations at him at the moment could be fatal. If Danny thought she was blackening his name with Zoe it would put the tin hat on everything, and Bill might not have had a degree in mental health, but he knew how vulnerable someone with post-traumatic stress disorder could be – and it would be miraculous if Danny wasn't suffering from that by now.

So he drove back to his flat and spent the next week getting Danny's things in order before he was due back at work. What he did get was an update by Sean about St Michael's which he passed on to Nick when they went for a curry together after his first week back.

"They found the dumping site for the two girls," Bill told him as he dunked a poppadom. "The joys of working in forensics!" and he rolled his eyes. "The forensic team had the results from the bodies from Bristol, which helped, and amongst other things, apparently the rat shit on the corpses matched the same stuff they found at the grave site – the little furry bastards had had a fair old feast, sadly. You were right, Nick, de Arce did need blood. What is tragic is that the one girl was pregnant, so in effect he took three lives."

Nick shuddered. "And I reckon he'd have seen that as significant. Threes are important in some many religious rites."

"And the samples which got taken from off the stones matched with the girls too. There's no doubt about it, I'm afraid, de Arce made his human sacrifices."

Nick took a hefty swig of his beer. "I take no pleasure in being right about that. However, I have something which I think will brighten your day a little."

"Oh really?"

Time's Bloodied Gold

"That Anglo-Saxon sword we saw being brought through – they found it at Kyrewood Graves farm, you know. So I managed to swing it that I was the one who went and picked it up, because your lot wanted it authenticating. I tell you, Bill, I was wondering what the hell to do about it, because on the one hand it gives us archaeologists a chance to study a pristine example, but on the other, how on earth was I going to explain it being here in that state? So I carefully tucked it away in a drawer and told your guys that I'd have to run a lot more tests on it, but that it was possible that it was just a very good fake."

"I can see why you'd do that," Bill admitted. "It's a lot easier to convince people that a bunch of rogues were flogging clever fakes to the Americans than bringing the real thing through time."

"That was my thought. Well you could have knocked me down with a feather when I went to have another look at it on Friday. I thought what with everyone else having cleared off as early as they could at the end of the week, it was as good a time as any for me to get it out and look at it without someone coming up and peering over my shoulder. I didn't really get chance to inspect it when I picked it up you see, I was just making sure it was stored safely and properly in its original wrapping." Nick gave a bemused shake of his head. "It's changing, Bill!"

"Changing? How?"

"Well for a start off, the blade is rusting, and rapidly!"

"Oh, my God, it's like de Arce's body all over again, isn't it? It's reverting to the state it should be in in this time!"

Nick nodded. "That's what I think. Now that won't affect the gold and jewels, but any of those collectors who bought stuff with an iron element in them are going to have one hell of a shock when they open up their cabinet, or whatever, and find that their secret prized possession is falling to bits before their eyes."

Bill found himself starting to grin. "So they'll get their comeuppance without anyone lifting a finger? Marvellous! That's what I like to hear. And they'll never be able to trade them on for anything like the money they paid for them, will they? So I doubt any gallery or museum will get robbed by paying for something like that, because what would be the point of selling? And they can hardly ask for a refund. ...Oh and by the way, Reznik's body was found in the Thames down by the Isle of Dogs, so he'll tell no secrets."

"What about that Tomek bloke you mentioned?"

Bill sat back contentedly as he watched his chicken pasanda arrive, then grinned again. "Ah, the illustrious Mr Miskiewicz! Strangely enough, he's been conspicuous by his absence in Birmingham, and then Jason got a phone call from Joe Connolly. Apparently, after Joe had been to break the news of his cousin's death to him he went abnormally quiet, so they began wondering if he'd been called down to London too, and was going to turn up like Reznik. Well the Met kept their eyes peeled, but he didn't show up there, and he didn't pass through any airport, but then out of the blue, we got handed the information that someone who keeps an eye out for bad lads lording it on the Costa del Sol sent in a report that Tomek Miskiewicz has turned up there. It seems he's been keeping a very low profile there too, and the thought is that he might be heading for Morocco sooner than later. The West Midlands lads are chuffed, though, because while the trafficking gang is rudderless, they've been able to go in and do a grand mopping up job. So even if the Polish gang send someone new in to take his place, they'll be starting from scratch. They won't wholly go away – they never do – but their claws have been hugely cut for several years I'd say."

Time's Bloodied Gold

"I'm glad about that," Nick declared. "You could almost say everything had turned out alright except for the toll it's taken on Danny. Any news from him?"

Bill shook his head. "No, but with the gang out of the way, I can at least be hopeful." Nick was the one person Bill had been totally honest with about where Danny was heading. "I think he'll want to see what mischief de Arce was planning in what he knew as Spanish Haiti and we know as the Dominican Republic. I was deliberately vague with Jane and just said Haiti in case she dropped it out to anyone else. All my instincts are screaming at me that that's where he is."

"Maybe time for a holiday to the Caribbean in the summer, then?" Nick asked with a mischievous wink, and with a grin Bill replied,

"I do believe you could be right."

Before we get to the notes which give you some back ground on the story, thank you for taking the time to read this book.

I hope you would like to read other books like this, and the fastest way to do that is to sign up to my mailing list. I promise I won't bombard you with endless emails, but I would like to be able to let you know when any new books come out, or of any special offers I have on the existing ones.

Go to ljhutton.com to find the link

If you sign up, I will send the first in a fantasy series for free, but also other free goodies, some of which you won't get anywhere else!

Also, if you've enjoyed this book you personally (yes, *you*) can make a big difference to what happens next.

Reviews are one of the best ways to get other people to discover my books. I'm an independent author, so I don't have a publisher paying big bucks to spread the word or arrange huge promos in bookstore chains, there's just me and my computer.

But I have something that's actually better than all that corporate money – it's you, enthusiastic readers. Honest reviews help bring them to the attention of other readers (although if you think something needs fixing I would really like you to tell me first!). So if you've enjoyed this book, it would mean a great deal to me if you would spend a couple of minutes posting a review on the site where you purchased it.

Author's Notes

Firstly I would like to say that I have nothing personally against the Polish people. In making the gang Polish I was simply following the available government information regarding human traffickers, and sadly Poland is definitely top of the list for countries that traffic people of all kinds to the UK. Close behind when it comes to women being trafficked into prostitution, in these statistics, are the former Soviet Baltic states of Latvia and Lithuania, hence the references to them in the story. I was also using the official information available when I located the gang in this country in Walsall.

What is rather more of an unexpected and disturbing coincidence is the origin of the name Walsall, which I have referred to. The late, great place-name expert, Margaret Gelling (who I was lucky enough to meet on several occasions), gives the *-halh* ending as referring to a hollow, meaning a shallow basin of land, or land liable to flood because it is low-lying. But the *walh-* is more surprisingly pertinent, because in Old English it really did have two meanings, as Nick tells Bill. *Walh* meant Welsh, i.e. the Anglo-Saxon settlers' neighbouring Celts, who are also sometimes referred to as Britons as distinct from *Angles* (English), and is where our modern name originates; but also because of that, and because the incoming Anglo-Saxons were in the ascendency over people who probably had a very low status in the declining years of the Roman era and beyond, it also clearly means a slave or serf in other clearly documented contexts. The laws of King Ina of

Wessex (688-94), which are some of the earliest surviving English legal documents, refer to freed *wealas*, and in this context it definitely implies Welsh slaves, not English ones; while even as late as the ninth century, *wealas* seems to have meant native Britons of very low status living within English territories. Only as late as the eleventh century does the term *wealas* become synonymous exclusively with the Welsh and Cornish people living across the borders from the English. That modern Walsall should therefore have a name which meant the 'valley of the slaves' in Anglo-Saxon times, and should currently be an area where foreign people are traded against their will, was something which certainly made me gasp when I realised the association!

The whole issue of slavery in Anglo-Saxon England is a piece of genuine history, as is Bristol's association with it. Anyone wanting a more in-depth account of what went on should read *Slavery in Early Mediaeval England* by David A. E. Peltret, but in essence what went on is what Nick explains to Bill in the story. Domesday Book gives us a snapshot in time of what life was like at the end of the Anglo-Saxon era, and there are mentions of slaves in it, although by then the word more often used is *theow*. Although slaves were increasingly rare by 1086, nonetheless the Anglo-Saxons had taken slaves in previous centuries when there was trading of slaves from warring kingdoms, but confined to within the geographical boundaries of what we now call England. However the main traders in slaves in the era we're looking at in this story were undoubtedly the Vikings, which meant both Danes and Norwegians, depending on which part of the country you're looking at.

London and York were both Viking slave trading centres, with York primarily exporting slaves to Scandinavia, but Bristol is recorded as being a place where people were bought (in the very real sense of cash changing

Time's Bloodied Gold

hands) from all over England to be exported to Ireland where there were major Viking bases. (Dublin began as a Viking settlement.) The near contemporary biography of Bishop Wulfstan of Worcester describes how slavery at Bristol was an 'ancient custom', and because of that it was particularly hard to eradicate there. It describes how young people of both sexes could be seen roped together, with their beautiful appearance being considered a temptation to the barbarians (i.e. the Vikings), and who therefore would likely end up in prostitution – some things don't change despite the passage of centuries when you consider the number of trafficked people who end up in the sex trade in this century. The same Bishop Wulfstan joined forces with the newly arrived Norman archbishop, Lanfranc, post-1066 to put pressure on William the Conqueror to halt the slave trade, but it took some persuading because of the lucrative tolls which were paid to the king from that trade. Finally in 1102 the Council of Westminster outlawed slave trading within Britain, but Bristol remained a dangerous place to visit for at least half a century after that date because of Irish traders (i.e. naturalised Vikings), who would seize the unwary and sail off with them!

And finally, if anyone thinks I have been rather hard on the Church, the Catholic Church within England as represented within the Worcestershire Domesday entries (bearing in mind that we are still several centuries before Protestantism had been even thought of, and therefore all Christian churches in England were by definition Roman Catholic in those days), had more slaves in just its four great religious houses in the shire than all of their lay counterparts. The men within the Church may have been the movers towards banning slavery, but the Church was more reticent than the nobility to grant existing slaves their freedom. Primarily this was because of depictions of slavery in the Bible, and therefore it was justified by the reasoning that slaves of the Church were therefore slaves of God – hardly a consolation for those condemned to toil in the monastery and abbey fields for nothing more than their keep, which was arbitrarily decided by the monks in charge of them. If slaves in Imperial Rome could lead a comparatively secure life, the same cannot be said for these poor souls.

If anyone wants to know more about Opus Dei, look it up on line, but be aware that some web sites have a heavily biased viewpoint in its favour, and do not necessarily tell the whole story! And I imagine everyone knows at least a bit about the Spanish Inquisition. What is far less well known is how long the Inquisition, both in Spain and elsewhere, lasted and still had a shocking amount of power and influence. There is plenty of literature out there on the subject, but be warned, it's not for the faint-hearted!

Ramón José de Arce y Rebollar (1757 – 1844) really was the archbishop of Burgos, as was his position as Grand Inquisitor in the last days of the Spanish Inquisition, and the dates I have given are correct. His appointment to the Patriarchy of the West Indies was rather more unusual, especially as by this time the role had been merged with the office of Vicar General of the Spanish Armies in the West Indies. That gave him an awful lot of power when you factor in the influence he would have had as the Grand Inquisitor. This was a man very used to having and wielding power. He is very coyly described as having 'retired' from the West Indies posts in 1815 at the end of the Napoleonic Wars, but others were appointed to this post after him right up until 1963, unlike the Spanish Inquisition, which never really recovered its power after the Peninsular War ended.

Time's Bloodied Gold

However, the real de Arce died in Paris on 16th Feb 1844, but such a character was far too good to waste!

There is no village of Kyrewood Graves, although Burford (just across the river from where I have located it) is very real. Kyrewood and the Kyre area are also real, as is the hamlet of Callows Grave, but none of them have any association with people trafficking – especially from another time!

There is no pub called the *Fox & Goose* in Tenbury on the Berrington Road or anywhere else. I needed a pub I could make seriously dodgy and didn't want to malign any of the other lovely pubs in the town. Tenbury is a very pretty little place to visit, especially in the summer – please don't let this put you off visiting.

Equally, there is no hotel called *The Eagle* in Leominster. Given the dirty dealings going on there I didn't want to discredit any of the real establishments! However, West Street is real, as is the approximate location of Danny's flat, although the details of the house have been altered.

Shropshire, Herefordshire and Worcestershire are remarkably devoid of stone circles and standing stones. Of course this doesn't not preclude them having being dug up out of fields before surveys were being taken of them, but there does seem to be a singular absence of them surviving around here. On the other hand that did give me some room to take artistic licence and invent the remains of one incorporated into an early churchyard. Early churchyards were almost inevitably circular, that is true. Investigate any old church going back to the twelfth century or before and you'll find a circular churchyard attached to it – which was what gave me the idea in the first place. However, the church in Aberdeenshire is real and it does have standing stones in its graveyard, although not built into the actual walls of the church.

So there is no St Michael at Brimfield Wood — which does not exist either, although I have located it approximately in the area of Brimfield Hill and Middleton Wood. Normally, dedications to St Michael are rare in churches, and the few instances tend to come with the added 'All Angels', (unlike St Gabriel, who can appear as a lone dedication), but the exception is this area, which has an usually large number of St Michael's churches. Why I do not know, but it is a peculiarity of the Worcestershire-Herefordshire border.

Deconsecrated small Norman churches, on the other hand, are far more common in Herefordshire and Worcestershire. Many of them are like my fictional St Michael's, small single chamber churches with no special space at the east end for the altar, or just a small area added on for the altar. In fact they could easily be mistaken for farm buildings in size and shape. I was thinking in particular of tiny churches such as St Michael at Michaelchurch near Ross-on-Wye; Urishay Chapel whose dedication is unknown; St Mary's church, Edvin Loach; and St Bartholomew's church at Lower Sapey, which is actually in a farmyard and was the inspiration for the dig in *The Room Within the Wall*, although in this instance it has to be said that it does actually have a proper chancel, albeit tiny.

And then we come to Danny's predicament. I wish I could say that this is just the product of my imagination, but it isn't. Anyone who wants to see how badly some undercover officers have been treated should look online at the case of Mark Kennedy a.k.a. Mark Stone. Regardless of what you think of his relationships with the people he was supposed to be watching while undercover, it's almost impossible to understate the way he was abandoned by those who should have supported him. He, too, started out with the required support around him, but ended up being left to fend for himself with dire consequences. What's worse is that since his case came to light, other officers have spoken out about how they, too, went undercover thinking that they were enhancing their careers, then found that when they returned to normal life that they were told that there was no longer a place in the police force for them. Given the risks these officers took, to treat them in this way is just plain wrong in my eyes, and once I had found out about this I always knew that one day it would find its way into one of my stories.

Also by L. J. Hutton

Green Lord's Guardian
The next in the Bill Scathlock series

A Finnish boy in Britain who isn't what he seems, an attempted abduction by Russian thugs, and an off-duty detective who takes on more than he expected!

When DI Bill Scathlock foils the abduction of Finnish schoolboy Tapio, things soon take an unexpected turn. What is Tapio's secret, who or what is hunting him and why? The links back to Finland, its mythology, and his au pair's family, weave an ever more tangled web, and as the violence escalates Bill needs a wholly different kind of back-up than his colleagues normally provide. More than a boy's life is at stake as Bill fights to guard him against evil.

L. J. Hutton

The Rune House

A detective haunted by a past case, a house with a sinister secret, and a missing little girl! Can DI Ric Drake rescue her and find redemption along the way?

When DS Merlin 'Robbie' Roberts hears he's got a new colleague it's the last thing he wants, and especially when it's Ric Drake – infamous, recovering from a heart attack and refusing retirement. But when a modern missing child case links to one from Ric's past, and to a mysterious old house on the Welsh borders, they find a common cause. Do the ancient bodies discovered under a modern one hold the clue to both girls' fate, and does the house itself hold the key? As the links to the past keep getting stronger, Robbie and Drake must find a way to break the strange link before more children fall prey to Weord Manor's ancient lure.

Printed in Great Britain
by Amazon